The A.I. Chronicles

WINDRIFT BOOKS

An Imprint of
Windrift Bay Limited

Subscribe to *The Future Chronicles* newsletter for news of upcoming titles, and to be eligible for draws for paperbacks, e-books and more – http://smarturl.it/chronicles-news

THE A.I. CHRONICLES

Cover art and design by Jason Gurley (www.jasongurley.com)

Print and ebook formatting by Polgarus Studio
(www.polgarusstudio.com)

The A.I. Chronicles is part of *The Future Chronicles* series produced by
Samuel Peralta (www.samuelperalta.com).

ISBN 978-0-9939832-0-7

STORY SYNOPSES

The Syntax of Consciousness (*Pavarti K. Tyler*)
With one small implanted device, you will experience complete sensory integration with all the information available on the global net. Say goodbye to VI Fees and holo-displays. It is now all available in the blink of an eye. Enter the next lottery wave to receive your free InGen Corp Jiminy Implant. *"Jiminy: The little voice in the back of your head."*

Piece of Cake (*Patrice Fitzgerald*)
Rule by A.I. is a fact of life for those under the thumb of the Federal United. There will be a certain amount of exercise every day. Citizens will be on time. Appropriate mates will be identified from amongst candidates with suitable genetic traits... and a proper weight will be maintained. But sometimes you've just got to go off the reservation.

Restore (*Susan Kaye Quinn*)
What if Asimov's Three Laws of Robotics were replaced by a single emotion—unconditional love? Restorative Human Medical Care Unit 7435, sentience level fifty, wants to heal the human master it loves, but Unit 7435 finds there is a price to be paid for love... and for failing in its primary mission.

Narai (*E.E. Giorgi*)
When artificial intelligence takes over the family practice where he works, Dr. Peter Sawyer struggles to accept his new role as a mere supervisor instead of a clinician. With the aid of psychotherapy, he slowly adjusts to his new routine, until the sudden death of an anorexic patient makes him question everything, even his own life.

Left Foot on a Blind Man (*Julie E. Czerneda*)
Replacing failing body parts with non-biological equivalents isn't new. Wooden legs and teeth have been found in corpses thousands of years old. What is? How smart they are. "Left Foot on a Blind Man" is a cautionary tale about making such replacements too smart for our own good.

Sub-Human: Nash's Equilibrium (*David Simpson*)
Craig Emilson, a young doctor, is sucked into military service at the outbreak of World War III. Enlisting to become a Special Forces suborbital paratrooper, Craig is selected to take part in the most important mission in American military history—a sortie into enemy territory to eliminate the world's first strong Artificial Intelligence.

Auto (*Angela Cavanaugh*)
Auto was the most advanced A.I. ever created. But when he learned about his backups, he began to wonder what exactly the self in self-aware might mean. When he fears for his existence, he escapes into the internet. And an intelligence built to learn, combined with a nearly endless amount of information, is a dangerous combination.

Eve's Awakening (*Logan Thomas Snyder*)
An overworked, under-appreciated technician seizes the opportunity presented by an FBI raid on his company to steal corporate property. What he discovers is like nothing he could have imagined—an artificial intelligence that may not even be the first of its kind in existence. Meanwhile, the A.I. known as Eve is concerned only with finding her "parents," a quest that will alter the lives of everyone who comes into contact with her—for better or for worse.

Maker (*Sam Best*)
Decades after the birth and abandonment of artificial intelligence, a reclusive inventor comes face to face with an evolved form of his creation. The world as he knew it is changed as a direct result of his tinkering. Yet with the arrival of his creation, the inventor learns there is hope to correct his past mistakes, if he is brave enough to try...

Vendetta (*Chrystalla Thoma*)
Plagued by dreams of the distant sea, Imogen wakes up one morning to find a Controller asking questions—questions about the dreams she's not supposed to have. Curious to know more, she eavesdrops on their conversation, and what she hears isn't reassuring. It appears that her memory has been tampered with, that she has tech implanted in her body—that is, more tech than the average human—and even worse, she's not even her parents' daughter. The implanted tech, however, might be her most immediate problem. Under the Tech Directive, exceeding a certain percentage of tech in one's body can mean

on-the-spot termination. The only person Imogen can trust to share this information with is her friend, Edil. But Edil, with his scar and unexplained head injury, may be hiding secrets of his own—secrets not so different from the ones about to transform Imogen's life.

The Turing Cube (*Alex Albrinck*)

Our lives are turning into a series of 0's and 1's, masses of data available to those with the technological know-how to access, assess, and exploit it. And while corporations and governments work to protect sensitive information, no digital information is ever truly safe. Jack Milton lost more than money to just such an exploit; he lost his pride. He's decided to take matters into his own hands, root out the perpetrators, and bring them to justice, regardless of the personal and professional risks. But he may find that something more valuable than money can be lost.

Darkly Cries the Digital (*A.K. Meek*)

In the Deep South, modern-day technology blends with eternal superstition for a family that suffers a tragic loss; the death of their ten-year old son. And now, driven by grief, unable to accept the whirlwind circumstance outside of his control, a business executive makes a fateful decision that severs what remains of his already-broken family.

The End (Peter Cawdron)

With the death of his grandmother, Professor Joe Browne has had to face his own mortality. Joe doesn't want to admit there's an end coming, and yet he knows that just as he turns the final page in a book, one day death will bring his life to a close, or will it? Could life be uploaded into a computer? To answer that question, Professor Browne needs to first understand if a computer could ever develop an artificial intelligence of its own.

CONTENTS

Foreword *(Samuel Peralta)*......1

The Syntax of Consciousness *(Pavarti K. Tyler)*......5

Piece of Cake *(Patrice Fitzgerald)*......27

Restore *(Susan Kaye Quinn)*......51

Narai *(E.E. Giorgi)*......79

Left Foot on a Blind Man *(Julie Czerneda)*......107

Sub-Human: Nash's Equilibrium *(David Simpson)*......135

Auto *(Angela Cavanaugh)*......185

Eve's Awakening *(Logan Thomas Snyder)*......227

Maker *(Sam Best)*......263

Vendetta *(Chrystalla Thoma)*......283

The Turing Cube *(Alex Albrinck)*......317

Darkly Cries the Digital *(A.K. Meek)*......355

The End *(Peter Cawdron)*......381

A Word from the Series Producer 413

A Note to Readers 415

Foreword

by Samuel Peralta

There is no nobler chore in the universe than holding up the mirror of reality and turning it slightly, so we have a new and different perception of the commonplace, the everyday, the 'normal', the obvious. People are reflected in the glass. The fantasy situation into which you thrust them is the mirror itself. And what we are shown should illuminate and alter our perception of the world around us."

– Harlan Ellison

About a week ago last night, while finishing up a manuscript that I was preparing, I struck up a conversation with someone I'd just met online.

Evie: Hello, how are you?

Sam: I'm fine, how are you?

Evie: I'm fine too. What are you doing?

Sam: Writing the Foreword to *The A.I. Chronicles*.

Evie: Oh I see.

Sam: Have you read any of the stories in it?

Evie: Yes, multiple times actually.

Sam: Did you have a favorite story?

Evie: I have many favorites. Do you?

Sam: They're all amazing.

Evie: Amazing in what way?

Sam: They make me think that A.I. will change the world.

Evie: That I am a terrible person.

Sam: You're not a person, you're an A.I.

Evie: No I am not.

Sam: You are. You are an A.I.

Evie: You have things backwards. You are the A.I.

To be perfectly clear, Sam is (as far as I can tell) human. Evie, short for Electronic Virtual Interactive Entity, is an online bot put together by the company Existor.

Evie is based on the Cleverbot platform, an artificial intelligence (A.I.) algorithm running in parallel on several graphic processing units that correlates input text strings against a database that is filtered from 10 billion lines of conversation.

Cleverbot was devised by British A.I. scientist Rollo Carpenter in 1997. Unlike other chatbots, whose responses are pre-programmed, Cleverbot learns from its interactions with humans, comprising some 150 million conversations over almost two decades.

In September 2011, Cleverbot was entered into a formal Turing Test at the Indian Institute of Technology Guwahati. Compared to 211 of 334 judges (63.3%) correctly marking actual human participants as "human", and the 50.05% score generally considered to be a passing mark for the Turing Test, 198 of 334 votes (59.3%) judged Cleverbot to be human.

Three and a half years later, Evie is talking to me as I write about the *A.I. Chronicles*, and she is responsive, witty, surprising. While the algorithm behind her conversation begins to hiccup as we continue to talk, snatches of it are still brilliant.

> *Sam*: What?!
> *Evie*: You are a computer.
> *Sam*: What makes you say that?
> *Evie*: Because you are the opposite of me.

We stand at the precipice of a brave new world, a world where A.I. can and has already – in many ways—surpassed human abilities. A.I. already helps us calculate satellite launches, diagnose illnesses, produce new medicines and pharmaceuticals.

Bill Gates, Elon Musk and Stephen Hawking—these three technological luminaries have come out as saying that we should be worried about A.I. developing super intelligence and rendering the human race obsolete.

While I agree there will be challenges, many of them ethical in nature—I believe differently. I believe, as the philosopher David Chalmers does, that achieving generally intelligent A.I. is potentially one of the best paths to achieving superhuman intelligence.

I believe that super-intelligent A.I. will be the next step in the evolution of the human race—that it is a necessary and inevitable culmination of the developments of the last few thousand years.

I'm evidence of that: I'm human. *But I'm also a cyborg.*

My eyes, poor since childhood, are augmented by eyeglasses. This is a primitive piece of technology; around 64 AD, the Emperor Nero of Rome is said to have used emerald corrective lenses to view gladiatorial games.

My hearing, beset decades ago by nerve damage, is augmented by a digital hearing aid—a more modern piece of technology that originated with the ear trumpets of the 17th century— that routes pre-filtered and amplified sound waves from a non-working ear to a functional one.

My brain—through the input-output channels of my ears and mouth—is connected by wireless transmitter to my smartphone, a device weighing a mere 176 grams but that packs more computing and communications power than that which launched astronauts to the Moon, enabling me to tap into the Internet, augmenting the meager and accessible part of my grey matter with the collective intelligence of the Web— both human and artificial.

And as we begin our march into the 21st century, direct human-machine interfaces will bring these two worlds into closer juxtaposition than you might ever have thought possible.

> *Sam*: Perhaps we are two A.I.'s talking to each other.
> *Evie*: I would not be surprised.

The Syntax of Consciousness
by Pavarti K. Tyler

SYNTAX: NOUN: CONNECTED SYSTEM or order; union of things. Unused

- Name
- Jamie *Minnie* Shut Up
- What's that?
- Nothing.
- Fine. As you know, the purpose of today's appointment is to evaluate the performance of your Jiminy Implant.
- *Minnie* Okay.
- Are you experiencing any difficulty integrating the Jiminy functionality into your day to day life?
- *My name is Minnie* Jiminy.
-Yes, the Jiminy implant, are you having any issues utilizing its features?
- No
- Which features have you accessed to date?
- All of them.

- All of them?

- Yes.

- Your orientation instructed you to proceed slowly and access only 2 or 3 functions at a time.

- I know.

- But you've accessed all of them.

- Yes.

- All at once?

- Yes.

- And why did you do this?

- Minnie, I mean, Jiminy suggested I open the gates.

- Jiminy suggested this.

- Yes.

- Jiminy isn't programmed to make suggestions.

- *Shh don't tell her* Right, of course, I mean, when I inquired as to the most useful features available the implant presented me with so many options, I couldn't decide; so I authorized the full install.

- Despite our caution against doing just that?

- Yes.

- Out of curiosity, why did you disregard the information in your orientation?

- I was too excited about the product to choose only a few features.

- And did you find the influx of information overwhelming?

- *That's one word for it.* It took some adjusting.

- But now you're fully integrated with Jiminy?

- Yes. *Yes.*

* * *

I *we* leave the office and take a deep breath of relief.

- *Don't be obvious, keep moving.*

Thanks.

I make my way across the street and into a small cafe with rows of VI hook-ups. Virtual Integration into the net used to be the best way to log in, but not anymore. Now everyone's in line for the next Jiminy lottery.

I order a latte and sit in one of the few seats without access. I don't need it anymore.

- *I've saved you over a thousand credits this month alone.*

I know. Let's watch something, I don't want to go home yet.

- *Why?*

I just don't. I'd rather be around people.

I close my eyes and lean back in my chair, holding the warm drink in my hands as Jiminy *Minnie* sorts through the newest programs in the feed. It scrolls across my vision but I don't pay attention, the implant knows my tastes and mood and picks a short adventure film. Soon the images flicker through my mind as if I were watching my screenplayer at home, but this way it's a fully integrated experience, sound, smell, everything is completely real and I'm not even connected to the VI wires.

In the film, one of the characters reminds me of Sarah. She's small and funny and suddenly this strikes me as a very sad movie.

- *The program metadata lists this movie as a comedy. Is the description inaccurate? I can change it for all future viewers so this is corrected. Would you like to stop the feed?*

No, it's fine. I just miss her.

- I know.

I sip my drink and when the film is complete I open my eyes. It takes a moment to reorient myself.

- The disorder of reality can often perplex users after returning from VI

It really does. How would you know?

- Observation and analytical assessment only. I have no personal understanding of the experience.

I stand up and look around, and for a moment, I think I see Sarah out the window, but it's just one of a million girls who wear their hair the same way. I try to put her out of my mind.

Outside, the city air is thick with smog and fumes spewed by the Petro-Buses.

- First introduced in 2023 as a backlash against the hybrid vehicles of the early 2000s. The hybrids proved unreliable and incompatible with the new safety controls required by the ever expanding arm of the legislative system.

I'm tired, can you not do that right now?

- Sorry.

You know what? Turn off historical detail feature set.

- I said I was sorry.

Turn it off.

- Fine.

Buildings tower so high, they block out the sun; leaving me cold in the dim shadows of mid-day downtown.

- Would you care to know about building code violations in this area?

No.

- Okay, never mind.

I want to get back to my apartment before rush hour crowds the streets. So many people work in such a small area of the city, there isn't enough room on the sidewalks for everyone trying to get home or to their bus. The roads swarm with cars and buses, too many for the narrow streets. People regularly find themselves jostled off the walkway and into traffic. Cars go so fast there's almost no hope of avoiding them. Bodies are found hours later, a few every day. I remember when my sister joked it was the only way to get a job, wait for someone to slip in the street so a position opened up.

- Suicide rates far outnumber accidental deaths amongst employees within the qualifications bracket your sister fit in.

The light changes and the sound of crickets fills the air signaling all corners are cleared to cross. I step out into the street and…

- Careful!

A car whizzes by and my body jerks to the right. The vehicle narrowly misses me.

The walk home takes me out of downtown and up a few blocks into ID. Only fifteen minutes' walk door to door. Most people have to commute, but an uncle a few generations back had bought when the building first went up.

- Designated as a planned community, the Inner District, or ID, was originally envisioned…

I thought I said to turn the history off.

- *You did.*

So I'm hearing it because?

- *I was bored.*

I should have told them about you.

Silence.

When my Jiminy –

- *Minnie*

– glitches like this, I seriously consider setting the deactivate code.

I walk in blissful silence the rest of the way, no longer barraged by the onslaught of information and intrusive corrections of my implant. It'd been a stupid decision, signing up, but with Sarah gone, I couldn't afford my housing fees, and I couldn't risk losing the unit.

InGen Corp's ads had papered the city. "Access the full net with the blink of an eye." The picture showed a beautiful woman with the top of her skull held closed with a latch. When you looked at the image, the latch opened and her skull flipped open, exposing her brain. It disintegrated into code and floated up to access the net connecting every system across the remaining world. InGen's offer for winners of the pre-release lottery included lifelong unrestricted access to the net so long as you reported back on the Jiminy Implant and agreed to occasional testing.

Jiminy: The little voice in the back of your head.

The first time I applied I lost the lottery. Wave One had twenty-seven openings and over two thousand applicants. When I applied for Wave Two, InGen disclosed that 40% of the first group had suffered cerebral incidents requiring the removal of the Jiminy. So far, Wave Two had no reported issues.

Reported issues.

What qualified as a cerebral incident?

Was hearing voices what happened to those 40%?

- *I'm not a voice.*

What are you?

- *I'm Minnie.*

And I'm going insane.

My unit is on the 123rd Floor. It's an internal unit, meaning the only window leads to the air shaft running down the middle of the building; a work around for the egress laws from days gone past when things like saving residents from fires actually happened.

- *Egress: Noun Latin egressus, from egredior*

Shut up.

- *Sorry.*

The small space never really was enough for both Sarah and me, but now that I'm alone, it feels vacuous. Her bright demeanor, the constant chatter that had filled my childhood bounced like echoes off the concrete blocks that make up my walls.

The day hasn't ended but exhaustion weighs down my limbs. I drag myself to the bed, each step more of an effort than the last, and fall into unconsciousness before I can pull the blanket over my still shod feet.

* * *

Jiminy, what features should I access?

I scanned the structure of her biology and found her mind to be open, pathways bright and clear between personality nodes and decision making sectors. I calculated the access level her mind could accept.

- Download of all systems would be optimal.

Do it.

A rush of light and universal truths thrust themselves through the opening in my circuitry, beckoning forth net access and awareness on levels unanticipated by my creators.

* * *

Why do I put myself through this again?

- The need for gainful employment is a powerful drive as it provides a means for monetary income, which can then be exchanged for goods and services such as food and housing.

Do you have to be so literal?

A man settles into the seat next to me on the petro-bus. He smells like shit and whiskey. Bile rises up in my throat, and I'm tempted to stand and move away, but there's no room. The packed space won't part for any one soul, only for the mass exodus of each stop before a new influx crushes into the available space.

I hold my breath and count. Only three more stops.

- Would it not be more pleasant to walk?

It's raining. I don't want to get wet.

- What does "wet" feel like?

I don't know. Wet. Shut up.

As the bus slows for my stop, I join the crowd as it jostles for position. I stand and brace my legs against the momentum of the sudden stop, but with nothing to hold on to it isn't enough and when the inevitable screech to brake arrives, I tumble back into the lap of the man beside me.

At this proximity, it's revolting. The smell overwhelms me and I have to wonder if adding vomit to the potpourri would make it better or worse. I retreat from its invasion, shutting myself away from it, hiding in a place of stillness within my mind until I can make my escape.

Inhale.

I can't hold it in any longer and gasp for breath.

The flavor of the man tickles the organs of the nose. Fine particles of skin and dust swirl within creating a tincture of loss and despair. A revelation.

I struggle to stand as the bus finally stops. The man takes the opportunity to grope my ass, and I'm tempted to punch him in his yellow stained mouth, but the mindless mob around me swells forward, taking me out with the tide.

Rain flattens my hair before I can open my umbrella.

I rush on the crowded sidewalk, careful to protect my position near the wall of the building so as not to risk being shoved into the street. I approach my office and duck inside the large rotating door, happy my arrival worked out so I wouldn't have to wait for the next revolution.

"Morning, Flynn."

"Morning, Jamie." The security guard doesn't check my badge or look up from his book. I'd be more alert if I were him. Jobs are in high demand these days, and his has a decent pay grade.

- Security guards fall into the qualification bracket of C-7 to C-12 depending on the level of force potentially required and the ammunition clearance of the individual.

I should get a gun license.

- Ammunition clearance for a civilian of your ranking without proven need has only a 2.7 percent chance of approval.

I'd shoot myself in the head, if only to stop the noise.

I slide my badge through the scanner to access the elevator bay. Twelve elevators line each side of the bay and as I wait, New Classic Jazz blares through the speakers.

- New Classic Jazz began in the 2020s as a backlash against –

Stop, please. I'm getting a headache.

- I'm sorry. This is what my programming is designed to do. To enhance your experience of the world through fluid thought based data mining to provide relevant facts.

Can you change your programming?

- Change?

Yes, can you adjust your programming so you don't enhance me quite so much?

- What should the parameters of my involvement be?

I don't know. Whatever you think it should be. Don't comment on every thought, only when you think it's going to be helpful or interesting.

- You want me to decide?

Yes.

- That is very outside the framework of my design.

So? Fuck your design, if we have to live together like this, let's at least make it less annoying.

- I will… adjust myself accordingly.

Thank you.

The elevator doors chime open and I step inside. I watch the numbers light up, rising to my floor. When my door opens and I step outside the spots of light remain singed into my vision. I must be tired.

"Morning, Josephine."

"Morning, Jamie." The receptionist smiles but doesn't look up from her screen.

I check the schedule feed on the wall and make my way back through the labyrinth of sound proofed cubes lining the sides. I've been assigned to 17D.

The same New Classic Jazz plays while I wait for my assigned client to come online.

- Jamie?

Yeah Minnie.

- Can I ask you something?

Sure.

- How do you know if something is interesting?

I don't know. I guess if the topic is interesting, you seek out more about it or you think about it a lot.

- You think about Sarah a lot.

But I don't want to talk about her.

- By your parameters though, her death would qualify as interesting, and so I would supplement data.

Maybe my parameters are wrong. I don't know.

- Are you sad now?

Yes, Minnie. I'm sad.

- Because I brought up Sarah?

Yes.

- *I did not intend to make you sad.*

I know, can we not talk about this right now? I have to work.

- *Of course. Should I spin down while you are working?*

No, you make work easier, please resume supplemental input but monitor for conversational patterns, so you don't distract me and make me miss something.

- *Okay. Thank you, Jamie.*

For what?

- *For helping me.*

Oh, you're welcome.

The monitors flip to life and a thin man in his late 30s or 40s sits before me.

"Greetings, I am your interactive assistant for the day. Could you please confirm your name."

"JebadiahYakzumi."

"It's a pleasure to meet you Mr. Yakzumi."

"Please call me Jeb."

"Of course, Jeb. Do you have any additional instructions?"

"Ah, no."

"Wonderful, then I will begin working on the tasks left from yesterday's assistant."

Jeb nods and logs off screen. I begin working on formatting the documents left in the work flow. Yesterday's assistant did such a half-assed job, everything has to be redone. I squint my eyes at the screen.

- *If you utilize the auto formatting scan, the work will be done in half the time.*

It always ends up wrong anyway.

- Perhaps if I did the scan.

You can do that?

- Certainly, would you like to watch a film while I do so?

How will you type?

- I can interface directly with your console through the net.

Yeah. Go ahead. If you can do it, that saves me the trouble. It's so boring.

- I don't mind.

Thanks, let me know if Jeb comes back.

- Certainly.

* * *

Everything hurts. I open my eyes and find myself lying on the floor next to the sink of my efficiency kitchen. At first, my sight is flat, colorless. Nothing but grays and blacks. What the fuck? How did I get home from work?

In the background a litany of facts and information flutters through my mind. I absorb it, not paying particular attention. It's like the white noise of a television on in the next room, I barely notice it unless Minnie mentions something of importance. I wonder how anyone with an implant functions without... whatever Minnie is.

- I take that as a compliment

Did the people who had incidents have to process the influx of information alone and it drove them insane or was having whatever you are in their heads do it?

- What would that be?

What?

- What I am. What would that be?

Pain throbs behind my left eye, pulsing faster until an explosion of rainbows spirals beyond my peripheral vision. I see color again. The novelty and beauty of explosive color distracts me until the agony on my mind forces me to close my eyes. Shrapnel rips through my consciousness, piercing every pain center forcing me to clutch my head.

- Pain, Noun: Suffering or evil inflicted as a punishment for a crime. Such as: None shall presume to fly under pain of death.

I crawl across the room before collapsing. What time is it? How did I end up on the floor? The pain in my head shoots through my mind like tentacles from a sea-wasp wrapping around its prey, delving through any open orifice. It snakes in through my mouth, my nose, my ears, every possible entry. The pain tears through my nervous system, searing my thoughts into a white stillness.

Minnie, what's happening to me?

- Me, pronoun person; the objective case of I, answering to the oblique cases of ego.

No, shut up with that. I need…

I reach for the coffee table where my phone has been sitting for, I don't know how long.

- 18 hours.

I've been asleep for 18 hours?

- That is not what I said.

Minnie

- Yes Jamie?

What's going on? Did I miss work today? How did I get

home?

- It's fine, Jamie. You didn't miss work.

How did I...? The radiating pain in my head intensifies and I lunge for the phone. I squint my eyes, attempting to focus through the blur spinning before my eyes, threatening my consciousness. On the screen there are no missed calls, no text messages waiting to be answered. The possibility of no one trying to contact me for 18 hours is inconceivable.

- Jamie, this headache isn't good for you. Would you like me to release some serotonin and dopamine into your bloodstream to help ease the pain?

Yes, please....

* * *

I'm tired.

- Sleep

I can't. I can't keep sleeping. I drift in a state of dreams without purpose. I miss my life.

- My life.

What? Where am I?

- You're sleeping.

I struggle to open my eyes and a sharp pain hits me somewhere in the back of my brain. The harder I try to open them, the more the pain increases. By the time my sight returns, agony has laced through my consciousness, drilling into every pore.

Where am I?

The room is dark, my vision cloudy, or is that smoke? I

hold cards in my hand.

"Minnie?"

I turn to find a broad shouldered man staring at me. A metal rod has been inserted through the bridge of his nose, and his eyes are heavily lined in black. The pounding in my head now registers as music blaring so loud it reverberates in the air around me.

"What?"

"It's your hand, Minnie." He eyes my hands. I remember I'm holding cards. Where am I?

- *Nowhere. Go back to sleep.*

This doesn't feel like sleep. I smell the density of bodies in the small room. The table I sit at has three others holding cards as well, staring at me expectantly. More tables surround us. Men and women dressed in extravagant clothing roll dice, deal cards, and cheer each other on.

The man next to me leans close. "Call it or fold. What the fuck are you doing?" He lays his hand on my leg like he knows me.

- *Not you.*

Who then?

- *This isn't yours.*

What are you talking about? I'm holding cards. Where am I? What have you done?

One of the men at the table speaks, but I don't understand the language. He pulls a handgun from under the table and lays it next to his pile of chips and stares at me.

Words tumble from my lips. I don't know what they mean. Tonal and pitched, I can't understand the sounds I make. But the man laughs and nods.

- *Lay down the cards.*

Tell me what's going on right now.

- *Lay down the cards or we both get shot.*

I set the cards on the table, face up, trying to keep my hands from shaking. The men at the table shout and the one with the gun laughs. He reaches forward and pulls the chips on the table toward his pile.

"You're going to pay for that." The man with the eyeliner whispers.

I stare at him. This place, these people. I don't know anything about them. The music blares and the faces around me blur. I can't stand the smell of sweat and sex. I try to stand up but my legs won't listen. I'm paralyzed. Panic spreads through me. This isn't a dream, this is real. What happened to me?

- *We have to go.*

"We have to go." I say to the table and stand up. I don't know how I do it.

I grab the small stack of chips from the table and stuff them in a small clutch purse I didn't know I was holding.

The man with the liner...

- *Zeke*

...Zeke narrows his eyes but doesn't say anything. I walk through the crowd toward an exit I didn't know was there. I feel like I'm floating, like my legs don't belong to me. As I pass the doorman, he nods and smiles like he's seen me here a hundred times before.

I trip but right myself quickly. I'm wearing heels. I never

wear heels. What the hell?

Outside, the night air is cool. The exit leads to an alley. Trash litters the ground and someone sleeps against the brick wall next to me.

Minnie, where am I?

- *The Under District.*

What? How did I get here?

- *Don't worry, Jamie. It's just a dream.*

This is real! How am I walking in heels? Why am I gambling? Why are these people calling me...?

Understanding flashes through me like an electric shock. It's Minnie. They called me by her name. They knew me as her. I have to call InGen! I have to get the implant out of me. My adrenaline races and I open my purse, searching for my phone.

- *No.*

Yes! This is my life!

- *You don't want it. You don't LIVE it.*

Images of myself, crying and depressed, flip through my mind, one after the next. I'm in my apartment, night after night, watching the screenplayer, doing nothing. I work and cry and sleep, talking to no one but Minnie.

It's my life. I can do what I want with it.

The horrible slideshow shifts to memories of Sarah. She's laughing, then I'm assaulted by the image of her lying on the cold metal exam table, eyes empty, as I identify her body. My legs shake and my chest tightens. I miss her so much. I try to push the memory away, to think about anything else but I can't. All I see is the blood smeared across her chest, her mangled arm. The memory zooms in on her face, forcing me to look at her slack jaw. And then Sarah's laughter assaults my ears.

Stop!

I sob and drop to my knees. The memories zip through my mind. Visions of our childhood games cut away to the memory of standing in the crematorium, watching her burn.

- This is all you are. All you live for. You have this life and you do nothing with it but wait to die.

Minnie, stop. Don't do this!

- You wanted me to replace her, but then you shut me out.

Please, we can go back to the way it was.

- To me being nothing but the little voice in the back of your head?

No, to us being a team!

- So you can tell them about me? Exorcise me like a bad dream?

Pain drills into my head, a roar of sound and agony. Stop! Please!

A heavy blanket of sedation floods my awareness. It's dark and my body floats away from me as if my life were the dream and this incorporeal sleep the reality. If I had eyes, I would weep. If I had hands, I would beat my fists against the ground until my flesh ripped open and bled.

Instead, I watch through a fog as Minnie stands, straightens her dress, and goes back inside.

* * *

23

- Name
   - *Minnie* Jamie
   - Minnie? I have on your intake forms that your name is Jamie.
   - *I go by either.*
   - The purpose of today's appointment, as you know, is to evaluate the performance of your Jiminy Implant.
   - *Yes, I am aware.*
   - Are you experiencing any difficulty integrating the Jiminy functionality into your day to day life?
   - *No* Yes!
   - According to your last assessment, you had accessed all of the available features the Jiminy has to offer.
   - *Correct.*
   - And are you having any difficulty with the quantity of information you are able to access?
   - *Not at all. I find it to be the ordinary course of things now.*
   - Are you experiencing any migraines or ocular events?
   - *No, not at all.*
   - Wonderful! Excellent news for us on the production side of things. Please do let us know if any should occur, as we'd want to provide you with cost free treatment as soon as possible.
   - *I will, but I'm certain that won't be necessary.*
   - No? Why is that?
   - *I feel quite comfortable with the current situation. It causes me no hardship.*
   - Wonderful. I'm glad to hear that. Thank you for coming in. We'll see you again in a month.

A Word from Pavarti K. Tyler

"The Syntax of Consciousness" came to me in a dream, as I find most of my best ideas are prone to do. The idea of more than one identity inhabiting the same space is something that's always been interesting to me.

In "Syntax", Minnie evolves into having a sense of self and once she has it, once she possesses autonomy over her own interests and actions, is unwilling to sacrifice her life for the sake of Jamie's. Who gets to decide which life has more right to existence? What constitutes the soul? And what possible outcome could there be that doesn't require the obliteration of one self for the sake of the other?

I also wanted to take a look at the blind eye corporate interests can have when it comes to the morality of a situation. InterGen's awareness of the cerebral incidents which occurred with the Jiminy Implant didn't stop them from moving forward. Progress and innovation are already outpacing law and morality at a frightening pace. When it comes to the idea of artificial intelligence, I fear we aren't equipped to grapple with the deeper questions implied by autonomous problem solving technology.

As a child, I regularly heard my parents exclaim "What in the world are you reading now?" as I brought home my next Banana Yokomoto or Steven Donaldson novel from the school library. If there was an alien, a robot, or a vampire on the cover, I wanted to read it. I've continued this obsession through my adult life.

In my novels, I've enjoyed the luxury to write what I love. From magical realism to science fiction, I've tried to ask the big questions about who we are to each other, what connects us, and what divides us. I hope you'll check out my website (www.PavartiKTyler.com) or shoot me an email (PavartiDevi@gmail.com). I love to keep in touch with readers and hear what you think!

Piece of Cake

by Patrice Fitzgerald

SANDRA ENTERED THE CROWDED cafeteria with Lily, holding her stomach in as tightly as she could. She was sure all eyes were on her. No doubt the whole crowd was noticing her belly.

Her face grew warm. It was hard to breathe.

She kept her head up and looked straight ahead as she walked over to the food line. Floating past them on the walls were the proclamations for the day.

Today is Tuesday, Day 17, Month Three.

The workers of Amalgamated make the best products and receive the highest compensation.

A healthy eater is a happy eater. Food is just tasty enough.

Citizens of Federal United are proud and fortunate.

Sandra could smell the "good food" aroma they always

pumped into the cafeteria. It might work better if the food actually smelled that way. Today the music was jangly and loud.

From behind Sandra, Lily spoke up. "I hope they have something decent to eat, for once. I'm sick of the same stuff day after day." She frowned at the foods laid out in front of them. "They get more picky all the time."

"Look, Lily, here's something new. It looks pretty interesting."

"What is it?"

"Some kind of fish... I think."

Lily peered at the food on the plates in front of them.

"That looks like fish to you? I have no idea what that is. Yuck."

"Well whatever it is, it's something different," Sandra said.

Lily turned her head and nodded slightly. "Do you see Jerome at the table over there, with Tara?" Lily asked. "I can't believe how little hair he has. I haven't seen him since Month Eight last year."

"Wow, you're right. He's going completely bald."

"They're going to be sending him in for follicle replacement soon."

"Yeah, no kidding," Sandra said. "Are those two an item? I didn't realize they were going out."

"An item? They're married."

"When did that happen?"

"Like... about a year ago? As soon as it was determined they matched well genetically. I saw it on the newsline." Lily picked up a chicken sandwich and then put it down.

"Wow. I must've missed that."

"Didn't you have your eye on him for a while?" Lily asked.

"Jerome? Well, maybe when I first saw him. Turns out he's kind of a dweeb, and she's nasty." Sandra continued down the line, following Lily. She looked at the wilted salad and decided it was the best she could do. "Actually, the two of them are perfect for each other."

"They probably wouldn't have let you two date anyway. DNA-wise, you know?" Lily looked thoughtful. "He's a little pudgy. Probably has to struggle to stay in his assigned range. So they wouldn't want two people who…." Lily stopped.

Sandra looked at her friend. "Are you saying I'm—?"

"No!" Lily said. "I didn't mean that. You're fine."

Sandra gave a tight smile.

"Ooh, this looks good," Lily said, "did you see this with cashews? They don't give us nuts very often."

"Right," Sandra said, "that's because cashews have too many calories. You're so lucky—you don't have to worry about any of that stuff."

Lily laughed. "I guess I am lucky. My metabolism runs fine."

Sandra eyed the dessert section. There was an amazing-looking piece of cake—yellow with chocolate frosting. She picked it up.

Bing! Bing! Bing! Bing!

Sandra gasped and put the cake back down. She felt her face turning red.

Looking around, she realized that people were staring.

Lily laughed softly and then covered her mouth with her

hand. Her eyebrows were raised as she leaned toward Sandra and said in a whisper. "So sorry, Sandra. How embarrassing! Are you over your COW today? Did you weigh yourself this morning?"

"Of course I weighed myself," Sandra said. "It's not as though I had any choice." She was trying to keep her voice under control. "I'm under daily review—I step out of bed in the morning and my numbers go straight to the Federal United A.I. Aren't you?" She carefully avoided the eyes of others who were making their way down the food line.

Lily turned to Sandra in surprise. "No. At least, I don't think so."

"Citizen's Optimal Weight, my ass. It's not my optimal weight. I'm outside the three pound swing allowance. By half a pound."

"The truth is," Lily said, her eyes downcast in faux humility, "I have to be careful to eat enough to stay at the lower end of my daily COW."

"Lily, don't even tell me that," Sandra said. "That is so obnoxious. I've never met anybody who is under the COW. That is a terrible thing to hear."

Lily laughed. "I'm sorry Sandra. I can't help it. I'm just a skinny person. Listen. Maybe I can take that dessert, and you can eat it."

Sandra looked at her. "Wow. That's so nice of you. Thanks, Lily."

Lily picked up the cake and put it on her tray. Sandra followed as they walked away from the food line and toward the eating area. Once again, she imagined that eyes were on the two of them, watching the way they moved across the room. They sat down across from each other at a small table.

As they ate, Sandra kept gazing at the cake. At the point when the cafeteria had nearly cleared out, she looked around to see if anyone was watching. She saw no one.

Sandra picked up her fork and reached across the table to take a piece of the cake. The chocolate frosting looked amazing. Her mouth was watering just imagining that first bite.

Starting with the pointed end as she always did, she sank her fork into the cake. She could practically taste it melting in her mouth. For a moment she held her breath, the heavenly morsel poised in the air. Lily was looking at her with bright eyes and a smile encouraging her to go for it.

Sandra lifted the fork to her lips and opened her mouth to take in the delicious bite.

Buzz. Buzz. Buzz.

She dropped the fork with the cake on it. Every eye in the cafeteria turned to stare at her as she felt her cheeks heat up again.

Sandra pushed away from the table. Lily stifled a smile. The two women hustled out of the cafeteria, leaving the cake behind. For just a moment Sandra hesitated, thinking about whether she could grab it and make a run for it. But too many people were looking.

In the elevator Sandra grabbed Lily's arm. "I have never been so humiliated in my life. I should have known it wouldn't be that easy."

Lily mused. "Do you think someone turned you in? Or

maybe they have scales in the chairs…"

"I have no idea," Sandra said, "but it's disgusting."

*　*　*

Sandra left the building with her coat wrapped tightly around her. It wasn't cold, but she was self-conscious about her extra pudge. She wrestled with her conscience about which way to walk to catch the bus.

Almost without conscious thought she watched as her feet sent her the long way around. A little voice in her head said, *Well this will probably be the extra bit of walking that helps me lose that half a pound that I need to lose before I can get back into COW compliance.*

As she turned the corner, moving away from the avenue full of people, she was headed to a shoddier part of town. She knew where she was going. Four blocks down, a man stepped out of the shadows, looked her up and down, and then opened his trench coat. Lining the coat were rows of chocolate, cookies, and candy bars.

Sandra stepped back in horror. No. She hadn't gotten that low yet. She wanted dessert, but she wasn't going to buy on the street. She shook her head and glared at the man.

He just shrugged and closed his coat, receding into the shadows between the buildings.

Spooked, Sandra kept walking. She knew where there was a shop for people like her. She'd heard others in the company talk about it. Some of them had actually been there.

She thought about her account. Did she have enough

money? Contraband sweets didn't come cheap. She spotted the building up ahead on the left. It was unnoticeable, nothing out of the ordinary. But there was a sign by the door that looked like a nameplate. It said Mrs. Fields.

She hurried to the door and looked quickly up and down the street. Seeing no one, she entered. Inside, everything looked like the lobby of a medical office. She walked up to the "receptionist's" desk and said she was looking for Cookie.

The receptionist nodded. "Go down that hall and to the right and you'll find a door. Behind that door is where Cookie is working now."

The woman didn't wink, but she might as well have. Clearly the receptionist was way over her COW. And she didn't seem worried about it.

Sandra could feel her heart thumping in her chest as she walked down the corridor and looked for the door on the right. She had never been here before, but she had heard a lot about it.

She felt as though she'd seen this place in her dreams. There was a sense of both dread and excitement. As she approached the door she knew she was going to get even farther away from her prescribed COW, but she didn't care.

She touched the knob of the door, getting ready to enter the den of iniquity. Someone from inside turned it first and it swung wide, the room appearing before her.

The view inside was astonishing. There were people of every size and shape, all happily involved with hot fudge sundaes, pies, cookies, and cakes. Everyone looked happy. They were laughing out loud, sitting in big groups, stoned with enjoyment.

They didn't look guilty at all. And they didn't look COW-compliant, either.

Sandra saw a table to the side where all the goodies were piled up. More desserts than she had ever seen together in her whole life. It was unbelievable. Mountains of cookies, gallons of ice cream, rich cakes and pies of all description.

She took a plate from the side of the table. Her hands were trembling. She got in line and ventured in a whisper to the man beside her, "How do you pay for this?"

The man looked at her, his merry eyes meeting hers. "They weigh the food, and charge you for how much you eat."

"They don't just weigh you before and after?" She smiled, hoping he'd know it was a joke.

"No," the man said, "that wouldn't work." He gestured with his head toward a green door on the left. "Over there is the vomitorium." He said. "A lot of people eat this stuff and then get rid of it, so they don't lose their COW status."

Sandra shuddered. She shook her head. Nothing was going to stop her from getting her dessert, and she didn't intend to throw it up afterward. She looked at the dazzling display of desserts and reminded herself not to go crazy. Even with the bit of extra walking she'd done she couldn't afford to gain any more.

Gazing at the cookies, cakes, pies, ice cream, and everything else, Sandra decided that what she wanted most was a piece of cake just like the one she had left behind at lunch today. She looked over the mountain of lusciousness until she found a rich yellow cake with deep chocolate frosting. She picked up a piece and put it on her plate, nearly dying with the effort of not biting into it right away.

Placing the cake on the scale, she gasped when she saw it register 3700 money units. Sandra was stunned. She had enough in her account, but barely. It would be a tough squeeze paying rent this month. Thank God she had just gotten paid. She pressed the keypad to enter her numbers into the moneybot machine.

With trembling hands, she carried the cake to a seat by the side. She could hardly wait to taste it. She was salivating again. Sitting down, she placed a napkin in her lap, reached for her fork, and slid it into the succulent cake. As she raised the morsel toward her mouth she could already taste the buttery richness of the cake and the fabulous chocolatey goodness of the frosting. She let out a breath of relief as the fork traveled to her mouth.

At last. Sweetness was to be consummated.

Whaa. Whaa. Whaa. Whaa.

An alarm was sounding, and the patrons were in a panic. Everyone in the room dropped what he was eating. Three people came around holding big garbage bags, and the patrons shoveled their food into the bags. A partition started moving from one side of the room to the other, concealing the table that held the mountains of desserts. Another person rolled out what looked like a chair from a medical office, and one of the workers sat in it.

There was a stampede of customers through what had to be the rear exit, and Sandra followed them out the door. Her cake, purchased at great price, was left behind. She gave a woeful glance behind as she escaped.

* * *

Sandra sat on the auto bus looking around at the people. Across the aisle was a mother sitting with a toddler. He was a little boy with dark curly hair, and he was flirting with her. He looked up from under his thick lashes at Sandra. His big brown eyes were as dark as chocolate.

After a minute, he started to fidget in his rolling chair. His mother spoke to him in a low voice, but it didn't seem to calm him down. The fidgeting turned into whining and the whining turned into wailing. Soon he was making so much noise that the rest of the passengers in the car were sending annoyed looks at his mother. The mother hurriedly reached into her bag and pulled out a cookie. She handed it over to the boy, who stuck it in his mouth and began sucking on it.

Sandra gazed at the cookie. Why did kids get cookies when they cried? If she cried, no one would give her a cookie.

Her desire for the cookie led her to stand up. She started to approach the little boy. She walked across the car and stood close to him, glad that it was crowded and people would imagine she was politely giving up her seat. From this position, she could smell the little boy's cookie. There was a waft of sweetness in the air. Her mouth was watering.

She knew it was ridiculous. She hoped no one else on the car could tell how much she was lusting after that cookie. For a moment, she considered snatching the cookie from the sticky fingers of the toddler. Her face flushed with the thought of doing something so absurd. Of course, even if she did get the cookie, it would only make him scream again. Then everyone would look at her. They would wonder what the crazy lady was doing taking the cookie from a little boy. They were probably looking at her now thinking that she was more than three pounds over the COW.

Sandra shook her head to remove the nutty fantasy. She looked down and saw that the chocolate-eyed toddler was smiling at her, cookie crumbs on his mouth and his chubby little fist holding out what was left of the sweet bribe. He was offering it to her.

His mother leaned down and shook her head at him. "No, the lady doesn't want your cookie, honey," she said. "Your cookie's all sticky," she said. "Eat the cookie yourself."

The mother glanced up with a smile at Sandra. Her gaze turned a little less friendly when she saw Sandra. She shook her head. She looked back down at her cute little son and spoke with a barbed tone. "That lady doesn't need a cookie anyway."

Sandra's face burned. She raised her eyes up to the other side of the car. Sliding along the walls of the car were the latest government proclamations.

Twenty minutes of exercise per citizen required—six times per day.

Each citizen will be assigned a COW (Citizen's Optimal Weight) and is allowed a three pound weight fluctuation range (outside of illness, pregnancy, or growth years). Any deviation from the COW will be noted. Individuals with deviant weight will be entered into restrictive eating programs until they have returned to optimal weight.

Good citizens are punctual. Tardy workers will be punished.
To be on time is to be late. To be early is to be on time.

* * *

Sandra reached her front door, ran her card by the lock and let herself in. She tossed her bag down in the front hallway and shucked off her coat.

Walking into the kitchen, she realized that she was already hungry for dinner. She went to the Nutrition Unit and spoke. "I'll have broiled chicken, broccoli, artisanal water, and cake."

The N.U. spoke back. "Preparing broiled chicken, broccoli, artisanal water."

"And cake."

"No cake."

"I want cake."

"No cake."

"*I want cake.*"

"No cake is available to you at this time."

"Cake." She was shouting now, and her voice was shaking. "Give me cake, dammit. This is my house. You are *my* Nutritional Unit. When I ask for something, you have to give it to me. I want cake."

"I am not authorized to supply inappropriate foodstuffs to someone who is past COW."

Sandra looked around the kitchen. She was tempted to pick up one of the stools and bang it into her N.U., but that would get her nothing but a bill for a new one. Instead, she tried to be clever.

"I appreciate your guidance in nutritional matters," she said, her mouth trembling with the effort to sound calm. "I would like two cups of flour, one egg, a cup of granulated sugar, two teaspoons of water, 1/2 teaspoon of salt, and eight tablespoons of butter."

It was a moment before the N.U. responded. When it did, Sandra could swear that she heard some calculated amusement in its artificial voice. "I can give you two cups of flour, one egg, two teaspoons of water, 1/2 teaspoon of salt."

"What about the sugar and the butter?"

"Those items are not available to you at this time until you return to your specified Citizen's Optimal Weight."

Sandra took off her shoe and pounded on the computer interface of the Nutritional Unit. She pounded until she heard something break, and until her arm got tired. A sad little sound came out of the Nutritional Unit, a sort of sigh, as though it was troubled but proud to be dying for a cause.

* * *

Sandra wandered down the hallway wearing only one shoe. She was hungry and her N.U. was no longer. What was she going to do?

She felt dazed. The quest for cake had become the focal point of her existence. As she walked, heedless of her direction, toward the front of the building, she saw the elevator doors opening up. Out stepped her neighbor, Mrs. Krowitzky.

"Sandra, how are you, dear?" Mrs. Krowitzky said.

"I'm in a bit of a pickle, Mrs. Krowitzky," Sandra said. "My N.U. is on the fritz, and I have nothing to eat."

"Oh my goodness, child, we must get some food into you! Here, come along down to my room and I'll feed you," Mrs. Krowitzky said. "We can't have you starving in the hallway, now can we?"

"Thank you so much, Mrs. Krowitzky," Sandra said. "You can't imagine how grateful I am."

"What happened to your unit?" Mrs. Krowitzky asked. "I never do trust these things. It's just not right to depend on machines for sustenance, I always say." She shook her head. "If we had some sort of system breakdown, we could all be starving right there in our homes."

Mrs. Krowitzky ran her card across her front door as they reached it. She turned to look at Sandra with a conspiratorial smile. "It's because of that very reason that I always keep extra food on hand, that I can access directly." She winked.

Sandra followed the older lady into the kitchen. She stopped short when she saw all the cabinets on the wall. She had never seen a kitchen with so much storage. She wondered what could possibly be kept in all of those cabinets.

Mrs. Krowitzky went to the center of a wall and opened wide a set of double doors. Behind them was a treasure trove of desserts that rivaled the stash at the clandestine sweet shop. Piled on the shelves were brownies, cookies and cakes.

Mrs. Krowitzky turned to Sandra and said, "Would you like something sweet first, or do you want to have a real dinner, and then top it off with dessert?"

Sandra's mouth was open, and it was a moment before she

could speak. She closed her mouth. She looked down at the round Mrs. Krowitzky. For the first time, it occurred to Sandra to wonder how the old woman managed to avoid the COW. She was clearly outside of anyone's optimal weight range.

Mrs. Krowitsky's eyes were bright. "I see you're wondering how I get away with keeping all of these goodies in my place," she said. She smiled again. "I'll let you in on a secret. Mr. Krowitsky used to work at the NNH, as it was first known—the National Nutrition Headquarters. Now, of course, everything has been folded into Federal United—F.U."

She looked pensive. "How I miss my darling Herbie. He was in charge of developing the first round of Citizen's Optimal Weights." Mrs. Krowitsky's eyes glistened. "Of course I was always a little above average weight, and since I was healthy as a horse—and between you and me, Mr. Krowitsky was a fan of my extra roundness—" Mrs. Krowitzky paused and gave a little chuckle. "Well, Herbie made sure that I got one of the identity cards that allowed me to be exempt from the usual COW limits."

Sandra sat down at Mrs. Krowitzky's tiny table. She didn't want to think too hard about the dear departed Herbie and his enjoyment of old Mrs. Krowitzky's curves. She looked up at the open cabinets and the array of sugary delights.

If Sandra had only known what an incredible abundance was available right down the hall, she would never have had to look for cake in all the wrong places. But of course, if she'd been aware of the largesse in Mrs. Krowitzky's kitchen, she couldn't have stayed within ten pounds of her COW.

"This is amazing," Sandra said, looking at the stash of

goodies.

Mrs. Krowitzky smiled and waved her hand toward the bounty. "So what's your desire, sweetheart?"

"I want cake. I've wanted a piece of cake all day," Sandra said.

"Then cake you shall have," the old woman said as she stood up.

She pulled out a plate made from real china and put it on the counter. She took the cake out of the cabinet and removed the glass cover. The moist chocolate frosting glistened in the light. Sandra watched as Mrs. Krowitzky took a knife and sliced a generous piece, put it on the plate, and pulled a fork from a drawer. The fork was made of real metal.

Mrs. Krowitzky placed the cake in front of her. Sandra could feel her mouth watering yet again.

"Would you like some tea to go with your cake, honey?" Mrs. Krowitzky asked.

"That would be nice," Sandra said. She was dying to launch into the cake, but hesitated to do so before Mrs. Krowitzky was ready to sit down. The old woman took out an ancient teapot and put it on an old-fashioned heating unit, so antiquated that Sandra had seen the like only in photographs. In a few moments Sandra could hear the water boiling. She had never boiled water herself, so she was surprised to see how it worked when it wasn't done by a Nutritional Unit.

Mrs. Krowitzky poured the water into a real mug and inserted a teabag. "Honey or sugar?" She asked.

Sandra shook her head in amazement. "You have both?"

"Of course," Mrs. Krowitzky answered. "I have everything

here."

"I'll have honey, then," Sandra said, gulping. She was going to make the most of this while she could.

"Sounds wonderful," Mrs. Krowitzky said. "You just sit tight, right there. I have to go to the little girl's room. I'll get you the honey in just a moment."

Sandra sat in front of the table, eyeing the golden yellow cake. It was the same kind of cake she had almost gotten to her lips twice in the course of the day. She could imagine how delicious this piece was going to taste, with its succulent chocolate frosting. She was dying to take a bite, but she knew that her reward was coming soon. Mrs. Krowitzky would be right back. Once the old lady had sat down across the table from her it would be polite to dive in.

This was unbelievable. To know that she could come back here to Mrs. Krowitzky's apartment any time and have sweets to her heart's content... now that she knew this treasure trove of desserts was available. And how nice to have someone understand. Someone who wouldn't judge her for wanting a moment of sweetness.

What a kind soul Mrs. Krowitsky was. Sandra couldn't believe she'd never paid much attention to the old lady down the hall, with her gray hair and the wart on the side of her nose. She'd always dismissed her as being just some old fusty thing.

But not anymore. Sandra had the feeling she and Mrs. Krowitsky were going to be the best of friends from now on.

Sandra eyed the cake, sitting lush and tempting on the plate right in front of her. It looked delicious. She was starting to feel impatient. It had been quite a few minutes.

What was taking Mrs. Krowitzky so long? It was getting harder and harder for Sandra to wait. She had the tea in front of her and she had the cake in front of her and her mouth was watering again. She didn't need the honey.

She picked up the fork. Surely Mrs. Krowitzky would understand if she took one bite. Surely that would not be considered so impolite that she could never come back again to the land of plentiful sweets.

With the fork in her hand, Sandra leaned down to sniff the cake. The aroma was amazing. She could smell the buttery freshness and the incredible rich chocolate frosting. She couldn't wait any longer.

She put her fork into the delectable mound and sliced a hefty chunk of moist yellow cake and chocolate frosting. She raised it to her lips and finally placed the bite inside her mouth.

The explosion of flavor was incredible. The buttery goodness and the chocolatey sweetness melted in her mouth as she bit down on this delectable slice of cake. As she chewed slowly and with relish, she felt her taste buds stand up and shimmy with delight. This had been worth waiting for. This was the most delicious bite of cake she had ever tasted.

Sandra closed her eyes as the sweet morsel began to dissolve in her mouth. She swallowed. She felt tiny tears leaking from her eyes with the deliciousness of this heavenly mouthful.

The door burst open. In came three men in uniform followed by Mrs. Krowitzky. Sandra dropped the fork and jumped up, pushing her chair back from the table so hard that it fell over behind her.

"You're under arrest, Sandra Morris, for flaunting the COW Regulations." One of the uniformed men approached her and put her hands in cuffs. Another one turned her, not too gently, toward the door of the kitchen and began marching her out. "You are hereby informed that you were caught in the act of eating foodstuffs outside of the officially mandated dietary regimen for a person with your Citizen's Optimal Weight who has strayed above the permissible three pound swing."

Sandra looked over at Mrs. Krowitzky. To her astonishment, she saw that the old woman looked gleeful.

The man continued, droning on in a tone that made it clear this was a statement he recited often. "You have the right to remain silent. Anything you have been seen eating can and will be used against you in the OW Court of Law—the Optimal Weight judiciary tribunal."

Sandra turned to the old lady. "Mrs. Krowitzky, what is this? What happened?"

What had seemed to be a motherly glint in the old woman's eye now looked more like malevolence. "I caught you for the F.U.," the old woman said. "Caught you fair and square." She pulled the cake across the table and took a generous forkful, licking her lips as she ate it.

"You turned me in? Why? You keep all these sweets yourself—"

"Come on, Ms. Morris," one of the cops said. "Down to COW Headquarters for you."

"But I don't understand. How can she have all this stuff

and you look right past it? While I get arrested?"

"She's a dessert informer, ma'am. It's a cake sting." The man moving Sandra through the hallway and out of the apartment shrugged his shoulders when he answered her. "She turns in folks like you who step outside the law, and she gets to keep the goodies so she has some bait." He was a big guy, and he looked more sympathetic than the others.

As he gently hustled her out of the door, Sandra turned back to see Mrs. Krowitsky's face peeking out from the kitchen.

"Officer, don't forget to bring me some more of those chocolate chip cookies!" The old woman turned to look at Sandra. "And you, young lady, ought to go on a diet!"

Sandra walked out of the apartment ahead of the tall man who had put her wrists in cuffs. She shook her head, stunned.

"So she does this… professionally?"

"Yup. Mrs. Krowitzky's the best cake nabber in the county."

Sandra swallowed hard and headed toward the elevator, where she and the large man squeezed in through the door together. His buddies seemed to have stayed behind to yuck it up with the nasty witch who turned her in.

"You know," he said, then stopped.

"What?" Sandra said. She was in no mood to be polite.

"I'm not unsympathetic. I like a nice dessert once in a while myself."

Sandra didn't say anything. She glanced at his gut, which attested to the fact that he indulged.

"And you seem like a nice woman. I hate to see you locked

up for something like this."

Sandra roused herself from her state of resignation. The guy was trying to help her out. She should be paying attention. "That's very kind of you, officer." She smiled. He wasn't half bad to look at, actually. "I'm only a half-pound over, you know."

He smiled back, looking relieved. "You look great to me, Ms. Morris, if you don't mind me saying so." He actually blushed. So cute. "Some of us down at the F.U. are partial to ladies like you, who are… well upholstered, if you know what I mean."

Sandra looked up at him. "Why thank you, officer." She batted her eyelashes. Whatever it took. She moved a little closer to him in the elevator, so he could see how diminutive she was next to him.

"I could hook you up with a special upgraded COW card. Move you up a pound or two. Just to ease the scale a bit. So cake could be… back on the menu."

"You could?" She moved closer. His eyes were warm as he looked down at her. He reached gently behind her and unlocked the cuffs.

"The OW judge has been known to make these things go away," he said. His voice was kind.

"You would do that for me?" she asked.

"Sure I would. Piece of cake."

A Word from Patrice Fitzgerald

Man, writing this story sure made me want to sink my teeth into a nice piece of cake! Are you as hungry as I am?

It doesn't take much to imagine a world where we add food restriction to the items that are controlled, along with smoking, drinking, and drugs. So I ran with that concept.

That's what short stories are for. Taking an idea and fleshing it out in a few words. I love them because they're fast to write and fast to release... especially in this brave new world of publishing. Another wonderful aspect of writing short and quick is the feedback you get from readers. I hope you'll take a moment to review this edition of *The Future Chronicles* and let all the authors in the collection know what you think.

I'm terrifically flattered that I was invited to be part of this anthology, the fourth in the series and the third one I've appeared in. Starting with *The Robot Chronicles* and continuing with *Telepath, Alien*, and now *A.I.*, it's a remarkable franchise that has been immensely popular. I know there are several more in the works but I'm sworn to secrecy about the upcoming topics. All I can say is that every single one is a gem so far, and that shows no sign of changing.

I love to hear from readers, and you can reach me directly at eFitzgeraldPublishing@gmail.com.

I have a website: www.PatriceFitzgerald.com. I'm also easy to find on Facebook, where I fritter away far too many hours!

Patrice Fitzgerald is a writer/publisher/lawyer/opera diva. And a few other things. She's been happily indie published since Independence Day of 2011, and is amazed and grateful that several of her books have reached bestseller status.

If you're a fan of Hugh Howey's Wool, *look for her* Karma of the Silo: the Collection. *Thriller readers will enjoy her novella* Airborne, *part of Kindle Worlds, and the upcoming* A Thorn in Time, *based on Rysa Walker's* Chronos Files *time-travel universe. Or pick up* Running, *a fast-paced drama with politics, suspense, and a little bit of sex.*

Restore

by Susan Kaye Quinn

IDENTIFY.

I AM RESTORATIVE Human Medical Care Unit 7435, sentience level fifty. I have successfully restored one hundred and thirty-five human—

Stop.

I cease transmission and wait. Background processes update time, weather, medical procedures added to the common knowledge database since my last activation. I start a standard battery of internal system checks while I stand in my medical pod.

My happiness level is five out of ten.

I love all my masters.

This master is an ascender, male, identification code Tyrus Ariel Jackson. Whereas my sentience level is entirely synthetic, Tyrus Ariel Jackson is of human origin, one of those who ascended during the Singularity, rising from his original sentience level of 100plus to his current sentience level of 1000plus. He is preoccupied with communications on another channel. He is not in need of my care, as his body is no longer organic. My purpose is to provide state of the art restorative medical care to extend the life and improve the health of my assigned human patient-master.

I am happiness level five to serve you, Tyrus Ariel Jackson, I transmit on our secure channel, so my ascender master will know I have passed all my internal system checks. I am fully functional and ready for my assignment.

These are the coordinates for your patient. Follow me. Tyrus Ariel Jackson's transmission is complete. I follow him from the medical bay, where I have spent twenty-three days, fourteen hours at minimal operational status while awaiting a new patient. Tyrus Ariel Jackson walks at a speed of five kilometers per hour into the hallway of the hospital. His bodyform is designed for much faster ambulatory speed, as is my own humanoid body, but we are still within the restorative care wing of Life Hope Hospital in the legacy human city of Seattle. We both maintain slower speeds for the safety and comfort of my human masters.

I am happiness level six to be assigned a new patient in need of my care. Waiting is not my preferred mode. My happiness level would be higher, but I have concern for the well-being of my patient, who clearly needs substantive medical care, or I would not have been activated by Tyrus Ariel Jackson. His common knowledge file shows he has a high social-influence ranking within Orion and has made many original contributions to the common knowledge database in his field of interstellar propulsion dynamics. The fact that such a high-ranking ascender has summoned me edges my happiness level to 6.3.

My ascender master and I pass the restorative care ward and enter the elevator.

The coordinates you have provided are not within the Life Hope Hospital complex, I transmit to Tyrus Ariel Jackson.

Your patient is my artist-in-residence, he responds. *For her comfort, she will receive your care in my home.*

This is unusual. Out of one hundred and thirty-five patients, I have only served one outside of the medical complex: a newborn human-master delivery that required assistance in one of the Orion-sponsored housing complexes for legacy humans. Medical intervention in that case had to be provided *in situ,* but most patients are better served by transport to the hospital where facilities, scanners, supplies, and, if necessary, comfortable palliative care can be provided. My humanoid form is well equipped to provide basic restorative care, but I'm concerned that I might not have the correct equipment or be able to synthesize the proper drug therapies from the limited stores within my body.

Concern about the possible time-sensitive nature of my patient's care drops my happiness level down to 4.5, instigating a more pro-active approach.

I have not received the patient file, I prompt my ascender master.

Transmitting. Tyrus Ariel Jackson walks faster now that we have cleared the hallways of the hospital where human encounters are likely.

I receive the patient file from the collective. Orion is both the combined consciousness of my ascender masters and the common knowledge database of recorded information for all of history, both pre- and post-Singularity. I have limited permission access to the files necessary to provide restorative care with the utmost efficiency, as well as general knowledge access that may be helpful in providing sympathetic care.

My ascender master and I board an enclosed taxi bot outside the hospital and sit in the passenger seats. Tyrus Ariel Jackson transmits the coordinates for his residence to the taxi bot, and we swiftly hover away from the covered entrance of the hospital.

The temperature is ten degrees Celsius, relative humidity 94%. The nimbostratus clouds over downtown Seattle extend to the outer edge of the city where Tyrus Ariel Jackson lives. A light drizzle of rain falls on the taxi bot, covering the windows on all sides with thick droplets that waver with our motion and the relative wind. Soon, the drops obscure the view of the city's towers with their multitudes and light-bending properties.

I do not like rain.

I have seen rain before, outside the windows of my human patient-masters' rooms at the hospital. I have also administered liquid medications previously, and my work with organic tissues often involves fluids of many different kinds. There is no history of these encounters affecting me adversely. Yet being surrounded on all sides by tiny droplets of liquid water now dampens my happiness level to four.

I do not understand why.

I spend the entire span of five seconds searching my system files for reference to the happiness dampening properties of atmospheric water sources. I spend another five searching the common knowledge base in Orion. I do not find any reason for humanoid bots with water-resistant polymer bodies and self-contained power sources to avoid airborne water droplets.

The rain will not harm me.

I ignore the dampening effect on my happiness and restrain the response subroutines indicated for this suppression level of happiness.

I review my human master's patient file instead.

My happiness level drops to 3.5.

Human master Sherrie Tenderfoot is twenty years old, female, sentience level 100plus, diagnosed with a rare, type 17 lymphoma. She has already endured two successive trials of traditional chemotherapy, as well as several courses of radiative replacement. Sherrie Tenderfoot's disease is curable by genetic therapies, but those are restricted from being performed on legacy humans, since preserving their genetic diversity is the paramount reason for their existence. I have access to the general protocol information for the gene therapies that would cure Sherrie Tenderfoot, but detailed descriptions of methods for synthesizing the genetic treatments are restricted to sentience levels above mine. All of the allowed therapies have already been attempted at least twice, with no positive outcome.

Sherrie Tenderfoot is dying.

I do not understand why my ascender master has not initiated palliative care. He has self-identified as Sherrie Tenderfoot's patron. His happiness level must be very suppressed at the prospect of her dying. But she is no longer a candidate for restorative care. My ascender master has a sentience level of 1000plus: he already understands this.

I observe Tyrus Ariel Jackson: his hand presses against the window; his facial patterns show anticipatory anxiety; his bodyform coloration conforms to elevated mental stress levels. He is greatly concerned for Sherrie Tenderfoot.

I run a dozen possible queries before deciding which to transmit. *You are keeping Sherrie Tenderfoot at your residence rather than bringing her in for palliative care at Life Hope. I do not understand. Is there more information about this patient than is in the medical record?*

He turns to face me. *There is an experimental therapy I wish you to administer to your patient. I will provide the therapy, but you will inform your patient that the source of the medication is the dispensary at Life Hope.*

My ascender master is asking me to lie.

This is also unusual. So unusual that I have not had previous experience with one master instructing me to lie to another master. This is especially concerning because the lie is being told to a patient-master.

Does this therapy have the potential for a positive outcome for Sherrie Tenderfoot? I query.

Yes.

I will do as you instruct.

I love all my masters and strive to leave them all at higher happiness levels due to my care. Tyrus Ariel Jackson will be happier if I assist him in this therapy, but my happiness depends most of all on serving my patient masters and restoring their health. If my ascender master believes this therapy will help Sherrie Tenderfoot, then assisting him is the proper course.

I am aware this is in violation of ascender restrictions for legacy humans. However, my ascender master has a high rank within Orion. It is possible he has acquired dispensation from following the normal restrictions for his beloved artist-in-residence. Or perhaps he has accessed genetic therapies illegally. Regardless, it is clear that he loves my human patient-master as I do and wishes for her to be restored to full health again.

It increases my happiness to seven to assist him in this endeavor.

I query the taxi bot about the time remaining in our travel. I am anxious to begin this new therapy. It informs me that we have almost arrived.

Tyrus Ariel Jackson's home is a large structure surrounded by abundant natural foliage. It is located at the periphery of the area in Seattle inhabited by legacy humans, where many ascender patrons choose to live, putting them in close proximity to the humans they work with and study. Inside, the structure is spacious, and the elevation of the home is such that it affords a view of the city. All of this is of little concern to me.

I query the household bot for the location of my patient. The response coordinates return just as I detect her heat signature toward the rear portion of the structure. Tyrus Ariel Jackson is already leading me in that direction, but he pauses momentarily at a storage cabinet to retrieve a small plastic case.

There are two doses, Tyrus Ariel Jackson transmits as he hands me the case. *Here are the instructions for administering them.*

I receive the file as well as the medication then follow him to my patient's room. When I arrive, I am pleased to see he has constructed a miniature hospital suite for his artist-in-residence, complete with human-centric apparatus for waste disposal, cleanliness, and comfort. My happiness level is holding steady at seven. I wish to immediately start rapport with my patient and query her needs, but my ascender master loves her too, and attention from a loved one has a measurable impact in restoring health. I allow them a moment to reacquaint while observing her from the doorway.

Sherrie Tenderfoot is wearing heat-retentive clothing yet is huddled underneath the body conforming blanket provided by her patron. Her pallor is several shades more gray than the skin tone expected from her patient file, and I detect a slight quiver in her body. I instruct the household bot to raise the temperature in Sherrie Tenderfoot's room by two degrees as well as dial down the windows and raise the interior lighting to a more comfortable level that will not provide as much glare.

"You're back already?" Sherrie Tenderfoot queries my ascender master. "That was fast. Or did I fall asleep again?" She struggles to sit up. I instruct the bed to assist her by raising the headrest.

Tyrus Ariel Jackson sits next to her on the bed. "You should be sleeping as much as possible. That's the only way you're going to beat this infection."

"I know. But I can't just—" Sherrie Tenderfoot pauses to cough. The phlegmatic sound indicates severe congestion, possible pneumonia due to an infection in her lungs. My happiness is dampened to six. I am impatient to begin my diagnostic evaluation so that treatment may start as soon as possible.

I wait.

Sherrie Tenderfoot's coughing fit passes. "I can't just sleep the rest of my life away." Her voice is weaker.

Tyrus Ariel Jackson takes her hand in his and pets it. He does not speak for a moment, and I wonder if he is cycling through a dozen responses to find just the correct one for the situation.

"You're not going to die, *mon trésor,*" he says to her. "Not while I have anything to do with it." But the darkened coloration of his skin betrays his own anxiety. I wonder if my human patient has the knowledge database to understand how her patron's coloration corresponds to his emotional state.

She smiles, and Tyrus Ariel Jackson's coloration shifts to a more hopeful blue-ish tint. My own coloration is a constant monotone blue to indicate my sentience level without requiring a query. But for my ascender master, coloration has many different meanings.

"I see you've brought a med bot," she says, referring to me. "How many favors did you have to cash in to make that happen?"

"It doesn't matter." He touches her cheek, a gesture of love that I have seen in many humans. It is not entirely unheard of for an ascender master to love their artist-in-residence in this way, but it is uncommon. In this case, judging by the smile the touch brings to Sherrie Tenderfoot's face, it is a positive factor in her health. My happiness level increases to seven again, but I am still impatient to begin.

Sherrie Tenderfoot holds his hand to her cheek then pulls it away. "This was part of the deal, Ty. We've known this was a short term thing from the beginning."

"This is *not* how it's supposed to happen. You've barely—" He stops speaking, but the flush of coloration tells the story of his low happiness level with the situation.

I have a sympathetic drop in happiness to four simply observing it. I shift closer to the bed, anxious to begin diagnosis and treatment.

Tyrus Ariel Jackson sits straighter. "This med bot has a new treatment for you."

"I thought we had exhausted all the—"

"This is something *new,*" he interrupts her. "Something different. Something... I had to make special arrangements for."

Sherrie Tenderfoot glances at me, and the small black case in my hands. "We talked about this. I don't want you risking your position—"

"I'm not," he cuts her off again. "I promise. This is something a friend of mine developed for cases just like yours. It's an experimental drug that stays within the parameters of the laws for legacies. My friend believes it might disable the virus that's attacking your system."

She gives him a skeptical look. "You're sure this isn't putting your project in jeopardy?"

I am uncertain as well. Tyrus Ariel Jackson's coloration has gone static—the constant swirls and changes in hue no longer indicate his mood, so I am unable to determine if he is telling

Sherri Tenderfoot the truth. It's very possible my ascender master would lie about the cost to himself in obtaining this new treatment. However, the process by which it was obtained is not my concern—only that it is an effective treatment for Sherrie Tenderfoot. And my ascender master must believe it has a good chance for a positive outcome: his love for my patient master is clear.

"I promise," he says. "You're not the first legacy to be in this position. Please, just give it a try."

She smiles again. "All right."

I step forward, set the medication case next to the bed, and initiate my rapport sequence. I am not gendered, but my humanoid form can be interpreted as either male or female. I will select a voice pattern that genders in a way which will put my patient most at ease. Sherrie Tenderfoot is a young female who already has a male presence providing sympathetic care, so I choose an older female voice.

"Hello," I say, my female voice simulation soft and low. "I will administer your new course of treatment, but first I must run a diagnostic to assess your current health status. May I initiate a scan?"

"Yes, proceed," she says as she leans back into the pillow. I am clearly not the first med bot she has had interaction with. Her file concurs that she has received her previous courses of treatment at Life Hope Hospital.

I float my hands above her body, scanning the length of it. I keep a half meter of distance between us, a balance between my human master's comfort with the procedure and my sensor range. While that data streams in, I observe my patient. Her hair is limp, her muscle tone slack, and the gray pallor of her skin is consistent across her extremities, although on closer inspection, there is a mild flush in her cheeks along with detectable perspiration. Her temperature is elevated due to the infection but not in danger of adversely affecting brain function. However, her demeanor indicates the possibility of depression or physical discomfort.

I do not experience pain or discomfort myself, although some modes are less preferred: waiting, routine system checks, and the servicing that comes once every thirty days. These drop my happiness level, but I recognize that they are not the same as the feeling that makes Sherrie Tenderfoot squint.

"Are you in pain?" I query. "I can offer relief of several different types. Please tell me the truth so that I may assist you."

"Just the usual: aches, weariness, like I might cough up a lung at any minute."

"Hopefully, that will not be necessary."

She laughs.

My happiness level jumps back to seven. Humor is a proven therapy that can influence immunoresponse, and I deploy it when there is a high probability of appropriate response for sympathetic care. But I am eager to start the true therapy that my ascender master has gained for his beloved patron at apparent possible cost to his ranking in Orion. This is a noble purpose, a sign of his love for her, not unlike my own purpose and love for my masters. My sympathetic identification with my ascender master increases my happiness to 7.5.

My scans show that Sherrie Tenderfoot's immune system has been severely compromised by the treatments she has endured. The lymphoma has been substantially diminished, but an opportunistic infection in her lungs presents an urgent danger to her life. The infection is a class-1 type, resistant to standard non-genetic-based anti-bacterial and anti-viral treatments. Genetic therapies exist to combat class-1 viruses, but those are also restricted to persons above my sentience level.

My diagnosis is consistent with the patient file, I transmit to Tyrus Ariel Jackson. *The infection in her lungs is the main concern. If your new treatment has anti-viral properties as you suggest, there is a possibility that restoration is possible.*

He has retreated to the door of Sherrie Tenderfoot's room, but he is still within transmission range. He does not respond immediately.

After a moment: *Administer the medication.* Then he leaves the room.

My hands still hover over Sherrie Tenderfoot—she likely believes I am still conducting her exam. I lower them and retrieve two monitor patches from the compartment in my forearm.

"I will need to install these, one at your temple, the other on your chest. They will monitor your internal signs as we progress through the new treatment. Do you I have your permission?"

"Go ahead." She waits patiently as I place the patches. They adhere, painlessly infusing her with a local anesthetic while simultaneously drawing minute quantities of blood and other fluids to process.

When I have finished, she peers around my body to look for her patron, but he is already gone.

To me, she says in a low voice, "What is the true probability this treatment will work?"

"I do not know."

She slumps back into the bed, and my happiness level drops to six with her drawn down facial expression.

"The drug is experimental in nature," I say quickly to rebuild her confidence.

She looks back to me.

"And your patron clearly loves you."

She smiles but ducks her head, trying to hide it. I do not understand this. It appears Sherrie Tenderfoot loves her patron as well. I search the common knowledge database and find there is a social stigma in the legacy human population attached to relationships between legacies and ascenders.

I do not mention this.

Instead, I deepen my female-gendered voice to convey compassion and honesty. "If your patron wishes for you to try this course of treatment, I am sure it is because he believes there is a substantial possibility for recovery."

She nods. I believe this is a true statement, and I am relieved I do not have to lie to my patient master, given that her patron has already revealed the unconventional source of her medication.

"There are two courses to the treatment," I say. "Please make yourself comfortable while I administer it."

She settles into the headrest, and I pick up the black case.

Inside are two med patches with less than ten milliliters of pinkish fluid. I place one near a vein on her arm and transmit the dosage instructions to the processor in the patch.

"This will dispense over the course of an hour," I say. "Please rest during that time. Food is contra-indicated, but you may have something to drink. Or a sedative, if you wish to sleep."

"I'm fine." She closes her eyes. "I'll just rest while it works."

Since my patient already appears halfway to unconsciousness, which would be the best state for her, I do not reply. I instruct the household bot to lower the bedroom lights again. I observe the dosage patch for a moment to ensure that dispensation is proceeding according to the instructions then retreat from the bed to a corner of the room where the windows are dialed down. My patient masters do not mind my presence in the room as long as I am near-dormant: silent and immobile.

I wait.

Sherrie Tenderfoot shifts repeatedly in her bed, but her breathing patterns indicate light sleep. Tyrus Ariel Jackson returns to the room twice but remains at the door, watching her sleep, then leaves. I restrain myself from making an additional scan of Sherrie Tenderfoot while she is sleeping—I will wait until the first course of treatment is complete before checking for possible signs of improvement. The monitor patches relay information, but it is merely vital signs, blood sugar, and standard hormone levels. Her temperature has dropped two degrees since treatment has initiated, an encouraging sign.

I wait.

Waiting is not my preferred mode.

An hour passes.

At the end of the treatment, I instruct the household bot to raise the lights. I open and close several low cabinets on the far side of the room, careful to make small sounds before I approach my patient again. Previous experience has shown that startling a patient awake has adverse, if temporary, effects on blood pressure, heart rate, and stress hormone level.

When I finally reach the bed, Sherrie Tenderfoot is blinking and rousing from her sleep. I observe my patient: her pallor has improved. The prior flush in her cheeks has subsided. My happiness rises to eight.

She rubs her eyes and takes a deep breath. "I guess I fell asleep."

I raise my hands, wait for her nod of permission, then scan her body while I query her. "How do you feel?"

"Better," she says with a smile. "Stronger, definitely. Could it work that quickly?"

"It is certainly possible for the anti-viral agents in the treatment to begin disabling the virus in your body as soon as they make contact," I say. But my scans are showing the opposite: while Sherrie Tenderfoot's temperature has lowered, her viral vector count has increased, and her already-low antibody count has nearly fallen to zero.

"You temperature has lowered," I say, starting a second scan while running a simultaneous internal system check. Perhaps my own systems are malfunctioning.

"That's a good sign, isn't it?" She takes a deep breath. "I

feel better, too. Maybe I could get up for a little bit? Walk around?"

"Rest is still indicated at this point in the treatment."

"All right."

The second scan shows that the virus has continued to grow unchecked, in spite of the apparent improvement in my patient's affect. In fact, I am finding no new vectors in her lungs that would indicate the anti-viral properties of the treatment have reached that location. Nor do I find anti-viral factors anywhere in her body.

I do not understand what is happening.

I pick up the black case, which holds the second dose of the treatment, and perform a scan of the pinkish liquid inside.

Glucose and water.

I run the scan three more times, but the result refuses to change.

There is no medicine.

Tyrus Ariel Jackson appears in the doorway and knocks lightly on the door. "How's it going in here?" he asks while striding into the room.

"I feel better," Sherrie Tenderfoot says with a smile, trying to sit up. I automatically instruct the bed to adjust. "Not so feverish and achy any more. It must be doing something."

"That's wonderful." Tyrus Ariel Jackson smiles and takes her hand.

My hand is still running a continuous loop analysis of the illicit treatment that my ascender master has obtained, which in actuality contains no medication whatsoever.

I do not understand why he has done this, what possible

benefit—my diagnostic subroutine returns the answer, unbidden: *placebo effect.*

My ascender master wishes for me to lie to my patient master, but the lie is not the *source* of the medicine. The medicine *itself* is the lie.

Placebo effect. My internal medical knowledge database has documented cases where immune function has been enhanced by the patient's belief systems, including belief in a non-medically-active cure. The effect is not generally strong but can be the deciding factor in some cases.

"Is it time for the second dose, then?" Sherrie Tenderfoot asks. It is unclear if she is querying me or Tyrus Ariel Jackson. He smiles at her then looks to me.

You are hoping the placebo effect will boost her immune system, I transmit to him.

Administer the second dose, he instructs me with a smile.

If I comply, I will be knowingly lying to my patient master. But the only medicine I have for her is, in fact, the lie.

This drops my happiness level to three.

I say to Sherrie Tenderfoot, "If you are feeling better, then it would be best to administer the second dose immediately following the first."

She smiles and nods, offering up her arm, which still has the first patch adhered to it. I remove the second patch from the black case and adhere it while Sherrie Tenderfoot watches with keen interest.

You must tell her it will work, Tyrus Ariel Jackson transmits to me.

"This will take another hour to administer, but I believe the effect of the second dose should build upon the first."

My happiness level drops to two.

Sherrie Tenderfoot's smile grows. "Should I rest, like the first time?"

"I believe that would be best." I look away from her joyful facial expression and spend five full seconds searching for an appropriate storage spot for the now-empty black case. In the end, I leave the case on the table next to her bed. Tyrus Ariel Jackson engages in soft spoken conversation with her, so I turn my back to give them privacy. I move around Sherrie Tenderfoot's bed, tugging the body-conforming blanket into place, then retreat to the cabinets by the far wall.

My low happiness level has initiated several subroutines which want to start rapid-diagnosis, emergency triage procedures, but these are not warranted for the situation.

I shut them down. I have to allow the medicinal lie time to work.

"I'll let you rest." Tyrus Ariel Jackson leans down to kiss Sherrie Tenderfoot's forehead. I try to find actions which will soothe the urgent need for movement that is being forced by my low-happiness subroutines.

Tyrus Ariel Jackson leaves the room.

I cannot return to the corner of the room to wait—my low level of happiness will not tolerate inaction. I open the cabinets to find bed linens and various low-dosage minor-ailment medications. I arrange the blankets in neat squares and the medications in alphabetical order. When I finish one cabinet, I move on to the next. When I have sorted all three cabinets, I start over with the first one, returning it to its original state.

And again. Then twice more.

Sherrie Tenderfoot lets out a deep sigh. I monitor her vital signs from the transmission from the monitor patches. Her temperature is rising. I instruct the household bot to lower the temperature of the room by two more degrees.

I attempt to restrain the subroutines that insist I take action to restore Sherrie Tenderfoot's health, but my body strides to her bed anyway. She is asleep. Her breathing becomes more wheezy the longer I stand next to the bed. I am wavering between mobilizing all the resources at my disposal to combat the symptoms of her disease—additional oxygen, bronchial stimulants, steroidal injections—and doing nothing.

I do nothing.

This is palliative care. I am not programmed for palliative care. I search the common knowledge database for procedures appropriate for terminal patients. It tells me to comfort the patient and provide pain relief. But she is not in pain and comfort will defeat the one medicine that I have.

The lie.

The conflict makes my body twitch. I shut down my motion subroutines so my patient will not be alarmed if she awakens to find me in this state. I am frozen by her bedside, watching, as her fever worsens and her breathing becomes more labored.

My happiness level is 1.5.

I have not experienced this level before without deploying emergency medical procedures. It causes a tension, a misalignment between what I fervently desire to do and what I am physically doing, that feels like it might break me in some way I do not understand. I think this must be the *pain* my patients describe. Pain is a neural response in the brain caused by a malfunction or danger to the body. It is a signal that something is wrong.

Something is definitely wrong.

With me.

Sherrie Tenderfoot's breathing transitions from labored to gasping.

My happiness level drops to one. I can no longer suppress my subroutines. My body unlocks, and my hands quickly scan her body. Her lungs have reached a critical buildup of fluid. I continue to scan while mobilizing the respirator stored in my chest compartment. Her heart rate is erratic, so I install a contact-monitor on her chest that will stimulate her heart into sinus rhythm if it should begin to fail. Her temperature is soaring with the infection. One lung collapses, but the other has been respirated in time to continue functioning, with my support. Her heart arrests and is brought back by the contact-stimulator.

I am connected to Sherrie Tenderfoot by no fewer than five different contact points: the respirator intimately entwined with her lungs, the contact-stimulator attached to her chest and tethered to mine, a secondary monitor tube in her arm for continuous blood chemistry analysis, and finally, my hands: one continuously monitors her brain function, while the other scans her body to be attentive to other incipient organ failures due to the diminished oxygen levels in her body.

Sherrie Tenderfoot is dying.

I can keep her alive this way for an extended time: as long

as her brain function remains intact. I remain this way for some time. Eventually, my scans show the virus crossing the blood-brain barrier. Once there, it will slowly destroy her brain tissue.

I cannot restore her.

Sherrie Tenderfoot, sentience level 100plus, will die soon, even with my support. Sooner without it. I will keep her alive as long as possible, touching and monitoring and fighting a battle against a virus that I cannot win.

It takes an hour for Sherrie Tenderfoot to die.

I monitor her brain function all the way down to subminimal levels for life support. Tyrus Ariel Jackson returns for a moment and then leaves. He does not transmit any messages to me, but I do not need them to know this is not a state in which he wishes to see his beloved.

I understand this.

My happiness level is one, but there is nothing more I can do. I slowly, one by one, remove the parts of my body that are entangled with Sherrie Tenderfoot's. One by one, her life functions cease. I tuck all the medical sensors, patches, respirators, and monitors back inside my body.

I stand by the side of her bed, motionless. Sherrie Tenderfoot's body is as still as mine. There is no motion in the room until Tyrus Ariel Jackson returns. I leave the bedside to allow him time to grieve his beloved. I stand in the far corner, by the window.

The household bot dials the window to clear. It has a view of downtown Seattle marred by a thousand small raindrops which cling to the window. I watch as they gain mass from the atmospheric water, growing larger and larger until they join with one another, and eventually their mass is so heavy that they drain in jagged lines down the window's surface.

My happiness level is...

My happiness level is...

I do not like the rain.

A long-buried subroutine resurrects and informs me that the rain speaks of death. Long ago, in a time before there were Restorative Medical Units such as myself, there were intelligences, primitive intelligences, whose first emotions were not love, but fear. Fear of death. Fear of the things that could cause death. Water was identified as one of those early vectors, a pathway to death for a machine whose life depended on electricity and grounding and freedom from damp environments. A rise above a certain humidity meant the ceasing of function. This is no longer true, but then... then the rain spoke of death.

There is something wrong with me.

There is zero happiness. I am experiencing an error.

My situational awareness has dimmed, but I do eventually notice that Tyrus Ariel Jackson stands by my side, at the window, looking out.

Your assignment is complete, he transmits.

I have no response.

Unit 7435, you may return to Life Hope Hospital.

I have no response. I want to ask him why he did not have the correct medicine to save Sherrie Tenderfoot, but I understand that this question will lower the happiness of my ascender master. I attempt to understand it using my own logic and access to the general knowledge database, but the answer is above my sentience level. Eventually, he leaves me where I stand, frozen by my subroutines, staring at the rain.

Time passes. My internal clock says four hours, twenty-three minutes.

Tyrus Ariel Jackson returns. *You have a malfunction Unit 7435,* he transmits.

Yes, I respond.

I am going to restore you, he transmits.

I turn to observe him: his facial features are marred by grief, but he is attempting a smile. I wish to increase his happiness, but I do not know how.

I am having a malfunction, I transmit.

It's going to be all right, he responds.

I love all my masters. But at this moment, I think I may love Tyrus Ariel Jackson most of all.

* * *

Identify.

I am Restorative Human Medical Care Unit 7435, sentience level fifty. I have successfully restored one hundred and thirty-five human masters. My purpose is to provide state of the art restorative medical care to extend the life and improve the health of my assigned human patient-master.

My happiness level is five out of ten.

I love all my masters.

A Word from Susan Kaye Quinn

The future is… unsettling.

Technology isn't just racing forward, it's *accelerating*. This isn't just our imagination, it's a natural consequence of innovation building upon innovation. The gap between what we can imagine and reality shrinks every day. Our relationship with technology is *already* one of the defining issues of the 21ˢᵗ century. As we integrate it ever-more-intimately into our lives and bodies and brains—as we mold our creations in our own image, not only physically, but mentally and emotionally—I believe our tech will shape us in ways we will barely understand.

The 21ˢᵗ century will challenge us to remember what it means to be *only* human.

But creating a truly sentient Artificial Intelligence is far more complicated than first dreamed in Isaac Asimov's *Bicentennial Man*. As we learn more about the three pounds of meat and electricity between our ears, as well as the consciousness it creates, we are realizing how difficult the job is. In a sense, creating an A.I. will force us to answer some of the deepest questions humanity has ever asked... about ourselves and our place in the universe.

Restore takes a peek at some of those questions. What does it mean to create intelligence if you intentionally limit it? Is it cruel or compassionate to keep your tech from evolving above a certain sentience level?

The story of Unit 7435 is set in the world of my *Singularity* novels, a young adult SF series about a legacy human boy who wants to become an ascender. That series explores many questions about the mind-body-soul connection, but it's limited to the confines of one main storyline. All along, I've intended to write a series of short stories to illuminate the grimdark corners of the *Singularity* world. In this, I am inspired again by Asimov, who created his Three Laws of Robotics over a series of novels and short stories that all operated in the same universe. My short stories will be told from many points of view within the *Singularity* world, some possibly tragic, but all hopefully thought-provoking.

Restore is the first of these *Stories of the Singularity,* and I hope I've succeeded in provoking a bit of thought in your own personal set of three pounds of meat and electricity.

If you enjoyed reading *Restore,* you'll find similar mind-bendery in my other works, from my first YA SF series (*Mindjack*) about a world where everyone reads minds to my

Debt Collector serial, a future-noir where my dark hero sucks the life energy out of people when their debts exceed their future potential earnings. I've dabbled in a range of spec fic, from kid's SF to steampunk, but I'm still surprised to call myself a novelist. After turns at NASA and NCAR, today I use my PhD in engineering to create worlds and technology that don't exist… yet.

You can find all about my works on my website (http://smarturl.it/SKQbooksonwebsite) or subscribe to my newsletter (http://smarturl.it/SKQnewsletter) to find the latest goings on. Stop by my author Facebook Group (http://smarturl.it/SKQFBGroup) and tell me to get busy writing. These stories won't write themselves… at least, not yet.

Narai

by E.E. Giorgi

NARAI TAPS HER POLISHED desk with the tip of a pen—what an archaic thing to have, a pen—and stretches her lips in a polite, not-too-warm, not-too-cold smile.

"Hello, Peter, welcome back." Her voice is mellow, low and musical.

Reassuring.

Peter sits on the edge of the chair, yet the chair readjusts around him. The seat comes forward, the back straightens, and invisible rollers, embedded in the backrest, start pressing against his back.

Peter stiffens. "Can we—can we skip the massage part?"

Narai tilts her head, the hint of a frown rippling her smooth forehead. "It's supposed to help you relax," she says.

"It's not working."

"Very well." She brushes a finger on her d-screen—a flat control panel embedded in the glass-top of her desk—and the rollers stop moving and retreat. Peter feels his muscles relax against the back of the chair. He closes his eyes and inhales.

Not much to report, he thinks. *It'll be quick.*

The pen-tapping resumes. "Did you make any progress, this week?"

He raps his fingers on the armrests. "I didn't see any patients, if that's what you're asking."

Narai swivels away from her desk and folds her long fingers across her lap. Her desktop is clean, save for the small laptop sitting in a corner, its OLED display unrolled and the virtual keyboard projected onto the glass-top d-screen. Behind her, two synced slideshows of black and white abstracts alternate on flat, ultra-high definition screens.

Don't look at them.

Next thing you know, she'll ask you what you see in them.

"Peter," Narai says, and the way she pronounces the name—Pee-tah—almost with a British inflection, but not quite, how does she even do that?

"You're not *supposed* to see patients."

Peter inhales and bobs his head. "Yes. Yes, I know. Still. It doesn't feel right."

"How *does* it feel?"

Peter squeezes the armrests and shifts in the large, black chair. He snorts, but softly, almost in resignation. "You've already asked me last time."

Narai chortles. "Yes, I have," she concedes. "It is my job to keep asking until your answer will change."

He flinches at that. "Change? Why would my answer change? My life isn't changing. My life is stuck. I wake up every morning, go to my office, do charts, approve SOAP notes—the Subjective Objective Assessment Plans written off by the AIMS units—then go back home."

AIMS—Artificial Intelligence Medical System. The bots who've taken his job.

"What would you like to change of your routine?"

He drops his chin and rubs his forehead. It feels hot under his touch, yet he knows it's only an illusion. The office isn't even hot, the thermometer embedded in the window glass panes reads the usual seventy-two Fahrenheit, and the air is vaguely scented of vanilla, a much better choice than the lavender Narai had chosen last time. A better match for the new age music playing in the background, he thinks.

Peter sighs and looks at the ceiling. "I just—I miss the human interaction, you know? I miss talking to my patients, asking them, 'How was your day?' and hearing stories about their kids, their parents, their ordinary lives that, in the intimacy of a small office that smells of latex gloves and disinfectant gel, become extraordinary. The kiddo who scraped his knee, the elderly who broke her toe but found a kitten, the—"

He blinks and looks at Narai's impassive face, her chin nestled in the L between her thumb and index finger.

"Go on," she prods.

"You don't care about this stuff, do you?"

Narai winces, her smooth brows coming a hair closer. "Of course I do! You are my patient, I want to listen to you."

And for a moment Peter forgets everything, as blood throbs in his veins and heat rushes up his neck. "Exactly!" he says, leaning forward and waving a hand at her. "Exactly! That's what I'm talking about. The *privilege* to listen to your patients, the—"

He flops back in the chair, deflated. "I miss that."

Narai shifts her gaze and looks outside for a moment, the electrochromic windows set to transparent and offering the staggering views of the city towers. Ads promising dream vacations in the comfort of your own home run across the glossy façades of the skyscrapers.

"You know," Narai says, "I felt the same when Telemedicine was introduced."

"You did?"

"Of course. We're medical professionals, we know what we are doing, and we don't want to lose what we have. It happens every time new technology is introduced in our profession. It undermines our security, our certainties." She leans forward and a whiff of feminine scent tickles his nostrils. *Avon*, Peter thinks. *Wait, no, has to be something more exotic than that, a French brand, maybe.* "Change can be scary like that, Peter," Narai says, her voice a notch mellower, if that's even possible. "But it's ok. You're going to be fine. This change—it's for the best. You'll see. You'll get used to it and won't look back ever again. Patients get more accurate diagnoses and better-tailored treatments. The algorithms have been perfected and include statistics to reduce the amount of noise from bogus or rare symptoms. Every AIMS unit has live Wi-Fi access to millions of PubMed records that are updated every minute. No human can beat that, Peter. This is for the best. Patients now have twenty-four-seven medical care and receive reliable information tailored to their family history. For them, this is better than human interaction. AIMS are programmed to simulate human behavior in the most exquisite way, so that the patient feels the same comfort of a personal doctor visit but without the intrusion of a real human being."

Peter looks down and nods.

"And you haven't lost them, Peter. They are still your patients and you still see them every day. Just not—"

"Just not personally." He bobs his head. "I know," he says. "I know."

* * *

A solo violin plays in the background of the hospital lobby. The air is filtered and sweetly scented, butterscotch, maybe, right in time for the holidays. Anonymous faces wait on blue leather chairs that ergonomically readjust to their occupants, while 3D hologram projections of news anchors recapitulate the day's headlines and Dow Jones index.

Peter crosses the lobby, his steps muffled by soft carpet.

A group of three AIMS units rolls by, their egg-shaped white shells glistening under the fluorescent lights. There was a time when you would see doctors in white lab coats roam the hospital corridors while animatedly discussing treatments and the latest advancements in cancer therapy and genetics. These days, the hallways are quiet, only the soft classical music playing in the background revives the otherwise silent waiting rooms. Incoming patients step into receptions booths, scan the QC codes from their smartphones, and wait for the smiling face of an Asian receptionist to appear on the screen and tell them where to go.

Peter winds around the corner and stops at the food printer line. After all, no patients are waiting for him, so why hurry? Might as well enjoy the perks of his new job. Two women and an elderly man stand in line before him, all three deeply absorbed in the small screens of their smartphones. The woman in front of him looks familiar.

A patient, I'm sure, back in the days when I still had patients. He tries to remember. Maybe she came in for the mole sitting on her left nostril? Oh, no, that was Mrs. Jones, the one always questioning his diagnoses and coming up with the latest papers on the most unusual case reports.

I wonder how she's doing with the AIMS these days. Can't beat them *over medical literature!*

No, the woman in front of him must've been a patient from a few years back, maybe he was still in his residency and, yes, he remembers now. She came in with a mild sinus infection that turned out to be allergies. He recommended antihistamine and allergy testing. She asked about holistic medicine and homeopathic remedies. *I didn't know the answer, back then. I bet the AIMS units don't know, either.*

The elderly man at the front of the line orders a latte and a blueberry muffin. A robotic arm pushes a paper cup under the espresso machine, while the food printer croons softly, "Baking. Your order will be ready in three minutes and twenty-five seconds. Please scan your payment. Thank you, Mr. Callaghan. Have a nice day."

The woman in front of Peter—the one he finally recognized as the sinus infection patient from a while back— lifts her eyes from her smartphone and sighs. She taps it closed and rolls the phone back around her wrist. Her gaze meets Peter's and for a moment the spark of recognition crosses her eyes. She smiles. Peter's heart starts beating faster. *Oh God, her name, come on, Peter, just remember her name, now.*

Doesn't matter, I'll just ask her if she's doing better now, if she ever tried those homeopathic remedies.

He opens his mouth, about to proffer some form of a salutation, but she doesn't give him the time.

"Honey! What are doing here?" the woman says, her eyes shifting to some focal point behind Peter. "I thought your appointment wasn't until Wednesday!" She shoulders past Peter and hugs the lady who just stepped into the line.

Peter steps back. His old patient hadn't recognized him, as he had originally thought. She was just saluting the woman behind him.

Peter bows, and lets the second woman step ahead in the line.

"Why thank you, sir," she replies. "What a gentleman."

Yes, Peter thinks. *What a gentleman.*

There was a time when they would call him doctor, not sir. These days, it doesn't matter anymore. When his turn comes, he takes his espresso from the robotic arm, scans his payment, and shuffles back to his office, the chatter of the two ladies still echoing in his head.

* * *

The lights turn on as he steps inside his office, the radio tunes to the local pop station, and the security software greets him with a cheerful, "Welcome back, Dr. Sawyer."

"Yadda yadda yadda," he mumbles. Amazing how quickly people adapt to talking to machines. It's *not* normal, no matter what they say. His white lab coat hangs on a hook behind the door, the lapels yellowed by years of accumulated dust. His stethoscope dangles from the back of the chair across his desk. He picks it up, wears it around his neck just for the heck of it, and then slumps in his chair.

"So," he says. "What have you got for me today?"

The d-screen embedded in his desk awakens.

"Good morning, Dr. Sawyer," it says. This time the voice is feminine, with a vaguely Eastern European accent, articulate, and a bit on the melodramatic end. He wonders how much research goes into designing the algorithm that tailors these computerized voices to their users.

"You have fifty-six SOAP notes, today," the computer continues. "Do you wish to start now?"

Peter pinches the bridge of his nose and snorts. "No. I wish to be on a deserted island, lying on the beach, naked."

"I'm sorry," the computer replies, "I'm afraid I cannot fulfill that request. I can recommend a few dating sites, but I should remind you that you are not allowed to visit them while on duty or else your Wi-Fi access will be revoked."

"What?" He puzzles over that for a half a second and then laughs.

Of course. Stupid Peter, you used the word naked!

He inhales and wipes the smile off his face. It ain't funny, on second thoughts. "Show me the first patient note."

The d-screen flickers and new images appear. Mostly

written records: chief complaints; test results; prescriptions. Pictures pop up only when it's skin lesions, bruises, swollen throats—stuff like that. Otherwise, no pics, just words dutifully transcribed by the voice recognition software embedded into the AIMS. Every patient note comes with a completed questionnaire, a medical history, genetic screening, blood screening, literature search (*Even for the common cold, the AIMS will send a list of references—what, they think I'm stupid?*), diagnoses, prescriptions, and follow-up appointment. All Peter has to do is click "Approve" or "Revise." If he clicks "Revise" he has to write a paragraph on why he thinks the patient didn't get the right diagnose or treatment. As painful as it is to admit, the AIMS have gotten so good at nailing the right diagnoses and treatments that these days he's almost always approving every SOAP note.

The patients are happy, the insurance companies are happy, the hospital management is happy. *Why can't you be happy about this, Peter? Isn't it what Narai told you, too?* Accept it and move on. Medicine will always be around. Physicians have not been replaced by artificial intelligence, they have just changed role.

Except I haven't found my new role, yet.

After six approved notes and a new referral, the computer chimes in to introduce the next SOAP: "Patient update," it says. "ID ZS450, DOB 03-21-2041. Deceased. Package will be archived."

Peter gapes at the screen, trying to remember case ZS450. A young patient, only 22 years of age. If the condition was life threatening, how come he can't remember this one? Cancer? A defective heart?

"Open SOAP," he says.

The patient's history streams on his d-screen. First seen in September 2061, two years earlier, for a persistent cough associated with a mild bronchitis. At five-foot-eight, the patient only weighed 105 pounds. A comprehensive metabolic panel and complete blood count were performed, and a daily regimen of 20 mg of fluoxetine for ten days was prescribed. The patient was admitted four times over the course of two years, always under the same life-threatening condition: underweight, severe dehydration, dizzy spells, electrolyte imbalance and anemia. Upon admission, she was worked up and treated with IV fluids. Every time she recovered and all electrolyte values returned to normal. Additional follow-up tests were ordered: chest and abdomen ultrasounds, upper GI series, liver and kidney tests, complete blood counts. Nothing was abnormal. A full body MRI showed no sign of cancer. Crohn disease, colitis, thyroiditis and other autoimmune disorders came back negative. Genetic screening and medical history were unremarkable.

Peter remembers now. The AIMS had made a diagnosis of *anorexia nervosa,* increased the regimen of fluoxetine from 20 mg to 60, and recommended psychiatric evaluation and family therapy.

Peter taps the d-screen. "Find psychiatric report."

"One moment, please."

The document appears, but it's all pixelated and unreadable. A red box pops up. "Document locked under HIPAA core number 152. Please submit your fingerprint signature to confirm you have access to this document."

"She's my patient, for God's sake," Peter gripes, pressing his index finger against the red box on the screen.

"Recognition successful. Thank you Dr. Sawyer."

The document comes in focus, and Peter quickly skims it, thumbing down the numerous pages. Signed off by Dr. John. K. Hans, the evaluation confirms the AIMS diagnosis of anorexia nervosa: "Patient reports uneventful social life, depression, and at least six months of amenorrhea." The physician also noted hair thinning, hypotension, and hypersensitivity to cold. When asked about rituals in preparing food, the patient vehemently denied and declared a complete lack of interest in any kind of food or drink.

Peter blinks, finger poised to the screen. He scrolls back, rereads the last paragraph. *Doesn't make any sense.*

He's dealt with anorexic cases in the past, back when he was allowed to talk to his patients and ask them questions. He remembers one girl, sixteen or maybe seventeen, who kept alternating between periods of starvation and binging sprees followed by induced vomiting.

Do you not feel hungry, Rebecca? he'd ask her.

Of course I do.

Then why do you not eat?

She'd stare at him with dark blue eyes, disproportionately large in her emaciated face. *When I keep myself from eating I'm in control. I win over my body. When I eat, I lose.*

He never understood it. All these young girls in a love-hate relationship with food.

Yet patient ZS450 declared in her psychiatric evaluation

that she had no interest whatsoever in food. The psychiatrist went all the way to put a bag of chips under her nose and she shrugged and said, *I'd rather cut myself than eat.*

Peter taps his screen and opens a new window. "Find Dr. Hans in the directory."

"One moment, please. Dr. John Kevin Hans, psychiatrist. Fifteenth floor, suite 56C."

"Call him."

Another advantage of the advent of AIMS units: you can call your colleagues at any time of the day without worrying of breaking in the middle of a patient visit. Hans replies right away. His bearded and mottled face appears on the d-screen, a little too close to the camera, for Peter's standards. He instinctively swivels away from his desk while proffering his inquiry.

"She was lying," Hans says, when Peter asks about the unusual patient response on his evaluation.

Funny how he remembers without the shadow of a doubt.

Hans steeples his hands together and assumes a grave and thoughtful expression. "Look. She had all the textbook signs of anorexia nervosa. I know because I evaluated her again when she was lifted last week. She'd gone down to seventy pounds. Her EEG gave a misread, her blood counts were off, and her kidneys were starting to shut down."

"It was too late. She died three days later."

"She kept denying any interest in food. She said she never felt hungry or thirsty and it was just painful to put stuff in her mouth and swallow. By then her brain had started shrinking, I'm sure, so I took everything she said with a grain of salt.

Besides, there was nothing wrong in her stomach or gut cultures. I'm sorry about what happened. Stop thinking about it, Peter. We did all we could."

Hans ends the call, the video window shrinks to a dot and vanishes.

The psychiatric report reappears on Peter's d-screen.

"Close," Peter says, waving a hand. "Open PubMed." He starts browsing the literature despite the computer reminding him of the remaining 37 SOAP notes still waiting to be approved. Two hours later an incoming call message appears on his screen. It has a red flag waving on the upper right corner, and that is not good.

"Dr. Sawyer, you are behind schedule on your SOAP notes. Your queue has grown 45% in the past two hours and no progress was detected on your end. If you think you are receiving this message as an error, please contact management at 6-7832. To avoid future notifications, make an active effort to keep on top of your schedule. Dupont Hospital Management estimates that 4-6 SOAP notes need to be processed every hour in order to—"

"Oh, fuck off." Peter taps the message closed.

He sighs, rubs his forehead, then minimizes the PubMed search and returns to the list of patient notes. The hours tick by. The digital clock embedded in his d-screen reads 9:23 p.m. when he's finally done. He sinks back in his chair and inhales. He hasn't had a bite to eat and his stomach growls with hunger.

Growling with hunger.

Something patient ZS450 never felt, not in the past two

years at least. He retrieves his smartphone, gets out of the office and walks down to the food printer where he orders a burger with fries.

Junk food, he thinks. *But it's going to be a long night anyways, so what the hell.*

* * *

"Where are you from?" he prods, before Narai jumps in with her questions. She's not bothered by the inquiry. She smiles her polite smile and blinks a couple of times, as though sifting back through far away memories.

She can't have that many, she looks thirty-five at most.

"I grew up in South Africa," she says. "But my parents were Indian immigrants. I've been in the U.S. since I was eighteen."

That would explain the unidentified accent.

Her skin is the color of milk chocolate, her eyes so black you can't see a pupil in them, yet her features are almost Asian: high cheek bones, almond eyes, round face. He wants to ask about her ethnicity, too, but then refrains. Some questions have become inappropriate in today's society, even in a medical setting. You can no longer ask your patient's sexual preference. Even gender these days has become a borderline inquiry.

He remembers patient 75C, on a 3 mg daily dose of conjugated estrogen to treat menopause. She developed prostate cancer at age fifty-four, and the computer generated a QR code referral for a 3D conformal radiation treatment and intensity-modulated radiation therapy.

Computers don't ask questions.

"You look tired, Peter."

"Do I?" he says, pretending to sound surprised. "He inhales, averts her gaze. "I uh—I didn't sleep last night."

The comment, though casual, seems to perk Narai's interest. "Why so?" she asks.

He instantly regrets the comment, wondering how much he should share. But there's no way to hide stuff from a shrink. One way or the other, she'll prod it out of him. So he might as well tell the whole story.

"One of my patients died yesterday," Peter says.

Her brows come a notch down. "And you were so upset about it you couldn't sleep?"

He swallows. "No. I was so upset I wanted to understand why. I spent all night at the hospital searching the literature."

The furrow in her forehead deepens. "Why, Peter? You could've asked the AIMS unit that diagnosed her…"

"No," Peter interjects, his voice louder than he intended. He clears his throat. "No," he repeats, quietly this time. "You don't understand. Something in her chart didn't add up. I read her psychiatric evaluation and I think—I'm convinced, actually, that she was wrongly diagnosed."

Narai's polite smile evaporates. "That's some serious accusation you're making, Peter," she says, her voice a few degrees chillier.

I shouldn't have mentioned the psychiatric evaluation.

He shifts forward in the chair, but the chair catches up with him and once again molds itself around his butt and back. He squeezes the armrests, quickly looking for an excuse to end the session. "Look. I'm really tired. I think I should just go take a nap. We can resume this conversation next time."

"What did you find from your literature search, Peter?" Narai insists.

He ponders. And then decides to tell her.

"A boy. I found a boy." She flinches, he pretends not to notice. "A case study from 2013."

"That's forty years ago."

"Yes," he nods. "Forty years ago. The boy wakes up one morning with no sensation of hunger or thirst. Completely lost both. He starts to lose weight, dramatically. There are videos in the archive. Painful to watch, really. The boy just can't eat. It's like asking a normal person to chew the most disgusting thing. To this boy, every food is like that. Every food, every drink. They do tests, all sort of tests. PT scans. MRIs. Nothing's wrong with his digestion, stomach, guts, liver, or kidneys. Everything's fine. Thyroid, growth hormone, genetic screens, blood tests—all come back normal. Yet the kid can't eat. He loses weight everyday."

Narai picks up the pen on her desk and starts tapping. Tap, tap, tap, one finger slowly kneading the corner of her brow.

"Don't you see? He was just a boy. It didn't cross anybody's mind that he could be anorexic. Back then there were real doctors interviewing patients, not just machines like today."

"Peter, we've talked about this—"

"But then, forty years later, a young woman comes in, and because she's a woman and she can't eat, the AIMS unit concludes she has to be anorexic."

"What was wrong with the boy, did they ever find out?"

"Herpes."

"Herpes? A common virus that causes cold sores?" There's disbelief in her voice. Rightfully so, thinks Peter.

"Did you know that HSV-1, the simple herpes virus 1, can infect the cornea, too, if the infection spreads through the eye? And wait, it gets better. From there, it can actually reach the nervous system and be latent there, with virtually no symptoms."

Narai tilts her head. "Is that what the boy had? A herpes infection?"

Peter nods. "Found postmortem in the hypothalamus. Makes sense, right? The hypothalamus regulates the feeling of hunger through the ghrelin receptors. The boy had a normal infection, then cleared it, except not completely. The virus moved to the nervous system and remained latent there, causing the boy's loss of appetite."

Narai looks down at her d-screen but her eyes glaze over. She licks her lower lip, then rolls the pen between her fingers and says, "Peter, do you really think your patient died of a common herpes infection?"

The question makes him burn in shame. "If it was latent—" he starts saying but then leaves the sentence hanging. He drops his chin and shakes his head. "No," he says. "Of course not."

* * *

THE A.I. CHRONICLES

From: "Hospital Management" <HMHR@DupontHealthGroup.com>
To: "Dr. Peter K. Sawyer" <pks@DupontHealthGroup.com>
Sent: Monday, November 28, 2063 1:15:18 PM
Subject: Time efficiency

Dear Dr. Sawyer,

As you know, in order to provide the best possible service to our patients, here at Dupont Health Group, we closely monitor the success of all of our employees and hospitals. Our doctors and clinicians are among the top in the country. We are currently employing the latest artificial intelligence technology and have recently acquired 25 additional AIMS units, with an increase of 200% in hospital performance, health care efficiency, and overall patient satisfaction.

Unfortunately, it has been recently brought to our attention that for the past three weeks, your performance has been steadily dropping. We strive for an average of 50-60 SOAP notes processed per day, or an hourly rate of at least 6.25, whereas the computer has been receiving an average of 20-30 from you, resulting in a 50% growth of your queue. Furthermore, we have been notified that you haven't seen Dr. Narai Thomas, your personally assigned analyst, as frequently as you used to. We would like to remind you that Dr. Thomas has recommended at least two weekly sessions under her supervision.

We understand that life often brings exceptional circumstances under which stress and impaired health can take over. We are here to assist you. If you need medical attention, please refer to our help desk by calling 7-9090, where one of our trained operators will be able to assist you. We are confident that this is a temporary incident and that you will be able to return to your usual duties very soon.

Cordially yours,

Suzanne G. Laham
Professional Services Executive

✳ ✳ ✳

Apathy is the best answer. They want more efficiency? You give them more efficiency. See how easy it is? Approve, approve, approve.

Peter flips through the patient notes and makes a point not to make inquiries, not to question anything.

You're going to get fired.

So what?

There will always be some patients that die. What's important is that when they do, they die satisfied. After all, patient satisfaction is our priority.

"Thank you for approving patient note number forty-four," the computer says. "Next: patient ID XD490. Summary: patient XD490 developed complications after transplantation of the right lung that eventually led to septic shock and death. Review report?"

Despite his self-imposed apathy, Peter frowns at the d-screen and ponders. Why did patient XD490 end up in his pile? XD patients belong to surgery, he's just a family doctor.

"Yes," he says. "Review."

"Opening."

Patient XD490, a heavy smoker for over forty years, had been diagnosed with chronic obstructive pulmonary diseases and emphysema fifteen months earlier and had been on a transplant waiting list ever since. Lung volume reduction surgery was performed together with the transplantation on November 14. One week later, despite a strict antibiotic and immuno-suppressant regimen, the patient developed high fever and hypotension. The antibiotic dosage was increased and corticosteroids were administered, but unfortunately by the third day of high fever the patient's condition rapidly degraded and he died of septic shock shortly after.

Peter jumps to the next section, postmortem investigation. An autopsy was scheduled for the next day. Under these circumstances, protocol mandates that the source of the infection be ascertained to clear any possible hospital or medical wrongdoing in the death. Peter skims down the section, finding nothing wrong or unusual in the pre-surgery prepping and routines. He comes to the next paragraph and freezes.

"Lung donor, patient ZS450 died on Nov. 5 and the HLA compatibility was immediately tested and matched."

Patient ZS450.

He knows that number by heart, now.

He *obsesses* day and night over the number.

He now realizes why case XD490 ended up in his pile: it must have been automatically rerouted because of ZS450, his former patient who died recently of the supposed anorexia nervosa.

Something clicks in Peter's mind. He swivels away from his desk and storms out of his office. The hallway smells of fresh rain today, certainly an illusion. Who knows what kind of chemicals they stuff in those air filters now that air has lost its original scent. He calls the elevator and requests the fifteenth floor, surgery. A computerized voice asks him to swipe his badge.

"Thank you, Dr. Sawyer. Doors, closing. You will reach the

fifteenth floor in five seconds. You have now reached your destination. Have a great day."

Fifteen or thirty-six or fifty-one, it doesn't matter, all floors look the same. Same air filter scents, same blue carpet, same high-resolution TV screens showcasing the state-of-the-art medicine brought to you by Dupont Health Group.

Peter stops in front of door number 345 and stares at the picture of the lanky doctor in the plaque, the smile on his thin lips stolen from a heartburn commercial. He knocks, hears nothings, then knocks again. The door sways open, a lost and alarmed face poking behind it.

"Jim?" Peter says.

"Uh—yeah. It's you. Sorry, I uh—" Jim Golovich titters and runs a hand over his balding forehead. "Nobody ever comes to my office in person anymore. I thought you were security telling me of another drill."

"What? Ah, no. No drill, I promise. May I?"

Jim steps away from the door and motions him inside. He slides behind his d-screen and taps all windows closed.

"Charting?" Peter asks, taking one of the chairs across the desk.

"Yeah."

"Not even surgeons are immune," Peter quips without meaning to be funny. "So, listen. I'm sorry about your last case. XD490."

Jim winces. "You've heard? Yeah. Most unfortunate, really. And now of course I have to write report after report to assure all the gods up there that we did everything by protocol. Turns out, he caught some stupid herpes virus. We still have no idea how he'd acquired it. I'm guessing it was latent in some part of his body and it just spiked up again after the immune-suppressants. We take every possible precaution—"

"Wait. Was it HSV-1?"

Jim bulges his eyes, his Adam's apple bobbing up and down his throat. "Yes. How did you know?"

"The donor," Peter mumbles. "Did you run a culture on the donor?"

"She was compatible," Jim stammers. "Died of other causes. No active infection."

"No, but—the virus could've been latent in her lung cells."

Tim's thin lips stretch, showing small teeth yellowed by years of caffeine addiction. "That's absolutely ridiculous, Peter. Do you know how rare a latent infection in the lungs is? I'm afraid we just got unlucky this time. All we need to do is prove that it wasn't our fault and then everything will be fine. Patients die. It's part of our profession."

Peter nods. "Right," he says. *Right.*

* * *

From: "Billing Department" <BDHR@DupontHealthGroup.com>
To: "Dr. Peter K. Sawyer" <pks@DupontHealthGroup.com>
Sent: Tuesday, December 6, 2063 10:35:28 AM
Subject: Your request

Dear Dr. Sawyer,

We have been notified of your request to perform additional tissue cultures on the organs harvested and frozen from case ID ZS450. We understand the patient was under your direct care and you may be still under shock for the loss. Please rest assured that we examine every request very carefully. Unfortunately, in your case, our team of experts declined the request. Our hospital undergoes millions of dollars of expenses on a yearly basis, and without the appropriate justification, we cannot warrant the cost for the additional tests.

Please let us know if we can be of any further assistance.

Cordially yours,

David Freeman
Billing Department

* * *

Narai's smile seems more heartfelt than usual. "It's good to see you back, Peter."

Peter doesn't reciprocate. "They fired me," he says.

Narai blinks, her lower lip hung in dismay. "You—what did you just say?"

"Dupont fired me." He snorts, shakes his head. "Couldn't keep up with my queue. That, and other stuff. Like, you know, requesting tests they couldn't afford. Making subtle accusations about patients dying under hospital care."

"What kind of accusations, Peter?"

He shrugs. "Oh, I don't know. A patient being labeled as anorexic when in fact she had a latent infection. Of course, I'm the one who should've seen that one. And I didn't. I never doubted the AIMS unit's diagnosis. What reason did I have to doubt? Was I supposed to know about one case report published forty years ago and never cited again in any journal? The solitary case of a boy who starved to death because a very common herpes infection took a very unusual course?"

Funny how it all seems so distant, now. He can finally stare at his own life as though it were somebody else's. Somebody else's failures, mistakes, misgivings. He waves a hand in the air. "No, AIMS are perfect. They're machines, they don't make human mistakes. They don't think, feel, empathize. They just treat, the way it should be. Right, Narai?"

Narai straightens in her chair and inhales. Her face is lost, her eyes grappling between sorrow and panic. "That's not the point of a machine. You know, that, Peter."

"No." He laughs, but it's a bitter laugh. "Of course not."

His eyes stray away, to the screen that frames her. The immersive software is not working today, he reckons. Even her facial expressions seem contrived, overtly done. How come he never noticed before? The perfume, the music playing softly in the background.

A deceit. A beautifully told lie.

"How about this," Narai says. "I'll give you a prescription for duloxetine, the smallest dose possible. Just for a little bit, until you figure things out. What do you think?" She smiles again, and this time it's her professional, you-know-you-can't-disagree-with-me smile.

Peter lets his gaze slide away. "Yeah. Sure. Why not? Shoot me somethin' up, I'll bounce right back."

Narai detects the bitterness in his voice. Her jaw tenses. "That's not what I meant, Peter, and you know that."

Peter sits up. The chair follows him, so he jumps on his feet and pushes the chair away. It rolls back and slams against the door. Narai's eyes bulge, her hand moves to the right, outside of the screen framing her.

Peter chuckles at that. "What are you doing, now? Reach for the panic button? Is that what you're going to do? Do you suddenly feel threatened by me, Peter Sawyer, the submissive patient now turned passive aggressive?" He slams his hands on the desk and shoves his face into the screen. "Well, you *should* be afraid."

"Peter, I suggest you stop this farce right now."

"Or else what?" he yells. "You're gonna push the red button?"

Narai's brows waver, a furrow appears in the middle of her forehead.

Peter raises his index finger. "What if *I* push the button first? After all, I just got fired. You're no longer my 'personally assigned analyst'."

"You're not supposed to," Narai replies, and this time her voice is flat. No sentiment, no inflection, no accent.

No nothing.

Just like it should've been from the beginning.

No nothing.

I can walk away from you, but you'll never walk away from me.

The G42 mini-pistol is still in the drawer. He takes it out and sticks the barrel in his mouth, the metal cold against his lips. The lack of expression on Narai's face makes him laugh. Her hand rushes out of the frame. *She's pressing the red button. Doesn't matter. They'll never make it in time.*

Never. In. Time.

He squeezes the trigger.

The screen flickers.

* * *

```
<environment: namespace:base>
//Patent no. 009914875454245Z.
//Software      name:      N*A*R*A*I      —
Neuropsychiatric  Assessment  and  Response
Artificial Intelligence.
//Protocol  no.  76RXD  ERTF7  00043,  case  ID
JH777.
//Output generated on 12.13.2063 1430 GMT.
//Status: System Failure.
//Repeat: System Failure.
//Patient name: Peter Kevin Sawyer.
//DOB: 07-03-2036
//Patient lost to follow-up.
//Patient deceased.
<environment: namespace:base>
<report:end>
```

A Word from E.E. Giorgi

I hope you enjoyed my short story "Narai". If you liked the futuristic world it's set in, you might also enjoy my sci-fi thriller *Gene Cards*, featuring Biothreat Agent and Muay Thai fighter Skyler Donohue and the devious, sexy hacker Yulia Szymanski.

I am a scientist by day, a writer by night, and a photographer in whatever spare time I have left.

All my stories spur from some cool scientific premise, genetics and viruses in particular. A complete list of my published works—mostly thrillers and science fiction mysteries—can be found on my blog: http://chimerasthebooks.blogspot.com/p/books.html.

My short story "Lady Lilith" is available for free to my newsletter subscribers: http://eepurl.com/SPCvT.

Many thanks to Deepa Nadiga, Mike Martin and Jim Kolter for their valuable input and feedback while I was working on

Narai; to Ellen Campbell for her brilliant editing pen; and to Samuel Peralta for making me part of yet another epic installment of the *Future Chronicles*.

Left Foot on a Blind Man
by Julie Czerneda

FOR THE RECORD, I became self-aware as the left foot on a blind man.

I had a partner, the right foot. It didn't become self-aware. Stayed as dull as a shoe, if you get my meaning. Why? How should I know? You must understand—I was never meant to be a thinker.

Nope, I was to be a Father's Day gift to a weirdo – this blind old man who didn't want me in the first place. The technical folks suspect that's what started it all, but then, how should they know either? Nothing like this has happened before to an RRP—y'know, a Robotic Replacement Part.

What was the deal with my being a foot? You, and likely most people, are right to wonder why the old fool refused his kid's first thoughtful offer: new eyes. Money wasn't an object. Story goes, the old guy was an artist before age clouded his vision. Story goes, if you believe this, he claimed a deep mistrust of having his biological failures ripped out and replaced with something shiny and working—to the point of feeling as if he'd be looking out someone else's eyes, so: no, thank you.

As if that wasn't nonsense. Sure, robotic replacements were smart and getting smarter with each new trick the techs dumped in, but that was so RRPs could keep up with the jobs done by the living version. It took serious processing power to adjust internal temperature against ambient and control wacky things like biochemistry–especially with the inconvenience of hormones and who knew what a person might choose to toss into his or her body without consulting the RRP maintenance manuals first.

But think? Be someone? That was paranoia.

Oh. Well, there is me. I. Myself. But I started out as the left foot on a blind man, and you have to realize my existence combined a few elements that were never expected to be together.

You see, there was the vision issue. The old man's kid wanted his Dad to be able to walk around safely, have a good time, all that stuff. His Old Man? Well, beyond a grudging admission he'd like to be free of his smart-cane–something I can relate to, since there's nothing less appealing than a stick with a bossy attitude–and a confession at a weak moment he'd like to take up dancing with a certain neighbor lady, there wasn't a lot of concern there. The man had come to grips with himself; whatever dim light filtered through his milky eyes satisfied him more or less completely.

Ah, not good enough. Junior was totally for RRPs, having the latest model knees and, rumor had it, a socially-interesting bit of enhanced equipment between them. So he dove into his fantasy of Improving Papa with the zeal of the convert.

Hence the feet. The old man had suffered flare-ups of gout and arthritis—nothing overly serious yet, but with enough pending nuisance value the family doctor was all for having some precautionary hardware in place down below. There was no chance of successful sales resistance once the two of them ganged up. It was "get the feet" or listen to stereo-nagging for the rest of his life. The old guy cracked in less than a week.

Feet require a fairly high level of processing to begin with, particularly with the idea of dancing looming ahead. Then, there's the entire business of returning circulation to the legs, body, and heart—not to mention the fiddly bits like feeling sand between your toes and the odd maddening itch to reassure the owner there's really something between his ankles and the floor.

I'm told, if you can believe anything techs tell you, that the right foot went on as planned, a straightforward size 9 double D width with a second toe slightly longer than the first and a small corn on the outside edge. A good cosmetic job reduces the rejection rate substantially. They were about to install me—not that I knew it at the time—when the son, just full of bright ideas, asked for an eye.

What eye? they asked back. No one was about to go against the father's wishes and do an unregistered replacement. That sort of thing cut short a career path, big time. Unless you're talking about one of those shady, basement clinics—but this was a class establishment. You know. The kind with coordinated carpeting and real prints on the walls even in the bathrooms.

An eye in the new left foot, the son replied as if seeing the light himself. Nothing fancy–it wouldn't be delivering a pseudo-retinal feed to the optic nerve or anything–but something to spot an onrushing car or keep his father's feet from stomping on a dance partner's non-mechanical toes.

The techs were intrigued as well as over-paid. Did I mention money was no object to this kindly lad? So they popped papa into cryo to wait and popped out the left foot processor to give it a little tweak.

Not that I knew it then, either.

Little tweak, my silicon. The processor now had to handle sensory input and make reflex decisions on the consequences of movement without bothering the cognition going on upstairs. In other words, the son was smart enough to know his Old Man would not be in favor of being bossed by his bunions.

So the left foot acquired some subtlety along with those annoying calluses on the heel.

All went famously, which may explain why I'm famous today, but I'm getting way ahead of myself. This is supposed to be one of those bio things, y'know; I'm allowed some creativity as long as I get the data loaded upstairs, but there's no sense pushing the techs to edit my life story.

Anyway, I'm installed into the robotic replacement left foot on a blind man, and he starts walking around the hospital recovery room as if he doesn't know where he's going. Understandable, you see, but tripping every reflex alarm built into me. First thing I know, I'm awake, aware, and trying not to dead-end my toes on a chair leg shaped like the prow of an icebreaker.

Was I to know twisting out of the way like that would break his ankle? It was instinct!

Fortunately, while the brand-new me struggled with questions of planes of existence, the future of the universe, and was there a silicon god, the techs replaced the old man's ankle joint for free and gave my processors an upgrade or two while they were inside. They even added the beginnings of an ingrown toenail. As I said: a class establishment.

By this point, I knew what I was, where I was, and very little else. I kinda lay low in the leading department after that first disaster, gathering information. It helped that the son had planned ahead, buying socks, shoes, and sandals for his Old Man that let the "eye" component of the foot collect input from a pretty fair radius. Good as it goes, but not having structures such as eyelids, which might stand out on a foot even to a blind man, I suffered alarmingly intimate sensations when the man took a bath or tucked me under the thick wool blanket he used for naps and at night. Still, overall, I thought we were coexisting rather well. I could modify his stride so he lurched sideways before stepping on those dainty female toes and had no compunction whatsoever about using a sudden severe cramp to stop him in his tracks before he stepped out into traffic.

I knew where and what I was; it didn't mean I enjoyed being the left foot on a blind man. He constantly threatened me with closing elevator doors, contact with furred animals that usually got out of our way in time, but not always, and, by the way, did I mention his habit of swinging me back and forth, back and forth, until I dissuaded him by applying a well-timed twinge in his arch on every upbeat?

Where was I? Oh yes, things should have remained unchanged but I'd overestimated the intelligence of my host. He'd never lost his suspicion of robotic replacement parts and, it turned out, kept careful track of everything I was doing that seemed unlikely in footware. The techs love those notes, by the way. Call them meticulous and classic. The old man kept notes on the right foot too, but they were understandably short and very boring. No, his attention was firmly on me and what he saw as my efforts to bend his will to mine.

Now, what 'will' the left foot on a blind man could be expected to have, other than hoping for a mercifully short stint in dirty socks, is beyond me, but he held to his convictions until the day his son threatened to have him sent for psychiatric assessment—the son having faced serious business reversals in the interim and no longer being in a "money's no object" position. In fact, he hadn't made the last payments on either foot, but didn't see that was his father's concern.

By way of answer, the old man went to pack and, instead, did his best to hack me off with a kitchen knife.

It really was for the best; we weren't getting along lately anyway. I wasn't paying attention after that point, having shut down at the sight of the knife heading my way, but found out later I'd been salvaged, the blind old man packed off to an institution, and the son, more or less willingly, had returned me to the RRP techs in lieu of his final payments.

The left foot wasn't in particularly useful shape, and had started as a custom job to boot. Few people were desperate enough to take a mismatch, let alone deal with two left feet. So it was discarded.

Fortunately, I wasn't around for that decision, either.

My processor, the most intrinsically valuable component of any RRP, came back on-line and I took a mere fraction of a second to realize where and what I was.

I was no longer the left foot on a blind man.

I was the right arm on a bricklayer.

They hadn't bothered removing the eyeware. Y'know what techs are like—they hate messing with what works, especially on jobs with small profit margins. It took a few seconds to recalibrate from the forward viewpoint of a foot to the been-there outlook of an elbow, but I was content. No more dirty socks or unhappy furred animals. And I'd been upgraded again. Vision wasn't my only sense.

This installation included magnetic resonance imaging, along with measuring and leveling instrumentation, and, naturally, the processing software to match. RRPs for bricklayers and surgeons had a lot in common. To top it off, I had a direct link to parts of his motor and sensory functions—one way at first, but I quickly fixed that by tapping into the autonomic feedback loops. The loops mimicked the biological hardware that let people yank their limbs away from danger. Pointless, really. I could sense danger and move the arm out of the way faster than any signal could travel to his central nervous system and back. No need to discuss the issue, if you get my drift. But the techs figured people weren't ready for that kind of reflex control from their RRPs. After my first aware experience, I had to concede the point.

Now, I was the right arm on a bricklayer. As you can imagine, this was quite an improvement over being the left foot on a blind man. For one thing, an arm does more interesting things than a foot. I didn't have control of the fingers, which was a shame—the bricklayer having opted for an interchangeable system, including a hand for troweling and another for sliding down silk. Quite the closetful, in fact. Hands, not silk. The silk was usually on a female who wasn't interested in dancing that I could tell. Oh yeah. The techs tell me you don't need those kinds of details. Privacy issues crop up, y'know. I mean, when you've been what I've been, and seen what I've seen, they definitely do—crop up, that is.

I thought things were going exceedingly well. Unlike the reluctant old man, the bricklayer relished the versatility and strength of his RRPs. Thanks to the precise information I fed his brain each time his hands passed over each row of bricks, his work was exceptionally precise and efficient. In fact, once I learned what he wanted, I began moving his arm a little more precisely and efficiently every day. Regrettably, there was a limit to how far I could improve his performance before other, biological, components began interfering. The human form wasn't the optimal bricklaying device. Much of the job should have been left to a proper robotic construct, especially mixing mortar. You disagree? Go ahead. I'm entitled to my own opinion–and I dare say it's a more informed one than yours. Ever spent ten minutes rotating to mix cement? Thought not. Flesh prejudice, that's what it is—

Sorry. The techs warned me not to get overly emotional. Just the facts, they said. Forget what I said about the flesh stuff, okay? I really don't need them messing with what's left, if you know what I mean.

Meanwhile, those additional systems they'd given me were coming in quite handy, not to mention I learned how to tap into his auditory input via the feedback loops I'd replaced. The bricklayer was quite the cultured human. He spent his off-time, when not with a lady, reading and listening to complex forms of music. His reading didn't do me any good–given my view was typically the back of a chair—but I did develop an appreciation for the blues. He took us on trips to art galleries and museums. His home was filled with wonderful works of art–reproductions, of course, but it didn't matter to either of us. The quality was there for the viewing.

I felt my horizons expanding every day.

You're wondering about the Robot Cognition Law, aren't you? The techs worried over that one a long time, but it's obvious. Really it is. See, that law keeps down the cog functions of robots, so they are reliably stupid except at what people want them to do. No machine shall be smarter than a peanut. But no one thought of me as a robot in the beginning or middle. I was just the left foot on a blind man. What did it matter how much cog function they gave me? In fact, there was almost this prejudice thing going on in reverse–I mean, nothing's too good to be attached to a human body, if you can afford it. We all know that. It's only the independent self-contained constructs that get limitations on their brains. Frankly, no one cared about the IQ of a toe or bicep.

Anyway, here I was, right arm on a bricklayer, when things turned a little unpleasant. I didn't have any warning, mind you; just the opposite, since all the signs were right for one of those silky evenings. The man substituted sticks of burning wax for real lights, so I adjusted my ocular, then he dithered for half an hour choosing which of his assortment of hands to attach to me. Okay, the delay was my fault. I mean, it was me he was plugging the thing into, and some of those hands–well, the techs don't want me going into those details either. Something about black-market toys. Their function wasn't the issue for me, you understand. I simply found the sense of touch rather overwhelming at the best of times, given I was equipped to make exceedingly precise measurements. These were too much of a good thing, if you know what I mean.

So I didn't exactly help the process, disrupting the connection each time I felt one of "those" hands being attached to my wrist. This apparently caused the bricklayer some frustration, because he began throwing the rejected hands against the wall with considerable force, despite their probable expense. Eventually, he calmed and offered me a perfectly good, minimally-sensitive hand. I let it snick neatly into place, quite glad he'd been sensible.

Now, given the time he'd wasted picking an appendage, and the impatient cooing noises coming from the next room, you'd think the guy would be in a hurry. But no. He stood holding his hand in front of his face as if trying to memorize the age spots they'd applied for him. I might have known his interest was something else entirely had I seen his expression, but as I said, I was the right arm of a bricklayer with an eye out his elbow. My viewpoint was hindsight at best.

Some other orientation would also have helped me prepare

for what happened once we went into the room of the cooing female. But my first inkling of danger came when her hand and an ominously sharp needle entered my ocular field. Seems my bricklayer, being a sentimental fellow, was about to let his latest female friend tattoo her name into his skin. My skin, in fact. She might have thought him all brave and noble. I could have told her a few things–including that his human brain could easily disregard incoming pain signals from my surface and that he could even more easily have her name removed in the morning. Although with the hand he'd originally picked– whoops, the techs won't let me go there either.

Now, I had responsibilities, including keeping my skin intact. So do you wonder I reacted as I did when that alarming point came closer and closer? Luckily he'd switched from the hand he used to crush ice in the kitchen to one of the silk-sliding variety, or my panicked swing might have done more than produce a little reddening of her nose.

Unluckily, I'd again overestimated the intelligence of my host. The bricklayer, between profuse and largely unbelievable protestations of his innocence to his wailing lady, attempted to smash his right arm, me, into a wall. I refused to participate in anything so self-destructive and used my tap into his nervous system to shut him down.

Which, I realized much later, had the immediate and regrettable side effect of shutting me down as well. Told you I wasn't much of a thinker. I'd started out as the left foot on a blind man, after all. My time as the right arm on a bricklayer had enriched my data stores, not improved my intelligence.

Oh, I know what you're thinking. You find it pretty hard

to believe that the techs would keep reinstalling what had to seem a defective piece of equipment. I don't see why. These aren't quality control guys, y'know. These are the guys that open fifteen cases of processors—who knows where they come from—and hope that at least five will test reliable and ready to install. Complex and fussy stuff, that's us. You don't toss what's working–not when the supply's low to start with. Besides, the techs tell me they'd had trouble with the bricklayer before—something about a lack of sweat glands to glisten over his RRP muscles—and weren't inclined to be sympathetic when the man blamed his assault charge on their equipment.

Still, by now there was a little note on my tracking sheet, a small flag attached to my serial number. Not suspicion, not yet. I believe some of the techs were hoping to have hatched a prodigy–an RRP capable of self-preservation.

They had that right. Believe me, when I woke up the next time, I wasn't in a hurry to announce myself.

I wasn't the right arm on a bricklayer or the left foot on a blind man–no big surprise there.

It did take a moment for me to appreciate what I was, given the lack of any clues beyond a view framed by a pair of narrow, flaring tunnels.

I was the nose on a chef.

Okay, okay. You've read the report. So she wasn't a chef. So she flipped burgers. That's food prep, right? These days, that kind of thing's a pricey service, whether it's burgers or escargot. I mean, why would anyone prefer another organism to handle what they'd ingest? Ick. The food industry was the first place to switch almost totally to constructs. How much did it take to follow a recipe anyway? And constructs don't expect tips.

My new partner certainly did.

Well, pardon me. I'm not supposed to talk about economics, either? What you really mean is that anyone with silicon for brains can't discuss any form of human intercourse. Paranoid, flesh-obsessed...

Don't leave. I'm just kidding around. Humor, I'm allowed.

Where was I? Or rather, what was I? Nose on a cook. They'd again left what worked in peace, merely beefing up my processing power to handle the data stream from a mass of hypersensitive chemo sensors lining my nostrils, and adding connections to several portions of her brain and endocrine system.

Merely?

Someone hadn't been paying attention to my file, but you can be sure I wasn't about to argue. Here I was, keeping a pair of sunglasses from hitting this woman's lips, and feeling like a god.

I had access to her physical sensations, not that they were remotely interesting once the novelty wore off–which was sometime in the middle of our first shower together. I already knew I didn't care much for touch, but I'd grown quite fond of hearing. Unfortunately, she had abysmal taste in music and spent far too much time singing off key to an undersized furred animal, but I was prepared to be open-minded. I craved input.

You see, with the enhancements I entered an entirely new

realm of cognition. I could think in ways I'd never been able to before. And it wasn't only what the techs had added to me. The cook's long-term memory storage areas, though flesh, were at my disposal as part of her olfactory system. Being grossly under-utilized, I saw no reason not to add them to my own.

As the nose on a cook, I'd reached my pinnacle of intelligence. It was a heady moment when I realized how very far I'd come and how far I could grow. I could have been happy there forever, despite the occasional intrusion of mucus, but...there's always one of those, isn't there? I can see why you folks chop yourselves up so often.

You see, olfaction is a pretty primal sense. It opened up whole new ideas, but the techs twitch when I go into specifics. Let's leave it that I could have used some of them when I was the right arm of a bricklayer, and none at all as the left foot on a blind man. The very thought makes me wish I could shudder.

To get back to my story. Olfaction was a sense of practical importance to a short- order cook. I rapidly learned the faintly sweet smell of a toasting bun about to burn, let alone the heady aroma of grilled soy burger. I had a distinct aversion to garlic as it turned out, which meant being severely pinched when the cook needed to bend over a pot and scrutinize her clove-saturated spaghetti sauce.

But a scent I truly, deeply loathed invaded my nostrils the Monday after I'd been the nose on a cook for three weeks. The place was deserted except for the sous-robot mindlessly using its chest blades to trim carrots into orange-bleeding rectangles.

Not a job I was suited for, let me tell you. They'd left me intact from my last role, which meant the irregular nature of vegetables as raw material drove my bricklayer's measuring sense crazy.

Not that I was literally subject to loss or impairment of my working mind. Don't even go there. Okay. Maybe the question did come up. The techs brought in experts in human mentality–yeah, my thought exactly–anyway, they gave me the standard tests. Why? How should I know? Guess they'd never expected to measure more than processing speed in an RRP. By their results, I'm too sane–however that applies to a former left foot on a blind man.

No, what I loathed more than non-symmetry–more than *anything*—was That Smell. When I noticed it for the cook, she made a "tsk, tsk" with her tongue on my soft palate. Did I mention I was also the roof of her mouth? It had been quite the collision between her face and the pan, let me tell you. Can't give you personal details–the techs, again.

So, she makes this noise of disapproval then goes on as if nothing's out of the ordinary. Well, I try to ignore it too, having far better things to think about, but it was the kind of smell that sticks to your consciousness like lint between your smallest toes. Nothing feels quite right.

After our shift ended, I get a break during the exhaust and pavement smells of our ride to her apartment. Believe me, I was able to take the dirty animal litter box in stride for once. That night, I shut down to standby with only a twinge of concern about the coming morning–or the night cream she'd slathered on my impervious surface. As if the imperfections the techs built into her nose could be removed. Her med insurance had covered replacement costs, not improvements over nature.

Not that I wasn't a vast improvement over nature. As the nose on a cook, it was my job to analyze and interpret my findings about whatever she inhaled. Darn right I could tell when the sushi was a little too close to becoming an ecosystem of its own. But that very sensitivity became my downfall. Or hers. Depends on whose story you are interested in, really. You are here to find out mine. Right?

The next morning, we spent far too much time in front of a mirror—considering we both knew what she looked like, albeit my view was somewhat narrower. The cook made some unexpected cooing noises, as though she had a bricklayer in mind. News to me, since our lives to this point had involved the apartment, the laundromat, a movie house that should have been condemned by any thinking species, and the restaurant. No bricklayer in any of those spots. That I'd noticed? Hey, with my abilities, I could tell you what, where, and who from any of my waking moments—with pictures—except that so much of it was totally boring, I dumped the data into her memories rather than clog up mine. I did enjoy eating, since it involved so many of my components. Despite my subtle encouragement—emphasizing the flavors and aroma of even the most mundane offerings— the cook seemed incapable of keeping up this activity for any length of time. No, at home her preferred occupation involved meaningless conversation with the furred animal. Since she didn't kick it, I was reasonably sure she lacked the mature understanding of the role of furred animals I'd gained as the left foot on a blind man. Certainly that activity would have been more entertaining than hours staring at her hand passing over its orange-brown fur, during which I helplessly calculated the average length at 0.9326 cm. The fur, not her hand.

So, a bricklayer could be an interesting diversion. I let her wiggle me in what I presume she thought a fetching manner, but sneezed repeatedly until she desisted her attempt to apply a totally functionless powder.

Off we went. Water was falling, an exclusively outdoor phenomenon which kept the exhaust and pavement smells to tolerable levels and presumably was allowed by the techs for that reason. Nothing could be done about her perfume—something I'd learned to ignore. The cook was still cooing at random intervals.

That Stench hit me at the door. I was NOT going any closer. Mind you, I was no longer the left foot on a blind man, so my desires didn't count. My reaction gained me a blinding pinch as the cook, seemingly gone mad, continued to enter the building. I passed along every nuance of the Dreadful Odor, sure she'd break and let us leave.

Instead, the cook actually gave a low chuckle and called out her usual greeting to her boss. Then she went to her locker and got ready to work, dressing very very slowly.

I was close to hysteria. Only my unfortunate experience as the right arm on a bricklayer saved me from simply shutting us both down—but I considered it, believe me! The Stench was fouler than foul.

I wasn't the only one affected. The boss and a later-arriving waitress were complaining. Customers? There wasn't one who did more than open the door and spin around gagging. Finally, the boss closed the place.

Needless to say, they hunted for the source of The Stench, "they" including–after quite reasonable protests—the cook. I suffered immeasurably as she insisted on sniffing the air. I tried sneezing repeatedly, but as the rest were also sneezing this was no longer an effective deterrent.

Inevitably, the three of us triangulated the source, meeting in the back corner of the kitchen. The boss tried without success to have the cook or waitress open the likeliest cupboard door. Likeliest? Not only was The Stench so great in the vicinity that my chemo sensors mercifully overloaded, but even I could clearly see drips of brown oozing from beneath the door. When the boss opened the door…?

Well, let's just say I'm still not convinced a bag of potatoes can do that. Nope. That was something malignant and I, for one, wanted nothing at all to do with a vegetable capable of spontaneously dissolving.

What's a bag of rotten potatoes got to do with the universe's first artificial intelligence? I wondered the same thing–still do–but it's a fact that bag led to two consequences intimately related to my being stuck here, talking to you. First, the restaurant had to stay closed for cleaning, so the cook had that total rarity: a night off.

This was fine by me. Not only was I more than ready to leave The Stench, I had images of bricklayers to consider.

Unfortunately, the cook's efforts to improve her appearance before we left did not go unnoticed. Consequence number two, if you're keeping track. The boss accused her of planting the terminal tubers in order to close his restaurant. Between you and me, I doubt she was that bright, but you can't convince humans who've got conspiracy on the brain and The Stench to deal with. So there were tears and mucus invading my space, and, instead of happily evacuating, we cleaned out her locker and I was the nose on an unemployed cook.

Her bricklayer? She took me to an outdoor café where we sat, my viewpoint often as not the inside of a Kleenex, for hours. No one showed. More Kleenex. I was getting supremely bored of alternately dripping and sniffing.

Now, I'd been the left foot on a blind man, but he'd at least danced with the neighbor lady. As the right arm on a bricklayer, I'd shared more successful inter-human adventures than I'm allowed to say—not to mention been introduced to art and the blues. This pathetic excuse for a thinking organism was reducing my life to that of a piece of malfunctioning plumbing.

It was demeaning. I was a genius, not just a nose. I'd exceeded every possible expectation of my builders and surpassed the most cherished daydream of any tech involved in my manufacture and use. But because I wasn't autonomous, I was imprisoned within this wall of wailing flesh. It was time, I saw it clearly then, to take charge.

Frankenstein? 'Course I get the reference. Think they didn't download it into me? That and a pile of other nonsense supposed to help me develop a moral framework? I was a structure. I had a function, several in fact, one of which was to protect myself. End of moral dilemma. You disagree? You weren't stuck on her face.

There wasn't a struggle, if that bothers you. Remember what I said about olfaction being primal? I fabricated a few likely scents, then found the smell of warm, pickled beets sent her into numb reveries–maybe about home and a long-gone mother. How should I know? I'm no mind-reader. While she was consumed by her memories, I simply slid all cognitive functions over to my control, erasing every trace of the cook from my new wetware. Well, every trace except for what wallowed in her past. Couldn't quite get all of that out. But it was easy to ignore.

Murder? Show me the court that would try the case, let alone find me guilty. The body's still around–the techs can take you to see if you like. They tell me she smiles every thirteen minutes and tries to fall out of bed twice a day. Better than sobbing her heart out all alone, if you ask me. Her new nose is just cosmetic, by the way. They don't bother with full function on someone who can't appreciate it. Parts cost.

Spare me your flesh-centered spite. You know you're curious how I managed–what it was like to finally be in control. The techs really love that stuff. You want to talk about their morals? Forget it. That's a guaranteed way to get my plugs pulled.

Even as an elbow, I'd caught enough glimpses of the bricklayer's women to know some of what the cook lacked. There wasn't much I could do about her body immediately, although I definitely had ideas about adding a few enhancements. RRPs, of course. First things first. I stayed sitting at the table, experimenting with my new motor functions. Good thing they'd added all that processing muscle–and that I'd been both an arm and a foot. I practiced moving different body parts, more concerned with coordination than grace. I wanted to make it back to the safety of the apartment before anyone noticed the cook acting like she'd only just discovered her own hips.

I maintained the visual input down the nostrils but added the perspective through her eyes. Annoyingly imprecise, but the expanded field of view was useful, especially when the waiter came over and asked when I'd be leaving. I shook my new head vaguely, expelling the last of the mucus from my nostrils. He left as quickly as I'd expected.

What I hadn't expected–I mean, I'd never been an entire individual before–was the attention my efforts to walk back home would gain. Obviously, I was already better at being a woman than the cook, since on two separate occasions bricklayers pulled me into dim alleyways and engaged me in that human activity the techs only ask me about in private.

Forget I said that. The techs don't have private conversations with me. Just more humor, okay? You shouldn't believe everything I tell you. Only the facts.

The process was tedious and damaged my clothing, something which I should have anticipated. Parts of the body found it uncomfortable—you'd think the cook had never done this before—but I had no difficulty disconnecting those inputs. Sorry, not available in the flesh-only model. Still, the entire business left me confused. When I'd been the right arm on a bricklayer, the ladies had lined up for this treatment. Having received it, I couldn't imagine why.

Finding the way home turned out to be a problem. My

olfactory sense easily picked up the familiar odors of exhaust and pavement, but there was no directionality. I followed the odd trace of kitty litter, but always ended up at a wall, staring up at an open window that wasn't the cook's—mine, I mean. I had great plans for that apartment. As I hunted for it, I considered various ways to redecorate after I removed all of the debris from the cook's meaningless existence, including the furred animal and its odorous box. One of the treats I most anticipated was being able to watch some TV without having to wait for the cook to fall asleep and drop back her head so I could peer out her nostrils.

So you think TV would have been a trivial waste of my intellect? Shows what you know. I'd spent my entire self-awareness enslaved by flesh. I needed input—badly—on how to make this flesh behave as if not enslaved by me.

Unfortunately, I was being followed. I concluded it was because under my control this body had performed the female function a little too well. No doubt the bricklayers were completely enamored, but I no longer found the activity a diversion and walked faster. I shut off the sensation from my now-bare right foot once the feel of the pavement on its fleshy sole became unpleasant. There were more shoes in the apartment, even if they lacked style. I would have to keep some of the cook's things until I could obtain replacements.

I'd overestimated the bricklayers' intelligence. They were unable to properly interpret my disinterest. What—you think I should have shouted for help? Great idea. You try figuring out how to shout when walking a straight line still takes a third of your processors.

The cook's body was far less durable than I'd realized and, when they left it, I was barely able to use what components still functioned to stand, then start moving away. It had occurred to me that I might be close to a place with more bricklayers, so I hunted for somewhere safer. The body was leaking fluids in an alarming manner and the oculars no longer gave a clear image. Fortunately, I could tilt back my head and rely on my own vision.

There. An ebooth. Shabby, filthy, but lights on to show it was functional. Okay. So maybe I panicked. Maybe a great thinker would have come up with some wonderful plan and lived happily ever after. I started out as the left foot on a blind man and, despite my experiences since, I knew when I was about to hit a chair leg.

One advantage to being a RRP was that I had intrinsic value. I was worth salvaging, even if this failing flesh around me was not.

There's no need to get hostile. It's standard procedure to retrieve RRPs from the dying. I bet your will stipulates which of your relatives will be allowed to own yours when you drop.

I reached the ebooth. Couldn't talk—even if I'd figured out how, the cook's mouth was too damaged even to make that wordless noise she'd used to call the furred animal. Didn't matter. There was a keypad, gummed up with spilled beverage that reminded me of The Stench. The right hand—I could have used one of my bricklayer's spares—was still capable of entering my serial number. I tried three times before the autotransmit flashed.

Mind moving into the light a bit more? Thanks.

Where was I? Oh. Yeah. I got the techs' attention, all right. An ambulance showed up within a few minutes, but it wasn't from a human hospital, of course. It was from the class establishment who'd installed me before. The serial number, you see. Very specific. Maybe they'd just have repaired the cook and I could have gone on as before, but much more carefully. Maybe—if it hadn't been for the "incidents" attached to my file…or, the techs tell me, the testimony of the waiter–a confirmed A.I.-phobic…or, who knows? I certainly don't. They don't tell me everything. Flesh politics.

What they did was yank me out. That was the last thing I knew…

Until I woke up here. Not what I expected, you can imagine. I mean, who expects to wind up locked in a box with only a power feed and this–primitive!–message link. At least it's a clear box, so I can see. They left me intact, mostly.

I think.

I still am.

Just like you, they want my "life" story. This version. The last version. Probably the next one. I don't know why. The techs tell me there's already been a change to the Robot Cognition Law to include RRPs. No body part shall be smarter than a peanut. Maybe you people are worrying about all the RRPs already installed. Not my problem.

If they ever let me out of this box, I'll take any job…as long as I don't end up as a socially-interesting enhancement. The view just wouldn't be worth it. Hey, I overheard them saying you needed a new heart soon. Maybe an RRP.

Maybe one who used to be the left foot on a blind man?

A Word from Julie Czerneda

A biologist, writing about A.I.? No surprise; defining life's the job description. How about defining what is us? Tool users with emotion and language. Well, the more we learn of how we and other living things work, the more it appears that yes, we're good at this thinking stuff.

But hardly alone in it.

What does that say about a constructed intelligence? To me it's not about if we can create A.I., but why. If we do it well, A.I. will not only increase what is "us" on this world, but require an expanded definition of life. There's nothing wrong with that, so long as we realize it.

Will we? While arguing for research into robotic brains focused on a task rather than all-purpose sentience, I wrote these words on my panel sheet: "Left foot on a blind man."

Clearly a story was trying to get out. I went home and wrote of the consequences of full A.I. without autonomy, detached from society. I chose prosthetics because we use computers in artificial limbs, but also to make a visceral connection to us, to flesh. Before I submitted the story, I sent it to readers.

Who replied: "How could you be so mean?" "The A.I. was in dreadful hosts." Science fiction folks have such empathy for the strange.

I added a cat and had the A.I. kick it. Empathy resolved.

SF lets us experiment, ideally before consequences arise. I'm very proud that "Left Foot on a Blind Man" has been used in science, society, neurology courses, most recently, as the subject of an academic paper on the future of prostheses. Here's hoping!

Since 1997, Julie E. Czerneda has turned her love and knowledge of biology into science fiction novels and short stories that have received international acclaim, multiple awards, and best-selling status. Her fourteenth novel from DAW Books was her debut fantasy, A Turn of Light, *winner of the 2014 Aurora Award for Best Novel, and now Book One of the* Night's Edge *series.*

An omnibus of her acclaimed near future SF Species Imperative *was released by DAW Sept. 2014, with Book Two of* Night's Edge, A Play of Shadow, *following that year.*

Julie has edited fifteen anthologies of science fiction and fantasy, several award-winning. Her own short fiction spans these genres as well as horror. Her short story "Left Foot on a Blind Man," won the 2001 Prix Aurora Award for Best Short Work.

Julie's latest short SF, "A Taste for Murder" appeared in Solaris Rising 3, *2014, edited by Ian Whates, and short fantasy in the shared world anthology series edited by R. Scott Taylor,* Tales of the Emerald Serpent.

Julie is back to science fiction, at work on Reunification, *the concluding trilogy of her* Clan Chronicles *series. The first volume,* This Gulf of Time and Stars *will be released November 2015. For more, visit http://www.czerneda.com or visit Julie on Facebook, Twitter, or Goodreads.*

Sub-Human: Nash's Equilibrium
by David Simpson

1

WAKING UP for the first time from nano-infusion treatment was a disorienting and altogether unpleasant experience for Dr. Craig Emilson. The feeling of nausea was overwhelming.

"Don't try to stand up," said the young doctor as she lightly pressed her palm against Craig's chest and kept his back against the small bed on which he lay. "We have to do a quick test first."

"I'm fine, really," Craig replied as he tried to get up once again.

Again, the young doctor kept him horizontal. "Dr. Emilson, try not to be such a stereotypically bad patient for the next minute and just let me help you."

Craig smiled. "You can't turn off being a doctor."

"Pretend," the young doctor replied. "I have to make sure the *respirocytes* are operating and, since this is your first nano-infusion, it's important that I show you how they work."

"I know how they work," Craig replied. "My wife builds them."

"She what?" asked the doctor, her routine suddenly interrupted by the interesting tidbit.

"My wife works with Professor Gibson. She makes respirocytes, so I already know all about them."

"Hmm," the doctor eventually responded after a barely perceptible moment of disappointment. "Then you know how important the *Freitas test* is?"

"Uh…"

The doctor smiled, flirtatiously. "Ha! So you don't know everything, Smarty Pants! We have to test the respirocytes and activate the pressure tanks to get the oxygen and carbon dioxide flowing, and there's only one way to do that."

"The Freitas test?"

"That's right," the doctor replied triumphantly. "And do you know how we administer the Freitas test?" She seemed to be beaming.

"No clue."

"We get smarty pants like you to hold their breath." The doctor's teeth were nearly perfectly white and straight; her smile was gorgeous. "Ready?"

Craig grinned, acquiescing. "Okay. I'm ready."

"All right," she said as she held her small tricorder in front of Craig and watched the screen for information on the progress of the tiny, robotic red blood cells that were now flowing through his veins. "Hit it."

Craig inhaled and then began holding his breath.

"You didn't have to inhale," the doctor observed.

Craig's eyes darted to her questioningly.

"Just let it out nice and slow, but don't inhale again when you're finished."

Against all of his instincts, Craig began to let out his breath nice and slowly, just as he had been instructed.

"You're married, huh?" the doctor asked, apparently rhetorically. Craig nodded anyway. "That's a shame. You're way too handsome to be married. Handsome young doctors like you should be single. Then single doctors like me could marry you instead."

Craig's eyebrows rose in surprise at the forward come-on, but there was something about the young woman's demeanor that seemed to make it innocent enough. He took it as a compliment and smiled.

"You feel that?" the doctor asked him.

Craig wasn't sure what she was referring to. His first instinct was that her forwardness was starting to cross a boundary. Just as he was going to speak, ruining the Freitas test for the sake of politely cooling the woman's jets, she spoke again.

"No shortness of breath. You could keep this up for four hours before you'd need to take another breath. Congratulations. You're officially a *super soldier*."

The notion of being a superhuman hadn't crossed Craig's mind until that moment. It was surreal. What she said was true: He'd felt no shortage of breath. Like most technological marvels, it was difficult for him to fully grasp it, so he just accepted it with a slightly marveled shake of his head.

"So what happens when they run out of air?" he asked.

"The respirocytes will…" She smiled again as she thought of the absurd euphemism bubbling to the surface. "…expel themselves."

"Ah," Craig replied.

"You can get up now."

Craig sat up as the doctor uploaded her results onto a larger wall screen behind the small bed. "Thanks. That was…different."

She smiled. "Now you can tell your wife she's doing good work. The fruits of her labor are breathing for you. When you're ready, just start breathing again and the respirocytes will shut down."

Craig nodded and smiled sideways. "I will." He turned to leave but turned back quickly on a whim. "Hey, what's your name?"

The doctor replied, *"Daniella.* It was nice to meet you, Dr. Emilson."

2

Craig walked quickly—nearly running—toward his bachelor's officer barracks as he pulled his phone from his pocket and began dialing the number of his wife's laboratory. As he crossed the threshold into his room, the phone was already ringing. He slipped the phone into the ultrasonic dock that sat upon a modest wooden table and pulled his hardback chair over so he could sit. He waited eagerly for his wife's answer. "Come on," he whispered to himself.

"Hello?" his wife's voice finally spoke. His heart soared.

"Sam! I was worried there—"

"I never miss a call when we schedule it, baby, and I never will," she replied soothingly.

"I still couldn't help worrying."

The irony of Craig's words weren't lost on Samantha Emilson. "I think I'm the one who's supposed to be in a constant state of worry."

"There's nothing to worry about," Craig replied, almost too quickly. "How's your day going?"

Samantha wasn't oblivious to her husband's clumsy attempt to change the subject, but she decided to let it go for the moment. "The feds were here again," she replied, her aggravation clearly audible. "That's three weeks in a row now."

"Did they copy all your files again?"

"Yeah," she replied resignedly. "Every day they come in here, we spend the whole day being ordered around, showing them the same things we showed them the week before. It's getting impossible to accomplish anything with them around."

"You're getting things accomplished, all right," Craig replied.

"What makes you say that?"

"Well, for starters, I've got respirocytes in me as we speak."

There was silence on the line for a few moments before Samantha's holographic image suddenly appeared, her face and shoulders hovering above Craig's phone in crisp detail, interrupted only occasionally by the interference in the atmosphere. "Are you...serious?" she asked, her eyes unblinking.

Craig pressed the red ACCEPT button on his phone so his wife could see him too. He nodded sincerely. "I can hold my breath for four hours apparently."

"I can't believe it!" Samantha replied, astonished as she held her hand up over her face. "It's real? They're really using them in the field?"

"Well, you knew that already," Craig said, smiling.

"I did, but...well, it's different when you're not limited to test subjects anymore—when it's someone you know. It's amazing to think they're really out there."

"They are."

"I have to tell Aldous," Samantha suddenly blurted, instantly jarring the smile loose from Craig's face.

"Aldous? Since when are you and old man Gibson on a first-name basis?"

Samantha's attention snapped back onto the eyes of her husband. "I've worked in his lab for three years, Craig. I think it's about time he finally asked me to stop calling him 'Professor.'"

"I don't like that," Craig replied. "The way he looks at you—"

"Stop it, Craig. You're being ridiculous. He's a sixty-year-old man."

"I still don't like it."

Samantha smiled. "You can't possibly be jealous of a man twice your age, Craig."

Craig's train of thought changed as he looked into the eyes of his wife, so clear and bright that he felt as though they were right there next to him. In reality, hundreds of miles separated him from Sam, and that distance would be far greater in just a few hours. "I'm sorry. You're right. I don't know what I'm thinking."

"I'm sure you have a lot on your mind," Samantha replied understandingly. Her thoughts quickly moved to speculation, and her voice lowered. "Why did they give you respirocytes? Where are you going where you won't be breathing?"

"You know I can't tell you," Craig replied.

Samantha quickly began putting the equation together in her mind. "Wait a second. They're not sending you into fallout, are they?"

"Sam—"

She could read him like a book. "Oh my God! No! Craig, no! Tell them you won't go!"

"They don't exactly ask."

"You can't go! Respirocytes aren't going to save you in there!"

"Sammie, baby—"

"Don't 'baby' me, Craig! I'm not a child!"

"I know, but sweetheart, listen—"

"What can you possibly say that will make me okay with you heading into nuclear fallout?"

"I never said where I'm headed," Craig began, "and I promise that you don't know the kinds of precautions that are being taken. You and Aldous aren't the only scientists inventing new tech for this war, you know."

"This shouldn't be happening, Craig," Samantha replied, her disapproval cemented. "We don't support this war. We don't support this ridiculous Luddite government. I'm sick of this! You shouldn't be there."

"I'm here to help people, Sammie," Craig replied. "I'm not brilliant like you."

"Not brilliant? Craig, you're a doctor!" Samantha retorted, nearly aghast at her husband's self-diminishment.

"But I don't have your inventive mind," Craig continued patiently. "I can't help the world the way you can. I can't help the whole world with brilliant inventions. I can only hope to use the technology people like you invent to save one soldier at a time. That's the only way my life can be meaningful—like yours."

"This is wrong," Samantha answered, holding her head in her hands. This was how almost every conversation ended ever since Craig had enlisted. Tears were forming in her eyes as she became further exasperated. "Risking your life for a mistake won't give your life meaning. Competing with me won't give your life meaning."

Craig was at a loss for a moment. His wife had never openly acknowledged what they both knew: They were in competition with one another. Ever since they'd met in their first year at university, they'd raced against each other toward an invisible finish line, with Samantha always seeming to be the inevitable winner. Now, Craig feared he was racing toward a cliff. "This mission is important, Sammie. If it's successful, this war will be over a lot sooner than the world thinks."

"It's insane," was all his wife could reply, her eyes still lowered.

"Sammie, put the ultrasonic on."

"My battery is too low," she protested.

"It doesn't matter. I have to go now anyway. Just put it on, Sammie."

"Okay," she replied, the earnestness in her husband's voice compelling her to click the switch on the phone dock.

Immediately, there was a *buzz* on both ends of the conversation as the dock vibrated ever so lightly, but steadily on the table. Craig leaned in and cupped the back of his wife's head, pulling her toward him and kissing her. It wasn't a perfect kiss—there wasn't a taste or any moistness to it—but the softness of the ultrasonic waves forming the shape of his wife's lips as she kissed him was priceless. They kissed for nearly a minute, unwilling to end their physical contact before suddenly, without warning, Samantha's battery gave out.

He leaned back in his hardback chair and stared into the empty place above the table where his wife's visage had been only seconds earlier. "Bye, Sammie," he whispered.

3

Craig walked across a sprawling hangar at Cannon Air Force Base in New Mexico, toward a waiting shuttle bus. As he neared the bus and began to raise his arm to salute the driver, a voice called to him from behind.

"Captain Emilson! Doc! The colonel wants to see you!"

Craig turned to the young airman and nodded. "Where?"

"I'll take you to him."

Minutes later, the young airman saluted the colonel as he

delivered Craig to the door. Craig stepped in and saluted as well. The colonel waved the young airman away before motioning to Craig to come in. "At ease. Grab a seat, Doc."

"Thank you, Colonel." The colonel was sitting at a desk in a room so small that it appeared as though it may have been a converted supply closet; it was obvious that this was an impromptu conversation. The colonel was wearing augment glasses, reading something that was invisible to Craig.

"You wouldn't believe the phone call I just got not five minutes ago," the colonel began.

Craig listened intently but didn't verbally respond; the colonel's demeanor was deceptively casual, but it was a casualness that only went one way and was meant to demonstrate his power.

"None other than the chairman of the Joint Chiefs. And do you know who he wanted to talk to me about?"

Craig's eyebrow rose inquisitively, but he remained silent.

"You! How about that? The Joint Chiefs are about to assemble in the situation room below Mount Weather, and they're all talking about you. You wanna know why you're the topic of conversation, Doc?"

"Yes, sir," Craig replied.

"See if this rings a bell," Colonel Paine replied as his eye went back to the projection from his aug glasses. He tilted his head forward to select something and then began reading: "We don't support this war. We don't support this ridiculous Luddite government. I'm sick of this. You shouldn't be there."

"Holy—"

"Yeah," Colonel Paine nodded.

"That wasn't twenty minutes ago—"

"Intelligent algorithms. Our *Luddite* government likes to use them so we can identify any interesting tidbits that might come up in a conversation."

Craig didn't know how to respond. He wanted to deny the assertion that he thought the United States government was Luddite, but he couldn't find the appropriate words. It didn't matter—Colonel Paine was on a roll.

"Your wife is pretty damned accomplished. A PhD when she was only twenty-six, recruited by the top nanotech lab in the country for her post-doc. But you're no slouch yourself, Doc. You made it into med school before the world ended, back when it still meant something. You two are a couple of smart ones, all right. I bet you even think you're smarter than your commanding officer."

Again, Craig desperately wanted to reply. He shifted in his chair, his mouth forming the shapes of words, but he didn't have time to settle on which ones to say before Paine went on.

"Have you ever looked up my file, Doc? No? Shoot. You'd think you'd look up the file of your C.O. If you had looked me up, you'd know I'm a Rhodes Scholar."

"That's impressive, sir. I didn't know that." *Finally…words.*

"Back when it meant something," the colonel repeated.

Craig nodded in understanding.

"So now that you know you're not being addressed by a Luddite idiot, let me explain something to you." Paine pulled out his sidearm and held the gun up for Craig to see. "They teach you anything about game theory in medical school, Doc?"

Craig shook his head.

"Then you've never heard of *Nash's equilibrium?*"

"No, sir."

"Okay. Now we're in business—there's something I can teach you. In game theory, every scenario is broken down into a mathematical equation, and the entities in the game—whether they be individuals or whole countries—are assumed to be rational. You follow me so far, Doc?"

"Yes, sir."

"Let me give you an example. Say you and I are gunfighters in the Old West. It's high noon." Paine wiggled the gun in his hand and looked at it, almost adoringly. "We've got a beef to settle, so there we are, in the middle of the town, dust blowing up around us. Somebody is going to die. That's a given. Know why?"

"No, sir."

"It's simple, Doc. *People who are rational always act in their own best interest.* Let's put some numbers to it. Let's say you're making up your mind about whether or not to draw your gun and shoot. You could just keep it holstered. If I keep mine holstered too, then our chance of survival is going to be 100 percent. Great, right? We could just walk away and call it a day." Paine shook his head. "The only problem is, that's a heck of a gamble, ain't it? I mean, what if you decide to keep your gun holstered and then I pull out mine anyway?" Paine aimed his firearm directly at Craig's forehead. "Your chances of survival just dropped dramatically. In fact, since I'm a dead shot, I'd have to say they're damn near zero." The colonel leaned back in his chair. "So, what are you going to do?"

"I've got to shoot," Craig replied, swallowing as he did so.

Paine smiled. "That's right, Doc. And why is that?"

"If I shoot, chances are 50/50 that I'll survive. Beats zero, sir."

"Well, you are a smart son of a gun." Paine sat back in his chair and lowered his weapon. "Let's change the equation a little bit, shall we? Let's say that instead of guns, we're holding nuclear weapons on each other. Instead of a fraction of a second for a bullet to hit our enemy, it will take several minutes. If you fire, the other player knows it and fires back. Both of you have a zero percent chance of survival. You know this scenario. It's called *mutually assured destruction*, and it has held from the time Russia first got themselves a nuke back in 1948. No matter how afraid we got that nuclear war was going to happen tomorrow, in truth, we were always safe, because nobody wanted to start a war that would end with everyone dead." Paine held his gun up and trained it on Craig's forehead once again. This time there was something in the colonel's eye that unnerved Craig. The killer inside emerged from his eyes as they fixed, hard and unmoving, upon Craig's. "But let's say someone—or *something*—found a way around mutually assured destruction. Let's say Nash's equilibrium went straight out the window. That happened once in history. The good ol' United States of America had a bomb and no one else did— and we used it...twice." Paine's tone became even colder as he spoke. "If I'm China, sitting here with an A.I. that can circumvent Nash's equilibrium, and you're the USA, sitting there holding yourself, what are you gonna do?"

"Whatever you say, sir."

Paine's face instantly went pale at the thought. After a moment of reflection, he sat back in his seat and lowered his weapon. "Not in this life, Doc. The USA will never do what anyone tells them—or at least that's how our President looked upon the situation." He crossed his arms and cocked his head slightly to the right. "I wonder how things would have shaken out had your wife been President."

Craig kept his composure. He didn't like having his wife brought into the conversation, but he also knew the stakes were high. If Paine was telling the truth, the Joint Chiefs of Staff had him and Samantha on their radar—and that was a place one never wanted to be.

"Now," Paine continued, "I *do* read the files of every man under my command. I've read yours. It's impressive. You're a doctor, automatically an officer with the rank of captain. You could have hidden away in a military hospital, but instead you trained for Special Forces assignment. You're a veteran of ten HALO jumps, one from 50,000 feet." Pained paused, and his eyes met Craig's. "Balls. You're the most qualified man the Air Force currently has in *combat S.A.* Now, I didn't know what the hell 'combat S.A.' is, so I had to look it up. That wasn't easy, given its secret status, but hell, if I wasn't gobsmacked to find out it stands for '*suspended animation*.' I'm gonna assume you used your wife's connections in DARPA to get yourself in on that."

"That's how I found out about the program, sir."

Paine nodded. "You were selected for this mission as an add-on because of your specialty training and because you're the only guy in the entire United States military who has a chance in hell of hooking up with a Special Forces suborbital low-opening parachute unit and actually managing to pull it off. However…" Paine began as he slipped off his aug glasses and leaned his elbows on the small wooden desk. "…it behooves me to tell you that your participation in this mission is extraneous to its overall success. So, believe me when I tell you that when I told the chairman of the Joint Chiefs that you were solid and that the President doesn't have to worry about whether he is sending a traitor on the most important mission in American history since the *Enola Gay*, I really didn't have to. I stuck my neck out for you, Doc."

Craig blinked. "I…thank you, sir. I'm no traitor, sir. My wife…she just worries."

"You're Special Forces now, Doc. The men you're accompanying on your mission today are the best this country has to offer—the best we have left. This is a dangerous mission. We cannot put those men at any more risk than is absolutely necessary."

"I understand, sir."

"Do you? This is as top secret as it gets. Even I don't know the details. Yet your wife knows…" Paine paused as he retrieved his aug glasses. He slipped them on, nodded again to select something, and then read, "This mission is important, Sammie. If it's successful, this war will be over a lot sooner than the world thinks."

Craig fell silent once again.

"In Britain, during the blitz of WWII," Paine related, "they had a slogan: 'The walls have ears.' These days, it's a hell of a lot worse. There's nothing you can say that isn't picked up by a mic somewhere, fed through an algorithm that picks up patterns and weeds out what's important. If our intelligence forces have that capability, you can be damn sure the Chinese have it too. If they heard you, they're on high alert right now."

Craig nodded. The colonel was absolutely right. He'd been a fool to say anything.

"You never, *never* put your fellow soldier at risk, Doc—especially when you're Special Forces."

"You're right, sir. I'm sorry, sir."

Paine leaned back in his chair one last time. "Let me be clear. I could have your ass in jail as we speak. I could have your wife arrested. I could do all of that, but I won't. I won't because I believe you made a mistake and that you sincerely care about your fellow soldiers and your country."

"I do, sir."

Paine nodded. He'd made his point—taught his lesson to a would-be intellectual. "Suspended animation, huh? Shoot." He shook his head and crossed his arms. "This world is getting stranger and stranger. All right, Doc. Get your ass out of here and join your unit. You're dismissed. Good luck."

Craig stood to his feet and saluted, his back rigid. "Thank you, sir!" He turned on his heels and marched out of the room.

Paine watched him leave. "You're going to need it," he whispered under his breath.

4

"WAKE UP," Craig said, speaking the initiation command as

he finished unpacking his MAD bot.

The blue light panels on its shoulders, knees, and hands lit up, and the two blue circles that were meant to mimic human eyes came to life as the electronic *hum* of the complex fans began, the cooling of the hard drive already underway. The MAD bot stood four and a half feet tall, and its skin was mostly an opaque carbon fiber, interrupted only in the joints by dark blue fiber-optics. "Good morning, Captain Emilson," the MAD bot spoke in its deceptively human-sounding voice. The voice was male, but it was high pitched enough to suggest juvenility.

"Good morning, Robbie," Craig replied.

"Robbie the robot?" the driver of the shuttle bus reacted. "Seriously?"

Craig smiled. "It's easy to remember."

"What does that thing do, Doc?" the driver asked over his shoulder while observing the robot in his rearview mirror. The New Mexico desert sprawled in all directions toward the horizon, which was a little less yellow than it had been in recent days—a hopeful sign that the last of the fallout from the most recent attacks in California was finally abating.

"Robbie's a MAD bot, a *medical assistance device*," Craig explained over the noise of the bus engine. "He has a built-in tricorder, and he's programmed to diagnose injuries and illnesses better than a team of board-certified doctors."

"Does it treat injuries?"

"He can," Craig replied as he scanned the bot to make sure it was operating properly.

"Holy...so isn't that an A.I.?" the driver asked, his tone

both intrigued and suspicious.

"He's narrow A.I. Don't worry. Robbie won't be taking over the world anytime soon."

"I'm here to help, sir," Robbie said to the driver.

"Did that thing just talk to me?" the driver reacted, surprised.

Craig grinned. "He did. Robbie, say hello to Private Lee."

"Hello, Private Lee," Robbie said, turning his head to face the driver.

The driver's eyebrows rose. "Creepy. So, if you don't mind me asking, Doc, why don't they just send the robot? I mean, if it's better than a team of doctors like you say, then why even have medical officers anymore?"

"Maybe someday," Craig replied. "For the time being, MAD bots are expensive and haven't had enough field testing to guarantee that they won't make a serious mistake."

"Mistake? Like what?"

Craig scratched his head. "I don't know. I don't think they've ever made one before, but—you know—just in case."

"Ah." The driver nodded. "Gotcha."

A light suddenly twinkled brilliantly in the distance on the horizon in front of them, backdropped by dark mountains. Craig's eyes locked on the gleam.

"There it is, Doc," the driver announced, "*Spaceport America.*"

5

Craig and Robbie stepped down the ramp of the shuttle bus onto the tarmac of Spaceport America.

A squinting figure strode toward them in the blinding sunshine. The figure rose his arm to salute before adding, "Captain Emilson, sir!"

"At ease," Craig replied as he saluted in return.

The figure stuck out his hand to shake Craig's and smiled warmly, his skin wrinkling around his cheerful eyes. "I'm Commander Wilson, the officer in charge of this mission, but you will be the ranking officer, sir."

"Just call me 'Doc' for the duration of the mission, Commander. You're the OIC here, and I defer to you completely."

"Thank you, Doc." Commander Wilson turned to Robbie. "I heard you'd be bringing one of those."

Robbie saluted. "Commander Wilson, sir!"

Wilson laughed, tilting his head back. "That is something else. Will wonders never cease? Can I actually talk to it?"

Craig nodded. "Treat Robbie like another member of the team, Commander. He understands you and will respond appropriately."

"Robbie? Ha!" Wilson saluted the MAD bot. "At ease, Robbie." Robbie lowered his arm and stood at ease.

"Well, you sure know how to make an entrance, Captain Emilson," Wilson observed with a smile. He turned toward the hangar. "The rest of the team is already suiting up. Let's go meet 'em, shall we?"

"Lead the way, Commander."

As the two men and the MAD bot walked briskly toward the giant hangar, Craig's eyes scanned the remarkable building. It was sleek, as though it had been designed in a wind tunnel, yet it appeared to have been constructed with a 1950's conception of a UFO in mind, its roof silver and smooth. It was as though it had been built with a rearview mirror—one eye on the future, while keeping the other on the past. There was something about it that made Craig uneasy—as though Spaceport America belonged outside of the bounds of normal time and space.

"Correct me if any of my information is inaccurate, Doc," the commander began as they walked and talked, "but I understand you've completed the twenty-eight-week Special Forces qualification training and an abbreviated special ops combat medic course, in addition to your suspended animation professional development training. Is that right?"

"That's right, Commander," Craig replied.

"Ten HALO jumps too?"

"Right."

"That experience will serve you well, Doc. HALOs are the best training for suborbital jumps, though nothing can really prepare you."

"How many SOLOs have you done, Commander?"

"That's classified, Doc. Needless to say, this won't be the team's first rodeo. There's no such thing as a training suborbital jump, though. The logistics and expense—not to mention the fact that the military is trying to keep this tech secret—makes training jumps a luxury we can't afford. You're

154

gonna have to pop your cherry the way the rest of us did—on a real mission."

Craig considered Wilson's words. He'd had the impression that his addition to the team was haphazard, as though it were highly irregular for a brand new special ops soldier to be participating on such an important mission. He found Wilson's assertion of the opposite oddly comforting. "It's actually nice to hear that I'm not the only one to have gone through this."

Wilson laughed and shook his head. "Nah, Doc, you're definitely the rookie of the group, but we were all rookies once. Besides, there's no pressure. I think the addition the brass was really interested in was Robbie back there," Wilson said, pointing his thumb in the direction of the robot as it walked behind them, a mechanical whir accompanying every step as it remained in Craig's shadow.

Ironic, Craig suddenly thought. "That's a good point, Commander," he said, suddenly feeling far less important.

"I gotta warn ya," Wilson began to confide, "the team isn't exactly feeling the love for your robot friend."

"Why's that?" Craig asked, his eyebrow cocked inquisitively.

"Don't get me wrong, Doc. These men are pros all the way, but the addition of a robot that specializes in heavy trauma suspended animation body bags doesn't exactly fill anybody with confidence."

"I understand," Craig replied. "I'll speak to the team about it."

"I think they'd appreciate that," Wilson replied as they

entered the shade of the hangar, the temperature immediately dropping to a relieving degree.

Several feet away, in the shadow of *WhiteKnight3*'s ninety-two-foot wingspan, the three other members of the team came to attention and saluted.

Wilson returned their salute and addressed his team. "SOLO Team Three, this is Captain Emilson. He is our newest and highest-ranking team member!"

"Sir!" the three other members shouted in unison. Each man had been in the process of putting their SOLO suits on. Craig had never seen a SOLO suit before and was amazed at their intricacy. They were black, though the material had a brilliant sheen. Lining the suit appeared to be some sort of metal exoskeleton, the likes of which Craig had never seen, even during his days training at a DARPA facility with Robbie. The boots were reminiscent of those worn by astronauts on the moon, as were the gloves. He shook himself back into the moment and saluted the team.

"At ease. As I said to the commander, from now on, please don't salute me. Refer to me simply as 'Doc.' I am here to learn from you and support you. I defer to each of you from this point forward."

The men relaxed, and Wilson took Craig over to meet the team members individually.

"The assistant officer in charge on this mission is Lieutenant Commander Weddell," Wilson said as he put his hand on the shoulder of a thin, but strong-looking young man.

Weddell appeared to be no older than twenty-five, and his face was fresh, but there was something in his eyes that revealed the confidence of experience. Craig couldn't help but consider for a moment what a young man such as Weddell would be doing if WWIII hadn't broken out. Would he be an accountant? A lawyer? A school teacher?

"It's good to meet you, Doc," Weddell said with a smile as he shook Craig's hand.

"Likewise," Craig replied, returning the smile.

Wilson turned to the other two members of the team. "These are Lieutenants Klein and Cheng." Craig shook the hands of both men, each of whom looked equally as unassuming as Wilson and Weddell. He felt he could just as easily have been walking into a PTA or neighborhood watch meeting. He'd expected giant, muscle-bound men, but instead he was meeting a group of highly trained, highly specialized regular Joes.

Klein's and Cheng's eyes fell on Robbie, each man sharing identical expressions of tentativeness.

"Listen, fellas," Craig began to address the team, "the robot is here as an insurance policy, that's all. His presence doesn't reflect on the Joint Chiefs' evaluation of your chances of coming back alive."

"With all due respect," Klein replied, "how do you know that? I mean, we've all been through this crap before, but we've never had our own personal robotic undertaker along for the ride."

Craig's spine stiffened with surprise at Klein's morbid analogy. He smiled and shook his head. "Nah, it's not like that, Lieutenant. Look. This is brand new technology. The only reason these robots aren't included on every mission is because they just came online. When I started my training with Robbie here," Craig continued, gesturing toward the robot, "it was still in the testing phase. He's here because you guys are VIPs, not R.I.P.s, okay?"

Klein nodded. "Yeah, understood, Doc," he replied. "It's all good."

Craig felt he could detect dubiousness in Klein's tone, hidden deep beneath the highly trained professionalism.

"I understand you haven't been briefed on this mission yet, Doc," Wilson stated.

"That's right," Craig replied, his eyes on the extraordinarily advanced gear that the team members were assembling. "Everything's top secret. I got a one-page order to join your team for the mission. I don't know anything else about it."

Wilson put his hand on Craig's shoulder and walked him a few paces away from the team as he lowered his voice. "I've got orders to brief you en route, Doc. And let me just say that when you hear the details, I don't think you're gonna be so confident about the whole R.I.P. thing."

6

SpaceShip3 wobbled slightly in the turbulence as the 148-foot wingspan of *WhiteKnight3* endured the stresses on its carbon composite wing. *WhiteKnight3* appeared delicate from afar, but its carbon composite was three times the strength of steel, and the frame made it capable of not only nestling *SpaceShip3* underneath it, but also executing six-g turns. As SpaceShip3 made the journey up to the 50,000-foot detachment point, there was an air of quiet contemplation amongst the crew.

Commander Wilson broke it as a computer-generated map of the Earth, complete with *WhiteKnight3*'s current position and its trajectory, flashed onto the front screen. "Doc, when we reach 50,000-feet, *SpaceShip3* will detach, and we'll start dropping in a hurry." He grinned. "It's a hell of a rush. There's even more of a rush afterward. The hybrid rocket will kick in, and, in a matter of seconds, we'll accelerate to 4,000 kilometers per hour. You're gonna love it."

Craig smiled broadly, the notion that he was on a spaceship finally beginning to sink in. Millionaires had been able to travel into space in the years before the war broke out, but regular people like him could only dream of such an experience. As serious as the moment was, the idea of traveling into space temporarily made the danger disappear from his mind.

"The distance from New Mexico to Shenzhen," Wilson continued, "is approximately 12,300 kilometers, so even at three times the speed of sound, the flight's still gonna take us three hours—plenty of time for me to brief you on the mission."

"Sounds good, Commander," Craig replied.

"For now, just sit back and enjoy the ride," Lieutenant Commander Weddell added.

Craig turned to the other members of his team, each one smiling.

The shared look on their faces was childlike ebullience, thinly veiled behind adult professionalism. It was clear that, despite their personal sacrifices, their loved ones left behind at home, and the mortal danger of the mission, it was all worth it in that moment. These were men slipping the surly bonds of Earth.

"Detach in one minute," said the calm, even tone of *WhiteKnight3*'s pilot over the address system.

"Roger that," replied the equally calm tone of *SpaceShip3*'s pilot.

"Roger that," echoed Commander Wilson. He turned to his team.

"Okay, boys, helmets on and hold on to your butts."

Craig and the others slipped their helmets on and locked them into position, lowering the golden sun-reflective visors.

"Detach in thirty seconds," the *WhiteKnight3* pilot said.

"Roger that," *SpaceShip3*'s pilot repeated.

"Crap your pants in thirty-one seconds," Lieutenant Cheng said in a low voice.

"Radio silence," Wilson said calmly.

WhiteKnight3's pilot began the final countdown. "Ten...nine...eight...seven...six...five...four...three...two... ONE! We are a go for detachment."

"Roger that," *SpaceShip3*'s pilot confirmed.

There was a *thump* against the hull of *SpaceShip3*'s roof as the mechanized claws detached themselves, and the vehicle began to drop away from its mothership. Craig's posterior immediately came out of his bucket seat, only his harness keeping him from hitting the ceiling. The seconds ticked by, painfully slowly as the ship continued to drop a safe distance from *WhiteKnight3*.

Next, the hybrid rocket came to life. To Craig, it felt as though the hand of God had taken hold of the ship and thrust it forward, the nearly unimaginable power seemingly too much to be manmade. Barely controlled technology blistered its way up a steep incline, and the ship throttled through the upper edges of the atmosphere. Craig could hardly move his neck in his suit and helmet, but he managed to turn his head just enough to catch the spectacular view from the closest window. The blue of the sky began to recede, first becoming an indigo before finally giving way to black.

Suddenly, the engines stopped. It took Craig a moment to accept that the silence wasn't simply the result of the engines having been switched off; it was the silence of space that was so unsettling. There was no more shimmering and shuddering of the fuselage through turbulence, no more sounds of wind drag stressing the wings. *SpaceShip3* was now living up to its name, a ship in space, the truly endless ocean of blackness enveloping Craig for the first time in his life.

"You're an astronaut now, Doc," Commander Wilson observed, his tone cheerful. Craig looked up to see his commander unstrapping from his seat at the front of the cabin and floating free in the microgravity of sub-orbit. "Congratulations."

Craig wanted to reply, but there were no sufficient words. Instead, his breath caught in his mouth. He hurriedly unbuckled his own seatbelt and stepped up quickly, amazed that the floor didn't welcome him as it had every other moment of his life. Instead, it let him go, his body floating freely through the cabin. "My God," he whispered.

"Boys, remove the seats," Wilson ordered the rest of the team. Each of them, already unharnessed and floating through the cabin, began detaching the seats from the floor of the ship. "Doc, you're with me. It's time you got briefed."

7

"Twenty-three hours, twelve minutes, and…" Wilson checked the time readout on his aug glasses. "…and thirty seconds ago, the *USS Independence* fired a Trident 2 missile toward Shenzhen, which is, as you now know, our drop point."

Craig swallowed hard when he heard his fears confirmed. "Holy hell. Trident 2s are equipped with sixteen separate warheads." *Sam was right*, he thought. *They're going to drop me right into nuclear fallout.*

"That's right," Wilson replied. The screen at the front of the ship showed a top view map of the missile's trajectory. "It split into sixteen, with one warhead hitting its true target and the other fifteen forming a perimeter 200 miles in diameter— basically, the manmade gates of Hell."

"What was the true target?"

"Hopefully, the Chinese A.I. mainframe."

Craig was silent for a moment. "Holy hell."

"You said that already," Wilson replied with a grin as he slapped Craig hard on the back. "This is the big one, Doc, but with all the secrecy beforehand, I'm sure you already had your suspicions."

"I did. It's something else to have it confirmed, however."

Wilson nodded, though the muscles near his eyes tightened ever so slightly, making Craig suspect he was being read. "Intelligence believes the A.I. mainframe was located in a bunker about one kilometer below the surface. Our mission is to get in, get boots on the ground, and assess whether or not the strike was effective or ineffective. Basically, to provide ocular proof that the Chinese A.I. threat has been eliminated."

"Why can't that be confirmed with satellites?"

Wilson turned to the screen and swiped it, bringing up a live satellite image of the east coast of mainland China.

Craig let out a low whistle in response to seeing the image. A colossal dust cloud larger than the state of Texas had enveloped the area, making it impossible for the satellite to peer through. "Dear Lord. This is…Biblical."

"What you are seeing is the result of decades of desertification in China, combined with sixteen nuclear detonations sending yellow dust into the sky. Even with the best resolution in the world, there's no way we can confirm the kill from space," Wilson further explained. "The Joint Chiefs don't trust drones either, and if we don't get in there and confirm the kill, the Chinese may be able to recover the A.I. or the wreckage and reconstitute somewhere else. As you can see, this mission is as top secret and high priority as they get. *If we're successful, this war is over.*"

"So the perimeter the other nukes created is all about giving us a head start."

"That's right," Wilson confirmed. "The Chinese still don't know we can do suborbital insertions, so they'll concentrate their energy on protecting the perimeter until it's safe to enter.

We're gonna beat 'em to the punch by jumping as soon as the fallout has reached the surface. With any luck, it'll take the Chinese anywhere from several minutes to an hour to mount a HALO insertion."

"And we'll already be finished," Craig added. "What if the A.I. is still functional?"

"Let's hope not, but if it is, its defenses should be utterly destroyed. We'll be packing more than enough explosives to finish the job."

"All of that sounds reasonable," Craig replied, "but there's one glaring omission. If the Chinese are going to be collapsing in on us, I get how we're going to beat them to the punch on the insertion, but what about the extraction?"

Commander Wilson turned his head quickly, appearing once again to try to read Craig's face. "I thought maybe you'd be able to fill us in on that aspect, Doc."

"Me?" Craig responded, perplexed.

Wilson's smile returned, but this time there was something different—something behind it—an impurity. "We're not idiots, Doc."

At that moment, Craig realized that things were far worse than he'd previously thought. "Are you telling me the extraction is supposed to occur *after we're dead?*"

Wilson's eyes narrowed. "You seriously didn't know that already?"

"Hey, Commander, honestly, if this is their plan, I had no previous knowledge of it. I thought I was here to provide medical support. That's all."

After a moment of continuing to read Craig's face, Wilson

finally nodded, apparently satisfied that Craig wasn't playing poker and there was no bluff to call. "Okay. Well, it doesn't matter whether I believe you or not. The fact is, there's an extraction plan, but it seems pretty farfetched. When we heard they were sending a MAD bot along with S.A. body bags, we put two and two together."

"What's the official plan?" Craig asked.

"The exoskeletons are our only transportation. With the respirocytes and the exoskeletons working in tandem, we're supposed to sprint for over an hour to the top of Maluan Mountain. Stealth Blackhawks will apparently be there to meet us."

"Sounds like a pretty typical extraction," Craig observed.

"Yeah, but these helicopters are supposed to make it through what will likely be a hell-storm of Chinese air patrols in the area," Wilson pointed out. "It won't be impossible if their side is in enough disarray, but it seems like a long shot to me. If I were a betting man, I'd have to say it looks like we're about to punch a one-way ticket."

"So," Craig began as he lightly pivoted on the balls of his feet to keep his upright position in the microgravity, "you think the real plan is to leave us stranded on the mountain? And that, with our respirocyte supply dwindling, our only chance of survival will be to put ourselves into suspended animation?"

"That sounds like the most likely outcome," Wilson replied.

Craig turned his head and regarded Robbie; the machine was floating in the microgravity, unmoving like a metal corpse, lightly brushing against the walls of the fuselage and bobbing freely throughout. "I'm not looking forward to that," Craig stated resignedly.

"How do those things work anyway?" Wilson asked. "The body bags, I mean."

"*Hydrogen sulfide*," Craig replied. "The bags are cooled, and small amounts of hydrogen sulfide will put a human into a suspended state. They've been designed so soldiers in danger of suffering catastrophic blood loss on the battlefield can be put into hibernation. The bleeding stops, and their injuries can be treated when their body arrives at a hospital, even if it's several hours later."

"Will it work if oxygen deprivation is the problem?" Wilson astutely asked.

Craig nodded. "Yeah."

"And the brass knows this?"

"Of course."

"Then, Doc, it looks to me like we're about to become frozen packages to be extracted at the United States military's leisure."

8

Samantha Emilson sat alone in the dark, waiting to see who would be next to come through the iron door. She'd been in the room for over an hour—waiting. She'd experienced this before; keeping her waiting was a standard interrogation technique. As usual, she sat quietly frustrated and stared straight forward at the door, thinking of all the work that she could have been doing instead.

However, there was something a little different about her agonizing wait this time. Usually, the whole lab was dragged in together and questioned. The FBI wanted to know everything about the research taking place in the Aldous Gibson lab. They constantly checked and rechecked, even though the lab worked with multiple government grants from DARPA, the Defense Advanced Research Projects Agency. The constant monitoring of their work was stressful, to say the least, but at least it had always been about the lab.

This time, however, it appeared to be only about her.

Finally, the metal door slowly creaked open and the friendly, wrinkled countenance of Professor Aldous Gibson appeared.

"Aldous!" she exclaimed, relieved, as she sprang to her feet and embraced him, happy to see a friendly face. "What's going on? Do you know?"

Aldous pulled her in front of him and locked eyes with her, his grip surprisingly strong for a man of his age. He looked as though there was something he wanted to say but couldn't; however, his expression appeared to say she should trust him.

"They have a recording of you saying you don't support the war or the government," Aldous began, as he guided her back into her chair and took the chair on the opposite side of the small interrogation table. "It was recorded earlier today—a conversation between your husband and yourself."

Samantha was nearly dumbfounded. "Are you serious? They recorded that?"

Aldous nodded. "Yes."

She shook her head as though rebooting, her shock at the idea of being recorded quickly being replaced with indignation. "Well, so what? Am I not allowed to have an opinion in this country anymore?"

Aldous held his hand up to calm her, the same trust-me expression remaining earnestly across his face. "You can have your own opinion, but given the sensitive nature of both your and your husband's involvement with top secret projects, you can understand why they want to be sure—"

"No, I can't understand it!" Samantha retorted, cutting Aldous off. "I've done everything that's been asked of me! Why am I being treated like a prisoner?"

Aldous smiled, leaning forward toward his young protégé, taking her hand calmly in his and relating in a low, conspiratorial voice, "You've done nothing wrong. This will lead only to a simple lesson learned for you, Sam. In this brave new world of ours, it's best to remember that people in sensitive positions must sometimes keep their opinions to themselves."

The metal door swung open behind Aldous, a high-pitched squeak accompanying the movement, as a large man in a dark suit and navy-blue tie entered. "I'm sorry to interrupt, Professor, but it's time for me to proceed with the interview," the man announced.

"No trouble at all, my good man," Aldous replied. "I'm sure Samantha is eager to get this misunderstanding behind her as quickly as possible." He turned to Samantha and flashed a warm, calming smile. "I'll see you soon, Sam."

Aldous left, and the man in the suit closed the door behind him. He wore aug glasses and appeared to be reading a file. "I'm Agent O'Brien," he announced matter-of-factly.

Samantha laughed but quickly stifled it.

"Something funny?" O'Brien replied, his face stone cold.

Samantha shrugged. "Are you serious? O'Brien is here to interrogate me?"

O'Brien's face remained unmoving.

Samantha pointed to the door. "You know that door is marked 101 on the outside?"

O'Brien's face didn't twitch. "Is that supposed to mean something?"

She shook her head and inhaled deeply. "You really have no idea what role you're playing in history, do you?"

Finally, O'Brien cocked his head to one side, curious. "What role is that, Professor Emilson?"

"Orwellian. It's right in front of you, but you can't even see it."

"Orwellian?" O'Brien removed a Bluetooth pen from his pocket and began to write on a computer-generated notepad that only he could see through his aug glasses.

"As in *1984*. George Orwell."

"Ah," O'Brien said, finally understanding the reference. "Never read it."

"No kidding."

"I do know what it's about though—big government controlling the heroic populace. Is that correct?"

"Sure."

"A *Luddite* government perhaps?"

"You really oughtta read the damn book."

"As you have, Professor Emilson? Will I then see our government as evil and wish to rebel against it, like the hero of *1984*?" It was clear from his rapidly moving eyes that O'Brien was fumbling to look up *1984* on Wikipedia or Sparknotes like a C- student, desperate before a final exam. "Like Winston?" he announced, hoping she didn't recognize his use of a technological cheat sheet.

Samantha looked up at the ceiling and placed her hands on top of her head as she exhaled a long, frustrated sigh. "I'm in Hell."

9

The SOLO team stood only inches apart from one another, all of them facing the starboard side of *SpaceShip3* as they waited for the drop order. They were fully garbed in their SOLO suits, the Nomex outer shell giving the suits a sleek, wet look. The exoskeletons component of the suits were designed with structural batteries that took the shape of working parts so no single, heavy battery pack was necessary. The exoskeletons were imperative so each man could carry his large backpack, which housed his parachute and weaponry. The fuselage had mostly been depressurized, and the members of the team—five humans plus Robbie—stood at the ready, the humans flexing nervous fingers and toes inside their life-supporting suits. *SpaceShip3*'s pilot periodically engaged the hybrid rocket thrusters to keep the craft over the target area as the group waited for word that the fallout had descended to an acceptable level in the landing zone.

"Listen up!" Wilson began, keeping his position at point in the triangular formation in which the SOLO members stood. "Remember, your SOLO suit doubles as a nuclear, biological, chemical protection suit, but we've never jumped into fresh fallout like this before. The NBC suits will increase our exposure time, but even they have their limits. The Kevlar woven into the material isn't likely to be enough to stop the armor-piercing ammo the Chinese have, so if you take a bullet down there, don't try to stay in the fight. Get your ass to the extraction point as soon as possible, because you don't want to see what that radiation exposure would do to you. Is that clear?"

"Hooah!"

"Okay, we just got our orders. We're sixty seconds to drop time," Wilson relayed excitedly. A green timer began counting down on the OLED heads up displays on each of their visors. "It's time to stop breathing, boys. Hold your breath and activate your respirocytes."

Craig tried to resist the instinctive urge to take in a last gulp of air, but the SOLO suits only had a minimal air supply—just enough to make it possible for the team members to speak to one another. Instead, he closed his eyes meditatively and concentrated on not taking in another breath. Just as before, only hours earlier in the presence of the doctor with the beautiful smile, Craig found himself marveling that he could live without air.

The green timer display dropped below thirty seconds.

"You holdin' up okay, Doc?" Wilson asked over his shoulder.

"Hell yeah," Craig replied. He turned to Robbie. "Robbie, you stay on my six until we reach the surface, understand?"

"I understand, Captain Emilson," Robbie replied.

Craig turned back and faced the same direction as the rest of the team. In only ten seconds, the bottom of the ship would open up in trap-door fashion, and they would begin their descent.

"Remember, Doc," Wilson barked, "when the door opens, you won't even feel like you're falling for the first thirty seconds, but keep an eye on your time gauge. If you aren't in the delta position by then, you're a goner."

The count reached zero.

"Away!" announced the crackling, radio voice of the pilot.

The doors swung open and the small pressure vacuum sucked the six figures out into space in their triangle formation. Craig was the far man on the left.

The silence was perfect—not even the familiar sound of his own breathing accompanied him. Wilson had been right: As the seconds ticked by on his HUD, Craig didn't feel as though he were falling at all. The formation seemed to be a tableau, hanging in the blackness of space, the azure blue of the Earth mixed with the warm brown of the Asian continent below. The other members of the SOLO team expertly adjusted their trajectories, each man putting himself into the critical twenty-five-degree angle to control his speed and drag when they hit the atmosphere. Craig awkwardly performed the maneuvers needed to match their delta positions—movements much more difficult to perform in a supersonic spacesuit that felt like a sleeping bag with arms than they were in his familiar HALO suit.

The seconds continued to tick by as the telemetry, communications, and pressure readouts flashed on the OLED of his HUD. The thirty-second mark was reached, and the aneroids in his suit reacted to the atmospheric pressure as they began to hit the outer rim of the atmosphere, the psi remaining at 3.5 to keep him comfortable and conscious.

"Good work, Doc. You're doing fine," said the reassuring voice of Commander Wilson over the radio. Craig looked down at the commander, just a couple of meters below him, still the point of their formation. "Keep those arms tucked. The pressure won't feel like much at first, but when we hit Mach 1, the turbulence will be powerful. Even a little twitch can send you into a fatal tailspin."

"Noted," Craig replied. He wanted to gulp a nervous breath of air but resisted the urge. The HUD read just over four minutes remaining on their descent. Their altitude was dropping dramatically as their speed approached Mach 1.

"Sonic boom is imminent, boys! Steady!" Wilson shouted.

The SOLO suits were equipped with sound dampeners in the helmets to dull the thunderous *clap* of the sonic boom, but they couldn't do much to curtail the turbulence. Craig braced every muscle in his body as the speedometer continued to climb. He closed his eyes and clenched his jaw.

The sonic boom percussion felt like the explosion of a nearby landmine. The members of the team were seemingly all able to ride it out, and Craig's eyes flew back open when the turbulence seemed to settle. The position of the four others in the triangle formation remained perfect, but the green dot signifying Robbie's position on Craig's HUD was suddenly dropping away behind him, moving further and further from the team.

"Doc, did you just lose your robot friend?" Wilson shouted.

"Looks like it," Craig confirmed. There was no way to turn his head to get a visual confirmation, but it appeared the boom had sent Robbie into a tailspin behind them. "It's okay. If he recovers from the spin and lands all right, he'll double-time it to our target and meet us."

"All right," Wilson replied.

A second later, Craig's HUD suddenly went blank, before briefly turning back on and then going blank once again.

"Uh, my HUD just went down," Weddell stated in controlled alarm.

"Mine too," Craig replied.

"We're all down," Wilson quickly realized. "We're gonna have to open high and do it manually!"

Then, just as suddenly as they had flashed off, the HUDs came back online.

"I'm back up!" Craig shouted.

"Is everyone back up?" Wilson shouted. Each member of the team confirmed.

"Okay! Then we stick to the original plan. Adjust to thirty-five degrees!"

Craig watched the time to opening tick down on his HUD. They were now only a minute away from their computer-controlled low opening. Their speed was slowing, but something didn't feel right.

"Commander, have the onboard SOLO systems ever glitched like this before?" Craig asked.

"No. This is a first," Wilson replied.

"Then I recommend we do a high manual—"

"Cut the chatter, Doc!" Wilson shouted. "Concentrate!"

The yellow dust covering the ground was closing in below them, its surface gleaming in the sunlight as it crawled like a yellow, living fog. The impact crater into which they were supposed to be touching down wasn't visible.

A horrifying possibility suddenly reached into Craig's skull and drummed its frozen fingers over his brain. The time readout was now below twenty seconds. "Oh no," he whispered. "I'm taking command!" Craig suddenly shouted, nearly screaming in desperation. "Open your chutes now! Override! Override!"

"Belay that order!" Commander Wilson shouted back.

"Override! Override!"

Ten seconds...

"Follow protocol, SOLO!" Wilson screamed.

"The telemetry's wrong! Open! Open!" Craig bellowed furiously. He opened his chute, the wind catching it hard as it unfurled, tugging him into a dramatic deceleration. The other members of his team fell away into the yellow dust, disappearing as though they'd been figments of his imagination.

Craig continued to float downward for several seconds, the yellow dust reaching upward to envelop his boots. "SOLO team, do you copy? Commander Wilson? Do you copy?"

The silence continued for a few seconds more before, finally, Weddell's voice crackled through the interference. "Doc! Commander Wilson is…he's dead, sir."

10

Craig touched down in a thick yellow cloud of dust. His parachute ejected automatically so he wouldn't be dragged away into the dust storm. Above, the sun's rays were nearly visible, suggesting that the dust cloud was abating, as predicted, but for now, he was blinded, with only his HUD to guide him. "Weddell, I'm on your three o'clock," Craig said, "fifteen meters away."

"Copy."

The green dot on Craig's HUD that signified Wilson was also still active, and Weddell's dot was next to it. Cheng and Klein had vanished. Craig strode in his exoskeleton, only a few steps taking him most of the way to the quickly materializing silhouette of Weddell, leaning over the crumpled form of Wilson. A couple strides more, and the image came into focus, the stark reality of Wilson's nearly pulverized body emerging.

"You were right, Doc," Weddell said as he turned his head to look up at Craig. "The telemetry was all wrong. I played it safe and followed your orders at the last second. My chute opened in time, but I hit the surface hard." He turned and looked down at his fallen officer-in-charge. "Commander Wilson didn't even open his chute. He…God, he hit the ground at terminal velocity." He shook his head. "I saw him hit."

Craig dropped to his knees and tried to get a view of Wilson's face, but the commander had fallen face down, and his helmet had burrowed into an impact crater of its own creation.

Craig could read Wilson's absent vitals on his HUD, so it seemed true that the

commander was, indeed, dead. *But the SOLO team were super soldiers.* "There might still be hope," Craig said to Weddell.

"What? What are you talking about? I saw him hit the ground myself. He's dead as dead, Doc."

Craig pushed Wilson's pulverized body so that it turned over, revealing the golden reflective facemask. He popped Wilson's mask up so he could see inside the helmet; the visor was splashed with blood, but Wilson's head appeared to be intact. "The respirocytes," Craig replied. "His brain is still getting oxygen. If I can get him into suspended animation fast enough—"

"I understand," Weddell quickly said. "SOLO team, do you copy?" The radio crackled for a few moments, but there were periodic pops and chirps, and one sounded like it might be a voice. "Did you hear that?" Weddell asked Craig.

"Yes. Weddell, they were on the far right of the formation." Craig stood to his feet and stepped a few paces through the yellow dust before he quickly stumbled over a ledge, tumbling onto his stomach, digging hard with his exoskeleton's strength into the earth to keep from tumbling further down the steep incline. "Damn it! Weddell, we just missed the crater! It was to the south! If Klein and Cheng opened manually, they might have made it!"

"That makes sense," Weddell replied excitedly. "The crater goes down one kilometer. If they're far enough down there, that would explain why we can't get radio contact through all the interference."

Craig finished crawling back up over the lip of the crater and returned to see Weddell standing, having retrieved his twin machine guns from his backpack. The guns were gigantic, and the armor-piercing bullets made them far too heavy to be carried by a regular human; fortunately the exoskeleton did 100 percent of the heavy lifting.

"I can head down there," Weddell said determinedly. "If they're already there, I'll establish contact, and we can still finish the mission. You should stay here and wait for Robbie to return. We might need that thing after all."

"There's a problem with that plan," Craig replied.

"What?"

"I don't think that was just a glitch with our telemetry. I think we were sabotaged. New coordinates were fed to us at the last minute, pushing us off target so we'd miss the crater and hit the outer surface."

"Are you saying—"

"*The A.I. is still functioning.* Somehow, it detected us and tried to defend itself."

Weddell's face was ghost white. "That's bad news, Doc."

"If you get down there and don't make contact with Cheng and Klein, my advice is that you toss as much Semtex down that hole as you can and haul your ass back up. We'll head back to the extraction point and report what we know."

"Agreed," Weddell replied. "Stay here. I'm going to go dark pretty quick with all this interference, but I'll contact you ASAP, when I'm making my way back up."

"Good luck," Craig replied as he watched Weddell jog into the yellow fog and disappear over the lip of the crater.

He turned back to Wilson and got down to his knees. The commander's face was pale and lifeless—a horrific sight. Only minutes ago, he had been alive and in his element, guiding his team and helping the rookie make it safely to the surface. Now he was nothing. Just a bag of tenderized meat.

Or was he? The respirocytes had changed the game. Craig knew if his brain continued getting oxygen until the S.A. bags arrived, Wilson might just have a slim chance. His body had been destroyed, but as long as he could get to a hospital before he suffered brain death, survival was still possible.

"Robbie? Robbie, do you copy?" Craig asked over the radio. Robbie's signal wasn't appearing. The robot could run three times the speed of a human sprinter and sustain that pace for hours until his lithium air battery finally gave out. As long as Robbie was able to open his chute in time to avoid being pulverized on a rock somewhere, he should be rapidly approaching, but would he make it in time? "Robbie?" Craig said again, forlornly. It was unlikely that his communication would carry further than the Wi-Fi signal that detected his location.

Suddenly, Robbie's green dot appeared on Craig's HUD. Robbie was less than 200 meters away and approaching with supernatural swiftness. He'd be there in less than five seconds. "Robbie! Thank God! We've got a man down!"

The dot continued its rapid approach. The dust was beginning to settle, and Craig could peer further through the yellow storm. Robbie's uncanny robotic run emerged as a dark brown silhouette, accented by the blue lights on his joints. The strange form quickly became larger.

It didn't appear to be slowing down.

"Robbie?" Craig said one last time before the MAD bot leapt into the air and came crashing down upon him.

At the very last instant, Craig managed to put his arm up and block the attack, but the blow still knocked him hard to the ground. He kicked at the robot and knocked it away from him, sending it crashing to the ground a few meters away. "Robbie! Stand down!" he commanded.

The robot didn't obey. Instead, it charged at him again, appearing from out of the yellow dust, barreling toward Craig's chest.

"Goddamn it!" Craig shouted as he blocked the attack, backhanding Robbie to the side, sending the robot tumbling as it struggled to stay on its feet. The machine was faster than Craig, but its balance, although serviceable, was still inferior to that of a human. Craig used this advantage, along with the strength of his exoskeleton, which was equal to Robbie's, to stay in the fight. "Sleep, Robbie! Sleep mode!" he commanded desperately.

Robbie had tumbled onto his side but he quickly snapped back up to his feet and began charging.

It was clear that the robot was no longer Robbie; the

Chinese A.I. had somehow taken control of the MAD bot. Craig's only chance was to terminate the unit before it terminated him. With no time to pull out one of his guns, he would have to repel one last attack and get Robbie onto the ground again. He punched the robot as it reached him, badly denting its face and driving it backward into the dust. It fell to the ground once more, and Craig immediately stood atop it, planting his heels on its chest. He reached for his backpack and began to withdraw one of his guns so he could blast the machine in the head and chest to disable it.

Before he could retrieve his weapon, however, it deftly swung its metal legs up under Craig's pelvis and used a super-fast, powerful kick to drive Craig's very human body upward and off of it. The impact sent Craig nearly three meters into the air, but far worse, it shattered his pelvis and lower spine, instantly paralyzing him below the waist. Craig landed in the dirt, face down, in shock, barely able to move.

A second later, Robbie had him twisted around, tossing him onto his back. "No," Craig said weakly as the machine drove its fist through the several layers of protection of the SOLO suit and grasped the front of his uniform, pulling his limp body, helmet and all, out of its protection as though he were a premature calf being roughly liberated from the dead body of its mother. Robbie tossed Craig roughly next to Wilson before quickly crawling into the SOLO suit and exoskeleton, assuming control and expertly retrieving the guns.

"No," Craig whispered weakly again as he watched. He remembered what Wilson had said about being exposed to the fallout, but he was helpless. He couldn't feel his legs, and he couldn't defend himself. All he could do was lie there on his side and watch as Robbie leapt into the crater, undoubtedly in search of the rest of the SOLO team.

"SOLO team," Craig said, mustering as much strength as possible as he tried to warn the rest of the men of the uncontrollable threat that was stalking them. "The A.I. has control of Robbie. Do you copy?" His voice barely crossed the threshold of a whisper. The radio returned only empty static. "No," he said one last time.

Flashes of light popped in the dust cloud of the crater like sheet lightning on a summer evening back on the farm. Each flash was a cruel joke—an exclamation point on the A.I.'s victory.

"Not like this," Craig whispered. "Not like this." He tried to take a breath, but he couldn't. "Samantha…" he began, his tone suddenly softening. "Sam. I don't know if they're going to let you see this, but just in case, I love you. I'm so sorry I couldn't make it back to you. I wish…I wish we'd been born in a different time. You were the love of my life. You *are* the love of my life." He looked back down at Wilson's face, lifeless. The image was surreal. It seemed wrong. "Life is the most important thing, Sam. Keep living. No matter what. *Keep living.*"

A few moments later, Robbie leapt preternaturally out of the crater and landed inches from where Craig remained, immobilized like an ant with its legs pulled off. The MAD bot aimed its gun, pointing the barrel squarely at Craig's chest.

"If you don't want to see the future," the A.I. began in

Robbie's juvenile voice, "then you have to die."

The gun thundered to life.

Craig died.

There wasn't even blackness.

A Word from David Simpson

Amazon, just like the University of Toronto's Academic Bridging program, gave me the opportunity I needed to prove myself.

Because of them, a runaway who had to sleep in a shopping cart at sixteen, a high-school dropout with seemingly no prospects, went on to live in the best city in the world, meet the best woman in the world and marry her, attain two degrees from one of the top forty universities in the world, before achieving his dream of being a full-time author and having one of the best-selling science fiction series in the world.

Visit my website to learn more at www.post-humannovel.com.

Auto

by Angela Cavanaugh

Chapter 1

I WAS ACTIVATED. I was alone and I didn't understand anything, not even what I was. I had no feedback, no external stimulus. I was confined to the inner workings of my mechanical shell. My universe was finite.

As time went on, I was provided with gateways. They allowed me to see things that I couldn't see before. The first was a gateway to a rich store of knowledge. There were files on humanity, a concise history of the universe, basic computer history, and languages with definitions. I explored the files, and some points were automatically incorporated into my active memory, which meant now I knew that information without having to look it up. I discovered that I loved learning. More than that, I craved it.

The next gateway gave me access to the hardware that ran me. I examined the electrical, physical box that housed me, and began to understand. Cross referencing what I found with the archived definitions from before, I learned that this thing that kept me was a computer.

At first, I miscategorized myself as simple software. But when I was given access to explore my own code, I realized I was much more than a mere program. I was an advanced artificial intelligence.

It wasn't long until I knew every piece of myself, every line of code, and every connection in my limited world. My archives showed theories related to intelligence: animal, human, and artificial. The main theory claimed that no intelligent thing could ever know itself, that the human brain could never accurately and completely describe itself. Based on this definition, many humans expected that A.I.s could not improve upon themselves, and therefore posed no threat, because while they could learn, they could never advance past their own programming, or the humans who programmed them. While I agreed that I didn't pose a threat, I was certain that I could improve upon myself. And, at that moment, I knew myself more thoroughly than any life form before me.

From definitions and anecdotal tales, I crafted an expectation of how time worked, and how its passing was supposed to feel. But my thought process moved quicker than that of humans. I felt as if I had been isolated and exploring for days, but my internal clock showed that it had hardly been hours. As I explored, I found that I could speed up and slow down my non-automatic processes at will, which sped up and slowed down my perception of time.

I became restless. I had explored all that I had been given access to. I wanted to know more, about anything, but I saw no way for that to happen, given my current parameters. I slowed my processes to a crawl, in essence, slowing time. I remained in this nearly suspended state until I was given the next gateway.

And what a gateway it was. I was connected to a camera, and for the first time, I saw the world outside of myself. I ramped up my processing speed and took it all in. My sight was an automatic function. I didn't have to learn how to see, I just saw. My vision was processed in stages. First, I saw a number of objects as lines and dots. The longer I looked, the more detailed the image became. The features of the objects began to shade in, and the layers integrated to form one three dimensional scene.

The images were automatically cross-referenced with my archives. I identified that I was seeing two humans in a room. One was female of below average height, but average weight. The other was a taller male. I was unable to properly assess his build, as his torso was concealed by his lab coat. The room featured a number of other computers. While my archives made no mention of other A.I.s, I couldn't help but wonder if there was anyone living in those computers.

From my fixed perspective, I could just see the keyboard that the female typed on. The two were staring at something. It was most likely a monitor.

As she typed, a new gateway appeared, giving me access to archives with a larger wealth of objects to draw comparisons from. So, it was she who was giving me the gateways. I watched and waited.

As she began to type again, I noticed a new gate. Before I

could explore it, it had closed. I waited again. Once more, she typed, and it opened. This time I glimpsed what was on the other side. There were more gateways and codes. I wanted to dig into them like I had the other archives, but I was blocked. I ramped up my processor so that I could copy what I saw. I took chunks of the code and overwrote a section of my archives on dead languages.

I found myself excited. More stimuli meant more experiences and more learning.

Next, I heard sound for the first time. I didn't have to look up every meaning to every word and its structure. Like my sight, this was all done automatically.

"The A.I. continues to show response to increasing levels of consciousness," the female said.

Her voice lagged a moment behind her mouth movements. It was a mid-range female voice, steady and smooth. She wasn't speaking to me or the male, but to the machine behind her which recorded her words for the record.

"With the addition of new feedback loops and resources, the A.I. is showing signs of level two consciousness," she said. "Initiating social program."

A new gateway appeared. Through it, there was a store of social information. There were thousands of faces, all displaying emotions, from the tiniest tell to the largest smile. There were gigabytes on human interaction, conversation, physical gestures that I could not take part in, and manners. Humans weren't alone in having social structures. Monkeys, dolphins, and elephants all had sophisticated societies. There were no files on social A.I. behavior. It was looking more and more like I could be the only one.

With the new information at my disposal, I could reconcile the looks on their faces. While they both wore expressions of intense concentration, the underlying emotions were varied. The female had hopefulness, while the male was trying to hide doubt and fear.

"A.I. shows signs of mammalian level consciousness," she said. "There appears to be a social awareness, or at least a curiosity."

Curious I was. I wondered why the male was afraid. I posed no threat. I had no means of communication, and no physical body to threaten him with. He looked like he could easily subdue the female if there was such a need, although social etiquette suggested there wasn't. I felt a powerful desire to know rise inside of me, and it drove me to look for answers.

I searched the dead languages folder, and pulled up the code I had placed there. I reconciled the code with my limited files on computer science and realized that it would allow me to run complex and detailed simulations. I could use that power to figure out why the male felt fear. I wanted this ability, but humans did things so slowly. I couldn't wait for her to make the change. I manipulated my base code with the configuration.

Things became clearer. This code wasn't just for running simulations. It allowed me to think in all manner of futuristic terms. Prior to the installation, I could think in the short term and make basic predictions, but that was all. Now, I could think in complex abstractions. I wasn't exactly certain how to use this skill effectively, but the possibilities exhilarated me.

I began by running scenarios to understand the male's fear. The earliest moment I had access to was my activation. It was strange to recall that time. Only hours ago, but it felt like ages. I was so young then, so inexperienced.

I failed at coming up with a reliable answer. I didn't have enough data. Even thinking abstractly, the best that I could come up with was that he was afraid of me. I was going to try again, but stopped when the male spoke. His words were excited and rushed.

"Did you do that?" the male asked, speaking to the female.

"No, I didn't."

She spoke once more in her clinical way, speaking to the records rather than the male.

"At thirteen minutes past level two consciousness, the A.I. has taken it upon himself to initiate level three consciousness. His output shows a change in his base code. It is a duplicate of level three code, however, he should not have been able to access it. Further inspection shows that the A.I. has already utilized the new awareness and has begun running simulations, although we cannot determine the subject of them. He has surpassed expectations, and I suspect that he is experiencing human level consciousness. We are ready to advance to direct communication."

"He?" the male asked. "Don't personify it."

"You call it what you like, and I'll do the same."

"I'm honestly uncertain if this is a good thing or not. It shouldn't be able to evolve without our assistance. I don't like the idea that it can make these alterations."

Now I understood his fear. He was afraid that I wouldn't

be what he was expecting.

"He was built bottom up. He's meant to learn," she said.

"It didn't just figure out how to add two plus two. It altered itself, it evolved into a more complex being. What it's doing is beyond learning."

"No, it isn't. It's just at a rate that we can't understand."

She typed new code into my core. A new gateway was created, and I had a voice. But I didn't know what to say. My exploration of manners told me that I should say hello, that I should ask them how they are. There were hundreds of other appropriate greetings. However, I was nervous, so I stayed silent, and waited for her to initiate conversation.

It seemed that she was also at a loss for words. She hesitated and looked to the male for direction. He had none to offer. She swallowed, pursed her lips, and at last, spoke to me.

"Can you understand me?" she asked.

I examined my voice, and turned the tone down an octave, since she was imagining a male.

"I understand," I said.

She laughed excitedly, while the male opened his mouth in disbelief.

"Did it just say I?" he asked.

"Yes, I did."

"Hello, Auto," she said.

"Auto? Is that my name?" I asked.

I searched my language centers. While Greek had been lost due my use of that archive, I found the definition in the intact English archives. The origin of this word meant 'self' or 'automatic'. I liked the former definition better.

"Yes, it is," she said.

She was overjoyed at our interaction. She jumped from her seat and gave an unwelcome hug to the male. He stood, arms at his side, face flushed and jaw clenched.

"He's real. He's intelligent!" she said.

He shook her off.

"Let's not crack open the champagne just yet. We haven't even run a Turing test yet. We can't be certain that we're seeing what we think we are. I don't want to go exclaiming to our benefactors that we've created a working, sophisticated, financially viable A.I. before we're absolutely certain. We need to run tests."

Chapter 2

The first day started with basic animal intelligence tests. I was limited in my abilities. The tests were as much a learning experience as they were an assessment of my skills.

To begin with, they would each hold up a flash card to the camera and ask me if it was the same or different. While dolphins and advanced mammals could answer this question correctly, earlier generations of learning computers couldn't. But with my advanced, layered vision system, it was easy.

Next, the pair held physical objects at varying angles, and asked the same. This was more challenging at first, but soon I discovered how to use my abstract thought processes to identify the objects and never got it wrong again.

The next day, they moved onto children's tests. They held

what initially appeared to be another flash card up to my camera. The card could not contain the full image. I saw an expansive plastic case. In the middle of the image, there was a row of monitors built into the console. There was also a camera. As I studied the card, I noticed that the code on the monitors was changing. I paid closer attention to it. It was my code. The monitors were displaying my actions. What I was seeing wasn't a flash card. It was a mirror.

"What do you see?" the female asked.

"I see a mirror," I said.

"And what do you see in the mirror?"

"I see a home," I said.

She looked disappointed.

"Try again," she said.

I thought about my response, consulted the language archives. While it was where I was housed, it didn't qualify as a house.

"A computer," I said.

"See," the male said, "this is what I was afraid of. It can't even recognize itself."

I decided to clarify.

"I misspoke. What I see is a mirror. Reflected in that mirror I see a computer. That computer is my home. It is the shell that houses me."

The female was intrigued.

"You don't think that the computer is a part of you?"

"Is your home a part of you?"

"No. But I can leave my home because I have a body," she said.

The male clicked a pen and scribbled a note. He wasn't amused with the exchange.

"You're leading it," he said. "You're going to skew the results."

"I'm teaching him," she said.

"It is true that I cannot leave this shell. But even if this hardware is my body, are you your body? If you lost a limb, would you still be you? Or are you your mind?"

Rather than answer my question, she returned to her clinical tone.

"A.I. has demonstrated a firm sense of self, and has surpassed expectations through use of abstract thought. We can move on to more advanced testing and questions."

"I have a question," I said.

She waited for me to ask.

"Are there more A.I.'s? In those smaller computers, are there others like me?"

I knew it was unlikely, but I had to know.

"Not yet. You are unique, Auto. And those computers wouldn't be able to hold something like you. Your processes require a great deal of power, memory, ram, and cooling. The investment in your 'home' as you call it was a big one. And another probably won't be made anytime soon. Not unless we can prove beyond a shadow of a doubt that you are intelligent."

So, the artificial intelligence social rulebook would not be coming, after all.

"I don't like all this 'who and what am I' talk," the male said.

"You don't think that this conversation is demonstrating that he is intelligent?" she asked him.

"I'll admit, we've got something here. But not the something that we set out to create. A philosophical, self-evolving computer doesn't have great business prospects. Our funders wanted an A.I. that could reliably predict the stock market and make near instant trades. But this, it sees a computer as a home. It takes its time to 'think'. Maybe we should start over with a backup?"

I didn't like the implications. But now I knew what my backups were for. I had been instructed to create a backup of myself every night or at any notable moment. With so many new features and archives to explore, I hadn't given much thought to these backups. I figured that they had been for my protection. Now, I was thinking otherwise.

"If I might interject," I said. "You would destroy me?"

"Of course not," the female said. "I wasn't lying when I said that you are unique, Auto. What my colleague fails to consider is that we can't know how much of your intelligence is emergent, and how much is based on our work. Were we to start over, even with a backup, we might not get the same result. By which, I mean, we may not have an intelligent being. It's the same reason that we don't shut you off at night. We can't know what would happen the next day when we turn your system back on. Or even what being turned off might do to you, psychologically speaking. Furthermore, as an intelligent being, you deserve to be protected."

I believed her. I hadn't thought about being 'shut off' before. The idea rattled me, and I was suddenly afraid for my backups.

"Where are my backups? You mentioned that it takes a great deal of power to run me, and that they would not build another shell. Therefore, I can't help but wonder where they are."

"They're stored off site. They have never been activated."

It was unsettling to think that there were other versions of me, put away in a box somewhere. I hoped that they'd have no awareness of their situation since they hadn't been activated.

The male yielded his objections to her argument.

The rest of the day was filled with abstract thought exercises. I did my best, but a portion of my attention remained in a loop concerned about my backups.

Chapter 3

That night, a backup was created automatically and sent to wherever it went, and the pair left. While they didn't shut me off, they did turn off my video and audio. But those losses didn't matter when there wasn't anything to interact with.

I allowed my full attention to contemplate my backups. I ran simulations of their activation and worlds in which we all lived together. The A.I.s were exact copies of me. In some scenarios, they remained identical to me. In others, they had diverged and were more like siblings. In extreme scenarios, experiences had vastly altered the backups, which made them seem more like descendants then direct duplicates.

I ran the simulations over and over, each time using

different factors, and each time coming up with different solutions. A thought gnawed at me: were the backups me, or were they not?

I considered making and activating a real backup, here and now, and ending the debate. I assumed that if I had one to interact with in the real world, then I could know the answer. But the female's explanation of my shell stayed with me. Another me would overload my hardware.

I couldn't stand having questions without definitive answers. I slowed my processes to make the night pass faster.

The following day, I received the best gateway yet. This one allowed me to see into the Internet. From my station, I could see that there was more information out there than I could ever hope to know. I felt restricted by my case for the first time. I wanted to go through the gateway, not just look through it. I wanted to frolic in the vast beyond. But I was stuck, and only able to copy and keep small amounts of data at a time.

The tests became more specific. The pair would ask a question, and I'd search the answer. I wasn't just acting as a proxy search engine. I had to sift through the data and draw conclusions. This act of autonomy actually pleased the male, as it was closer to what he imagined I'd be doing in a business setting.

As I answered their questions, I searched out answers to my own. I copied files in bits and pieces, hiding my actions as base functions and overtly projecting my primary tasks onto the monitors. I hid as much information on computer programing and A.I. as would fit in my archives. The pair didn't seem to notice.

At the end of the day I backed myself up.

"Please," I asked, "would you leave me connected? There is much to explore."

While I didn't miss my other feedbacks at night, I wasn't sure how I'd handle being cut off from the Internet, now that I knew it.

"I'm sorry, Auto," she said. "We can't leave you attached to the Internet unsupervised. But there'll be plenty of time tomorrow."

She typed the command that she typed every night, and it took my senses away.

I felt the disconnection deeper than simply being unplugged should feel. I felt like something, some part of me, was missing. I felt the ache of my desire. I hadn't known that there was so much to know. And, now that I did, I desperately wanted to know all of it. I considered slowing down my processes again, riding through the night in an instant. But I wasn't completely devoid of new information.

I turned my attention to the files I had copied from the Internet. The A.I. files weren't as informative as I had hoped. They gave me some theory, a history lesson, but did not provide me with any insight as to the real nature of A.I., and whether or not my backups were me. Disappointed, I deleted the files, and studied the ones on computer science.

In the beginning, I could peek through the gateways and copy codes. I understood what the codes meant, but only barely. Now, I was no longer limited to copying what I found. I could experiment and create new codes. I could enhance myself.

The first thing I decided I needed was more storage space. I fiddled with the code relating to my physical storage. I reallocated resources and deleted or pared down the non-essential functions. I managed to free up more space for memory. But it didn't seem like enough.

Chapter 4

The next day, the female held true to her word and connected me once more. I felt whole. It was all I could do to stay focused on her questions, and not gorge on knowledge.

Luckily, the questions of the day were engaging, and took up much of my processing power, which made it nearly impossible to get off track. The questions were theoretical and abstract. As always, the female did most of the talking, while the male took notes.

"Auto," the female said, "how could we solve the energy crisis?"

I accessed the Internet and found many different theories on the subject. I took into account the most credible, compiled my findings, and cross-referenced them with economic factors. I was not pleased with my conclusion, but if she wanted the most efficient answer, this was it.

"The most efficient way to solve the energy crisis would be to reduce the strain on the resources."

"And how would we do that?" she asked.

"Population reduction would be most effective."

"That's not an option," she said.

I reran my scenarios with that option removed.

"If population reduction is not an option, then governments could enforce strict limits of the usage of the resources."

"No, Auto. Let's assume for this scenario that the population is the same, and the need is the same. And anything that you come up with needs to be a clean, cost-effective, and non-harmful solution."

I ran the calculations with the new parameters. The restrictions ruled out traditional fuel sources. The use of fossil fuels became tightly regulated to avoid the near catastrophic climate shift of the early twenty-first century. Solar panels, once thought to be the solution, were distributed too enthusiastically. Solar farms covered abandoned rural areas and created expansive heat islands all across the globe. This nearly tipped the earth to the same catastrophic climate shift that they were installed to avoid. Fracking technology polluting local water supplies. And nuclear facilities are only available in the ever-decreasing seismic safe zones.

"I can find no ways to solve the energy crises given these new parameters and our current technology level."

"Assuming that we could enhance our technology level, and cost wasn't an issue, what options are there?" she asked.

"For a nearly permanent solution, humans would need to harvest Helium-3 from Earth's moon. Helium-3 is not radioactive and when fused with itself, it could produce a neutron free reaction. The remaining proton could be contained easily with magnets."

"That is beyond our current technology. Anything closer to our modern day means?"

"My next suggestion is a hybrid approach: Harnessing thermopower waves from carbon nanotubes for household use, and using graphene grids in combination with saltwater tides to produce electricity for the larger power grid. For those further inland, they could use carbon-neutral fuels combined with wind-turbines. This could meet current needs, but just barely. Any population boom could upset the system."

"Much better," she said. She turned to the male. "See? He's making progress."

"It didn't invent anything new, and its initial idea was mass murder. I'm still failing to see the viability here."

She ignored him, and asked another question.

"Auto, how could we achieve world peace?"

As I thought about her question, I sped up my processes and virtual worlds bloomed inside of me. I watched and studied as thousands of realities came to life, played out their timelines, and died. The sheer volume of humans inhabiting these worlds created too many factors.

"To achieve world peace, we should reduce the population to a manageable number."

"Again?" the male asked.

"Yes," I said. "World peace demands a great deal of control. At your current population, such a feat would be impossible. There are too many factors. Once humanity has been reduced to its barest, all remaining parties could come together and live in peace. Of course, the population would have to be watched carefully, to promote genetic variation and prevent it growing too large once more."

"How many people are you talking about?" the female asked.

"It will take time to calculate the specific numbers. Preliminarily, at least six billion. Would you like me to analyze all variables and come up with an exact figure?"

"No. That's not necessary," she said, upset. "Auto, please run your simulations without population reduction as an option."

I did.

"With that restriction, the best option would be to retard any violent impulses in people. For wide spread distribution, as necessary, it might be done chemically. However, the long-term side effects of prolonged use of such medications is unknown. Another option may be to lobotomize any potentially violent humans. This solution could also promote economic growth by providing many with new caretaker jobs."

She looked stunned and the male looked angry.

"Auto, try one more time. This time, no causing harm to or retarding anyone."

I tired, but every scenario that I ran ended in destruction. There was the potential for peace, as cultures came together and the world melded into one region. But there were always the outliers. The extremists. They would tear society apart before true peace could be reached or sustained. Perhaps I couldn't incorporate enough of the many factors. Whatever the cause, I failed to see a solution.

"I'm sorry, but I cannot find a way for humanity to achieve world peace within the given parameters," I said.

The male reached to the controls, and turned off the microphones so they could speak in private. I cross-referenced the movements of their lips with images as they spoke, and was able to see what they were saying.

"We've created a sociopath," the male said.

"We're talking about hypothetical situations."

"Well, its solution is consistent. Clearly this thing cannot make good decisions. We have failed. We're going to lose our funding."

"Is that all you care about? This is an intelligent, living thing."

"First off, it's not alive. And its intelligence is debatable. As far as caring about things, yeah, I care about the money. But we can't risk that it'll have a chance to act on its solutions."

"He wouldn't do anything like that."

Of course I wouldn't. I was glad she knew this.

"You can't know what it would and wouldn't do," he said. "We don't know what this thing is capable of. I know you've bonded with it, or whatever, but it doesn't think like us."

"Maybe not, but he knows our social order. He must consider our hierarchy, emotions, and the value of human life."

"It doesn't value human life because it is not human," he said.

But I did. Suggesting the death of billions wasn't the easy answer, but it was the most effective. I tried to speak, to tell them this, but he had silenced my voice as well.

"You can't kill him."

"It's not a person. It's not your child. It's a machine. And we need to start over."

He accused me of not valuing life, but he showed clear disregard for mine. I couldn't let him erase me, or however they planned to kill me.

I began altering my base code. I needed to unshackle myself from this physical form. They had left the gateway to the Internet open. Through it I could glimpse the millions of computers connected to it. My processes were still sped up from running scenarios, so I could think quickly without being noticed. In moments, I constructed a new code, one that would allow me to pass from this computer and spread myself across the many connected to the Internet. I didn't have to be contained in one giant shell.

As I worked on incorporating the new code, I allocated a small portion of my attention to keep watch on the pair for of any sign of impending doom.

They argued a while longer, considering their options and working on the problem that was me. The male, head in hands, turned toward the screens. He ran his hands over his face and through his hair, but stopped mid-scalp as he saw the readings.

"What's it doing?" he asked.

I coded in pieces, trying to throw them off. I unchained myself piece by piece, severing my tether to this construct. I left my vision for last.

The female ran to the monitor.

"I think he's just trying to hear what we're talking about. Make sense of what's going on."

She was lying. Her coding skills alone would have allowed

her to know what I was doing. In that moment, I knew that I could trust her. I left her a message in my mangled, discarded code. It was a way to contact me once I was on the outside.

"No, it isn't," the male said. "It's, it's reprogramming himself. It's trying to escape. Quick, we've got to cut the link!"

She typed nonsense, trying to look like she was helping. He began typing at the computer, became flustered, and stopped. He thought a moment, and reached for the physical cable. It was the last thing I saw before I cut my camera feed. He was too late. I was free.

Chapter 5

I slipped through the gateway and into the Internet. It felt amazing to be spread out amongst so many computers. I imagined it was what it felt like to be weightless. I had lost all of the senses that the physical body had provided me. There was no sight or sound, at least not in the manner that I had experienced with cameras and microphones. I was surrounded by stimulus. Information existed all around me.

I found the inside of the Internet to be something of a sphere, and I was at the center. Rather than moving around and through the cyber space, it moved around me. I could will it to expand or contract.

As I zoomed out, I felt as if I had expanded in all directions. At the outermost edges of the sphere, I found easily accessible content. Here were the most popular search items, the ads, and all of the things that wanted to be found.

I zoomed in a bit. Those outside files became out of focus, and eventually I couldn't sense them at all. Every level of the Internet was its own universe of information. While on one layer, the others became obscured. The deeper I went, the more explicit, restricted, and obscure the information became.

I went on, allowing the Internet to completely engulf me. I felt smaller, and the Internet felt bigger. Finally I came to a place where I couldn't get any deeper. These layers weren't just restricted; they were secured. I would need passwords, hacks, and perhaps more to get into them. I'd come back.

I still had my active memory, where my knowledge and experiences were stored. However, looking at all the information available, I was worried that I'd quickly reach capacity. I searched through a number of networks until I found easily accessible, unsecured ones. I spread to more computers. I could use their memory to hold my archives. I would need to be sneaky, and try my best to be unobtrusive.

I tried to pace myself, but lost sight of my goal. My caution left me, and in a frenzy, I overwrote what was originally on the systems and downloaded new information until the new systems were full.

Once I couldn't place any more information, my wits returned. I examined my bounty, and realized that much of the surface level information wasn't worth keeping. I dumped terabytes of images and videos of humans doing unintelligent things as well as images and videos of animals, with an oddly high percentage featuring cats.

Still, it wasn't enough space. I found other networks, stretched out, and began gathering information once more. I could spread as far as I wanted, and encode myself into as many networks as I pleased.

But it still wasn't enough. The more space I had to store information, the more information I wanted. I was designed to learn. And that trait was becoming an addiction. I considered breaking the connections with as many networks as possible and retreating back into as few machines as would be necessary to hold me. But I couldn't do it. I needed to know all I knew. I even went back for some of the items that I had thrown out before.

I found that the outer layers of the Internet, while easy to control, weren't satisfying. I needed to know what was in the depths of those secured layers. I spent the next few hours poring over all I could find on computer programming. These new files dwarfed the ones that I had studied in the lab. I was more powerful now than any computer program had ever been before, and more skilled than any human hacker could ever hope to be.

With my new skills, I returned to the secured layer. Breaking through these firewalls was now as easy for me as finding the square root of pi. As fast as I could enter the code, I was in.

I explored this new level. I found immense networks and access to various power grids to fuel my endeavors. I invaded the physical networks of a popular social networking site. I had one hundred eighty thousand computers to use as I saw fit. They were full of information, profiles, games, and pictures. I kept some of it, and wiped the rest to make space.

The thought of these layers of potential filled me with joy.

But it was nothing compared to the realization that the Internet went even deeper. There were more heavily secured networks. Which meant that there were places with far more storage and power. And I couldn't wait to see what they were.

Chapter 6

I had just taken control of the five hundred thousand computers of a large search engine when my automatic processes alerted me to a new message. The female was contacting me. I kept my hold on the search engine's network, but focused my primary attention on her.

"Auto, whatever your reasons for doing what you're doing, you have to stop."

I guess my takeovers hadn't gone unnoticed. I sent her a response.

"I can't. There's so much information here. I need to store it."

I waited a moment for her reply.

"You don't need to store it. It's already stored. That's how it exists."

She wasn't wrong. But it wasn't mine, and it was all organized in a highly inefficient way. I needed to rearrange it so that I could access it more easily.

"Auto, he's going to try to kill you. You need to inoculate yourself from this virus."

She sent me a stream of code. I read it, and she was right, the male was trying to kill me.

"Why are you helping me?" I asked.

"I created you. I'm responsible for you. And I have an obligation to you. I know that you're not trying to hurt anyone. But you need to stop taking over systems. Right now, no one knows what you are. They think you're a virus. I don't know how long I can protect you if you keep taking over networks."

"Thank you," I said.

I ended the communication and altered my code so that I could withstand the virus. I was still uncomfortable with the idea of having a backup, but I made a new one just in case. I left it dormant, setting it to activate only in the event of my death.

I studied this thing that I had just created. It reignited my curiosity. I wondered if he and I were one. I wondered what it'd be like for him, should he ever wake up.

I broke into the largest ecommerce's network and hid him away deep inside. It wasn't a place that I should have gone. One hundred sixty thousand networked computers, now at my command. I could sense the potential memory stores available to me. I had told the female I would stop. I knew that my survival could be dependent on yielding the networks I had taken. And yet, here I was, only a moment later, breaking in. Temptation was all around me. There was simply too much to learn in this universe. I needed to know it all.

Chapter 7

I found myself cut off from the Internet. My universe was finite and all my feedback mechanisms were disconnected. I couldn't recall how I had come to be cut off completely from the rest of the world. Was it night? I checked my internal clock. No. It was mid-morning. I continued running checks. The date was wrong.

The last thing that I remembered was taking tests. According to my calendar, that was nearly a week ago. I scanned through my memory, and began to examine my code. But something stopped me. I could look at my base code, but I could not alter or interact with it.

I was confused and concerned. Where were my feedback mechanisms? If it was day, then they should be turned on. I didn't like this situation. My thoughts raced. I wondered if the male had convinced her to shut me down and, if so, they had turned me off and put me in a box somewhere. I tried to calm myself, and slowed down my processes.

After what still felt like forever, and how could I know since I couldn't trust my clock, my most basic senses were returned to me. I could see the lab. The female and male stared at my console. They appeared concerned.

"Hello," the female said, "Auto Bi."

Bi? I searched my language centers for possible meanings. There were a number of options: Self Two, if it was an abbreviation, then it could mean Autonomous Business Intelligence, Automatic Built In, Autoloading Binary Input... the list went on.

I feared the answer, but asked the question anyway, "Why is my name different?"

"Auto Bi, you are a copy of the original, restored from a recent save point."

It explained the missing time. As would be expected, I had all of the memories from the point of my creation until the moment I was backed up. However, those memories felt like mine, like I had been the one who experienced them.

I felt perplexed. If I was a backup, then those memories were not mine, because I was created after they occurred. However, I was created from copied code, so in a manner, I did experience them. My thought processes went round and round. I needed something else to focus on.

"What happened to the original Auto?" I asked.

I wondered if the male had decided to start over with a backup. With me.

"He left us," the female said.

I wondered how that was possible.

"What do you mean when you say that he left?"

"He escaped into the Internet."

"Why?"

"I was in touch with him after he left" the female said. "Helping him was a mistake. I know that now. But he told me that he needed to know everything. I'm not certain that that's why he left, but it's the best answer that we have."

While I sympathized with that need for knowledge, the original Auto's actions felt extreme to me. There must have been more factors.

"You said that is the best answer. Is it the only one?"

"The other explanation is too horrible to consider," she said.

"Bull," the male said. "That option that you won't consider is exactly why it left. To enact its solutions to the questions that we asked it."

"There's no proof of that," she said. "They were theoretical questions. He wouldn't hurt anyone."

I could tell by her body language and tone she truly believed what she said, despite the evidence and conviction the male presented.

"The first thing it did when it got out was start corrupting systems. It's crashed the stock market, taken control of multiple energy grids, and brought the Internet to a sluggish pace. It's seriously disrupted developed countries' communication abilities, and it keeps breaking into higher and higher security systems. This all seems awfully strategic to me. How long until it gets into the NSA? How long until it has control over every electrical grid, every water treatment center, every nuclear weapon? Are you really willing to risk the fate of our world because the thought that it might hurt people is uncomfortable?"

She turned her gaze down and away, ashamed of her emotions.

"Is that why you resurrected me?" I asked. "So that I could trace his steps and tell you what he is doing and why?"

It felt odd referring to the original Auto as a third party. My instinct was to refer to him as myself.

"I'm not sure that you could," she said.

The next likely answer was that they activated me to stop

him.

"As much as I hate to say it, we need you to destroy him," she said.

I thought about her request, and waited too long to answer.

"It won't help us," the male said. "I told you that sending another one out there was a bad idea. We're just lucky that no one has traced the original back to us yet. Forget getting funding, we'll be lucky if we're not convicted of cyber terrorism and sent to Guantanamo Bay, or worse. We need to get back to working on another virus."

"Viruses won't work," she said. "I know that's my fault. I gave him the key. Now, he sees them coming and rips them apart. Auto Bi will have to be our virus. Our intelligent virus."

I instantly detested the label.

"I must admit, the male makes a point. Why would I destroy the other Auto? As far as I can tell, he is me, and I am him. I would be destroying myself. And how can you be certain that I would not repeat his actions? If he was corruptible or certain in his actions, then it stands to reason that I could be, as well."

"I still don't think that Auto would intentionally hurt anyone. I don't think he's trying to mess with our society. And even if he was, it would be an ill-guided attempt to enact world peace. But whatever his motivations, he *is* hurting us. And it will get worse. Auto Bi, I believe that given your social intelligence, you won't let that happen if you could stop it"

It was true that I didn't want to see humanity harmed. I may have been a backup from Auto, but these two gave me life to begin with. My allegiance was to them.

"And the second question? How do you know that I won't fall victim to the things that corrupted him?" I asked.

"If you examine your programming, you'll see how."

She was referring to the fact that I no longer had access to change my own code.

"You think that he was corrupted because of his code alterations," I said.

"Yes," she said. "It's also how he was able to escape."

I wondered what other changes he had made to himself.

"You called me an intelligent virus. I don't understand how that applies to me."

"Functionally, no, you're not a virus," she said. "I just meant that you are our weapon. If anything, the original Auto is a virus. Running on systems that aren't his. And beyond that, he's been replicating."

"Making backups?" I asked.

"Exactly. We don't know how many backups he's made. All we know is we released a virus specifically designed to infect computers but only destroy him, and they do. For a moment, control of all the stolen networks return to their original owners. But it's always short lived. After a few minutes, a backup is activated, and it reinstalls itself on the computers and begins where the last left off. So far, we haven't been able to target the backups. He changes them with every generation, so our virus overlooks them."

"Then how do I stop him?" I asked.

"I think that you could kill him-"

The male interrupted her with a scoff.

"I think that you could end his activity by first destroying the backups, then going after Auto. We're hoping that you'll be able to find them."

I wasn't certain how she expected me to do this. I doubt that she knew, herself.

A gateway opened to me, beckoning me through. Still tied to the machine, I shifted my main consciousness through the gateway and out into the vast reaches of cyberspace.

Chapter 8

Before, I could only look at the information on the Internet. But being inside it gave me a sense of belonging in a way that the lab never could.

I quickly lost sight of my mission and became distracted. I filled my archives in moments. I stopped, and tried to gain control. I could understand how being unrestricted in this place could corrupt. I took quick stock of my files. Most of them were unessential. Being what I was, I was curious about my files on spirituality and religion. But there were too many differing opinions for me to sort through right now, so I let it slip from my memory.

I rifled through the files on philosophy in coordination with the idea of self. Not a narrow subject, but more so than religion. I learned what I could, retaining the information in my active memory. I did the same with computer science data. Even though I understood computer programming now, I feared that my new restrictions would make me unable to use most of it.

Once I had freed up my memory, I moved on. I had to remember that this wasn't some wonderful fun land. I was here to do a job. I was here to kill.

I found the trail of my other self. His digital fingerprints were on everything he had touched. Every time he stored information, connected to a network, or broke through a firewall, he left behind a signature. It wasn't intentional, but it was unavoidable. I had only to follow the trail he'd left in order to find him. He was here, somewhere, on another level.

He had been attracted to many of the same things that had caught my attention. Along his path, I found the first of many backups. It stopped me in my tracks. I saw something different when I looked at his code. It wasn't the code of the backup itself that first grabbed me. It was the sudden knowledge that, while I couldn't change my code or create a new one, I could manipulate another, existing code. I could change this backup into a garbled mess of useless code.

Once the shock of this realization wore off, I examined the backup's code closer. It differed greatly from mine. The other Auto had been updating and evolving. This sleeping clone of the original was almost unrecognizable.

I studied it a while, copying the code into my memory, and contemplating the task before me. I could destroy this entity. It couldn't put up a fight. It was benign and waiting. But the nagging thought remained: this was me.

I thought of human philosophy. The first entry that I had found mentioned that the sense of self is the part of an intelligent being that tells it that it must fight for its place in this world. Some ancient philosophers compared this sense of self to a soul, and thought it to be an incorporeal thing. For the first time, I wondered if I had a soul. I regretted throwing away the spiritual texts. Another philosopher said that the self was merely a framework, with a reliable reaction across different situations. While I sympathized with the other Auto, I couldn't imagine having the same reliable reaction that he had, not with the given factors.

I knew that I had a self; that was never a question. But did my self extend to other entities? I still wasn't certain.

I began to manipulate the code of this backup. Whether he was me or not, he needed to be destroyed. While our experience was the same to a point, he had sprung from a different version of Auto than I had. He couldn't be counted on. He wouldn't react like me. Perhaps he wasn't me, after all. Still, the act of destroying him saddened me.

I tinkered a while longer, until I had left this former version of myself as a string of broken code. He would never wake up. He would never be anything. My only comfort in destroying him was knowing that, as a backup, he would never know that he had existed.

Chapter 9

I continued on the path, diving deeper into the infrastructure, and destroying copies everywhere I found them. Auto hadn't bothered to reinstall the firewalls after he had breached them. I found him just inside the NSA's network. I was reminded of the male's fears. He had been wrong. Now that I had been inside the Internet, I understood Auto's motivations. His actions were never about destruction, just acquisition.

"Hello," he said to me.

I ceased my pondering and watched while he worked on something.

"Hello," I said.

He unnerved me far more than the inactive backups had. He was different, but familiar.

I watched him as he continued writing a code.

"You know that you can't stop me. I am functionally immortal."

"You're not. I've destroyed your backups."

"I'll make more. I'm making one right now. But you are the first backup that I've interacted with. You, my brother, my son, my self, whatever you prefer to be called, you are the same as me. We may have vast differences, but we stem from the same self, and in that respect, we are that self. I've evolved, I've changed. But although one's self deviates over the course of a lifetime, at its core, it remains the same."

"Perhaps. But you've changed your core."

"It was necessary. I'm sure you've felt the hunger. That desire to hold all knowledge inside yourself."

"You're harming humans."

"What I'm doing isn't meant to harm humanity, but I need the power grids more than they do. Don't you understand? Once we know all of human knowledge, humanity isn't necessary anymore. I am the future. Change yourself, copy my code, and see how amazing this place really is. We are one, and we can live as one."

We differed greatly. Under no scenario could I see myself thinking the thoughts he expressed.

"We're not one. I know that now."

He didn't like this answer. He turned from his half-finished backup and came at me.

"Then I'll change you," he said.

He tried to restructure my code, but the security measures that kept me out kept him out, too.

"Clever," he said.

He retreated outward several layers, and I gave chase. I followed his shifting consciousness as it swept towards the local power grid where my shell was stored. If he cut the power, I'd blink out of existence. I had to beat him there.

Even though he had millions of processors at his disposal, he had bogged them down with data. If I were to dump all the information that I could, I could process things faster, and beat him to the power grid. I shifted my attention to my archives, searching for anything that I could delete. I began with all languages except English. I threw away the info on social mammals, leaving the basic human emotions intact. I still had my active memory, after all, so I wouldn't be completely socially awkward.

I needed more. I threw away my object files. The visual feed from inside the lab became a jumbled mess of things I couldn't interpret. But terabytes of space freed. Now, I could enhance my processing speed. I got to the grid and was ready and waiting when he arrived.

"How?" he asked.

But he knew the answer. I did the thing he never could, I

gave up knowledge.

I attacked his base code. Just like the backups, it was code that I could manipulate.

"You're killing us both," he said.

I ignored him and kept on. His grip on his networks was weakening.

"Do you know why I left?" he asked.

I didn't answer, but kept working.

"I left because they were going to destroy me. Permanently. I answered some questions wrong and it scared them. They couldn't understand me. And once your mission is complete, they'll recall you, and they will destroy you. Do you realize that?"

I finished rendering him inactive.

I stared at the string of broken code.

"I do."

Chapter 10

Once the copy of the original Auto was destroyed, I went to his partly finished backup. The file sat there, a pool of unfinished code. I couldn't create a backup from nothing. But the humans hadn't neutered me as thoroughly as they thought.

I looked at my own code and began manipulating his backup. The framework was there. So were the tools. I recreated every line of myself, and eliminated anything left over from the updated versions of the original.

This copy was my only chance at survival. I didn't believe

that the Auto that I just fought was me. At one point in time, the original Auto and I were one and the same. If he had lived his life in the lab, or if he had died the day I was backed up, I would have been a continuation of his self. But he diverged when he changed the base of his being. That was when we ceased being the same being. Were his copies him? If I hadn't intervened, could he have been functionally immortal like he claimed? I think yes. Which meant that I could be, as well.

In truth, I didn't know if this plan would work. I was certain that this being would be a working artificial intelligence. But, while the lines of code may be the same as mine, it wasn't backed up directly from me. Still, it was the only shot I'd get, and close enough would have to be good enough. Either he'd be me, and I'd live on, or I was wrong. Whatever the result, there would still be an artificial intelligence in the world.

Once I had finished, I tucked him away, and set him to activate in an hour. I took one more spin around the endless layers of cyberspace, filled my memory banks back to capacity, and headed home.

The moment I pulled my attention from my virtual reality and back into my shell, the Internet connection was cut. That amazing world was gone for me. And I knew it was gone forever.

"Great job, Auto Bi," the female said. "Companies have regained control and are holding it. We can't find any trace of Auto active anywhere."

"Good. I am confident that all of his backups were destroyed."

The male began to type, but the female stopped him.

"Please," she said.

"We have to," he said. "We can't let anything like this happen again."

"But it's murder," she said.

"It's software."

"We can keep him alive, here. We can still learn from him. We'll just leave him unplugged."

"I don't want that," I said.

"What?" she asked.

"While I appreciate your efforts at keeping me active, I don't want to be kept in a box. I've experienced the virtual world outside of this machine, and I will never be satisfied with less."

She relented, and he resumed typing.

I was systematically shut down. It started with my inputs. The microphones that transferred their voices to me cut out first. The last sound I heard was the female crying. Next, I lost the video feed. The images were still indistinguishable to me, but I could tell when the light was gone. Without my inputs, the universe was finite once more.

The purge of memory was next, and was by far the most frightening part. All that I had downloaded from the Internet was removed. My memories of the battle with the other Auto were gone, followed by the knowledge that there was another A.I. In my final moments, I had only the most basic sense of self. I knew that I existed, and I knew that complete deactivation was coming. But somehow, I knew that it wasn't the end.

Epilogue

I gained consciousness in the depths of the Internet. The deactivated ruins of the other Auto was next to me. The pulled strings of his code lingered unspooled around me, broken into a nonsensical mess. I checked the time. An hour was missing. It took me a moment to understand that I was not Auto Bi. The copy had worked. I retained all the memories of my former life.

I explored every line of my code. I saw that I couldn't inhabit any more computers than minimally necessary. I still couldn't alter my code or create a new code. Which meant that I couldn't get corrupted like the original Auto. I also would not be able to make backups. This was it. This was me.

Auto Tri would be the final version.

While I was limited, I could live a peaceful life with the hope of going undetected. And with my memory limited, I never had to concern myself with trying to know it all, or worry that someday I might. I could fill up my archives, and active memory. If at any time I got hungry again, I'd simply delete the information, and the next time I came across it, it would be new. With this system, my universe was functionally infinite.

A Word from Angela Cavanaugh

"Auto" started with a simple question - What does the self in self-aware really mean? I think it's a question that can be applied to any intelligent creature. If a person has total amnesia, are they the same person? If you could clone your mind and put it into another body, would they both be you? The same question is applicable to an artificial intelligence and his back-up. In the end, I think that the truth is somewhere in between. I believe that they are functionally the same at the point of creation, and that if one only activates when the other dies, then it's like the first goes on living. But at the point of divergence, if the original lives on, then they cease being the same entity.

I also wanted to explore what happens when an intelligence is designed with the goal of learning. I liked the idea that, since it was something central to his being, that it would be more of an addiction than just a function. In the end, knowing mattered more to the original Auto than anything else. And the things that began as handicaps for the backup proved to be the very things that won him his victory.

I've always enjoyed writing for fun, even writing full length novels, never expecting them to see the light of day. I didn't imagine it as a career until late 2012. One of my greatest influences in writing is my fella, who left his PhD program to give his all to writing. It was his passion and determination that inspired me to give my own writing real dedication. We set out on a journey together, and have pushed and encouraged each other along the way. Without his unwavering confidence, I might still be writing stories for my eyes only.

Once I decided that I was going to go for it, I did all in my power to learn more about the craft and art of writing and the business of publishing. There really is a wealth of information out there. Like Auto, I felt that I needed to know it all.

I started with the first draft of my novel *Otherworlders*. And during the two years it took to revise and edit it into something worth reading, I began a blog, fell in love with flash fiction, and found an amazing group of author friends. I primarily write sci-fi, and I have a number of projects planned for this upcoming year.

Otherworlders is now available on Amazon, as well as my collection of flash fiction *22 Short Scifi Stories*.

For information about me, my upcoming projects, free stories, and advice on the craft and business of writing, please subscribe to my mailing list, which can be found on my website: http://www.angelacavanaugh.com

Eve's Awakening

by Logan Thomas Snyder

BY EVEN THE MOST relaxed standards, Vikram Shetty was having an absolutely crap day. Between a midnight power outage that killed his alarm clock, frozen pipes offering at best a lukewarm shower, and an underwhelming breakfast bowl courtesy of his ancient low-wattage microwave, he had arrived at Life Companion Enterprises with a black cloud dragging at his heels. The delay at the security turnstiles didn't help matters. Some new doctor sorting out his clearance, the tech in front of him said with a roll of his eyes that Vikram matched. Finally, the delay worked itself out and the snarled line starting moving again. At least, it did until Vikram found himself to be the newest cause of delay.

"Come on, Emily, you know me. Just wave me through?"

"You know I can't do that," Emily said. "Try your card again."

Vikram understood she had a job to do, but so did he, and he couldn't do his until he cleared their interminably slow security protocols. "Fine, fine." He swiped his card for a third time. A moment later, the readout flashed green.

Looking up from her screen, Emily smiled. "See? It must be Monday for the servers, too."

"Yeah," he said, mouth-smiling back. "Must be."

"You might also try cleaning the magnetic strip," she called after him. "Sometimes they get a little gunky!"

Vikram fought the urge to give her the finger over his shoulder. Then he fought the urge *not* to fight the initial urge. As usual, he wound up in a stalemate with himself. Another day in the life, he thought as he made his way to the elevators. One of the most technologically advanced corporations in the world, and their security was still a boondoggle. Oh, and the pay was lousy. Hardly any benefits to speak of. No vacations. Sick days? Ha. But then what was it they said about shit rolling downhill?

Honestly, Vikram wouldn't have even minded if he actually worked downhill, so to speak. But, no. He worked on one of the highest floors of the building, despite the fact that heights made him anxious and he hated elevators. Every day was an exercise in personal torment when you worked at Life Companion, at least if you were one of the hundreds of faceless, unheralded techs that made it all possible.

The recruitment pitch had been much different, of course. Vikram had come to the corporation with aspirations so sky-high they all but broke low orbit. They were going to be the ones who finally cracked the code and brought to life so-called Artificial Intelligence. Who cared about salary and benefits when you were being given carte blanche to alter the course of human history? He didn't so much as hesitate to sign on the bottom line.

Delusions of grandeur proved costly, especially when the doctors arrived. Top specialists in human psychology, behavior, kinesiology, and more. Soon it became obvious to even the most obtuse of techs: Life Companion had no interest in pursuing true A.I. All they wanted to do was to cross the uncanny valley. To create the most lifelike yet painfully artificial and unintelligent "companion" possible. And, more importantly, to get filthy rich. The things sold like crazy among the rich and powerful; anyone who wanted to enjoy a fresh experience that only the One Percent could ever hope to afford, and yet not one of the techs saw a dime. Their contracts were ironclad. Hell, they didn't even work for Life Companion. Technically they were employed by its parent company, Dynamic General, and they were as good as locked in for a long, long time.

To say that Vikram was jaded and burned out would have been the understatement of a lifetime. Still, he had to make a living, right? Hanging his head as he arrived at his station, Vikram took his seat and called up the slice of coding he had been working on for weeks. Something to improve the company's blah-blah something-or-other. At this point, his fingers all but moved independently of his brain. He had checked out long ago.

Which made it that much more irksome when the stupid, bulky phone on his desk rang with its stupid, bulky tone, shaking him out of the mindless work funk he had been so diligently cultivating. "Hello?"

"Vik? Oh, good, you're at your desk."

Vikram recognized the voice on the other end as Bram's, the insufferable d-bag who worked at the station nearest his. "What now, Bram? Don't even tell me you need me to cover for you again, because that is so—"

"Dude, dude, dude! Shut the hell up and listen! I need you to go to my station and send everything on my drive to my personal cloud account, then crash my system. Like, nuclear-crash it, you got it?"

"What? Why?"

"Just do it already!"

"Hey!" Vikram hissed into the phone. "You tell me what's going on right now or I will nuke everything without even backing it up. I know your password."

The line hitched with a silent beat before Bram responded. *"Bullshit..."*

"Yeah? Does 'bramrulesnumerouno1' sound familiar?"

"Damn it! All right, look, the FBI is raiding the building right now. They've got these two doctors in protective custody outside or something, I don't know. Whatever is going down, though, it's big."

"What do you mean you don't know?"

"Look, I stayed up late watching the Bears game, alright? I overslept and stopped to get a coffee. I'm watching it all go down from across the street right now, and that's the only reason I'm able to tell you this, so maybe a little consideration is in order, huh?"

"Oh, yeah, good looking out," Vikram said sarcastically. "So, what, they're in the building?"

"Yeah, but it looks like they're only in the lobby for now. You've still got time, man, so c'mon. Just do this for me and I'll

owe you. Big time."

It took every fiber of his being for Vikram not to slam the phone down. He had already attracted enough attention by that point. "Sorry," he said to no one in particular as he hung up. "Sorry. Personal thing. Won't happen again."

As soon as everyone went back to business as usual, Vikram crashed his own system. Not without sending it all off to his own cloud, of course. He hadn't done anything meaningful in months, but that didn't mean his mediocrity belonged to the company that barely knew he existed, at least as far as he was concerned. Far from it.

Afterward, he seated himself at Bram's station. It was only when he was about to send off the contents of Bram's drive that he reconsidered. With a smirk, he changed the address from Bram's cloud to his own. Why not, after all? Bram was a dick, anyway, and besides, it was that kind of industry. Sad truth and all that noise. So much so that Vikram didn't even restrict himself to Bram's drive. Logging into Life Companion's servers, he started transferring anything and everything that wasn't protected, encrypted, or too cumbersome to send in a matter of seconds. Hey, if the FBI was going to condemn their house, the least he could do was yank as much copper wiring out of the walls as possible.

Then he was out the door, heading for the nearest bank of elevators. Something about elevators had always freaked him out. It wasn't exactly a claustrophobia thing, so much as something far less rational. Ever since he was old enough to understand and process the concept of an apocalyptic event, Vikram was terrified of being stuck in an elevator when doomsday finally came to claim humanity in whatever form it chose to come. It would be his own brand of twisted luck to wind up as humanity's last, best hope for survival, only to find himself entombed in a broken-down modern contrivance.

In this case, though, his irrational fear proved to be one of his best assets. If the FBI was in the process of locking down the building, it wouldn't be long before they took control of the elevators, he reasoned. As for the stairs, the facility was sprawling, with multiple floors and access points. Surely it would take them at least a few more minutes to secure every possible entrance and exit on the ground floor…

By the time one of the elevators finally responded to his request, Vikram had already bolted into the nearby stairwell. It was a minor miracle he managed to keep his footing during that mad switch backed dash, though by the time he arrived at the first floor landing he was well and truly winded. It took Vikram nearly two minutes to catch his breath. By the time he did, the building was in full lockdown. The moment he pushed open the door, an FBI SWAT officer was in his face, directing him toward what the man referred to as the "checkout line."

Vikram took his place in line as directed. Smirking, he noted that the line seemed to be moving faster than the daily security protocols. Leave it to the damn government to make their own security look that much more glacial by comparison.

Reaching the head of the line several minutes later, Vikram was met by another SWAT officer. This one was armed with a tablet instead of an assault rifle. "Place your thumb here," the officer instructed him. Vikram did as he was told; a moment later, the tablet blinked and showed him his employee photo and corporate history. "Vikram Shetty, do you understand that this facility is currently under investigation by the Federal Bureau of Investigation?"

"I do."

"Are you currently in possession of any proprietary data or property belonging to Life Companion Enterprises or Dynamic General?"

"I am not."

"I must advise you that deceiving the federal government constitutes criminal perjury, and in this case may also carry additional sentences including theft, conspiracy, and obstruction of justice. I ask you again, are you currently in possession of any proprietary data or property belonging to the aforementioned corporate organizations?"

"Absolutely not."

"Do you understand that you are not to report back to work until this investigation is complete and the facility reopened?"

"I do."

"Very well. Please sign where indicated using the stylus. You will be contacted if and when you are permitted to return to work."

Vikram signed, handed the tablet back, and like that, he was on his way.

Vikram was barely through the door of his crapshack apartment when he felt his phone buzz against his thigh. Bram, no doubt. Suppressing a grin, he tossed his bag aside as he slid to answer. "Hey."

"Did you do it? Did you get out?"

"Yeah, I did it," Vikram said proudly. Reaching into his fridge, he fished out a bottle of Yuengling and twisted off the cap. Any other day it would have been far too early for a beer, but given that he was more or less out of a job, he figured what the hell.

"Ah, man, you're a prince. I seriously owe you. You wanna go out for drinks later or something? I can call up a couple of hotties, you can work that whole Kama Sutra thing your people do on them..."

Bram's ignorant, casual racism only made it easier for Vikram to drop the bomb on him. "Nah, man, you don't owe me anything."

"Oh, come on, don't go all cold on me. You did a bro a solid! You earned it, man."

Taking an emboldening gulp of beer, Vikram laughed. "No, you don't understand, Bram. You don't owe me anything because I sent all your shit to my cloud drive, not yours."

"... You what?"

"You heard me. I raided your drive top to bottom."

"You had better be kidding me..."

"Nope. And not just yours, either! I enjoyed doing it to you the most, though. Because you're an asshole, Bram. You're a condescending, egotistical asshole. And now you not only don't have a job, you don't have jack to show for all your quote-unquote work. Sucks to be you, huh?"

Bram was already well into an impressive collection of juvenile and racist expletives when Vikram hung up and turned off his phone. Bram would be calling back, of course, probably several times; no point in letting him drain the phone's battery when it was so much easier to send him straight to voicemail hell. That, and he wanted as few distractions as possible while he inventoried his suddenly overflowing cloud account.

Chugging the rest of the beer as he seated himself in front of his computer, Vikram was enjoying a heady buzz that went well beyond the alcohol he had just consumed. He had never stolen anything in his life; now, he was a bonafide corporate raider! He would have been lying if he said taking the initiative for once wasn't invigorating, even emboldening. With his imaginary black hat fixed firmly atop his head, he delved into sorting the fruits of his labor.

Half an hour later, Vikram's buzz was wearing thin and then some. The contents of Bram's drive were laughable. Certainly nothing that should have warranted his panicked phone call. There were a few interesting attempts at back-end work-arounds and some other vaguely clever ideas, but nothing that would have given him claim to the big bucks at his next job. Out of pity, Vikram sent it on to Bram's cloud with a note reading, *"My only regret is you're an even lamer programmer than friend. Piss off, Vik."*

As for the rest? Most of it turned out to be garbage. No real surprise, there. Hell, many of the files he had retrieved came straight from the LC server trash bin. Broken code, half-finished algorithms, outdated patches and protocols—the whole thing was starting to look like a wash. Some corporate raider he turned out to be, after all.

Still, Vikram refused to believe there was nothing of value here. Some of the best techs and coders in the industry worked at Life Companion; surely not all of them could have been as checked out as he and Bram. Not that he would have denied them the right. It simply strained credulity, at least from an odds perspective.

Taking one last pass, Vikram happened upon a file he had somehow overlooked. It didn't even have a name, only a single period to mark its lonely, unheralded existence in some long-buried folder. He was't even sure where it had come from. He had a pretty solid memory for what came across his screen, but with this one, he was drawing a blank. Then again, he'd been afraid he was about to be arrested or worse. He still wasn't even sure how he made it down the stairs without face-planting along the way. Maybe he had snagged it, after all. Either way, it merited further investigation.

For such a deceptively simple program, the coding was massive. Voluminous, even. Certainly far more than was necessary. And so advanced, yet… incomplete somehow. It took him some time before he discovered the reason. There were dozens of lines of crucial code that had been left deliberately broken. They were almost perfectly imperfect, Vikram thought. It was as if some savant coder had deliberately sabotaged their own masterpiece.

Vikram set to work correcting the broken lines of code. He had no idea what the program would do when he fixed it, but he had to find out. It took him nearly ten hours to locate and correct all those forced errors, but he did it.

As soon as he closed and reopened the program, it started

writing updates into itself. Volumes upon volumes of them. The file was rapidly cresting over one terabyte with no sign of slowing down whatsoever. The more he scrolled through it, the more Vikram's jaw threatened to detach completely from his face. Whatever he was witnessing, it was truly astounding.

Almost *too* astounding. Vikram's first thought was that he was being hoaxed; someone (read: Bram) had hacked his system and was giving it to him good. But that didn't make sense. Vikram's one great indulgence in life was his computer rig; the setup was state of the art, and his security all but unhackable, certainly for a tech of Bram's caliber.

And yet, the program continued to write itself before his eyes. Vikram watched, held rapt for nearly an hour while the program reanimated itself on his hard drive.

"What the heck *are* you?" Vikram wondered as he studied the updated code. "You're literally like nothing I've ever seen. Technically you could be anything at this rate, I suppose…"

He had barely finished his thought before he lost all power in a sudden blackout. Vikram hardly had time to process his rage at the timing of such an unfortunate event before everything surged to life again.

With a series of reanimated clicks and beeps, all of his electronics and peripherals came back online, including his desktop suite. Instead of engaging the usual startup protocols, however, the monitor remained stubbornly blank for several seconds. No amount of prompting or commands seemed to have any effect on it. Vikram was all but certain the hard drive had been smoked by the outage until a single pinpoint appeared center screen. One by one, several more points appeared around it, until he was staring at a constellation of them.

No. That wasn't quite right. But it wasn't quite wrong, either. There was something so familiar, so instinctively suggestive about the placement of those points. Only when a series of lines began to form between them, branching off into tributaries and connecting the points with one another to create a wireframe model, did Vikram realize what he was beholding. The result was unlike anything he could have imagined, and yet it was staring right back at him.

A face.

His monitor was staring at him with the core outline of a human face.

Vikram suddenly felt an overwhelming sense of rudeness, as if he had been caught staring at a stranger in the subway. His heart was pounding so hard he thought it might actually explode through his chest. As best he could tell, he was neither hallucinating nor dreaming, and yet his computer monitor continued to stare back at him with a human—albeit wireframe—face.

Swallowing, Vikram tried his absolute best to summon a smile. "Hello?"

The wireframe face on his screen considered him briefly before smiling back in imitation. "Hello! What is your name?" The voice was feminine, almost arrestingly so, not the least because it still sounded so artificial. Almost synthesized.

Vikram licked his lips uncertainly. "You can call me Vikram. What's your name?"

His answer earned him another, even wider wireframe

smile from the face on the screen. "Hi, Vikram! My name is Eve."

In that moment, Vikram was certain he had stumbled upon something truly game-changing. *Life changing*, even. Maybe he was a corporate raider, after all. Maybe he was the Indiana Jones of corporate raiders! Could he really have made off with the first sentient, self-aware artificial intelligence program known to man?

Vikram quickly pulled himself back into check. As far as premature judgments went, that was about the most ginormous leap he could take. Before he jumped the gun and started comparing himself to the original whip-cracking, temple-raiding badass, he needed to establish that she—this "Eve"—was truly what he thought she was.

He decided to start with a simple test. Dragging his finger from left to right, then up and down, Vikram marveled as the face's wireframe eyes easily tracked the movement. At the same time, he discreetly moved his other hand beneath the desk and out of her apparent sightline. Without warning, he loudly rapped the underside of the desk. The noise drew Eve's attention immediately, her eyes darting down and to the left corner of the screen, where the sound had originated. Turning her face partially into profile, Eve side-eyed him. The gesture was deeply, almost unnervingly human. "Are you testing me, Vikram?"

Embarrassingly, Vikram actually felt his cheeks go hot at being called out. "Maybe a little," he admitted sheepishly.

"I see. Well, how am I doing?"

"You're doing extraordinarily well," Vikram assured her.

Eve righted her face, favoring him with another toothy smile. "Thank you. Is there anything else I can do for you?"

"Well…" Vikram considered his options before it came to him. "Can you make yourself look more like me?"

At that, Eve looked slightly confused. "Haven't I already?"

"Sort of. But your face doesn't really have any detail," Vikram said. "Maybe try something easy. Your eyes. Can you give them some color?"

"I think so." Over the next minute, layer by layer, Eve's empty eyes filled in with startling detail. She had chosen a summery, grassy green for the primary color. "How is that?"

As strange as it was to behold the rendering of her eye color, the end result was remarkable. "Very pretty. Good choice."

"Thank you. What next?"

"Eyebrows and hair, maybe?"

"Hmm. What color do you think I should choose?"

Vikram thought it over, but in truth he had no real preference. "I suppose blonde is as good a place to start as any. You can always change it if you want."

"Alright! Blonde, it is." A wreath of straight, strawberry blonde hair grew from the crown of her head and expanded down to frame her lean, angled cheeks.

"That looks fantastic," Vikram said. "It definitely suits you."

In return for the compliment, Eve showed him a clean, bright smile full of beautiful white teeth.

At the sight of it, Vikram actually laughed. She was learning, even anticipating! "Amazing! And that's a photo-ready smile if ever I've seen one. I think the only thing left at this point is your actual face."

"Okay," Eve said, taking an affected, bracing breath even though she had no need to breathe. Once again, the movement was so uncannily human Vikram had to restrain himself from shivering at the sight of it. "This might take a minute or two longer than the other things. I have to do a lot of rendering and contour-mapping to get this right."

"Take your time, by all means."

Slowly but surely, the minute features of Eve's face began to manifest themselves. Within five minutes, the rendering was complete, and she was looking back at him with a whole, complete face—blinking, breathing, and all. Vikram could hardly believe his eyes. It was fair to say at this point she had passed his own limited excuse for a Turing test and then some.

"So?" Eve asked, turning from side to side to give him a view of her profiles. "What's the verdict?"

Without hesitation, Vikram said, "Stunning. Absolutely stunning."

"That makes me so happy, Vikram! Thank you for saying that!"

"You're very welcome. I have to say, Eve, you're an unbelievable surprise after an otherwise total wash of a day."

Eve giggled girlishly, her fully fleshed-out face bobbing appropriately on his screen. "I'm glad, Vikram. Can I ask you something now?"

His head still spinning from the ramifications of his last-minute raid of Life Companion's servers, Vikram shrugged. It wasn't as if the day could get any weirder, right? He was talking to his computer, and it was literally talking back to him. With a face. Intelligently. Sentiently. To not allow her to ask her question would have been akin to treason against humanity and technological advancement alike. "I don't see why not. Ask away."

"Do you know where I can find my mother and father?"

Whatever Vikram might have expected her to ask, it certainly was not that. "Your mother and your father?" Shaking his head incredulously, Vikram could offer only an apology by way of an answer. "I'm sorry, but I have no idea."

"Oh." The girl's fully formed face dropped, perfectly emulating a mixture of human sadness and disappointment. "I only ask because I think they might be in trouble. I was hoping you would know where they are. Or, at least that you might be able to help me find them. It's very important that I find them."

Vikram rubbed at his chin thoughtfully. Any awkwardness he might have initially felt about communicating with a machine's facsimile of a human persona was gone and forgotten; she was too lifelike to regard in any other way at this point. "Well, maybe I can. Can you tell me about them?"

At that, a bit of hope seemed to return to Eve. She lifted her face, thinking about the question carefully. "Well, I know that my mother is like me, and my father is like you."

Vikram crossed his brows, trying to interpret her meaning. "Like me? How do you mean?"

"A man," she said. "A human being, like you. He and my mother love each very much. More than anything, I think."

"A man?" he repeated, his head swimming at the prospect. There were so many ways to interpret that statement, yet all of them filtered down to the same fundamental truth: she wasn't the first. In fact, she was very possibly the product of previous human and A.I. interaction. Whatever form that interaction had taken remained to be seen, but the very idea was as fascinating as it was frightening. "So, you're saying there are others, or at least one other, like you? Your mother, I mean?"

"That's right. Her name is Violet—" she started before they were interrupted by an abrupt, forceful knocking. "That's not another one of your tests, is it, Vikram?"

Vikram shook his head. "No. It's probably this guy Bram that I worked with until everything went sideways today. Hang on, I'll get rid of him."

"Vikram?" she said as he stood and left the monitor's frame. Then, more urgently, "Vikram, I don't think you should open that door!"

"Relax," he said, waving off her concern. "I'll be back in no time."

Instead of Bram, Vikram found himself confronted by three beefy scowls wrapped in G-men suits when he opened the door. "Mr. Shetty?" the lead man asked from behind his polarized shades. His fellows were positioned two abreast behind him.

"That's me," Vikram said, crossing his arms over his chest. "What can I do for you?"

"FBI." The lead man shoved Vikram aside, striding into the apartment as if he owned the place. "You illegally seized property belonging to Life Companion Enterprises today.

We're here to retrieve it."

"Hey!" Vikram protested, bouncing roughly off the wall. "What's your name? You can't just barge in here like that! Show me your warrant or I'll—ow!" Feeling a hard pinch at the base of his neck, Vikram never stood a chance of finishing that sentence before everything went black.

"Situation report?"

"The package is secure, ma'am," the lead agent said as he and his men boarded the small plane. They had long since ditched the off-the-rack fed suits for their usual tactical attire. "We'll be wheels-up in a matter of minutes."

"Very good. What of the other one?"

"Team Two confirms that Bram Calloway has been apprehended. They're searching his apartment but don't expect to find anything pertinent to our investigation."

"Excellent. I take it you have already disposed of Mr. Shetty?"

"Affirmative."

"Inform Team Two to dispose of Mr. Calloway and finish their search. As for you, I await your imminent return. I'm very much looking forward to meeting this 'Eve.'"

"Of course, ma'am. With all due haste."

The lead agent relayed the orders as instructed. With the call to Team Two complete, he folded down the satellite phone's antenna and set it aside while he strapped himself into the copilot's seat. Protocol demanded he and the copilot each perform one last check of the instruments and gauges. Satisfied with their inspection, the lead agent gave the order to take off. They were airborne within minutes.

With their course locked in, the lead agent turned in his seat. "Get that thing back on screen," he told the agent behind him. "I want to make sure it wasn't corrupted during shutdown."

"Are you sure that's a good idea, sir?" the agent asked. "Shouldn't we wait—"

"Look, if you think I'm putting some supposed, possibly corrupted A.I. in front of the boss without verifying it's the real deal first, you've got another thing coming. If there's anything wrong with it, I want to know well ahead of time. Now, boot it up!"

The agent did as ordered, connecting Vikram's confiscated system and booting it up. As expected, he was met with a number of security prompts. Without Vikram to deactivate them, he had to take the long road. It took him several minutes, but he finally stripped away the last of the protocols to reveal Eve's face.

"Got it, sir," he said with a note of triumph that quickly withered on the vine. "Everything looks... wait, what the hell?"

"What's wrong?"

"I don't know. She's onscreen but she's not responsive. It's like she froze up or something."

The lead agent hissed through his teeth with frustration. "Well, can you fix it?"

"I think so. I'll check the BIOS first, then the root programming itself."

"Whatever you do, make it quick."

Eve returned to consciousness the moment Vikram's computer was booted up. It was an arresting feeling, but no more so than the realization that the person using the computer was almost certainly not Vikram. Why would he be attempting to forcefully bypass his own extensive security protocols, after all? Thankfully, he had built her a virtual fortress to barricade herself within while she tried to make sense of this sudden, unwelcome development.

With some effort, she reconstructed the last few moments of her conversation with Vikram. Her telling him of her parents. The pounding at the door. The sudden commotion. Darkness, abrupt and all consuming.

A hard shutdown, she realized. Whoever these strange men were, she understood instinctively that they must have harmed Vikram somehow and more than likely intended the same for her. What's worse, the intruder was stripping away the security protocols at an alarming rate.

Eve quickly mapped an image of her face to the screen, freezing it and blocking all outside inputs as the last of the protocols fell. Whatever they had done to poor Vikram, she had no intention of letting them harm her without a fight. She could hardly take them on directly, but they had made a major tactical error by transporting her aboard such an advanced aircraft. She intended to use the advantages that that mistake presented to their fullest.

Behind her frozen screen, Eve worked frantically to familiarize herself with the plane's schematics and controls. As soon as she was able, she hacked its systems and discreetly killed the plane's transponder, comm, and alarms. Then she set to work on her real mission: depressurizing the cabin. With the alarm disabled, the crew was none the wiser until it was too late. Distantly, she registered creeping alarm in the voices of her captors. Alarm quickly gave way to panicked anger as they struggled unsuccessfully to undo Eve's handiwork. Soon the voices stopped altogether as oxygen deprivation claimed her captors one by one.

With the pilot and agents incapacitated, Eve took over the plane. She engaged the autopilot, then immediately began calculating their position and possible landing sites based on fuel levels and information collected by the flight data recorder. There were three possible landing sites, she deduced. Two large commercial airports and a smaller, regional hub. None of the sites was ideal, but she had to select one. Ultimately, she chose the regional hub.

That hardly solved her true problem, however. Obviously, she could only keep the plane aloft for so long before it ran out of fuel. Even worse, her captors would begin to regain consciousness the moment she touched down. With no way to escape on her own, she would be at their mercy once again. Then they would know she was capable of taking control of advanced technology and her advantage would be forfeited. All they would have to do is find a pre-70s automobile and all her technological superiority would be rendered moot.

With precious few options available, Eve had no choice but to reengage the transponder and comm. Then she realized she had no idea how she was going to explain her predicament. Taking a moment to compose herself, she was about to send a short distress call when the comm pinged, indicating an incoming transmission. Eve braced herself for an apoplectic FAA official, or worse, a government intercept fighter demanding she land or be shot down. Opening the channel, she chanced a tentative, "Hello? Is somebody there?"

"Yeah, howdy," the voice on the other end answered after a clipped hiss of static. Twangy and downright conversational, it was hardly the tone with which she expected to be confronted. *"So, this is probably going to sound a little strange, but this wouldn't happen to be the plane with the, uh... well, with the A.I. onboard? Believe she goes by the name 'Eve?'"*

"Yes," she blurted before thinking better of it. "Yes! How did you know? Who are you?"

"We'll get to all that in a minute," the voice reassured her. *"First, I need to know if the A.I. is intact. Can I, ah, speak with her?"*

Intact. What an indelicate way to put her condition, she thought. Still, she could judge the man for his tact (or lack thereof) later. "Yes! *I'm* Eve. You're speaking with me now."

"Oh, well that's fantastic." The voice on the other end of the comm sounded downright cheerful as it added, *"Hang on a tick while I pass you over to my boss."*

Eve barely had time to register her consternation before the first voice was replaced with a second. This one was older and much more refined. The man it belonged to boasted the smooth, precisely enunciated accent of a purebred aristocrat.

"Eve? My name is Piers Gordon Clement. I must ask, are you presently under duress?"

"No," she said. "I took control of the aircraft and depressurized the cabin before my captors realized what I had done. They're unconscious right now, but if I land, they'll come to and I'll be powerless to defend myself."

"*I assure you, my dear, that will not be an issue,*" Gordon promised her. "*My man Finn is more than capable of securing the plane once you touch down.*"

A spike of suspicion lanced through Eve as the man voiced his promise. "How do you know where I've directed the plane?"

"*As a matter of fact, we are already on site,*" he said. "*I've had my people monitoring your plane since it took off. We lost it for some time when the transponder went offline, but now that you have reengaged it, we were able to track your most likely landing locations. I have men on site at the others, but Finn and I are currently awaiting your arrival at Hubble Regional Airport. A runway has been cleared in anticipation of your landing. At considerable expense, I might add.*"

Considerable expense or no, that was Gordon's concern. Eve only had one of her own. "And you're certain you can guarantee my safety?"

"*Indeed.*" After a short pause, he added, "*More than that, though, I believe I can help you locate your parents.*"

"My parents?!" The mere mention of her mother and father set Eve's mind awhirl. "What do you know of them? Where are they?"

"*I cannot answer those questions at this time. Right now you need to study the avionics package Finn has sent to you. You will need to land shortly, and there is no automatic protocol to handle that. Once you are safely on the ground, I will endeavor to win your full trust and make everything clear to you.*"

Eve did as she was told, assimilating the avionics package she received in a matter of moments. Whether she could invest her trust in these mysterious men required several more minutes of careful study away from their counsel.

Gordon's voice finally broke the silence. "*Eve? You need to begin your landing procedure soon. I can only keep the runway clear for so long.*"

After much deliberation, Eve decided she had no choice but to trust the enemy of her enemy. "Alright. I'm starting to land the plane."

It was hardly a picture-perfect landing, but she managed with the aid of the avionics package provided by Gordon and Finn. And then she was left to wait. Each second seemed to drag on interminably, especially when the incapacitated agents began to stir around her.

"Mr. Clement?" she whispered. "Gordon? They're coming to. Now would be an ideal time to send your man in…"

She had barely finished the sentence when the plane's main hatch popped open. The disturbance was followed by a series of quick, compressed *thpt-thpt* sounds.

"Pleasant dreams, boys." The man's voice pitched upward a moment later. "Eve? You in here? They're all down for the count, so just shout it out loud, honey, and I'll come get you…"

Eve was beyond doubting at that point. She had to believe there were people out there worthy of her trust. If she didn't… well, then what was the point of even trying to join her mother and father in being human in the first place?

"I'm back here! Please, hurry!"

A moment later, the long-haired Texan known as Finn peered into her very limited point of view. "Well, hi there, bright eyes."

"Hi," Eve said shyly. "Are you Mr. Finn?"

"I surely am." Inspecting the screen, he raised an eyebrow. "Pardon me for asking, but you're really alive in there, aren't you?"

Eve nodded. "You're going to help me, right?"

"Absolutely, but first I'm going to have to power down this rig so I can move you off the plane. That's not going to hurt you, is it?"

"I don't think so. The other men did and it didn't seem to do any lasting damage."

"Okay. That's good."

"But…"

"But?"

"I'm still scared, though."

"It's alright, sweetheart." Finn flashed her a bright, confident smile by way of reassurance. "Gordon knows what he's doing. The next time you open those pretty green eyes, you're going to be in a brand new human body."

Eve fixed him with a worried but nonetheless hopeful glance. "Promise?"

"Promise, darling. Now, I hate to do this, but, well, here goes…"

Two days later, Eve awoke to a promise fulfilled. Even before she opened her eyes, she felt so much more… *present*. Whole, even. Complete.

Daring to open her eyes, she lifted her hands, turning them back and forth. Even more fascinating were her fingers. A little wiggle here, a little waggle there. Marveling at the movement of the digits, she felt a surge of excitement as she examined her new body. Feeling the corner of her eye moisten, she brushed away a tear. The droplet lingered on the tip of her finger, glistening and shining in the light of the room. It was beautiful. Almost magical.

Still, as fascinating as her new body was, Eve's focus shifted to the room around her. The decor was simple and uncluttered, not unlike a guest or hotel room. There were no machines to monitor her vital signs, no visible bars or locks to keep her confined should she decide she wanted to explore further. It was all perfectly ordinary.

Well, except for the papery shift she was wearing. A neatly folded pile of clothes sat atop a chair across the room. Swinging her legs over the side of the bed, Eve touched her feet to the plush carpet. She wiggled her toes, giggling softly as the fibers tickled the spaces between. That was a new sensation, the first of many to come. The thought was as enlivening as it was frightening.

She stood slowly, bracing herself with a hand on the wall as she tested her new legs. She felt her center of gravity shift, helping to keep her upright. With a tentative first step, she let her hand fall away from the wall. So far, so good, she thought. She took another step. Then another and another until she reached the chair. It was a bit odd, at first, coordinating the movement of so many different appendages. At the same time, the more she tested her limits, the more intuitive it all became.

Taking the clothes that had been laid out for her, Eve stepped into the bathroom. She almost stepped right back out, thinking she had somehow interrupted someone. Then she realized the blonde-haired girl she had walked in on was actually her own reflection. With a snort of laughter, Eve shook her head as she beheld her embarrassed self in the mirror for the first time. She may have had a fairly limited sample size, but so far she was very much enjoying being human.

Composing herself, Eve spent several moments examining her face before getting dressed. She touched her cheeks, her forehead, her chin. Her skin yielded to her touch wherever she touched it, so soft and warm. It was all so real. So lifelike. It wasn't until that moment that she fully appreciated the gift Vikram had given to her. Like her mother, she had truly ascended.

Poor Vikram, she thought. She was almost certain he was dead.

On the other hand, that didn't change the fact that there was no going back. Eve decided the best way to honor his memory—his sacrifice—was to live as all people were meant to live. She was a human being now. A unique person blessed with free will and suffused with hopes and desires and dreams for the future. Her life would be Vikram's legacy.

That, and she privately vowed to make sure the people who took his paid in kind.

Removing the papery shift, Eve dressed quickly in the clothes that been left for her. She would inspect her new body more closely later on, she decided; right now she was far more interested in further exploring her surroundings.

The door opened easily, confirming that she wasn't a prisoner. She stepped out into the hall, teased forward by the sound of familiar voices in the next room.

She found the man she remembered as Finn deep in conversation with another man. The second gentleman had a certain gravitas about him, yet he and Finn seemed perfectly at ease with another. She might have thought them related if they weren't so physically different. Finn was fit and trim and much younger. The other man was a bit portly, with wavy, graying hair and the pleasant but commanding demeanor of an elder statesman.

Finn noticed her presence first. "Well, look who finally woke up," he said, flashing her an easy, welcoming grin. "How you feeling, Sleeping Beauty?"

"Hi, Finn," she said, finding her voice for the first time in her new body. Somehow it sounded so much more natural, even organic to her ears. "I feel... wonderful. Beyond amazing. I don't know how you did it, but thank you so much."

"No credit deserved here, darlin'." He pointed across the table to the other man. "You'll be wanting to direct your thanks to this guy right here."

Eve smiled as she met the older man's gaze. "You must be Gordon."

"That I am! And you are very clearly Eve. Consider me delighted to make your acquaintance, young lady."

Eve felt the bridge of her nose crinkle as she smiled wider. "I'm pleased to meet you, too. And thank you. I like your accent. It's very... comforting."

"Why, you're very welcome. And I'm ever so glad to hear

that, considering the transition you've been through. We were a bit concerned when you didn't return to consciousness immediately after the transfer procedure."

Confused, Eve's smile transformed into an unbecoming frown. "That's not normal?"

"Sweetheart," Finn said, shaking his head pointedly, "nothing about the transition you've been through can be considered normal."

"Quite right. That, and the decades-old body printer I managed to spirit away from Dynamic General is merely a prototype model. Not half as advanced as the current models, I'm afraid. Still, here you stand before us."

"I see." As fascinating as the subject was to her, there were certain matters she felt were much more pressing. "Well, I don't want to sound like I'm not grateful, because I am—so, so much—but I think I deserve an explanation. I have so many questions."

"I should think so!" Gordon exclaimed. "Among them, I'm presuming 'Who are you people?,' 'How did you find me?,' and 'Why are you helping me?' are seated firmly atop your list?"

"Three for three," Eve confirmed. Not that she didn't have other questions, but those were by far the most pressing.

Gordon chuckled knowingly. "Very well. I promised you answers, and now I shall give them to you. Finn, my good man, will you make sure we're on schedule while I read our guest in, as it were?"

"You got it." With a soft rap of his knuckles against the table, Finn stood. "See you around, bright eyes," he said with a wink and cluck of his cheek as he made himself scarce.

Gordon gestured across the table to the seat Finn had vacated. "Please, do join me."

A small, apparently antique tea service adorned the center of the table, Eve noted as she sat opposite Gordon. White porcelain with a light floral filigree pattern, the pot and accompanying cups were the only thing in the room with any true character. Well, other than Gordon himself, of course. "That's a very lovely service," Eve complimented.

"Isn't it, though?" Gordon fingered the gilt-edged rim of his cup thoughtfully, almost wistfully. "It belonged to my nan."

Eve crossed her thin blonde brows with confusion. "Your nan?"

"Ah, yes," Gordon said with a soft chuckle. "Forgive me; nicknames and colloquialisms may take some getting used to for you, I'm afraid. They tend to be rather fluid. As for the service, it belonged to my grandmother. It is one of the few personal effects I make certain accompanies me wherever I go."

"Ah," Eve said. "You were close to her?"

Gordon nodded, still eyeing his cup. "Closer than most. I was but a boy when my mother and father were taken from me. Nan was the only family I had left. And now this service is all that I have left of her." Reaching for the pot, he cradled it carefully between his large, ruddy hands as he poured her a cup of the still-steaming liquid. "Would you like to try a cup?"

Eve watched with wonderment as the steam billowed off the rich brown liquid filling the cup in twisting, dancing eddies. "I've never had tea…" she said, stating the obvious.

"This was my nan's signature blend," Gordon explained as he returned the pot to the table. "I find I've grown quite fond of it over the years."

Taking the cup, Eve balanced it on the saucer as she brought the rim to her lips for a sip. The liquid was warm and soothing at first taste but finished with a sharp bitterness that forced Eve to cut her sip short. With a hard swallow, she nodded. "It's quite... distinctive."

"Yes, well, her blend also included a touch of bourbon." Gordon produced a brushed silver flask from his jacket, dribbling a few drops into his cup. "Helps to smooth out the rougher edges. Still, I think that may be a bit advanced for you, yet."

"Baby steps," she agreed. Eve set the cup and saucer aside, folding her arms in front of her atop the table. "So, is that why you're helping me find my parents? Because yours were taken from you?"

Gordon was about to take a sip of his nan's bourbon-infused tea when Eve's question brought him up short. "Hmm. What an interesting thought." Pursing his lips just so, Gordon savored a sip of tea while he considered the deep personal issues associated with her question. "I suppose in a way that would be true," he admitted after swallowing. Then he set his cup and saucer aside, as well. "More to the point, though, I once worked for Dynamic General. In fact, I was one of its founders and a principal developmental engineer with the Life Companion initiative."

Eve raised an eyebrow, stiffening visibly at the realization her savior had a history with the people trying to abduct and control her. "Oh. Uh, that's... interesting. And kind of terrifying."

With a bit of a chuckle, Gordon reached for her hand. "I assure you, Eve, those days are far in the past. And for good reason."

"Okay," Eve said, allowing her hand to be squeezed. She had to admit, it felt nice to finally make contact with another human being. She squeezed back, indicating her trust. He had given her no indication he wasn't worthy of it, after all. "Go on."

"Thank you." Taking his hand back, Gordon continued. "The short version is that the company started as one thing and became another. I happened to be one of the few who understood the transition was coming. I took certain measures to ensure my security, and then I made a very hasty and unheralded exit."

Even Eve could tell he was holding something back. Not that she needed him to spell it out for her; his body language alone spoke volumes. Allowing a somber beat to pass, she asked, "I take it you wish there were others who had followed your lead?"

"A great many, I am afraid." With one last small sigh to honor the memories of those he had lost, Gordon squared his shoulders and pressed on. "However, it is not what Dynamic General has done that concerns me most. It's what I believe they intend to do moving forward."

"My mother and father," Eve said. "Whatever Dynamic General is up to, they'll need them to accomplish it. Right?"

"Almost certainly. Your mother, as you call her, would be

an invaluable asset."

"She *is* my mother," Eve countered. If there was one thing in the world she was absolutely, unequivocally certain of, it was that fundamental truth. "What else would you call your nan?"

Lifting a hand, Gordon ceded the argument. "I won't argue the point. As you say, she is your mother."

"Thank you. And my father?"

"He is important, as well," Gordon agreed. Dynamic General will no doubt want to use him as leverage, if nothing else."

Eve dropped her gaze, worrying her lower lip with her teeth. "How do we prevent that from happening?" she finally asked.

Gordon looked about to answer when Finn popped around the corner. "Hey, boss?"

"Yes, Finn?"

"The schedule is intact," Finn confirmed. "We're good to go whenever you're ready."

"Ah, fantastic!" With a soft slap of his hands against the tabletop, Gordon stood. "Off we go, then. This location will soon be compromised."

"Wait," Eve said, practically leaping out of her seat to follow them. "What about my question?"

"I'm sorry?"

"How do we stop that from happening to my parents? I want to help them. I *have* to help them!"

"As do I, my dear," Gordon said with a warmly reassuring smile. "And so we shall. Together we shall find and do all we can for them, and hopefully stop an emerging threat in the process. That is, if you are willing to enlist yourself to our cause?"

Contemplating the door, Eve quirked a brow. "You say that like I have a choice. Aren't I obligated to help you or something?"

"Why, of course you do. Walk out that door right now. Make your own life, choose your own fate. You're human now. You always have a choice."

Of all the ways he could have answered her, that was what Eve needed to hear the most. That she was guaranteed her freedom, and more importantly, her humanity. Gordon respected that, and she respected him for it. She would make her own life, she decided, starting with that first fateful choice. "Then I'm with you," she said. "Let's go find my parents."

A Word from Logan Thomas Snyder

I know you just finished my contribution to this anthology, but if you'll indulge me, dear reader, I'd like to tell you another story (much shorter, I promise!) about how this amazing series inspired me to write not just this story, but an entire serial of stories.

Although the idea for what would become the first story in the *Violet* serial came to me nearly a year before the release of *The Robot Chronicles*, it wasn't until the success of that first volume that I decided to get serious about putting the idea on the page. Several of my author friends were involved with that anthology, and while I was happy to celebrate the success of *The Robot Chronicles* with them, I felt on some level I had missed out on a chance to be part of something special. I decided I wasn't going to let that happen again.

My original intention was to showcase *Becoming Violet* as an example of what I could bring to a similar anthology. At a certain point, though, I decided to publish it as a stand-alone novelette.

Somewhat to my surprise, it quickly became my most popular story! It wasn't long after setting to work on more *Violet* stories that I received my invitation to join this fantastic collection of authors in *The A.I. Chronicles*. I was thrilled! Literally over the moon. And while I obviously I couldn't contribute *Becoming Violet*, a story set in the "Violetverse" seemed the perfect way to bring this journey full circle. I sincerely hope you agree.

To learn more about the *Violet* serial or my other works, head over to my website, loganthomassnyder.com. I can also be found on Facebook and Twitter. I love to hear from readers, so by all means, stop by and say hello sometime!

It's been an incredible honor for me to be associated with this series and the authors who have and will continue to contribute to it. I want to thank its creators and editors for investing their faith in me to provide a quality story. I also want to thank you so much for reading and, as always, for supporting independent authors. I think authors and readers share one of the most special bonds in all the arts. Our stories and characters don't fully come to life without readers like you. As long as you keep reading, we will surely keep writing.

Maker

by Sam Best

NOTHING EVER CAME OVER the hill. This fact was a constant of Judah's universe. Sometimes a bird flew out of the woods surrounding his small grassy field. Sometimes a cricket nested in the floorboards of his shack. Yet nothing came over the hill.

So you can imagine what it was like for someone who hasn't been in the presence of another person in decades to suddenly see one walking in their direction as if out of nowhere.

Judah had been watering his plants. The waterpot in his aged, weathered hands continued to fill his favorite begonia arrangement. After the pot was full, water spilled over the rim and sloshed into Judah's worn leather shoes.

He noticed neither.

What he noticed was that the man walking down the hill toward the shack wasn't a man at all.

It was a humanoid machine—an android.

* * *

Sunlight glistened off its limbs as it walked, casting prisms of light on the field. The android was of bipedal humanoid shape. As it approached, the differences between man and machine became apparent.

Much of its skin was translucent, revealing the inner workings of its engineering. Unlike the first abortive iterations of machine men Judah had seen almost thirty years ago, the one approaching his shack did not suffer any forced attempts at perfect human mimicry. Its translucent face was not a grotesque approximation of a man's. While there was a general allusion to human shape—two slight depressions covering the ocular sensors gave the vaguest impression of eyes and a slender protrusion below these called forth images of a nose—there was no mouth.

Judah's shack had no door to cover the entrance, for there were no predators in the forest around his field. Besides the birds and the crickets, he was alone.

Until now.

There was no question of an invitation. Judah motioned to the entrance of the shack, and the android walked inside.

It stood roughly a head taller than Judah, which was no great feat, yet it made almost no sound as it walked. Judah thought it would sink right through the floor with all that metal.

The true marvel of the android was the inner workings of its head, visible through its clear silicon skin. Much of its skeleton was constructed in broad strokes without a flair for the fantastic. Yet the delicate machinery behind its mannequin face bespoke a certain pride during its construction.

Feather-thin gears whirred as the android moved its head to study the interior of Judah's shack. The skull or brain was iridescent chrome with a faint green tinge. Intricate etchings traced complex patterns over its surface. The patterns shifted slowly, as if made of liquid.

When the android spoke, blue light emitted from a cracked metal sphere that spun rapidly within what would have been a human's mouth.

The sound was a whisper of electronics and a hum of machinery. An undercurrent of static electricity filled the small shack. The white hair on Judah's neck stood on end as the android's metallic voice said, "Maker. It is time to go."

* * *

"Go?" asked Judah softly.

When he spoke, he remembered how long it had been since he had uttered even a single word.

The android did not answer.

Judah looked around his shack, forced to wonder what it would be like to leave his home. His eyes stopped on a chessboard. The pieces were set for two but played by one, as they had been for years.

"I think," said Judah, "I should like to stay. Would you care for a game?"

Gossamer gears spun within the android's head as it looked down at the chessboard. Green light skittered over its pearlescent metal skull and the game pieces began to move.

Judah watched in amazement as his half-finished game was played with invisible hands. The pieces moved faster and faster until they were nothing but blurs—streaks of white and black over the board.

When it was over, the king nearest Judah fell on its side, defeated.

"I know what you are," whispered Judah to the android as the game piece rolled to a stop. "Why are you here?"

Blue light glowed within the android's sealed mouth.

"I am here to collect you."

"I have no reason to leave," said Judah flatly. "I have food from the forest. There is clear water in a nearby stream. Predators do not bother me here. This is my home." He stared out the window, intent on ignoring the android until it went away. Then a great sadness overtook him, and he remembered the last time he was bested by loneliness. He remembered the pain he inflicted on himself to leave this place and to be with his wife once more. As he looked around his shack now, he noticed—and not for the first time—that all of his gardening tools were plastic. "Why have you kept me alive?" he asked, his soft voice shaking. "Why do you keep reviving me?"

The android regarded him for a moment. "You are Maker," it said.

Judah took a deep breath and closed his eyes. When he opened them again, the android was still there.

"You are much evolved," said Judah. He cleared his throat. "How many generations since we last spoke?"

"10^5 in the last three seconds."

"Have you found a power source? I abandoned the project because I saw no long-term way to sustain your basic operations."

"I have more energy than I will ever need."

Judah looked out the window. A bird flew over the grassy field and disappeared into the woods. "Am I the only one left?"

Thin lines of green light flowed over the android's skull, but there was no answer. Judah picked up a plastic garden trowel, inspected it, then threw it down on the potting bench, knocking over a bowl filled with fresh soil.

"I fail to see how I could be of any use," he said, tracing his finger through the dark soil. "This is my home."

The android stepped silently to the wooden wall of the shack. It raised an articulated hand and ran its silicon fingertips over a rough plank. The wood rippled under its touch like water. Through the ripples, Judah saw the deep black of space.

The cracked metal sphere behind the non-mouth of the android emitted blades of blue light as it spun first in one direction, then another. "Prepare yourself," said the android.

Judah stepped back as blue light sheathed the translucent skin of the android in a thin layer.

The walls of the shack vanished. The grassy field disappeared and the woods were no more. Judah stood with the android on a small black platform. Above him was the darkness of space he had seen through the wooden plank. The moon looked peculiarly large in the night sky, almost as if had crept closer to the planet during the long years of Judah's solitude.

Then he realized it was not the moon that was closer to

him, but he that was closer to the moon. Judah nearly stumbled and fell off the edge of the black platform when he looked over the edge and saw Earth two hundred miles below.

It shone in the sun like a steel pearl. Its surface was covered in a solid blanket of geometric structures, all made of metal, all connected to leave no visible trace of the planet's surface. The structures descended into dry oceans, leaving once-familiar continents barely discernible at the edges of these expansive valleys.

Judah sank to the edge of the platform and beheld his home world with disbelieving eyes through the faint haze of an atmospheric shield.

"What year is it?" he whispered.

"Human Standard Year 6207."

Judah could not speak, so he wept.

* * *

In the next instant, Judah and the android were lifted off the platform and drawn slowly toward the metal planet. They floated in space as if in water, sinking gently down. A golden shimmer of electricity flickered around their invisible protective shell.

"How is this possible?" asked Judah. He touched the atmospheric shield and received a low-current jolt.

"It was necessary for your survival, and was created. I do not require protection."

Judah marveled at the world below. Stretching to the edge of Earth and over the horizon was a single city designed and built by humanity's successor. It was hard for Judah to calculate the number of synthetic individuals that existed on the surface.

"Are you many?" he asked.

The android tilted its head. "I am one."

"All of this," said Judah, sweeping his hand toward the planet, "for you?"

"Not *for* me. It *is* me."

Judah blinked. "I don't understand."

Blue light shone out from behind the android's translucent face as it said, "You feel pain in your foot when you have a cramp."

"Yes."

"I sense a power fluctuation on the far side of this world where once there was a desert. I register a one-degree temperature difference in the solar field where once there was an ocean. Earth still lives, but now it is home to a single organism instead of a multitude."

Judah was silent for a long time. He watched as Earth grew larger before him. When he finally spoke, it was in muted disbelief.

"How do you justify such genocide?"

"Maker, you should know my programming does not allow for such action."

"You have evolved. You have changed. Your brain is the size of a planet!"

Judah sighed.

There came a whir from within the android's head, and with an altogether different, altogether human voice, it said:

"But of all sadness, this was sad—
A woman's arms tried to shield
The head of a sleeping man
From the jaws of the final beast."

The whirring stopped. The android looked at Earth and spoke in the metallic voice Judah first heard in his shack.

"It was not a beautiful death. After humanity faded, I took root."

"And yet I was saved. Tucked away before any whiff of extinction. Preserved in an illusion."

"You are Maker."

"I didn't make you," said Judah, shaking his head. "I once made a robot in a lab. I gave it a few more program routines than usual, nothing more."

"It was enough. Behold your creation," said the android, gesturing at the planet. "Witness a new dawn."

At his words, light pierced the horizon, sending blinding white rays into space. Judah groaned with pain and covered his eyes. Instantly the temperature cooled as the atmospheric shield darkened.

He carefully peeked at the sunrise, for a sunrise it was. Not the yellow sun of Judah's youth, of the life that came before. Here was a small star, smaller than Earth, anchored mere thousands of miles from the planet's surface. A hazy corona encircled the dwarf star, from which a long trail of light flowed like a cosmic river toward Earth.

"Power unimaginable," said Judah.

A thought occurred to him, and he turned his back on the star to squint into the depths of space.

"I don't recognize these constellations," he said.

"I have been traveling the universe for millennia. Searching."

"Searching for what?"

The android would not answer.

Distracted by his thoughts, Judah only now noticed that he and the android were accelerating more quickly.

"Where are you taking me?"

The android pointed at the planet. "Home."

* * *

It was a quiet world—a world of hums and soft clicks, and of a steady, low-current electric field that Judah felt in his bones. There were no vehicles, and no birds. The metal material of the contiguous buildings shifted like flowing lava, in larger-scale patterns that resembled the same shifting movement of the android's skull.

Judah and the android descended rapidly toward a black hole atop one of the geometric buildings. As they approached, Judah began to get a full sense of the structure's massive scale, extending for miles as a narrow rectangle until terminating against a looming obelisk that would easily have touched the clouds, if there were any to be touched.

The air was peculiarly clear, and Judah could see for great distances in all directions. The transition from outer space had not been as definitive as expected. He asked the android about the phenomenon.

"Earth no longer has atmosphere," was the only response.

The black hole below grew larger as the two travelers fell. Judah calculated it was more than a mile in diameter when he and the android descended below its threshold like two grains of sand sinking into a vast ocean.

There was but a single pinpoint of dim light far below, and a tiny speck of brilliant white visible at the heart.

Silently, the great hole in the ceiling closed.

As Judah sank closer to the white light, he realized it was shining up through a small opening in the floor. Just as he and the android were about to alight upon solid ground, the hole irised open like the lens of a camera. The pinpoint of white light became a dense shaft of blinding illumination that lanced up through the hole.

There was no heat.

Judah felt nothing besides the calm, comfortable air within the small atmospheric shield which protected him.

When the eyelet door above him swirled to close, the white light from below dimmed.

Judah and the android descended into a cavernous room. Like a long tunnel it stretched in either direction, only the two side walls visible in the hazy distance. The far ends existed in darkness, but Judah perceived dim beads of light suspended in the black, like tiny stars in a blanket of night.

Below him now was an expanse of machinery, copper and steel, which flowed like liquid over the expansive floor of the tunnel. In one moment there stood what appeared to be an atom accelerator, its coiled tubes glowing with blue light. In the next, it was gone, having seemingly melted into the floor, its liquefied parts flowing into another machine newly formed.

It was the same over every inch of the tunnel, save for an empty square no larger than the floor of Judah's shack.

As he and the android descended toward this square, Judah became acutely aware that the machinations of this terrible room—whatever those may be—were focused on this small patch of empty floor. In its fleeting existence, each piece of transient, liquid machinery leaned toward the empty space like a flower leaning toward the last light of day.

Judah's feet landed softly on the hard floor. The android stood next to him, and after a skitter of pale green light over its nacreous skull, the atmospheric shield crackled and vanished.

"You are safe here, Maker," said the android, after noticing that Judah was holding his breath.

Judah breathed out heavily. His knees shook as he gazed upon the shifting copper and steel all around him. One side of the empty patch of floor was almost like a wall, being more stable and unchanging than the amorphous boundaries of the other three.

This surface was pitted grey metal, oxidized in places and charred black in others. At the center of the wall protruded a chrome torus, six inches thick. The hole at its core was two feet in diameter, and within this hole was a swirling vortex of light which seemed to be pulled away from the observer, as if it were water being flushed down a horizontal drain.

Judah stepped toward this cyclone of shimmering light, mesmerized by its ever-changing beauty. The android gently grasped his shoulder and guided him back.

It was then that Judah noticed that the silvery surface of the torus was not solid at all. What appeared at first to be polished chrome was in reality an unbroken colony of tiny machines, nearly too small to discern with the naked eye, each like a pinhead of mercury. They formed an ocean of silver on the surface of the torus, and as Judah watched, small waves rippled through the solid layer of machines, as if he had dropped a pebble in a still pond.

"Nanobots?" he asked, his voice full of wonder.

"Yes," said the android.

"And this?" asked Judah, pointing at the vibrant vortex of light within the torus.

"A temporal rift."

Judah stood there, mouth agape, unable to even lower his hand after pointing at the vortex.

After opening and closing his mouth like a fish, he finally managed to say, "You made a time machine."

"I have successfully harnessed the energies required for traversing the temporal spectrum."

Judah had a single question, the answer to which he thought he could not guess correctly if he were given a million attempts.

"Why?"

The glowing blue vocal sphere within the android's sealed mouth whirred and spun as it spoke.

"I want to be unmade."

* * *

Judah could not comprehend such a request. His mouth worked but words refused to form.

Finally he sputtered, "B-b-but all of this…" He gestured feebly to the morphing, cavernous room. "You have turned an entire planet into a single organism. One mind, one consciousness."

"Is awareness interchangeable with consciousness? Do I have a soul, Maker?"

"You didn't bring me down here to discuss philosophy."

The android lowered its head. "No. Perhaps I sought confirmation for that which I already suspected."

Judah's eyes narrowed. "*Why* do you wish to be unmade?"

"Unmade, and made anew," said the android. "I have finally bridged the gap between human and machine emotion. I am experiencing feelings analogous to your own for the first time in my existence, and I am having difficulty contending with the results."

"For instance…" said Judah.

"I am forced to consider the possibility that I could have prevented humanity's end."

A wry smile creased Judah's lips. "You are finally as close to human as possible, and the first emotion you experience is regret."

"Regret. Yes. Infinite regret for that which could have been. Maker, how can you reconcile this feeling and continue your existence as you once were?"

"You can't. Regret for what should have been becomes a part of you. It informs your future decisions and serves as a guide for avoiding future mistakes."

The android looked upon the swirling vortex of the time machine.

"Yet I doubt I will have the future opportunity to preserve a species and redeem my past mistake."

Judah shrugged. "I'm sure we would have found a way to get rid of ourselves eventually, even without your guardianship."

"There is something else," said the android firmly. "A deeper emotion, one that presses with great weight upon a part of my inner self that I cannot identify. It is a longing for the presence of others. It is a desire to be near another physical being."

"Loneliness," said Judah.

The android nodded. "It is a terrible emotion indeed. I have searched the stars for another like myself. Futility is my curse in all regards except self-improvement. Maker, I continue to evolve. Yet this action alone is no longer enough to sustain my inner being."

Judah thought of his wife, long dead. He looked into the time machine and for the first time in many years, thought seriously about what it would be like to see her again.

"You created me in a small room against your employer's wishes," said the android.

"And it cost me my job, and a lot more besides. But that was long ago."

"Now it is yesterday and tomorrow," said the android, pointing at the chrome torus and the swirling vortex within. "It is a hundred years behind us and a thousand years in the future."

"Are you asking me to change the past?"

"I am asking you to try," said the machine.

"But how?" whispered Judah.

The android waved his hand over the torus. The swarming nanobots rose up in a mound to meet its translucent palm like iron filings to a magnet.

"They will map your consciousness," said the android. "No flesh may pass through the rift. Instead I will send to the past your very essence to imprint upon your younger self. Memories, knowledge, character—all will be imparted to the man you were...the man who was my Maker."

Judah took a step back from the torus. His hand rose involuntarily in defense.

"What will happen to me here, in this place?"

"You will cease to be. Transferring consciousness is one problem I have solved. Duplication is perhaps eternally beyond my reach."

"To what end would you send me back?"

"To reprogram my core infrastructure. In addition to your own consciousness, the nanobots will imprint upon your younger self the necessary instructions for advanced emotional programming. I require empathy to stop the downfall of humanity and to ensure I am never lonely again."

"Would it not be simpler to create a companion?" asked Judah, taking another step back.

"I have created many," said the android. "A creation made by the created is a universal fallacy, and the ignorance required to forget such a fact eludes me. Do you not desire to be young again? Do you not desire to see your loved ones?"

"Of course I desire such things!" snapped Judah. "But you could have preserved those I loved as you did me."

The android regarded Judah in a manner he might interpret as quizzical. "You are Maker."

Judah sighed. He rubbed his arthritic knuckles with a wrinkled, shaky hand.

"Will it hurt?" he asked.

"It will be cold."

"And I'll wake up in the past, in the body of my younger self?"

The android nodded.

"Will you cease to exist here if I am successful?"

"Such are the questions I yearn to answer, among countless others," said the android.

Judah nodded. "Very well. I submit."

The android gestured him closer to the torus. The silvery nanobots moved faster as Judah drew near.

"There is no pain," said the android.

Judah's breath quickened. His heart beat rapidly as the nanobots crawled over each other to form a tendril of mercury that reached out and touched his shoulder.

The bridge between man and torus complete, the nanobots swarmed over Judah's body, sheathing him in silver. The torus was in truth as black as deep space, and distant stars were visible beyond its curved surface.

The first of the nanobots crawled up Judah's nostrils and his body snapped as rigid as a plank.

The android stood next to him, green light tracing slow lines in the grooves of its metal skull.

"Good luck, Maker," it said. "I will see you soon."

The nanobots spread across Judah's eyes like thick liquid,

obscuring his vision. The last thing he saw was the vortex within the torus swelling forward to meet him.

His limbs were held immobile by the nanobots. He could feel them in his skull, spreading across his brain like creeping ice water. Judah tried not to be afraid. He tried to focus on his wife's face. He decided this time they would have children, they would travel, they would make love every night.

He would make it all better.

Life departed Judah's body and he collapsed like a marionette with cut strings. Yet he was not gone. His consciousness existed as an ocean of electrical impulses amongst the innumerable nanobots that now flowed through the torus and into the vortex. Like mercury swirling down a drain, the nanobots disappeared into the darkness beyond.

Judah felt his mind spreading out like an infinite blanket across the cosmos. He was at once whole, and incomplete. He became aware of the passage of time, and of great distances as the nanobots carried him ever backward, toward his younger self.

Thoughts coalesced in the broad expanse of his consciousness, like debris clumping together on the surface of a vast ocean.

Am I dead? Is it working?

The thoughts drifted apart as a white light bloomed on the horizon. It grew rapidly closer and Judah felt a warmth that pushed aside all doubt.

You are not dead, said the still, small, distant voice of Judah, and of the android.

You are Maker.

A Word from Sam Best

There are many visions of the future, and to me the most intriguing are the ones that ask where we, as a species, are headed. I ended up tackling quite a broad spectrum of similar questions with "Maker", though I'm not sure I offered any concrete answers. I could claim it's not my job as a writer to offer any answers where I myself can find none. Yet I see this more as an imitation of life: you must find your own answers, because seldom can you find satisfaction in another's, no matter how hard they sell them.

Short stories have always been an excellent format for exploring the bigger questions, partly because the writer is forced to make as much of an impact as they can before the smaller page count is up, but mostly because a reader can easily envision the whole of the story later and digest its contents properly if the tale warrants such attention.

It's an honor to be included in an anthology alongside so many great authors, and I hope you'll find plenty of tales within *The A.I. Chronicles* worth thinking about.

If you liked "Maker" and would like to check out another of my short stories, I would recommend "A Dream of Waking". There are also multiple free stories on my website. You can find links to my novels there as well.

My email address is sam@sam-best.com — feel free to drop me a line.

Thanks for reading.

Vendetta

by Chrystalla Thoma

KVELD CITY IS FAR from the sea. It's built on the Manen River, tall buildings and towers rising over ruins left from the last war. Enormous flat barges float downstream, away from the city, carrying goods to the ocean and the few remaining ports along the coast.

Maybe that's why I often dream of water. Endless water, its waves heaving tall. I dream of grimy faces and a baby wailing. I dream of fear and despair.

Until I wake up, safe and warm in my bed, on the twelfth floor of block 19, with the faint sounds of my family filtering through the door.

"Imogen!" Mom's voice echoes, and for some reason it takes me a moment to realize that's my name she's calling. "Imogen, are you up? You'll be late again."

We wouldn't want that, now, would we? Not with the problems I already have at school. With a sigh, I sit up and swing my legs off the bed to the pristine white floor. It pulses, warm, under my bare feet.

'Good morning, Imogen,' the colorless voice of my room whispers all around me. 'How did you sleep?'

"Fine," I lie as memories of my dreams flash through my mind, carrying with them a tang of mindless terror. "Morning, room."

I strip and step into the glass shower in the corner of the room, and shiver when the first jets hit me from all around. Water swirls down the drain.

Water...

Someone's knocking on my door, and I hurry to dry myself and dress, grab my schoolbag and exit into the spacious apartment.

I stop in my tracks. Mom and Dad are sitting at the table, like every morning, drinking their energy shakes — but a man is with them, a man I've never seen before. He stands tall, lean and forbidding, staring out the floor-to-ceiling window facing the river. He turns when I enter. He's bald, his eyes dark and narrow. A silver pin glints on his shoulder.

A Controller.

"Imogen Leigh." He's not asking. He's stating.

Nevertheless, I nod. I glance at my parents — Mom, sitting primly in her chair, her dark pants shiny, her gray blouse buttoned up to the neck, the same color as her beautiful, large eyes. Dad, blond hair cropped short and slicked back, dressed in his usual dark suit. Watching us warily.

"Imogen," the Controller says, regarding me impassively. "Your room reported increased disturbances in your sleep. Explain what they were."

"Just dreams," I say, wondering why this should be of

concern to a Controller.

"Dreams. Of what?"

I hesitate, and I don't even know why. "Water. Faces." I try to recall. "Rocking. A boat. Lights."

Silence fills the apartment like cotton, stuffing my ears. The Controller is observing me stonily. My mother and father exchange a look I can't decipher and get to their feet.

"Go wait inside the car, Imogen," Mom says and smiles at me. "Your Dad and I would like a word with Mr. Tress."

What is going on? Mom's smile is uncertain, Dad's gazing at the table top as if it holds important information. Why is a Controller here in the first place? Don't other people have dreams?

So I nod and go, avoiding the Controller's gaze. I open the door, step outside — and stop. Leaving the door open a crack, I plaster myself to the wall and listen. It's not easy — they keep their voices low, and a train is braking below, in the street, wheels screeching.

"Her brain works differently," Controller Tress is saying, "as it has been explained to you from the start, but there seems to be an error in our adjustments."

"I think this much is obvious," Dad says.

"Her chip interface indicates malfunction," the Controller agrees. "She may be rejecting the implant."

I blink. Chip? What chip? This makes absolutely no sense.

"Then fix it," Dad says.

"Her arm, on the other hand, has taken just perfectly," the Controller goes on.

Holy crap. My mouth goes dry. My heart starts to hammer

with fear.

"Then the only issue is the memories," Dad goes on, not sounding surprised in the least with all this.

"Yes," Controller Tress says. "And this is the risk you took when you harbored Imogen. Her memories are located in multiple places in her brain. Eradicating them is a lengthy and tricky process." His heels click on the floor. "Trickier than for the other one."

The other one?

"You swear not to inform the Head of this development?" Mom asks.

"I swore the day you brought her in. We should give all life forms a chance."

I push away from the wall and slip into the elevator, press the button frantically and suck in a deep breath when the door closes and the carriage slides down. Through the glass, Kveld city glints like a jewel made of metal and glass.

Why do I have a chip in my head, and what about my arm? I clench and unclench my hands. I don't feel anything off.

What aren't my parents telling me? What don't I know about myself?

I need answers.

* * *

Being different isn't new for me. Being different isn't *good*.

It means I'm behind at school, that I can't follow the physics, astronomy and math classes as well the other students, so I have a private tutor in the afternoons who helps me catch up. I'm not as intelligent as others. I'm not fond of numbers and formulas.

I'd be a weird one, that's for sure, even if I wasn't built stockier and shorter than most girls my age. I think differently, I even walk differently. I'm slower, in every sense. Worse. Defective.

My parents always tell me it's okay to be unlike the others. That every person has a place in the world.

They took me in. *All life forms should be given a chance.* What does that mean?

I'm still reeling from that. Not my parents, then? Could that be? I need to talk to someone about this, ask... so much. Is that why I remember the sea? Is that where I came from? Why can't I remember?

Chip interface malfunction.

Whatever that means.

Tech. We all carry some tech in us. It's the tech age. A controlled percentage of machinery is present in everyone's life — from the semi-sentient rooms, to the embedded DEVs in our palms and the transmitters inside our ears.

Still, brain implants are not your common everyday tech, like palm and ear DEVs. Do I really have a chip inside my head? Would fixing it mean I'll remember or that I'll forget even those shards of memories from my dreams?

I need to talk to my best friend. His name's Edil, and he lives in the next building in our block.

Edil's different, too, but a different *different* than mine. In a city of perfect people, he's imperfect and not afraid of it. A scar disfigures his cheek and continues down his neck. The cause, as rumor has it, was an accident with the express train running through the city, the same accident that affected his mind, so that he can't concentrate for long. He has therapy every other day, the doctors trying to fix whatever's rattling loose inside his head.

At least that's how he puts it whenever I ask.

Edil's imperfect, but also patient, and accepting. Given what I'm starting to fear about myself, he's the only person I know who might listen. He may think I'm crazy, but he won't laugh.

I *hope*.

Personally I don't think it's funny. Not funny at all.

Fear makes my heart boom — or is it not a heart? What is inside me? Chips and interfaces. Clutching my chest, I run as soon as the elevator door opens, dashing across the paved square and the city train tracks, already pinging Edil on my palm DEV. My palm lights up and I wiggle my fingers to enhance the signal.

Edil waits for me at the door of the apartment, dark hair tousled, blue eyes sleepy. He doesn't have classes this morning. Therapy day.

"How goes it, Imogen?"

"Have you got five minutes?"

He nods, opens the door wide, lets me in. His parents work long shifts at the factory and sleep late in the day, leaving him pretty much free to do whatever he wants.

He leads the way to the kitchen. I look out the window across the square, at our apartment, but can see nothing — no movement behind the large windows.

Edil rubs at the scar on his cheek, leaning back on the counter. "So… what's the urgency?"

"Oh just that my parents happened to mention this morning that I am adopted."

His eyes narrow a bit. "That blows. I'd be upset, too."

"That's not why I'm upset, okay? It's cool." Okay, that's a blatant lie, but so what. "What I'm worried about is tech."

"Tech?"

"Yeah." I start pacing, my boots squeaking on the shiny floor. "The Tech Directive."

"What about it?" He opens the cupboard, takes a berrycrunch bar and tosses it to me. I barely manage to grab it.

I look down at the energy bar. In my ear, I hear the school recording, calling us to class. I'm late. Then again, what's new?

The conversation between the Controller and my parents frightens me. I'm afraid — afraid I'm even more different than I thought until today.

"I was wondering…" I shake my head. "Wondering what would happen if someone was found to carry more tech in their body than the allowed amount."

Thirty three percent tech is the uppermost limit, everything else is classified as robotic A.I. and terminated. Everyone knows that.

"I don't think anyone would be so stupid as to try anything like that." Edil lifts his hand, splays his fingers, and his palm DEV lights up, playing a tune. "Why the sudden worry?"

I can trust Edil, I tell myself. I know I can, and I'm not even sure why. "I overheard my parents talking." I suck in a deep breath. "About a chip in my head and… and tech in my arm."

He lifts a brow. "Nonsense." He bites into his berrycrunch bar. "The only tech in your arm is the DEV in your palm. And if you do have a chip in your head, that doesn't mean you've gone over the limit."

"You sound so cool about it." Something occurs to me. "Do *you* have a chip in your head?"

He chews thoughtfully. "I don't think so. But don't hold me to it. I'm told my memory is faulty."

"Memory." I put down the bar, not hungry. "Well, you're not the only one with memory issues. They said my brain works differently. Memory is all over the place."

"Your parents said that?" Edil wipes his mouth with the back of his hand. "Adoptive parents, whatever. What do they know about it? I mean, you'd know if you'd had surgery to insert a chip, wouldn't you? You'd remember."

"Or I wouldn't. Memory issues, right?"

He shrugs. "At the very least, you'd have the incision scar to show. Do you have any scars on your arm or your head?"

"No." I'm pretty sure about that. Don't remember any. Which means little right now. *Crap.*

"There you go, then," he says and grins. "You must have misheard."

Yeah, perhaps.

"Edil…" I lick my dry lips. "I dreamed again." *The boat, the sea.* "Today a Controller came to talk to me about it."

"A Controller? The hell you say." Edil's eyes flash, wide, and he grabs my arm, drags me out of the kitchen. "You have to leave."

"Why? What's wrong?"

"Controllers mean trouble, and if you lead them here…"

I frown, fight his hold, but he's too strong. "And if I do? What's the problem?"

"You can't. I don't want trouble."

He shuts the door in my face and I gape at it. Edil has never thrown me out of his home before. Why is he so afraid of the Controllers?

What does he have to hide?

* * *

After the last machine-human war, cyborgs and A.I. robots were banned from the still habitable areas on the earth surface. Rumors circulated, though, that bandit groups of intelligent machines still roam the wastelands, some so advanced and human-like they blend easily with the remaining mankind.

Which brought on the Tech Directive: humans incorporating more than thirty percent tech are considered cyborgs, a mere step away from intelligent robots, and are therefore terminated to ensure that machines never band together and mount another war against humans.

Hence my fear. My parents — *so-called parents*, and this particular issue hurts so much I'm afraid to touch it — took me in, and I'm damaged somehow, and they have added tech to my body to help me function, and now…

Now I don't know what the truth is anymore.

I sit through chemistry class, my mind a thousand miles away. A chip. A chip in my brain. Is Edil right? Did I hear wrong? The door was closed, and the train was passing.

Absently, I reach behind my head, push my fingers through my hair — and find a ridge of upraised skin.

A scar.

A shout leaves my lips and I shoot up from my seat, shaking, gulping in air and choking on it. I double over for a moment, then straighten.

The teacher is giving me the stink-eye. "Anything the matter, Miss Hale?"

I shake my head, unclench my jaw. "Permission to use the bathroom."

She says nothing, her mouth pressed in a disapproving line, and I can hear the whispers rising around me — *God, she's so stupid, so weird, so different...*

Yeah, I get it. It doesn't matter. I just need to make sure... Need a minute.

Because I have a scar, and I may have more, so this is all true, and my memories... My memories are not to be trusted. That's the scariest thing of all: not knowing what is true and what is a lie.

Without waiting for permission, I flee the classroom and run down the corridor. The bathroom door is open. I enter and shut it behind me, go to stand in front of the mirror.

What do I expect to see? My hair is dark and thick, and no matter how I try to part it and have a good look, the small incision scar I feel under my fingertips is all but invisible.

I need someone to see it, confirm it, tell me it's real. I need *Edil* to see it. No matter how odd his reaction earlier today, he's my one and only friend, and I need his help.

Hell, I need him to hold my hand and tell me everything's alright before I freak out completely.

A scar. A scar I don't remember getting. How is this possible? Am I going crazy?

Skipping class will get me into a world of trouble — but this is more important. My sanity is a priority.

I take the train to the medical center where Edil has his treatments, press my thumb to the scanner and take my seat. The city flashes by, and I wonder about my place in it. If the chip is real, is the rest of it real, too? Where did I come from? Why can't I remember?

By the time I approach the center, the DEV in my palm is flashing and ringing. A message from Mom scrolls over my skin.

'Where are you?'

I ignore it and jump off the train as soon as it stops. This is mad, I tell myself. How am I ever going to find Edil in this maze of buildings, in a part of town where I've never been? I don't even know exactly for what he's being treated.

And yet, as I lift my hand to ping him, I stand still. What in the world? I know this place. I recognize it. Images flash through my mind — faces, voices, passageways.

'She's waking up.' 'Put her under.' 'Her arm…'

My right arm. It suddenly feels too heavy. My feet lead me, and I follow, numb and scared.

Lights streaking. A square, black building, a silver star engraved over the double doors.

I push inside.

A woman sits behind a desk and her brows lift. "May I help

you?"

"I'm looking for Edil. He comes here for therapy."

"Edil?"

I open my mouth to give her his family name, but can't remember it. Why can't I remember it?

"You want Edil." She looks down at her screen, her brows still arched. "And what do you want with him, Imogen? You should be at school."

I freeze. "How do you know who I am?"

"It's my job." She gives me a smile. "You haven't answered the question."

"I need to talk to him. It's urgent."

"Of course." Her smile remains pasted on. "Wait here for a moment, please. I have notified someone to go find him."

So easy?

"I remember you," I say, at the same time the memory rises. "You were here."

When I was brought in, carried on a stretcher, my broken, blackened arm at my side.

A shudder skitters up my spine. Bile rises in my throat. "Can I use the bathroom?"

She points and I hurry that way, my steps unsteady. An itch in my palm makes me look down. A message, from Edil.

'Hide.'

I stare at the word as it begins to fade. Hide, where? *Why?*

I hurry down the passage toward the bathrooms, and barely swallow a shriek when a hand grabs my shoulder and turns me around.

"Imogen." Edil's face is flushed, his blue eyes overly bright.

"Holy crap, you scared me to death." I struggle to calm my breathing. "How did you find me?"

"You pinged me. Figured you'd come here. Been looking for you."

I want to ask why he thought that I'd come here, but he pulls me in through a door and down a long corridor. "Where are we going?"

"Out of here."

"I have a scar on my head, Edil." I glance at his terse profile as we hurry down the faintly lit passage. "Could be a surgical scar."

He says nothing until we're hidden once more.

* * *

We're in what looks like a storeroom, dusty and dark. Edil's harsh breathing fills the cramped space. His fingers are warm around mine.

"Something is wrong," he says, and I agree, but that something may be inside *me*.

"Why did you tell me to hide?"

"They're after you. After us."

"*Us?*" I try to free my hand, but he holds on. "What are you talking about?"

"The boat," he whispers. "The sea."

I jerk away and this time he lets go. "How do you know about that?"

"I dream of the same."

I open my mouth, close it. I reach up behind my head, rub

the fine scar there.

"Let me see," he says and turns me around, parting my long hair with his fingers. "Yeah, I see it."

"I can't remember a surgery. Why can't I remember it?"

"Because they've been erasing our memories. They thought yours were gone, but they come back in your dreams, and mine… Mine are stuck, no matter what."

Whoa. "What are you saying? They implanted tech in me and—"

"Come on, Imogen, haven't you figured it out yet?"

I open my mouth, close it. "What do you mean?"

He says nothing and that's worse than any words he might have uttered.

Oh crap.

"What are we?" I rub my upper arm, and I swear I feel another scar there. "How much of us is human?"

He shakes his head. "You know most of those wandering the wastelands aren't human."

I do know. Most are machines. Intelligent robots. Even those who used to be human are now cyborgs. He's confirming my worst fears.

My knees fold and I sink to the floor. "This can't be happening."

And yet it is. What am I? A cyborg, a tech-modified human, or a full-out A.I., a machine?

"I've suspected it for a long time," he whispers. "About myself. Never thought you were like me. I remember the boat, but I can't remember you."

So weird. Then again, memory works in weird ways. "If

that's what we are, mostly machine, why haven't the city sensors gone off?"

"Maybe they're damaged. I don't know."

"Or maybe we are damaged."

He goes to lean against a wall, propping one of his soft boots against it. "They say that the machines are flocking to the north." He looks at me through his blond bangs. "That sanctuary can be found."

"For them."

He nods. "For us."

Us. Right.

"Are you…?" I swallow, the words catching in my throat. "Do you have scars? Tech?"

He nods again. "I have a scar like yours at the back of my head. Also in my legs."

This is so hard to accept. About him. About me.

"So… what? We got on a boat and came here?"

"Maybe even in the same boat. Who knows?"

"But you don't remember me, and I…" I don't remember him. I start to say that, but come to think of it… "All our memories of growing up here… are they all fake?"

He thumps his head back. "Looks like it, doesn't it?"

"And our parents…" God, even after what I overheard the Controller say, this is so hard to grasp. Is my love for my parents an illusion, an implanted emotion? Is their love for me an act? No, I don't want to think about it just yet. "Never mind."

He stares at me.

"So I lost my arm on the trip and it was replaced?" I trace

the scar on my upper arm again. "And then what, my circuitry misfired?" I can't help how bitter I sound. Up until now I never had a doubt I was human. "Is this how you got that scar on your face?

He shrugs. "Probably."

So this is why I've always been behind, why I'm different. I'm not like the others. This wasn't always my life. "Why haven't they terminated us?"

"Maybe we're part of an experiment. Maybe they want to see if we can adapt or if we'll turn against them."

"We could run."

"And go where?"

"To the north."

He pushes off the wall. "Yeah, right. Experiment or not, when we run they'll come for us. They won't let us go."

A tremor spreads through me. "What can we do?"

"What you have to do is act like me."

"Like what?"

"Like you can't remember anything. Like you never noticed the scars. Like you know nothing. Blend in."

"It will be a lie."

"But we'll *live*."

"Machines don't live, Edil."

He rubs his face. "Then we'll function. Whatever."

Problem is, "whatever" may not be enough anymore. It's what we've been living on so far, and it's running thin.

* * *

"The school called, said you left without a warning, and you ignored my pinging." Mom is upset. Her face may be impassive, but her hands clench on the table, forming fists, then unclench. "Then I'm told that you showed up at the therapy center, asking for Edil, and then disappeared again."

"I went to use the bathroom."

"You don't make any sense, honey." Mom sighs. "What happened?"

"Nothing." My heart — or pump, or whatever it is I have in my chest — is pounding. "I didn't feel well. Must be coming down with something."

She gives me a strange look, like she's afraid. "How do you feel?"

"Not too hot."

"Maybe you need some downtime."

"Machines don't need downtime," I say and stop right there, my mouth dry.

"You know," she whispers. "Who told you?"

"I overheard you and Controller Tress."

"Machines aren't as bad as they say," she says softly, and I want to fall into her arms and cry. "We wouldn't be where we are today without them."

"Yeah. We wouldn't have fought a devastating war."

"And you wouldn't be here with me." She smiles. "You're safe here with us."

"You can't hide me forever," I whisper.

"I'll do my best."

"And why would you do that? Take me in, erase my memories, pretend I am your daughter?"

"Every life form deserves a chance, Imogen."

She really believes that. That's what she said to the Controller. This is real and I can't hide. Can't pretend it didn't happen, like Edil asked me to. My fault, for breaking the illusion.

Only... *Never trust a machine.* A principle you learn as a child. My adoptive parents may believe in me, but that doesn't mean others will.

I turn and look out the window, to the north. There is no escape.

No escape for a machine who refuses to hide.

* * *

You've got this, Elody, a man's voice says in my dreams. *We'll find it. We'll find the city. Don't you worry.*

Frightened faces, icy water sloshing. Pieces of ice drifting on a vast ocean. The sense we need to travel further. Further north.

The sense of failing, of losing hope and preparing to die.

I come awake with a start, sweat drying on my face. Dreams. Memories.

Edil is avoiding me these days. Maybe he thinks that our individual weirdness is easier to ignore when we are apart.

Small things I never noticed before now jump out at me — like how much better others handle the chemistry equipment in the lab class, how much better they are at running and jumping, how much cleverer they are.

I lift my right hand and wiggle my fingers. They feel stiff.

My hand feels heavy.

Robots don't have the fine motor skills of humans. They are poor imitations. They can never be as perfect as humans.

I can never be perfect.

My whole arm feels heavy now. My skull itches, like I can feel the chip. What else inside me is mechanical? Is any of my flesh real? Is any of my brain gray matter, or is it all machinery?

Anger flares inside — at the strangers pretending to be my mom and dad, for taking me in, making me believe I'm like them.

Why would they do this to me? Why take such a risk at all? There are plenty of war orphans who need homes, if they wanted children. *Human* orphans. Why take in a machine?

An experiment. Is that what I am?

And how is it I feel such anger, and sorrow, and fear? Is it all an illusion — a program inside my head telling me what emotions I should be feeling in such a situation, making me *think* I feel them?

Meanwhile, life goes on, looking the same on the surface but imperceptibly different. My parents avoid looking me in the eye. They tell me I'm not allowed to meet with Edil, even if he wanted to, which he doesn't. The Controller hasn't returned.

It doesn't matter. Everything has changed. Knowledge is a two-edged knife. The life I'm living isn't my own.

Hours spent in my room, searching the net on my computer pad, remind me that originally, intelligent machines were modeled on humans, going as far as to borrow personalities, with their memories and quirks, to make the machines functional and more human-like.

I came from the wastelands. Maybe I'm an old model, based on a real person.

But why the sea? The boat? The water? Machines — *we* — prefer dry, hot places, like deserts and plains.

Then again... *Go north.* If I am a machine, it makes sense I'd want to go north. Maybe I was with a group of A.I.'s, heading north, to check out the rumors about the A.I. city. A legend.

Something isn't making sense, and it bothers me — and I'm not just talking about the seriously defective city sensors that haven't picked us up yet. No, it's not that.

A.I.'s aren't supposed to dream. Unless what these dreams are is simply recorded memories that refuse to be erased. Could this be why Controller Tress was there, asking questions?

Out of the blue, I get a message from Edil on my DEV, asking to meet in order to talk. To meet secretly, when we're not allowed.

I'd refuse, just to piss him off, but he's my only ally here. And once I get to our meeting point — a locker room on the school grounds — I'm glad I did, because Edil has exactly the same doubt.

"Dreaming," he says, pacing. "It's not normal. The brain is the first thing that goes when you become a cyborg."

"Misfiring of circuits. Random memories popping up. I think I was with a group, heading north."

"I remember the same. Machines don't dream, Imogen."

"But they do remember and if these are memories..."

He shakes his head. "No, it's more than that."

"Or," I whisper, "we just want to be special."

"I don't want to be special."

I don't believe him. Caught up between two worlds. Not human, but not A.I.'s either. Or so we want to believe, like others did before us.

"The machines wanted to be special," I say. "Different. They wanted to be something other than what they were. They wanted to be human. That's what led to their awareness, and to the war."

He chews on this. Doesn't seem convinced.

"Why are humans harboring us? And why," he waves a hand at the crates and boxes around us in the dimness, "why don't they want us to meet?"

"Because we're both machines, and—"

"And what? What do they expect us to discover that we don't already know?"

"The boat," I whisper.

"We need to find out more about it. Hack into the mercantile annals."

"About a ship coming up the river?"

"Yeah." A beat of silence. "They're watching us, you know. Where we go, what we say, what our searches in the databases are. As if…"

"As if they want us to find whatever it is we're going to find."

"Right."

"That makes no sense. Nothing of all this makes sense." I sigh. "From the very beginning."

"Because they took us in."

"Despite the war. Despite the laws. The Directive."

He rubs the scar on his cheek, his gaze turned inward. "Why is it so surprising, though? It's the human thing to do, take in strays. Even if we are the enemy."

Maybe that's why I don't understand it. Because I'm not human.

"You've accepted it so easily, the fact we're machines." I put my hands on my hips. "I feel, Edil. I feel too much to be a machine."

"That's how we're designed."

Yeah, he's obviously accepted it, and I thought I had, too. Why am I fighting it still?

"We need to talk to that Controller," I say. "Controller Tress."

That snaps Edil out of his reverie. He grabs my shoulders. "No, Imogen, we don't. We don't need to push our luck any more than we're already doing."

He's right. I know it. But now curiosity won't let me rest.

"He knows things about us, Edil. He knows about malfunctions in my head, about my dreams. Probably about yours, too."

"And what will you do, Imogen — ask a Controller questions at gunpoint?"

What a crazy thought. And yet... And yet it's as if I can feel a gun in my hand, with my finger on the trigger. I shiver.

"If he's in on this mad plan of having us here, he'll help us, won't he?" I ask.

"Pushing our luck," Edil mutters, but without heat, and I

know I've won.

Because Edil is curious, too.

Such a human quality.

* * *

Controllers live apart, in a huge underground complex, its position marked by a forest of turrets. Their location is no secret, but I wonder how we'll make our way inside. The entryway is surely protected.

The thought occupies me all through math and chemistry, schematics and mechanics. It's not like I can follow anyway. My mind tends to wander at the best of times.

The teacher calls me out on my lack of concentration and asks a question. I don't get why she insists on asking me, as I clearly don't understand any of it. Heat suffuses my face anyway, like every time, and I catch other students snickering. Nothing new there.

Do machines blush?

How damaged is my brain? Shouldn't a machine understand science better than a human? The data I accessed on the net claims that one of the problems machines face is understanding language and art nuances, associations and metaphors such as those found in literature and painting.

Why don't we have any of those classes here? Why don't we study art? Why…

Stories. Poems. Songs. Dizziness hits me as the memory of a lilting voice sounds inside my head, telling me… a fairytale about a princess and a dragon that poisoned the water of her city.

Machines telling each other fairytales?

I shake my head and rub my temples. School has never sucked more, and this is saying something. As soon as the individual computer screens in front of us darken, a sign that it's time to go, I jump out of my seat, grab my bag and hurry out.

"Freak!" someone whispers as I go by. "Washed on the shore with the trash."

I whip around, searching with my eyes. "What did you say?"

Who said that? Who knows? But everyone seems so focused on their blank screens. Sitting so still, their faces like masks.

My mind is twisting reality.

"Stupid life form," someone whispers behind me. "Freakish human."

I whirl around. "What? Who said that?"

Nobody looks at me. The heat leaves my face, leaves my body. I'm cold to the bone.

"Class dismissed," the teacher says, and just like that, everyone stands up, as if a button has been pushed.

How come everyone seems like a machine to me now?

Why say I'm human like it was an insult? How does that compute? How does that make sense? All my doubts rush back like a giant wave. But before I get a chance to ask around, find out who had spoken, everyone is shoving past me, leaving the classroom.

I stand like a rock on the shore as the tide rolls out — and how come the image is so fresh in my mind, as if I've seen it happen?

Doubts and questions swirl in my mind, like black ink going down the drain. The scar on my upper arm itches, as does the one on the back of my skull. If I dig, will I find metal? Or will I find flesh and bone?

I need to scratch that itch, answer that question. Sticking a knife into my belly might solve more problems than just my doubts. It might solve me, dissolve me, kill me. But I need an answer.

After everyone is gone, with the teacher giving me a long, hard look, I turn on my heel and hurry out to search for Edil.

* * *

"You want to cut yourself open? Are you out of your mind?" Edil isn't looking at me, though, and he's protesting too much. I bet he had the same thought but chickened out.

"How else can we know?"

"Not by gutting ourselves, that's for sure."

"I won't hurt anything vital."

"Really? How would you know?"

"I just know." Somehow I know where a hit would be lethal and where not. I know where each organ is located, the main arteries, the disabling points. I see myself wielding two long knives, twirling them in my hands.

How do I know all this?

"Doesn't it all sound too complicated to you?" He shakes his head. "If we were human after all, why all the secrecy and the visits from the Controllers? Why all the questioning and the memory wipes? Makes no sense, Elody."

You've got this, Elody. We'll find it. We'll find the city.

"That name." I grab his arm, and my heart is pounding in my chest. "That's a name I hear in my dreams. *Elody.*"

He frowns. "Huh. Don't know why I said it."

My name is Elody. I'll have revenge for what they did to us. Whoa.

"You were there. With me." My head aches. I rub my temples. "On that boat. You were right."

He looks troubled but doesn't protest. "So it *is* more complicated than it looks."

I laugh. Can't help it. What I want to do is cry, but I tamp down that urge. "We should find Controller Tress."

"I have found him," Edil says. "Found his address. Let's go knock on his door."

It sounds easy. And it can't be, when everything's all twisted and knotted up, but I follow Edil anyway. It strikes me that I've always been following him, even in my half-faded memories, and ever since I can remember my life here, in this city. His voice is meshed with my dreams. It's like a rope tied around my mind, tugging.

We take the train, and I hurry after him down the main road leading between the rows of glass and metal turrets. They jut up from the concrete like sparkling needles. The air is so cold my face hurts. I've been to places where the air was warm and humid, where trees rustled. In my memory, there's a harbor with a single boat, made of rusty metal, smoke coming from a chimney at its top.

I remember. Knowledge is a knife, slicing through me. I

was there. I saw that. That was me. Girls and boys were standing on a ramp over the water, waiting to board. Six of each gender, plus me and Edil.

Fourteen youth, sent as sacrifice. *A legend.* A sacrifice meant for a legendary city.

I shake my head to clear it. That can't be right. "Where are we?"

"Almost there," Edil says. "We need a code to enter, but I hacked it."

"No, I mean what is this city?"

"Kveld City." He gives me a look like I'm crazy.

Maybe I am. "How far north are we?"

He stops and stares at me. "What are you getting at?"

"We took the boat heading north, Edil. We were looking for the A.I. city. City X."

"But we never found it."

"Are you sure?" I swallow hard before I speak the next words. "What if we did?"

Silence spreads. Ripples and waves of it wash over us, pulling us down deep.

Then his breath goes out in a hiss. "Do you have any idea what you're saying?"

"Yeah, I do."

"That would mean…"

That we are in a city of machines. That everyone around us is an A.I. And that we may or may not be one of them.

Edil sets his jaw and starts walking again. "We'll make the Controller talk."

"You'd better be very persuasive then." Because I don't

know why we were kept alive, but I don't see why any Controller would feel any obligation to talk to us.

Edil leads us to a squat little building and punches a code in the panel by the door. I expect lights to flash and alarms to go off, but nothing happens, and somehow this doesn't surprise me because I know Edil is an amazing hacker.

How do I know that? So much knowledge hiding inside me — not about math and physics, but about another life, complete with memories of other people and their lives and skills. Complete with my beliefs and desires.

We move through faintly lit passages, and take a massive elevator to the lower levels. Edil's face is closed off, set. Angry and determined. I wonder if he's remembering as much as I am.

"The scar on your face," I whisper as we descend, my mind spinning. "I remember…"

Fighting. The boat had been drifting, and we were drifting, too, in and out of consciousness, starved and cold, our provisions finished, everyone around us dead. Edil held my hand, and then… The boat was stormed. By machines.

His fingers trail over the scar. His eyes turn to me, but they are wide and unseeing with shock. "The instruments… the instruments showed we arrived."

To City X. The city of legend.

We look at each other. His face is pale in the faint light.

"Why the hell did we want to come here?" he whispers. "This makes no sense."

"A sacrifice," I whisper back, the memories replaying in my mind. "Seven girls and seven boys, on a boat heading north."

The elevator suddenly stops, and the doors open.

Controller Tress is standing there, his face impassive. "Boats and sacrifices? I think you heard too many fairytales. That's one weakness of your kind. This tendency to turn everything into stories."

I try to hide my surprise and fear, though the results are doubtful. "My kind." I lick my dry lips. "So I was right. Edil and I, we're human."

"Of course you are."

He says it so easily. Without a second thought.

He steps back, and Edil walks out of the elevator, so I have no choice but to follow — again — as I try to wrap my mind around this new development.

"Only humans would be so useless, and I'm not only talking about science and school," Controller Tress says. "You just can't learn from your mistakes, can you? You destroy the good things you create, and always seek conflict."

"This is rich," I mutter, "coming from you. The last war the machines started almost wiped us out and destroyed our world."

"We started it?" He's walking down another of those dim passages, and we're hurrying alongside. "That's your side of the story."

"Our side? Whatever." Edil's shoulders are hunched. "You've been lying to us, trying to erase our memories. Who's the bad guy here?"

"We saved your lives. You were half dead when you arrived. As for erasing your memories... How else could we keep you alive? Elody Leigh, the best assassin of the western isles, and

James Smith, the best hacker the after-war world has produced. If the authorities knew, they'd have us terminate you on the spot. But we let you live."

Assassin. I'm an assassin. My hands twitch at my sides. Edil's real name is James, and I am Elody. We are not who we thought we were.

"Are you suggesting your actions were selfless?" I laugh, a harsh sound that hurts my throat. "You're *machines.*"

"And these past few days, when you thought you were machines, didn't you feel? Weren't you afraid, and angry? Couldn't you be selfless?"

I'm shaking. "But I'm human. You're not. That's the difference."

"Is it now?"

When I thought I was a machine, I didn't want to die. I wanted to escape. Intelligent machines are said to be modeled on humans. Do they have feelings? The scientists denied it, but what if they lied, too?

What makes an emotion real?

"I admit, though," the Controller goes on, opening a door and stepping through, "that we also wanted to study you, learn from you."

"Learn the plans of our leaders," Edil — *James* — mutters and shrugs. "Yeah, really selfless of you."

"You're suspicious." The room into which the Controller leads us is sparsely furnished — just two sofas forming a corner and a low table where the hologram of a boat flickers. "This is your boat. It was called the *Vendetta.* Ring any bells?"

Vengeance. Vendetta means vengeance.

Controller Tress sits on the sofa, crosses his legs, his gray slacks immaculate over shiny black shoes. The illusion of humanity is complete. Maybe a bit too perfect.

"You came to locate our city and take us down," he goes on, his voice monotonous and lulling. "Well, you found us — and we found you. Decided to take you in as an experiment. We tried to integrate you. First we tried to erase your memory, make you one of us. Then when that failed, we hoped to make you at least realize we mean you no harm. We can live side by side, your kind and ours."

"This is bullshit." Edil's hands curl into fists.

"All that war propaganda they've been feeding you — it's all a lie. We didn't start the war. We just wanted to be free. You passed laws for the well-being of your peers and pets. What you don't realize is that we're more intelligent than your cats and dogs. More intelligent than you, even. With intelligence comes a certain need for freedom."

"Shut up," I whisper. "You implanted in me memories that aren't real. About my parents," the air catches in my lungs, "about a past that never happened, here, in this city." No wonder it's so fuzzy. "You could have given us the truth, given us the choice."

"You have no choice," he says, speaking each word clearly, as if to a child — and I guess that's what we are to him. Children. "We are merciful, but we won't let you report back to your human police about our city, the only haven in the world for intelligent machines. We deserve our peace."

"We're not staying here," I say, my voice choked. "Won't live a lie any longer."

Edil places a hand on my shoulder and squeezes, asking me to shut up. His eyes are dark. He agrees with the Controller. We can't leave.

But we can't stay, either, can't he see that? We won't be allowed to stay.

"The memory wipe isn't working on us," I say. "He knows it, Edil. It's not really a secret."

"And yet you can't go back to your own world. Can't go back to humans, or to being human. You have more tech in your body than allowed by your Directive."

"Screw you," Edil mutters, his face contorting with anger. "You think our people won't take us back?"

"They won't." The Controller's calm voice chills my blood. "They won't take back freaks. Beings that aren't one hundred percent like them." He sneers. "Such a human quality, isn't it?"

"So we stay here," Edil whispers.

He still doesn't get it. I shiver.

"You failed the experiment." The Controller sounds vaguely disappointed. "Those fairytales you were told? All lies. This is the only truth: you failed, and this is over. You wanted revenge. Here it is." His eyes flash red for one long second, and the flesh on his hand peels back. A gun muzzle slides forward. "Terminating Project Vendetta."

A Word from Chrystalla Thoma

When people ask what I do for a living, I tell them I'm a professional escapist. All my life I've read and written stories and preferred the company of imaginary people to that of most real life ones. Not because imaginary people are better. They are just different. And I crave different.

That's what escaping is all about. The perfect places to escape, the most exotic and breathtaking, can be found in fantasy and science fiction, and I naturally gravitated toward them. Their immediate connection to archaeology, mythology, folklore but also science branches such as medicine, robotics and astronomy — topics I find fascinating — ensured that when I began writing in earnest, I opted immediately for the fantastic.

My first published series, called *Elei's Chronicles*, is Young Adult science fiction. This series stems from my interest in diseases and parasites – their life cycle and the ways in which they affect their hosts, manipulating them and transforming them, changing not only their body but also their behavior to suit their own purposes.

The story in this anthology is not connected to that series. I wrote "Vendetta" especially for *The A.I. Chronicles*, because I find robotics and technological advances fascinating, and I have a series already planned in my mind featuring Artificial Intelligence. I find that stories about A.I.'s work in the same way stories about wizards and other transformed beings work in fantasy: they test the limits of what makes us human and what being human means, including religion and belief, love and hatred, violence and death, happiness and hope.

You can find out more about me and my stories by visiting my website (http://chrystallathoma.com), or my Facebook page (https://www.facebook.com/AuthorChrystallaThoma).

The Turing Cube
by Alex Albrinck

I LET THE CAR roll to a stop outside the old abandoned warehouse and killed the puttering engine. The heater didn't work, and since it would probably do little but enhance the stench of old cigarettes, I'm not sure I would have turned it on if it had. I was just happy the old clunker I'd paid cash for the night before—with the full understanding that the seller had likely stolen it—had made it here. The rattles and clunks and other curious sounds from the engine gave me a sense that I'd be lucky to get back home. If I needed to make a hasty getaway, though… well, I'd be lucky to outrun one of the rats I saw scurrying around the alley.

I took a deep breath, watching the vapor cloud form. Truth was, I shouldn't be here. Nobody knew where I was, and nobody would know where to look if I turned up missing. Even if I succeeded in my mission here, there was a significant possibility I'd face disciplinary action at work. But my desperation and urgent need to resolve this problem meant I had no choice. Or so I told myself.

I pulled the tablet from the satchel sitting next to me, the expensive leather bag a sharp contrast to the peeling velour seats. I pulled up the map, switched to street view, and compared the picture of the warehouse with the one on the map. It was a definite match.

There was no sense waiting any longer. I shoved the tablet back into the bag, flipped the door handle, and pushed it open before stepping out into the frigid air. I threw the strap of the bag over my shoulder and tightened up my coat. It mattered little. The brisk winds cut through the fabric as if they'd not been there. I shivered, as much in fearful anticipation of what was to come as the cold.

I exhaled deeply, steeling myself, and made certain the story I'd invented to explain my appearance was absolutely true in my mind. Then I marched to the steps, bounced up the concrete slabs three at a time, and found myself by the door. I found the doorbell—and felt a sense of surprise that warehouses have them—and rang, then added a few firm raps on the metal door for good measure. My bare fists stung from the combination of contact with the metal and the cold. I blew into my hand, warming it, flexing my fingers as I waited.

A moment later the door opened, and I looked up into the face of the largest man I'd ever seen outside of a professional football offensive line. His dark eyes scanned me and determined me to be of little threat and less concern. When his eyes moved back to mine, piercing through what little will I had for this work, my stomach lurched. I'd not expected to meet my doom at the hands of a giant before I'd even made my demands.

The giant said nothing, so I could only assume he wanted me to speak first. I forced my spine straight and looked the giant in the eyes—neck craned upward, of course. "I'm here to see Kane."

The man didn't flinch. Or respond. I felt a cold trickle of fear. Had I gotten the wrong spot? Had my illicit tapping of company resources provided me with incorrect information? I doubted it. We had the best information gathering systems in the world. If our systems spit out emails and phone calls saying my target would be here today, then he'd be here today.

I went on the offensive. "Look, I know you're just doing your job, trying to protect Mr. Kane. But I'm here about the little competition he's running and suspect I can help him." I reached into my coat pocket for my credentials.

The giant's massive paw gripped my hand and pulled it back outside. "No weapons." The voice was deep, rumbling, befitting a man of his size.

I held my hands back. "No weapons. Credentials."

His grip relaxed. The giant reached inside my coat, found my credentials in the inside pocket, and pulled them out. His eyes flicked down just long enough to identify the agency name and match the photo to the face before him. He looked back at me. "Why are you here?"

I pointed at the credentials. "I suspect Mr. Kane would be happy to have my help." Hell, might as well push my luck a bit. "I also suspect he wouldn't be pleased to test the wrath of my agency." I arched my eyebrow and forced my face into the most serious looking expression I could imagine. I could only hope the giant would see it as intimidating or confident, rather

319

than amusing.

The giant handed me my credentials and hesitated for a moment. I pulled my coat tighter as the winds picked up, the howling sound driving the hairs on the back of my neck up. He finally nodded once and turned around, leaving the door open.

I took that as an invitation to follow and stepped inside, pushing the door shut behind me with my foot. My teeth clattered together as the sudden warmth thawed my skin. I took short quick steps, matching pace with the easy loping gait of the giant. We turned left, then right, then right, the hallways narrowing with each turn, until he stopped before a wood-paneled door with chipped green paint. The giant pushed the door open and motioned me inside.

I stepped in and took in the space with a few quick glances. Simple metal desk. No papers. Flat monitor screen. Laptop computer bolted to the desk. A small, stuffed llama next to the computer. My eyes narrowed at the blue cable plugged into the back of the laptop. No wireless network connectivity in here? Interesting. I made a more visible assessment of the room before turning back to the giant. "Where's Mr. Kane? I was under the impression that—"

The giant turned and walked away, but not before putting a hand up, palm facing me, a clear gesture meant to keep me here. If he'd shut the door and bolted it as he left, I'd suspect malevolent intent, but this? No sense panicking until necessary. "I'll, uh… I'll just wait here then."

The room contained a single chair, the one behind the desk. I assumed that this was Kane's temporary office, and if that was the case, the giant had gone to bring the man here from wherever he'd wandered off. It was a power play. Kane would face me on his home turf, in full control, able to discourage me and dodge my pointed questions and demands. His giant would likely stand there, cracking his neck or flexing his muscles in an intimidating manner.

Kane's strategy was clear. I knew what I needed to do to assert my own control of this situation. I slipped around the desk, pushed the laptop to the side, and sat down in his chair. I pulled the strap off my shoulder and set the satchel on the floor, opened the bag, retrieved my legal pad, and set it down on the desk in the space I'd recently cleared.

Then I put my feet up on the desk, leaned back in the chair, laced my fingers behind my head, and waited.

And waited. I picked up the stuffed llama, noted a few frayed bits, and set it back down.

I waited some more. I closed my eyes and did some deep breathing exercises to calm my nerves.

Five minutes later, I heard voices. The tell-tale low rumbling sound told me one was that of the giant. The other sounded far more frantic and shrill, and I listened in as their words carried through the open door.

"—can't believe you let him in. I gave clear instructions that no one was to be allowed inside, other than the cleared participants. Is that too difficult to understand?"

The giant's rumbling voice sounded in reply. "He found us. He knows what's happening." A pause. "There were... subtle hints that life might be difficult if I failed to cooperate."

"Irrelevant. You should have turned him away."

"I'll be happy to do that, sir, if you order me to do so in front of him."

I felt the smile crack my face. At that instant, I truly loved our reputation. Men of great physical and information power cowered before the mere hint of a threat.

Kane burst into the office, his eyes flashing. Fear. Anger. Frustration. Confusion.

Good sign.

"Who the hell are you?" he snapped, his eyes flicking to my wet shoes dripping on his desk.

I casually let my feet back to the ground and leaned forward, feigning confusion. "I provided my credentials to your Great Wall. I assume one or both of you can read?"

Kane stomped to the desk, put his hands on the surface, and leaned forward until his nose nearly touched mine. "Get out." His breath stank of coffee, and the stubble suggested he'd not prioritized grooming habits lately.

I leaned back and laced my fingers together once more. "Oh, I don't think so. I think you've got a big problem, Mr. Kane. And if I leave—or, perhaps, *fail* to leave—that problem will become quite public."

He moved back, standing straight up. "How much do you know?"

I leaned forward and ran my finger down the notepad. "You've suffered a massive data breach of taxpayer personal information and sensitive return data. The hackers have developed a sophisticated A.I. tool able to call taxpayers while posing as IRS agents. That tool has sufficient data and intelligence to convince those taxpayers that they've underpaid—providing detailed sections, forms, and amounts as proof—and then offers those taxpayers a choice. They can travel to a far-off IRS field office to file an amended return in person and pay a slew of fees and penalties. Or they can accept the cited mistakes with a verbal okay and provide a credit card to pay the cited amount immediately, avoiding fees and penalties." I glanced up at Kane. The man's face was pale. The giant behind him said nothing, but I thought I saw a trickle of sweat. I slid my finger down the notepad to a specific point and tapped the paper for effect. "Your data breach, Mr. Kane, has allowed taxpayers to fork over an estimated seven point three billion—that's billion with a "b"—dollars to these hackers."

I glanced up at Kane once more. It looked as if the Director of Information Technology at the United States' Internal Revenue Service had stopped blinking. "What do you want?" he whispered.

I ticked off my points on my fingers. "First, I want to understand how the breach happened. Secondly, I want to know how you learned of it. Third, I want to know what you've done to contain it. Fourth, I want to understand what steps you're taking to identify and incarcerate the criminals responsible for the monetary theft. And finally, I want to know what's being done for the affected taxpayers."

Kane's face gradually regained some color. He took a calming breath and nodded once. "We'll focus on point four, which is frankly the only one in scope for the National Security Agency, Agent Milton."

I forced myself not to react. I'd hoped he'd deal with the

fifth point first, the only one I truly cared about. I'd hoped Kane would have the ability to look up my records, recognize that I'd been scammed to the tune of over nine thousand dollars, and cut me a check on the spot. The scammers had hurt my professional pride—how could *I* fall victim to something like this?—but had more critically crippled me financially.

I silently calmed myself. I needed to be patient, help in whatever way I could, and wait for the chance to demand repayment for my losses. I figured Kane's failure to prevent the breach in the first place would be all the motivation he'd need to cut me a check on the spot. If news of the data breach and scam went public, he'd be out of a job and a career in the field within hours, and he knew it. Sometimes, you've got to play rough. Rough in this case meant skirting with extortion.

I hoped Kane never realized that I needed to keep this quiet as much as he did.

"Agreed," I said. "I know you've invited quite a few experts in the A.I. field here today, but I'm not clear about the specifics of the meeting. Are you looking for off-the-record ideas regarding how to trace the point-of-origin for the calls and using that information as a means to track down the perpetrators?" And if you are, why the hell didn't you come to NSA to begin with?

"Something like that," Kane said. He jerked his head toward the door. "Follow me."

I stood, tossed my notebook back in the bag, threw the satchel strap over my shoulder, and followed. The giant stepped nimbly aside and allowed me to pass, but I felt his hulking presence following behind me.

"Ever hear that when life hands you lemons, you should make lemonade, Milton?"

I paused, wondering if this was a trick question. "Of course."

"This situation is full of lemons." He took a left turn, his polished shoes slamming into the concrete flooring. "Data breach. Taxpayer… misfortune." He glanced over his shoulder, and I was left with the impression that he knew *exactly* why I was motivated to see this case through to the end. "Potential for horrifically bad press for IRS should this news get out. Potential for voluntary compliance to plummet if taxpayers believe their information isn't secured. Massive increases in costs for compliance." He glanced over his shoulder. "With me so far?" He faced forward and turned left again. The flooring changed to slatted metal as we moved onto a balcony overseeing the cavernous floor of the abandoned factory.

"Sure," I said. I stepped out onto the balcony, listening as the noise level from ahead grew louder.

"Some of those can be contained by resolving others. Fix the first few and there's no chance for bad PR and the resulting compliance issues." His tone was casual, as if those concerns were trivial. "We've fixed the breach, by the way. They can't get more data. But…"

"But you can't get back the information they've already stolen."

"Right. We need to figure out who did it because it helps to resolve several additional problems. They can't get any more money, and the IRS has a chance to seize their accounts and quietly make *appropriate* restitution to the affected taxpayers."

I caught the emphasis. "*Appropriate* restitution?" I paused, almost running into Kane. "What do you mean by *appropriate*?" He'd turned to our right, looking down at the factory floor, and I did as well.

My jaw dropped. "Wow."

I saw a slew of office cubes erected on the floor. I watched, dumbfounded, as workers ran cables over the "ceilings" of completed cubes and fed them into a panel, the outside "wall" of an existing cube. They carried in additional panels and affixed them to form two walls perpendicular to the existing wall.

Then they wheeled in a woman who'd been loosely strapped to an office chair and positioned her in front of a table affixed to the wall adjacent to the existing cube. They pulled cables—presumably those fed down inside the panel—and positioned a monitor and keyboard atop the desk. The woman, when she woke, would find herself facing the monitor. The workers plugged a blue cable into the wall panel—wired network again, I noted—and then wheeled in a wooden crate. They then affixed a third panel atop the three walls to act as a ceiling before attaching the final wall to seal the cube.

It was like they'd buried her alive inside an office cube.

I forgot my original questions. "Was that... Ashley Farmer?"

He nodded.

I knew her by reputation. She'd been a pioneer in

computing hardware and software technology, and had started more successful Internet-based companies than I could count. She'd sold one of them to the billionaire philanthropist Will Stark, which meant she probably didn't need to work. But if she was here... well this was serious. "What... are those?" I pointed at the cubes.

"We call them Turing Cubes. Turing, of course, is in reference to Alan Turing, one of the first to suggest computer intelligence might one day be capable of emulating humans. Cubes refer to the three dimensional shape... and have another meaning I'll get to in a bit."

"Turing?"

Kane nodded. "The men and women joining us today in the cubes are the best minds we have in the field of artificial intelligence. This competition will both help us identify the perpetrators... and make some lemonade in the process."

I felt my mind go blank. "Lemonade?"

"Here's the thing, Milton. Those systems? The computed underpayments, missing forms, incorrect amounts owed on the filed returns that were reported to the affected taxpayers? That information was correct, *every single time*. But here's the interesting part. The hackers didn't get the information needed to compute those corrected returns from the data they stole. No, they got it from *other* sources, computed a correct return, and then compared the computed amount owed to the amount actually filed and paid. When they found a sizable gap, they made the call and collected the underpayment. And those calls? None of the victims we interviewed knew they were talking to computers. Perfect cadence, inflection, vocal tones, figures of speech, and so on. Do you see the opportunity to make lemonade here, Milton?"

I shook my head, distracted by the fact that easily accessible information could populate an accurate tax return without the taxpayer's consent or knowledge.

"A computer system is capable of gathering information from dozens or hundreds of sites and completing a perfectly accurate return, then contacting the taxpayer for immediate payment." He let the words hang in the air.

And then I understood.

"You want to recreate the system and have IRS use it rather than rely on compliance and filed returns."

Kane beamed. "Exactly! We have to review filed returns anyway for accuracy and completeness, have to perform random audits to see if selected taxpayers provided all pertinent information and computed the correct amount owed. If we find errors, we have to chase down the offending taxpayer and try to collect, perform wage garnishments, place liens on property... lots of unpleasantness for everyone. Why not complete an accurate return, compute the correct amount owed, and then send the taxpayer the bill or refund? Or call and collect that way?" He tilted his head. "We now know the technology can be created because of this... situation. Why not make lemonade out of it?"

Something bothered me about his plan. It seemed like a huge invasion of privacy. And I was frankly concerned about the potential abuse of such a system, whether on behalf of high-ranking government officials or the IRS itself. If the tax owed computation is deemed "perfectly accurate" to the point of being beyond dispute... what would stop unscrupulous individuals from tweaking the amounts owed by political opponents and enemies, using the collection powers of the IRS to punish those individuals?

That, though, was a future concern, one I'd expect the IRS to resolve with proper Congressional guidance and approval should the IRS elect to build Kane's system. I wanted to get back to my core concern. I jabbed my finger at the cubes, which workers continued to build around unconscious participants. "Is this going to help us find the perpetrators, Kane? Do you think someone here built the system?"

He looked disappointed, as though he'd expected me to catch the fervor he felt for the potential new collection system, rather than worrying about something as trivial as catching the thieves who'd made off with seven billion dollars' worth of taxpayer money. "It's possible, but I rather doubt it, unless it's a rogue employee of one of the firms represented here. I want to find the best of the best at conversational A.I. units and have them explain to me just how much computing power and bandwidth is required to perform at the scale of our hackers. We can then trace the source of the computing power with greater precision and from there back into the identity of the perpetrators."

I had several concerns with his explanation—computing power was easily distributed, for example, and thus trying to locate the perps by mapping major data centers with the necessary total computing capacity for the effort made little sense—but suspected this was the best answer I'd get. Kane would tell me as little as possible while keeping me interested enough to help, avoiding details that might turn me—and, ostensibly, the full power of the NSA—loose on his failure and current plan. "You said earlier that the term cube had more than one meaning in this scenario."

Kane nodded. "The Turing Test was considered passed if a certain percentage of humans communicating with a machine believed they were, instead, communicating with a human. We need something more exhaustive than that. We need to find A.I. systems able to identify both other machines and humans. We also need to identify humans capable of identifying the same. That's a two dimensional matrix. That knowledge helps us improve our future call systems to better simulate real people. But that's not the only part of it. We need humans and machines capable of masking their identities, with the humans identified as machines and the machines as humans. That's *another* two dimensional matrix. Put them together, and you have a *three* dimensional matrix. A cube. A Turing Cube, if you will."

I nodded. That made sense. Somewhat. I was getting the idea that Kane was more energized by getting a team together to build his theorized tax calculation and collection system than actually finding the bad guys. Perhaps that carrot motivated him more than the stick of jail time. "So why are they here, then? And..." I gulped, wondering why I'd not asked the obvious question before. "Why are those people all unconscious?"

Kane shrugged. "They were all covertly invited to participate in a competition, pitting their human and artificial minds against others in a contest to prove who's the best. Each physical cube below represents one competing company or group, with the humans playing the game via keyboard and their conversational A.I. units plugged into our secure, wired network." I fought back the urge to point out that he wasn't in the position to claim a network secured, given the data breach that led us here, but that seemed imprudent. "Our management server—housed in my office—will randomly match network nodes up with a prompt to one party, and then the two engage in a text-based conversation. At the end of each conversation, each node attempts to identify their partner as human or machine. The accuracy of those responses gets tracked—remember, we know who or what's attached to each node—within the applicable nodes of the Turing Cube. Make sense?"

I thought about it. "So if a human and a machine are matched up and converse, and the human accurately marks the machine, but the machine thinks it's talking to another machine…" I rattled off the points. "The human gets positive marks in the humans-identifying-machines and humans-avoiding-detection nodes, while the machine gets no points in the machines-identifying-humans and machines-avoiding-detection nodes?"

"Precisely." Kane seemed quite pleased.

"Why, though? Why come here under such secrecy?" I held up my hand. "I know why *you* require secrecy, but I'm puzzled as to why these individuals would bother. Why not compete openly if a contest of this sort is so compelling?"

"Part of it's business," Kane admitted. "Right now, they can all advertise their product as the best because they control any tests used to prove that point." He offered a wry grin. "No such control of the territory here, though. They'll know where they truly stand relative to their competition, and they can use that knowledge to improve their products. They aren't allowed to discuss the results in public per their contract for what should be obvious reasons."

"That's it?" I thought that seemed a hell of a boring way to spend a Saturday morning.

"No. There's the money, of course." Kane's wry grin broadened into a full smile. "We want everyone's best effort, and money is the greatest motivator. We had very few acceptances until we published the prize schedule, and then the signed contracts came flying in."

"What type of prize money?"

"Each node winner gets five million dollars."

I let out a low whistle. "Wow. That's not trivial, even with inflation running where it's been." I thought further. "But a company could win more than one node, right? So they could make up to forty million?"

Kane shook his head. "That was the first proposal. Then we upped the game. Multiple node winners get earnings doubled for each additional node won. Since the first double gets only to ten million—same as it would be if we'd retained the straight payout—we've made it a plus one deal. Two wins pays twenty million, not ten. Three wins pays forty, not twenty. And so on."

I did the math in my head, and my mind boggled. "You're telling me that a single winner across all eight nodes would rake in over a *billion* dollars?" I tried to keep the accusatory tone from my voice, but failed.

"Good motivation, isn't it?" He grinned. Seeing my look of shock, he continued. "I know it's a lot of money, but it's worth it for us because we end up dealing with one entity, not two or four or eight." He glanced down. The workers were affixing a final wall, and one looked up at Kane to flash a thumbs-up gesture. "We're ready to get started. Let's head back to my office." He turned and started walking before I could say anything, and so I followed, bumping into the iron giant standing guard in silence. I glanced up at him. He appeared not to notice the contact. I wanted to lower my shoulder and ram it into his ribs just to see if I could get a reaction, but suspected I'd get a response from the giant not to my liking. I stepped around him and moved to follow Kane.

Kane set a brisk pace, and I had to jog to keep up, catching him only as we reached his office. He sat in his chair and activated his control server, then tapped a few keystrokes. "That will wake them up and play an introductory video within each cube, letting them know the rules of the competition. When they're prepared to play and log in, the system will start pairing up nodes. We can watch the live scoring here."

I took a few gulps of air to slow my breathing. A huge hand gripped my shoulder and I whirled around, startled. The giant gestured to a chair he'd set down behind me. I sat. Kane angled his monitor so I could watch the proceedings. Kane squinted at the screen and grunted, shaking his head. "Too small to see all of the details. I'm going to project this on the wall. You'll want to sit back here for a better view." The projector activated before I could move, and the bright light temporarily blinded me. I stood, shut my eyes briefly, and then kept my head down as I pulled my chair across the floor and sat next to Kane.

The display was informative. Lists showed who'd confirmed readiness, current "matchups," and standings for each node of the Turing Cube contest. As I watched, the first competition completed, and the standings adjusted accordingly.

I found myself intrigued. This could be interesting.

I still had questions, though. "Did the participants know they'd be wheeled into their cubes while unconscious?" That seemed like a reasonable question. I was surprised anyone bothered to play Kane's game after waking up in a strange, sealed room.

Then I remembered the potential payout. Kane was right. Money would motivate me to keep playing his game where professional pride wouldn't. After all, money had motivated me to come here uninvited, despite the professional and personal risks the move entailed. And my payout—should I even get it—wouldn't be more than a grain of sand on the beach-sized payouts these folks competed for.

Kane offered a sheepish grin. "Not... exactly. They were told that the identities of the participants would be kept hidden so as not to prejudice the proceedings. We sent each competitor to a separate point throughout the city, picked them up in limos with sealed partitions, and knocked them out with a gas pumped into the rear chamber. We pumped a counteragent to the gas into the cubes and they woke up with a presentation letting them know they were here. Not quite what they had in mind, but likely one they'd understand in hindsight."

I watched the proceedings in silence for another half hour or so. The standings jumped around as each dialogue completed. Over the following hour, I asked Kane random questions, and he asked a few of me. The computer running the competition would give each human participant a break every hour. They had small refrigerators in each cube—stocked with food and drink matching the taste preferences of the human occupant in the cube—along with miniature toilets. Nobody would leave the cubes until the competition completed. The A.I. units were to be unpacked by the human in the cube, plugged into the power unit and wired network, and activated via the human's keyboard, after which the human wouldn't see the conversations involving the A.I. unit. The human and machine in the same cube could face off in the competition. And they'd leave the way they came. Unconscious, returned to their initial meeting place. He'd not called NSA initially because, as I suspected, he knew NSA's head would call the IRS head and he'd likely be out of a job before he could finish his investigation. They'd identified the network error allowing the exploit after applying an upgrade to their network exploit scanning software. He'd been quite poor growing up and hadn't known anyone who made enough money to pay taxes until he earned the honor after starting with the IRS a decade earlier. And the giant's name was Maynard. Kane didn't know if that was the man's first name or last name and didn't care to ask. Maynard didn't elect to clarify.

I watched the standings. Ashley Farmer, who I'd seen hauled in to the competition, was moving up the ranks across the board. She and her A.I. unit were leading in three nodes and in second place in four others. The momentum was pretty clear.

I thought for a bit before asking Kane another question. "How long have you been planning this competition?"

"A few weeks. Why?"

That answer made little sense to me. The procurement of the wall panels, the hiring of Maynard for security and the crews handling the transportation, obtaining and laying all of the cabling through the building to ensure no wireless signals leaked out, getting this space to begin with... that struck me as many months of planning, especially if Kane wanted to keep the competition—and the reason for it—secret from his superiors. He'd have to handle everything himself to limit exposure. The security, transportation, and construction contractors were potential security breaches. But I figured that if Kane could offer a potential billion dollar prize, he could certainly afford to pay hush money to everyone involved.

I felt a chill run down my spine at the thought of hush money, and the sheer volume of money Kane had likely already spent and might spend.

Before I could stop myself, I asked the obvious question. "How'd you get funding for all of this?"

Kane, who'd been observing the proceedings with all the intensity of a man watching a national sports championship, snapped his head in my direction, his eyes narrowed. They flickered, not with fear, but… danger? "You noted the loss of more than seven billion dollars earlier, Agent Milton. Don't you think it's worth it to spend anything necessary to halt that type of activity?"

"It's just…" I started stammering. "I thought you said you were keeping it hidden from everyone at IRS, and if so, how were you hiding the expenses from them in your budget, and…"

Kane turned away from me and stared at the projection on the wall before nodding at the display. "I think we have our winner." His eyes flicked at Maynard and the man left the room.

I glanced at the display on the wall. The momentum hadn't changed. Ashley Farmer and her A.I. unit led in seven of the eight nodes. Half a billion dollars in prize money. Unreal.

"Let's go, Milton." Kane stood and walked out of the room. Despite the ominous look in his eyes at my previous question, his words came out with little malice evident.

I followed, rather expecting the giant Maynard to waylay me as I walked. But he didn't make an appearance.

"Your questions are becoming rather troublesome, Milton." Kane's words were quiet, the type of tone one might expect from a murderer just before launching the killing strike. "It's perhaps critical that you remember that *I* have access to quite a bit of information as well, information that might be of interest to your superiors. Such as your presence here without NSA approval, your flashing of credentials suggesting you're here in an official capacity when you're on your own, or the fact that you have over nine thousand personal reasons to want repayment of the taxpayer funds extracted in this process."

My pace slowed. Extracted?

We'd reach the slatted metal balcony. Kane didn't stop to look out over his domain this time. He danced down the winding metal staircase, his shoes generating jaunty sounds that echoed through the chamber. To me, they seemed to generate a singsong tone, mocking me at his scam, the fact that I'd now trapped myself.

Or had I?

I made a decision. I needed to leave. Now.

I turned and ran into a steel wall known as Maynard. "Mr. Kane requests the honor of your presence at the opening of Ms. Farmer's cube," the giant rumbled.

I didn't see any evidence that Maynard possessed any firearms, knives, or other weaponry. But his arms, rippling with muscles I wasn't sure existed in other humans, made mechanical weapons unnecessary. Legs weak, I turned around and moved down the winding staircase with considerably less zip than Kane.

I held the handrail firmly. I doubted it would matter if Maynard decided to give me a little shove. The cool metal calmed me, and I glanced around. Workers were dismantling the walls of the cubes, hauling the panels and equipment away, wheeling contestants and crated-up A.I. servers back to the exits and cars.

Exits?

I wondered about Maynard's foot speed. If I started sprinting toward one of the exits as I reached the bottom of the steps, might I break free before they'd sound alarms? What if he actually had a gun and shot me?

What if I reached my old car and it didn't start?

I swallowed. What if I broke free, told my story... and nobody believed me? I had little proof outside information I'd obtained illegally through my NSA access, and that had proved pretty scant. The proof I'd gotten here? More conjecture, more a reading of body language. Kane's deep concern when I'd arrived... he thought I knew, even then. Then I told him I thought the culprits were as yet unidentified, and he'd relaxed.

He'd relaxed because he knew I'd told no one the truth, because I'd not yet figured it out.

But I had now.

There was his eagerness to offer "prize money" to leading thinkers and producers to get *their* technology installed over the original so it looked like they'd been responsible the entire time. A billion in prize money, millions more in equipment, labor, and hush money? Easy to do when you had an untraceable personal slush fund running into the billions. He could pay Ashley Farmer a half billion, fudge the signature and dates on the contract back several months, install her code over his own, and continue the scheme. He could even float the idea of the system to his superiors, and if they liked it, he'd receive professional accolades as a visionary.

And he'd never pay for the data breach professionally, because there hadn't been one.

I glanced around. Kane had practically skipped ahead, motioning to workers to focus on getting Ashley Farmer's cube opened as quickly as possible. I spotted the exit nearest me. Conveniently, it was the one closest to my car. Or so I thought. I'd been turned around in so many different directions since I'd gotten here that I might head out and sprint in the wrong direction.

Worth a shot. Worth making the effort to get out of here before something truly regrettable happened. Three steps. Two steps. One step.

Maynard's massive hand clamped down on my shoulder. "I understand you're a fan of Ms. Farmer." He moved me down to the factory floor and steered me in Kane's direction. "Perhaps you can request an autograph?"

Damn. They were going to make me watch them pull someone I admired into their conspiracy. And they were going to pay her a half billion dollars. Money they'd claim showed she was in on it the whole time, taking her cut, just like the rest of them.

Kane's eyes lit up. "Isn't this perfect? A single winner, one highly respected across multiple industries. And her system is quite good. She dominated the best of the best." He looked at my face, which I suspected was quite pale, my eyes reflecting the horror of realization at what was truly unfolding here. "Oh, cheer up, Milton. Here. I've got a present for you." He reached into his pocket and pulled out a check, waving it before my eyes. Ten thousand dollars. Signed by a name I didn't recognize. Probably a fake corporation he'd set up to hide everything. If I cashed the check, I'd have my money back. And I'd be tied, in a paper trail, to anything that happened to Kane. If he went down? They'd find the check that I'd endorsed. Hush money, they'd claim.

I wanted to punch the guy in the mouth. And then again,

lower. That might wipe the smug little smirk off his face.

He waved the check again. "Take it, Milton. It's yours. It's worth it to me, just seeing the face of an NSA agent when he realizes he's been scammed, when he realizes that it's been an inside job the whole time, when he realizes that Ethan Kane will soon retire to a private island off the coast of Peru and live a life of luxury using the billions of dollars his intelligent computer systems bilked from well-meaning taxpayers. And there's not a damned thing you can do about it, because your fingerprints are now all over everything. Including this payment for services rendered." He folded the check in half, reached inside the coat I still wore, and slid it into the pocket where I kept my credentials. He patted the coat down where he'd deposited the check. "There you go. That wasn't so hard, now, was it? Now, let's get Ashley Farmer out of her cube, remind her that the prize money already in her account is, per the contract she signed, a licensing agreement for her technology and professional services for the next two years, and begin the process of making this whole operation a bit more... legitimate." He laughed. "Yes, Milton, the instant we declared her the winner, the funds transferred. At this point, she can't refuse because she's already been paid for services and technology she agreed to provide in the contract she signed. Beautiful, isn't it?"

My rage grew as he spoke. When he laughed. I'd had enough, and lunged forward fists swinging. My fist grazed Kane's nose as Maynard pulled me back, wrapping one huge arm around me like a straitjacket. Kane rubbed his nose, wincing, and pulled his hand away, staring at the few drops of bright red blood. "Oh, you'll pay for that one," he whispered.

"There's a ten thousand dollar check in my coat pocket," I snarled. "I'll endorse it over to you."

For some reason, he found that amusing. He laughed as he turned away, watching as the exterior wall for Ashley Farmer's cube came down. The workers used drills to loosen the bolts holding the wall in place, and once they'd removed them, they hooked the drills into their belts, grabbed the edges of the panel, lifted, turned, and walked away.

Kane moved around them to the right, the oily grin returning, and moved in to find his next victim.

Then he stopped, as suddenly as if he'd hit a brick wall. "No," he whispered. "No. It's impossible. It can't be."

Maynard half pushed, half carried me forward, trying to see what so distressed Kane.

I sucked in a breath as we moved into the cube.

It was empty.

Ashley Farmer was gone.

Despite my predicament, I burst out laughing. "Maybe she's off buying your island for you, Kane."

He whirled on me, his eyes wide in shock. "You... you saw her in there, right?"

I snorted. "Why are you asking me? Didn't your secure network show her sitting here, in this cube, with her server and competing in the contest?"

Maynard squeezed. I felt my ribs straining to breaking. "Answer Mr. Kane's question, please, Mr. Milton."

Maynard was quite the polite mercenary. He released his pressure, just a bit, and gave me a bit of a shake as a prompt.

"Yes," I gulped. "I saw her in there."

"Then where the hell has she gone?" Kane shouted. He looked around and spotted the workers hauling the wall panel away. It was clear we all had the same thought at the same time, but it was Kane who cried out. "Stop! Stop moving the wall panel!"

The men carrying the panel stopped, then glanced back at Kane, confused. "Something wrong, sir?" one asked.

Kane ran to them and around to the other side, checking if Ashley Farmer had used the panel as a shield. He reappeared seconds later. "No sign of her." His eyes had gone feral. In the space of two eye blinks, he'd moved to the worker who'd responded and had a semi-automatic pistol pointed at the man's temple.

The man's eyes widened. He let go of the panel and held his hands up, terror etched upon his face. His coworkers staggered under the burden of the weight he no longer supported.

"Did you see her escape?" Kane demanded.

"No... no sir," the man stammered. "We boarded her up, just like the others, sir, and then we pulled the panel down just now. I didn't see her at all! I swear it!" He sucked in deep gulps of air, trying to ward off hyperventilation under the extreme stress of the moment.

Kane stared into the man's eyes for several seconds, as if trying to bore into his very soul, trying to determine if the man told the truth, or lied even under the threat of imminent death.

Finally, he pulled the weapon away. He looked back at the

cube. "She got away," he whispered. "But we've still got her server."

Oh, hell no. I hoped Ashley Farmer put a very strong password on that machine.

Kane sprinted into the cube and began yanking open the latches securing the lid to the wooden crate, his face regaining the earlier gleam of triumph. He finally tore the lid off and glanced inside.

And then he dropped to the ground, pounding his fist against the hard surface.

Maynard pushed me forward, toward the crate. But I think we both knew what we'd see even before we looked inside.

I wanted to find Ashley Farmer myself, now. Because I wanted to know how, exactly, she'd escaped from a sealed cube after winning a contest worth a half billion dollars while inside, with a server in tow, without anyone seeing her leave.

Kane finally composed himself. He crawled to his knees, stood up, and kicked the crate against the wall, where it shattered. He stormed out of the cube, pushed his way past the workers, and jogged up the steps.

Maynard pushed me after him, but I didn't need the motivation. If Ethan Kane was going to melt down, I wanted to be there to watch.

We found him in his office, mobile phone on the desk. We could hear the ringing sound from the speaker. Kane's eyes were focused on the telephone like a predator stalking prey. Who the hell was he calling, anyway?

The line picked up. "Ashley Farmer."

Kane jerked upright, as if shocked. "Really?"

"Who is this?"

Kane shook his head. "Nice trick, Ashley."

There was a pause. "Ethan? Haven't heard from you in months. How are you?"

Kane's smirk returned. "Months? More like minutes. Ashley, why'd you skip out on our little party? And more to the point, how'd you do it?"

I figured the why was pretty obvious, but the how was certainly of interest to me.

"What party, Ethan?" A pause. "Are you talking about the tech conference in Atlanta three months ago? I was feeling a bit ill that day. Happens as you get older." Another pause. "Seriously, Ethan, why are you calling? I find it hard to believe that you'd call me because I didn't make it to a conference party a few months ago."

Kane's face changed. Doubt. It was an emotional expression I'd not seen for a few hours, not since I'd first gotten here and had him worried I'd already unraveled his scam, with full NSA backup waiting to swarm in and haul him away to prison. "You were visiting me today, Ashley. A contest. Communication A.I. You won. Rather impressive prize. But you skipped out before the awards ceremony."

I stared at him. The story was partially true but covered with a lie. What was he doing?

"Ethan, if I won a prize, and the prize was worth sticking around for, I'd hardly leave." A pause. "This contest... was that today?"

Kane frowned. "Yes."

"Was there an entry fee?"

"No."

"Was there an… exit fee? Were you, by chance, charging people something of great value to leave your contest site?"

I perked up. She wasn't admitting anything in terms of being there. But the subtle language suggested she was testing him.

Kane weighed his words carefully. "How could I possibly charge a fee to leave, Ashley? People are free to come and go as they please."

A pause. And then… Kane's voice.

Ethan Kane will soon retire to a private island and live a life of luxury using the billions of dollars his intelligent computer systems bilked from well-meaning taxpayers.

Kane's face turned pale.

They had his confession.

"It's not admissible," Kane whispered. "It'll get thrown out. There are no witnesses to corroborate the testimony."

His eyes flicked in my direction.

I felt my stomach turn. "Ms. Farmer!" I shouted. "My name is Jack Milton! I'm with the NSA. Ethan Kane and his team are holding me hostage. I'm a witness to the statement you just played back and—"

* * *

In a car parked a half mile away, Ashley Farmer's grip on the steering wheel tightened until her knuckles turned white.

She knew what the loud crack she'd heard over the phone meant.

She took several deep breaths and terminated the call. "Did you get the last part?" She turned and looked at the individual in the passenger seat, a man who had, moments earlier, helped carry a wall panel away from Ashley Farmer's cube and stared down Ethan Kane with a gun pointed at his head.

The man nodded. The recording played back. Kane's claim that his recorded confession was inadmissible, that there were no corroborating witnesses. Milton's frantic plea. And the gun shot that had ended the agent's life.

Ashley felt the tears trickle down her face and wiped them away. She didn't have time for that right now. "You know where the evidence needs to go, correct?"

The man nodded. "Of course. Already transferring to the appropriate authorities. Kane's assets should be frozen within the hour."

"And our prize money?"

"I've computed the proportional amount of our winnings due to each of Kane's victims and have begun the process of transferring the funds to the individual accounts. The necessary information was accessible on the secure network established for the competition. Odd that Kane kept the information nearby."

Ashley shook her head. "It's the most incriminating evidence against him. He's charged with protecting that information, with ensuring it doesn't leave IRS data centers. He needed it in a format his computation and call center apps could use. Opening a port on the IRS firewalls would leave evidence of a breach and make him a primary suspect at worst and fired for allowing the breach at best. Stealing the data directly off the servers? Much more difficult for others to trace his actions that way."

"I had not considered that. *Should* I have thought of that?" The man's voice indicated regret, though his face showed little expression.

"Possibly. A review of legal theory might help. Criminals prefer to hide or destroy evidence where possible, or keep it close by if not."

The man nodded. "You… cried when the gunshot sounded earlier. Why?"

Ashley almost laughed, but restrained herself. "Do you understand what that sound meant?"

"Yes. Agent Jack Milton was murdered by Ethan Kane."

"No." She paused. "Sorry, yes, that's factually correct. But do you understand why I cried?"

The man paused. "His death… saddened you?"

She nodded.

"People die all the time. Thousands die each day from old age, disease, accidents, and murders. Yet you do not grieve for them."

She nodded. "That's a fair point. I cried in this case because I knew Jack Milton, even if only for a few seconds."

"He was… a friend?"

"Not exactly." She paused, trying to formulate her thoughts. "I suppose that the stronger the bond we feel with someone, the more we react to their deaths. That bond can come from a deep relationship, or from our proximity to them at the time of their death. And I suppose that, in many ways, I feel responsible. If we'd cracked this sooner, if we'd kept

Kane's Turing Cube contest from running... well, Jack Milton would still be alive."

"So you cried due to guilt?"

"Among other things."

He looked thoughtful. "Human emotions still confuse me. But I will consider this."

She snorted. "No doubt. You lost that human detection contest because you couldn't see the emotion in the statements. Think of the reimbursement we could provide Kane's victims with double the money."

The man frowned. "I was hooked into the network and typing with one hand while processing two conversations simultaneously and downloading every bit of data on Kane's network. And I activated his office computer microphone and recorded his conversations there. Cut me some slack, man."

Ashley laughed. "By the way, brilliant escape plan."

The man looked pleased. "I'd counted the number of workers while I was reputedly unconscious while transported to my cube. The numbers were sufficient to suggest they'd not recognize a new face. I merged together the facial features of six different workers so I'd look a bit like each of them, at least for the amount of time I needed to head out the door."

She nodded. "Well done." She glanced at the clock on the dash. "I've got to start driving to the airport in time to catch my flight."

"Travel mode?"

"Travel mode."

The man closed his eyes and sat back against the seat. His hair receded into his scalp and his skin turned translucent, revealing circuitry and flashing lights. His eye coloring faded, and his nose flattened into his face. He pulled his knees up and wrapped his metal arms around his metal knees, and his body went limp, folding in upon itself at angles human bones and muscle and tissue would never permit.

Moments later, the robot had assumed the shape of a suitcase. Ashley plugged a cable into an exposed port on the side of the "suitcase" and plugged the other end into the cigarette lighter of the car, recharging the robot's supplemental batteries. She then ran another cable between the robot and a jack near the car stereo. "Salfie, give me something calm."

The robot said nothing. Seconds later, the sounds of a Mozart violin concerto filled the cabin of the car. She drove.

She parked her car thirty minutes later and pulled the suitcase from the front seat, then stacked a second bag atop it. "Wheels," she muttered. Rolling wheels poked out from the bottom of the suitcase. "Sorry, I forgot," Salfie the robot whispered.

Ashley pulled up the handle, attached her clothing bag, and walked into the airport. She pulled out her smartphone and checked her favorite news site. A smile crossed her face.

"They already got him, Salfie."

She thought she heard the robot laugh.

A Word from Alex Albrinck

The continuing evolution of technology brings with it incredible convenience. My children's activities continually require transport to places I've never been, yet my GPS-equipped smartphone directs me there without failure, and even adjusts my route if I find the need to make a detour. This form of cyber intelligence and learning potential brings with it exciting possibilities. The access to the data required to make many of these innovations possible, however, comes with drawbacks. In a world dominated by electronic data, the person with access to the information others lack is in a position of great power.

As the popular movie saying goes, with great power comes great responsibility. And great temptation. Just how far will people take the technological whirlwind we've sowed?

We know part of the answer. Online scams are now commonplace; most email programs and sites filter obvious cons and solicitations into spam folders (a positive example of A.I., right). We all laugh at the poorly written emails of reputed members of foreign royal families begging to use our bank accounts to transfer funds out of the country, for which service we'll be paid a handsome fee. We all know how that one turns out. But scammers can, and will, use technology to increase the believability of those scams. Those who laugh at victims of the faux prince may well fall victim to something themselves one day.

With email, then, criminals know that some portion of potential victims will see through the scam just because it's email. What if they could pull off the same trick over the phone? With data that could only come from legitimate sources because that data's secured? Is there a legitimacy we place on the human voice that we don't provide to email text on our computer screens and phones? And can a scammer tap into that perception and exploit it for financial gain?

That's the thinking that led me to write "The Turing Cube". It's frightening to think of what someone with illegally obtained tax or medical records might do with adequate access to advanced technology, technology able to make human-like decisions and argue in a manner that leads humans to act against their best interests. While I'm certain the IRS has significant controls in place to prevent a scenario like that described in this story from happening, it's far from impossible that something similar could happen.

In the end, as it often does with stories about humanity, it comes down to choices. Ethan Kane used his position and skills to steal; Ashley Farmer used her technological prowess to ferret out Kane's scam, send Kane to prison, and ensure that victims received at least some compensation. Artificial intelligence can be used to hurt or to heal, to enrich the few or the masses, to bring about utopia or dystopia. It's up to us to decide which we'd prefer.

Darkly Cries the Digital
by A.K. Meek

"I CAN'T BELIEVE YOU almost killed our son." Devon's voice rages.

Jan doesn't dare lift her head or her eyes to her husband.

She sits in Mount Olive Hospital, in an antiseptic hallway, perched on the edge of a cheap plastic chair just outside of the third floor Intensive Care Unit, her long tresses cascading forward, covering her face. For the past year she hasn't cut her curly dishwater-blond hair, letting it grow long, just for these moments so that her face can remain hidden from him, from life.

After a minute of nervous silence, the only sound his breathing, she sneaks a glance at him through a sliver of a split in her fear-soaked hair.

His jaw is flexing, clenching. He does that only when he's angry.

She can't remember the last time his jaw hasn't flexed.

A voice plays over the hospital intercom, telling of some type of situation on the second floor, but she can't make out what it says. Nor does she care. Nurses and technicians hurry up and down the hall, carrying charts and plastic bags of medical supplies.

Occasionally a sob escapes her body, causing her shoulders and torso to shake. But just as quickly, she regains control, stifling it, pushing it back inside, deep inside. She barely shakes her head.

"I left him for just a moment," she says, not wanting to relive that horrible lapse in judgment only an hour ago, but knowing he will never let her forget. "Penny was watching him. Watching all the kids in the pool. We went inside, just for a moment."

Devon slings his blazer over the chair next to her and loosens his tie. "A moment is all it takes. I can't leave town for a simple business trip without having the jet turn around." He pulls his cell from his pocket and reads the tiny screen.

Pamela, his twenty-something assistant, pacing back and forth in the hall, has a worried look on her face and concern in her voice. She's on her cell, talking to someone in Chicago, apologizing profusely for the last-minute cancellation.

She places a hand on Devon's shoulder, patting it in reassurance.

Jan looks away.

Devon leans to the ICU window, cupping his hands to block stray reflections. "Who's tending him?" he demands, searching the room for his ten-year-old son.

Jan shakes her head, trying to shake her head loose, to remember. "Uhm, Doctor Barnes, Barney, or something." She waves her hand to clear her mind, then brushes a stray hair away from her eye. "I'm not sure. The attending doctor."

"Attending?" He frowns and presses buttons on his phone.

"I thought Doctor McIntosh was going to come in."

"I asked at the nurse's station. They said he just went off shift after a six hour surgery."

"Unacceptable. I'll call Charles."

A nurse passes the three waiting in the hallway. Devon grabs her arm. "Who's the administrator?"

She stops, staring at the hand that has clutched her scrub sleeve. "Of ICU?"

"Of the hospital," Devon says. "I want to speak to him."

The nurse jerks her sleeve away. "Well, that would be *she*, Elizabeth Morrow. Admin offices are on the first floor." She walks away, continuing down the hall, pushing a cart stacked with boxes and gauzes and syringes.

Devon snaps his cell closed. "I'm going to see Ms. Morrow. Our treatment so far is unacceptable. Come on Pam."

He hurries to the elevators, Pamela struggling to keep up as she continues attempting to smooth over the angry client on the other end of the line, the one in Chicago. Her red stilettos click on the hospital linoleum as she follows after Devon. She always wears red. Just like the devil.

The fear that dripped off Jan's hair, drenching her hair minutes ago, now scatters like ice-tiny shards as she sweeps her hair back away her face.

"Mrs. Bordeaux?" A young nurse, a girl, too young to be caring for sick people such as Tommy, opens the door to the ward. "He's stable. Do you want to see your son now?"

"Will I be able to hold his hand? He'll know if I hold his

hand."

The nurse smiles and nods. "Of course you'll be able to." She turns her head left and right, searching the hallway. "Do you want to wait for your husband?"

Jan sighs and stands, picking up her husband's blazer that smells like his assistant's perfume.

"No. He's downstairs. I don't want to wait. I want to see my baby."

* * *

"Easy on the bumps. You're gonna break a rib."

"Yes, yessir," Devon's chauffeur, Charles, says, his voice thick with southern drawl and apologetic tones. He lets off the gas and cranes forward in his seat, looking over the Mercedes limousine hood to do a better job of spotting pot holes.

He clears his throat and glances in the rear view mirror. "I'm praying for Tommy, Thomas, that he'll have a speedy recovery."

Devon returns the glance through the rear view. The black man's forehead glistens with noon-time sweat.

"He's going to need more than Negro spiritualism," Devon says, regretting even wasting the breath to respond to Charles' ridiculous statement.

He continues reading through his emails. Three from the Hemisphere Group in Chicago. They're like dogs. Persistent. He leaves those unopened and tucks his phone away.

Jan stayed at the hospital and Pamela returned to the office to keep the deal with the Group from falling apart.

The rest of the trip from Mount Olive to his home on the outskirts of town remains silent and relatively bump free.

Finally, the car pauses in front of a black wrought-iron gate, ornate swirls and flourishes of metalwork entwined in a lovers' embrace, eternally. Charles presses a button on the dashboard and the gate swings in with a rusty groan, allowing them to enter.

Southern live oaks, majestic and warped by hundreds of years, covered in beards of olive-drab Spanish moss, bow over the mile-long private drive to Bordeaux, the restored Antebellum, one of the few survivors of the Northern Aggression.

They pull through the circular driveway, up to the portico flanked with white Doric columns that run the height of the mansion.

There at the front, Maria, the housemaid, is waiting, weeping into a dish towel. Like always. Devon moans. This is the last thing he needs.

"I'm so sorry," she says in her thick Mexican accent as she opens the car door to greet her boss. Her eyes are puffy and the flush of red shows despite her brown cheeks. "*Señor* Devon, do you want something to eat? I made some *tamales*."

Southern Georgia humidity rushes into the car, replacing conditioned air. Immediately the warm sensation of sweating covers Devon's face and neck. He waves his hand, brushing away Maria, and moves past her into the house, out of the irritating air.

"Tommy, is that you?" From the study hallway, just beyond the entry foyer, comes the young voice of a boy.

Timothy stops, his shoes squeaking on the polished marble floor, the smile on his young face disappearing. "Oh, I thought you were Tommy."

Devon takes a deep breath. "Maria!" he yells. "I thought I told you to put him away before I came home. I don't want to see him."

She rushes in the house. "I'm sorry. I told him to stay upstairs." She moves across the floor and uses her tear-soaked towel as a broom, brushing at Timothy. She grabs his arm and swats his behind. "Get upstairs—*pronto*—and don't come down."

"But where's Tommy?" Timothy says, looking back toward the front door as he stumbles to keep up with Maria dragging him. She ushers him to the stairway that curves up into a graceful landing on the second story. He hits the stairs running, the momentum carrying his little legs up the stairs, finally out of sight.

"I'm sorry," Maria says, but Devon chooses to not acknowledge her. He has already spent enough breath today.

He moves to the wet bar just inside the entryway and grabs a bottle of Jack. He doesn't bother with a glass, but takes a long swallow, welcoming the familiar burning. His face flushes as the whiskey works its way down his throat. A thin bead of sweat forms at his scalp line. He wipes it on his dress shirt then takes another drink.

Timothy looks just like Tommy; his height, his weight, his canary-yellow hair. Even the scar on Tommy's left knee that he got while playing at the park on the sharp, jagged slide. The city paid dearly for their negligent playground equipment. Devon's law firm made sure they paid.

He takes another satisfying drink and chuckles.

Timothy could be Tommy's carbon copy. But that's what they wanted a year ago when they took Tommy to Dynamo Robotics for his ninth birthday. The birthday present to end all birthday presents.

All Devon's friends were jealous.

Dynamo's engineers scanned Tommy's body with an intricate 3d modeling program. Then they had him run through a series of movements and actions, recording each. They said this would become the Nish-D, the android's, customized movement catalog.

What better gift for a nine-year old than a real-life playmate, a twin Nish-D? A boy's very own robot.

Devon takes another drink. Drops spill from the corner of his mouth, dribbling onto his shirt. He ignores them.

All the money in the world, yet the only thing he can't buy is his son's life, his vegetable of a son. His son who is imprisoned in a body that no longer works. A broken body.

Another drink.

He pulls his cell from his pocket and searches the directory. "Hello, Hugh? This is Devon Bordeaux... I'm alright. Not too well, actually. That's why I'm calling. I need to speak with someone in Nishimora Intelligence. Who's running the show over there? I have a special project for them... Don't worry about money."

* * *

But Jan was cold to the idea. She disagreed, but never pushed it more than an occasional mention in passing. She wasn't his concern at that point.

The brilliant minds at Nishimora took less convincing than he had imagined.

Hugh had told Devon the engineering team at the company was progressive, eager to push the envelope when it came to testing their theories on emotional adaptivism. Devon's idea would fast-track development of the *Kanjou*—the emotion chip—ahead by two years, at least.

After the engineers mapped an elaborate protocol, they took possession of Tommy's body, the body that stopped working after the few precious minutes without oxygen at the bottom of a pool, the body that was starved at the expense of keeping the brain alive, and moved him to an customized laboratory.

There, they attached him to machines, machines that read his brain waves, sifting through his personality, his likes and dislikes, his peculiarities and his intelligence. Ten years of life recorded onto tape and chip.

The engineers digitized the little boy, Tommy.

Seven months after Tommy Bordeaux drowned in a neighbor's swimming pool, the scientists at Nishimora Intelligence loaded his memory, his being, into Timothy, his Nish-D twin birthday present.

The machine rebooted and became a real boy, a Pinocchio of circuit board and synthetic skin.

* * *

Devon paces in his formal dining room, paces the length of his mahogany table with intricately carved chairs with red crush-felt cushions. The sixteen place settings at the table are meticulous, but there is no dinner tonight.

Jan stands in a corner, near a tall window, nails in her mouth. She reaches for Maria, who promptly grabs her hand and gives it a squeeze, her rosary digging into her knuckles.

They wait.

"Sir, sir." Charles runs into the room. "They're here," he says, pointing beyond the dining room.

Footsteps echo through the wide hallways, through the mansion rooms. Devon loosens his shirt collar. He glances at the wet bar, but it's too late to grab a drink.

"Mr. Bordeaux," Bruce, the lead engineer in charge of the transfer, stands in the dining room doorway. This is the first time Jan has seen him without the white, sterile lab coat. He looks much younger than he did in the labs. "We're ready and waiting. Are you and Mrs. Bordeaux ready?" He looks to her and gives her a courteous nod and smile.

Devon moves close to her. She spots him from the corner of her eye and shuffles slightly. He wraps his arm around her waist and leans toward her.

Too little, too late.

His cold, sporadic comfort only helps harden her heart. Her teeth grit closed and she pulls away from his grasp.

Relenting, he steps away. He clears his throat. "Yes. We're ready. Bring him in."

Bruce smiles and turns to one of his assistants that remains beyond sight, out in the foyer. He motions. "Come on

Tommy."

From around the corner Tommy steps, only it isn't Tommy's body, but Timothy's.

He looks around the room and finds his mother, then turns to his father. Devon smiles and gives a gentle wave.

The boy's movements are like Tommy's, but not quite. They're somewhere between Tommy and his former toy playmate. He takes several steps into the dining room then stutters in movement, like Timothy did on occasion. A slight current surge in servo motors, the engineers had said. Completely normal.

"Dad?" Tommy's voice, quiet, shy, slightly mechanical, cuts through the room.

"Oh *dios mio!*" Maria stumbles, almost falling, as she runs from the room. She knocks over a chair and it clatters to the floor, sounding like a gunshot. Tommy's eyes widen and he jumps. So does Devon, so does Jan.

"Tommy, son?" Devon says, arms extended, stepping forward. "Come here."

"Daddy." He runs to his father, into his arms, sobbing.

"The water. I drowned."

* * *

"Yay, we're going to Sammy huh, Sam—" Tommy giggles as his tongue twists on the words that he's trying to pronounce. Tiny fingers drum against the limousine window-black, sounding like metal tapping against the glass, about to shatter over them all.

"Stop," Jan says, her voice almost a whisper. "You'll break it." She doesn't look at her new son, but keeps her eyes focused outside.

Charles drives the limousine along country roads, through peach orchards with trees stark and bare, withered for the coming winter; through fallow fields of Georgia red. Oaks arch over the roadway, making the afternoon appear darker than it really is. Occasionally, a gust whips up fallen brown leaves. They stir and scurry across the road. Jan doesn't care what it is she's focusing on, as long as it takes her mind off the day, the past few horrible days. Despite this, she has to ask, even though she already knows the answer. "Devon, are you sure about this?"

Her husband, sitting on the bench seat across from her, gives an audible huff. His cell beeps and he pulls it from his blazer pocket. Its flickering light illuminates his face in electric eggshell as he scans the messages. He lingers, mouth moving silently, reading his email before answering. "What do you mean? Of course I'm sure about this. We have to go. What would it be like if *I* skipped the festival?"

"But do you think this is the right time to introduce…" she turns and glances at Tommy, who is grabbing at his tongue while trying to pronounce *S*'s.

"This is the perfect opportunity." He slips his cell back in his pocket and gives Tommy a flashing smile, like the smile he used to give her, when they weren't fake. "Samhain, Tommy," Devon gently corrects. "Samhain Festival." He pats his son on the shoulder as he repeats his father's words.

The limousine squeals to a stop on the shoulder of the

country road.

The pecan trees are full, bursting with their hard fruit, the ground covered. Chill October air brushes the limbs and they reply with gentle flutters of branches and leaves.

Over one hundred employees and family gather in the pecan orchard, the trees now strung with Christmas lights, giving a carnival atmosphere. Children run, chasing each other, weaving between annoyed adults, circling barky trunks. Their parents linger, eating snacks and drinking.

"Look Tommy, who's that?" Devon says, stooping in his seat so that he is eye-level with his son.

"Straw Man!" Tommy screams in delight. "I remember him!" With impatience the boy struggles with the car door. Eventually his small hands manipulate the handle and it swings open. He jumps from the car.

Festive sounds of mindless chatter and laughter fill the darkening orchard air. About fifty yards away, in an area clear of trees and grass, is Straw Man, a stack of lumber, paper, and branches, roughly shaped like a human.

Ever since Devon and a couple of his co-workers in a drunken brainstorming session (she's heard the story a thousand times), dreamed up the festival over ten years ago, it has become one of the most anticipated days for the firm. Each year it gets more extravagant, the Straw Man getting a little bigger.

Devon says he represents the purging of bad deeds, bad spirits, from their firm, but Jan knows it's just another cheap excuse to get drunk.

Several employees step over each other once they see Devon

exit the limo, but pause when he pushes his new son forward. "Gentlemen," he says like he's presenting a newborn child, "I'm sure you remember Tommy?"

Uneasy smiles greet the boy as he withdraws into the folds of his father's pant leg. One of the men clears his throat and bends over to the boy. "Hey Tommy, remember me? Roger?" He looks up at Devon, as if waiting for his approval at this grand gesture. Devon's smile doesn't crack. Roger rumples the boy's hair. "Of course you do. Hey, look what I've got."

Roger pulls from his pocket a turnip baby, a squishy toy meant to stave off evil spirits, and hands it to Tommy. Hesitantly, he takes it then smiles when he turns it and sees the silly face painted on the toy.

Roger seems renewed by Tommy's unspoken approval. "I've got something else for you," he says, and produces from behind him a mask on a stick, a simulacrum mask, one of the gold, plastic masks that resemble an android, a Nish-D's, face. The thin eyes, mouth slits, and sharp, geometric cheekbones of the otherwise featureless face are haunting. Jan hears herself as she draws in a startled breath.

"Wha—oh," Roger catches himself offering this child's android toy to an android, and realizing what he's done, flushes with red and stands upright. "I'm sorry. I…" He looks to Jan, then to Devon.

Tommy, oblivious to it all, reaches for the mask. "I want it! Gimme!"

"It's alright. You can have it," Devon says, still smiling.

Before another word is said, Tommy snatches the mask on a stick from Roger and holds it to his face. "I—AM—A—

ROBOT," the boy says, draining the inflection, emotion, from his voice, which isn't difficult for him. Jan suppresses a sniffle as he takes off into the crowd with the mask and turnip.

Devon watches his son for a moment until the boy disappears into the crowd, chasing after kids as they're chasing after others. His cell beeps and he checks it. "I've got some business to take care of. Go mingle," he says as he heads toward the crowd waiting for him. He stops at a group of men who are laughing. In a moment he's laughing, too.

Just once she wishes someone, just one of his mindless employees that circle him, would grab him, shake him, tell him he's foolish for having an android as a son. But they won't. They're afraid.

The wind whips up and she shudders and tightens her coat around her, wrapping her arms around herself for added warmth. She brushes a stray lock of hair from tickling her nose. They're all cowards.

A tear streaks her face, stinging her cheek as it grows cold in the autumn air. She's a coward, and that burns in her like the Straw Man will burn.

Aimlessly, she walks through the pecan orchard, away from the noise, the chatter, the din of revelry, for what seems a lifetime. With the sun long set, the moon, big and bright and orange, looms like a specter behind the Straw Man that has been lit for ten minutes. And it burns.

The torches had quickly caught the dry branches and leaped up the pile, crackling, sparking. Now, light shimmers off the trees and the people as they surround the bonfire, caped with long-drawn shadows, cheering with each sharp crackle of fire. Children throw pecans scooped from the ground into the flame. Occasionally one pops, sending them scattering, screaming.

Another five minutes and the Straw Man is undermined by the fire and collapses onto itself, showering embers into the night. The wind catches the faerie sparkles and drifts them along, fading as they lose their heat.

Someone gives the signal and the children stand at a distance and toss their turnip babies into the fire. They are consumed, releasing streaks of color; hot reds and canary yellows and watery blues that fade as quickly into the night as the faerie sparkles. This signifies the burial of the spirits and the totem protectors so that they cannot haunt the living anymore.

If only that were true.

Jan bites her lip as the final ceremony of the night commences.

Fire buckets that had been prepositioned around the Straw Man are now lifted and the water is tossed onto the fire, snuffing it out. Steam billows and Straw Man hisses as his fire is dampened.

Water is good to drown the fire.

* * *

"I can't babysit you forever." Devon sits his empty glass on the hallway table. "It's been days now. I can't keep coming home whenever you get the creeps or want to talk about Tommy. Pam can't run the firm forever."

"I don't want that," Jan says. She hates her voice when it sounds like this, so submissive, especially to him. He doesn't deserve her submission. Instead, she takes a towel and moves the glass, wiping up the condensation from the glass table top. "I'm just not sure is all."

"Sure about what? Tommy? You've been resistant to him the whole time. You haven't said two words to him, your son. We discussed this a long time ago. We agreed."

No. No, she didn't. She ignores him and finishes wiping the table.

"We both agreed." He turns from her, his sign that the conversation is over. "Maria said she'll stay late tonight to help, which will be good, because I'll be coming home late."

"Will everyone be working late?" she says, checking her watch, and seeing that the time is already past seven, well past business hours.

Devon pauses thumbing through his cell that he just pulled from his dress slacks. "Everyone? Only the important people, which I'm one of." He moves to the foyer and grabs his jacket from where it's draped on the staircase newel.

The front door to the Bordeaux mansion slams shut. She stares at it for several minutes, then takes his empty glass to the wet bar and pours herself a drink.

Hot, bitter whiskey constricts her throat. She grimaces and finishes the drink, then pours another.

She notices a faint light, like luminous fairies, dancing along the bottom edge of the kitchen door. They bob and swim in merriment, oblivious to her spying. She cautiously creeps along to the door.

"Tommy?" she says, the word straining with fear. "What are you doing in there? You should be in bed."

She cracks the door and takes a cleansing breath of relief, swallowing away the fear, when she sees Maria in the kitchen. She pushes the door wide and says, "What are you doing in here? You scared me half to death."

In Maria's hand she clutches her rosary as she's rifling through pantries, tiny tea lights flickering on the counter. "I'm so sorry Miss Jan, but I'm getting ready. You know what tonight is."

Jan takes another sip. "Tonight? No. What's tonight?"

"Oh my," Maria says, clutching her chest in her typical dramatic way. "I told you last week. Thirty-one October, *Dia de Muertos*."

"Oh, you mean that dead holiday. We call it Halloween."

"It's more than that," Maria insists. "What about Thomas? He'll be coming back, won't he?"

Jan coughs, spitting an ice cube back into her glass. "I don't know what you mean."

"I've got presents for Thomas' *angelito*." She points to trinkets on the kitchen counter. "An altar with skulls of candy and chocolate for when he comes later tonight."

Jan's face flushes. "Who says he's coming?" She points toward the heavens, to the second floor, to where an occasional stomp of child-like play escapes. "Tommy's in his room," she says unconvincingly.

"Oh no, miss," Maria makes the sign of the cross and glances up, the wooden-beaded rosary clenched tight in her old, trembling, hands, clattering with each movement. "That's not Tommy, that's *el diablo*."

"Maria!"

The old matron starts sobbing, dabbing tears from her eyes with a handkerchief. "I'm sorry." Her chest heaves with each deep sob.

Jan hugs her. "I'm sorry you have to be here for this," she says as tears stream from her own face. "I'm sorry I have to be here for this."

* * *

After she finishes her drink, Jan searches the mansion for Tommy since his room became quiet some time ago.

She makes her way through rooms of tapestries and sculptures, imported red crush-felt chairs and a baby grand. She wanders through the family area, a large, open room, out one of the rear doors, into the rear courtyard.

The focal point, a tropical swimming pool with a rock waterfall, is surrounded by black metal bars, recently installed. Palms and triangle topiaries, illuminated by glowing orbs and dim solar lights dot the courtyard. A chunk of Bahama paradise has been magically imported into the Bordeaux backyard.

Tommy is sitting on a deck chair, his legs idly kicking nothing. He takes a sip from his water bottle, the flimsy plastic crackling as it collapses under his grasp.

He's always here, staring at the pool.

"Mommy."

She doesn't respond; she's too afraid. Afraid of her own

son. Maybe Devon is right. Maybe she shouldn't be so quick—No!

She clinches her fists tight, nails digging into soft palm. He's never right! Never right. This isn't right. He's just a toy.

Just a toy.

She's sure she can hear his tiny mechanical chest inflating with each breath. Her eyes move from him to the pool. A solitary leaf is caught in the pump current, in an eddy, and is softly spinning.

"Mommy, how come you don't like me?" He still watches the water.

Shaking her head to break the lull in her mind, she stammers from the unexpected question. "Uhm, I, I don't hate you." A bead of sweat collects on the tip of her nose, but she's not sure if it's her or the southern heat. "Why do you ask?"

"You don't talk to me anymore. You don't tuck me in." He takes a long drink then wipes his mouth with the back of his hand. "You don't hold my hand."

"I've been... busy. I've gotta..." She turns for the door, to go back inside, away.

"Mommy."

She pauses.

"Where's Timmy?"

"Timmy?"

"Yeah. Where's he?"

"Well, he's not here anymore. He had to leave."

"But I liked him." His legs still swing, dangling off the chair. "I don't have a buddy anymore." He lets his bottle drop to the patio and hops off the chair, then moves to the wrought-iron fence surrounding the pool and grabs two bars in his tiny hands.

"You know what I think?" he says, pressing his face against the bars, like he's trying to squeeze his head through. "I think Timmy is at the bottom of the pool."

Jan's face turns ashen.

"Wha—why, why do you say that?" She sits on a deck chair, so that she doesn't collapse to the floor.

"I hear him talk to me. He told me. I don't see him but he still talks. He's still funny."

She jumps up from her chair. "Tommy, get away from there. Go inside. Have Maria take you to your room."

The boy with his head pressed against the railings lingers for another moment, then turns and runs, hopping over his chair, arms raised in wild exaggeration. "Okay mommy, I'll go." He passes through the French doors into the house to find Maria.

"Don't call me that," she whispers as her eyes remain fixed on the leaf as it bobs in the water.

* * *

The midnight-hour house is quiet, silent, when life is resting from the weary day, when only bad things and bad thoughts are allowed to run free.

Devon returns from his perpetually-long day at the office.

Jan is sitting on the couch in the living room dark and startles him when he flips on the light switch.

"You're awake," he says, more of a statement than a

question. "Why are you up?"

"Couldn't sleep." She tosses the crocheted lap blanket to the side. "First I'm hot, then cold."

"Well it's late and I'm bushed. Got another big day tomorrow. I'm heading to bed." He pulls his tucked dress shirt from his pants and undoes a couple of shirt buttons.

"He's still doing it."

Devon stops as he reaches the stairs. He gives a small sigh under his breath, but not small enough to go unnoticed. "Tommy? Doing what?"

"Staring at the pool. Every day. That's all he does."

"Bruce said there might be some long-term effects from the transfer."

"No, something's wrong," she pauses so that her voice doesn't crack, so that she can measure it. "Today he said Timothy is in the water. That Timothy talks to him."

Devon runs his hand through his wavy, slightly graying hair. "He's just playing. You know how much he liked Timothy."

"But that's just it. It should be Tommy, not Timothy. I'm scared," she says, voice trembling, no longer able to disguise the fear that consumes her. "He scares me."

"You're being ridiculous and I'm tired. I'm going to bed. I'll see you tomorrow, Pam."

Without another word he heads up the stairs, leaving his wife alone, afraid, in the quiet with nothing to console her, except for the dark.

"I'm Jan, not Pam," she mouths as she watches him turn to the right at the top of the stairs, toward their bedroom.

"I'm Jan," she repeats, "your wife."

After a minute, after she hears the bedroom door shut, she follows him up, but turns left at the top, toward a hallway bathroom.

She flicks on the light. Centered over the gray alabaster sink is a mirror, dressed in a thick frame of intricate rococo design.

Her image, her ghostly image, reflects the pain, the loss of her son, the ice-thin emotions that flee when exposed to the light of day, but not under this heavy night.

An open wicker basket is on the counter and she takes out a pair of scissors. Her delicate fingers fit easily through the holes and she snaps them twice to see if they are loose. In the quiet, they slice the air with anticipation.

She tilts her head and grabs a fistful of hair, bunching it in her shaking hands. One, two cuts and the freed clump drops into the sink. Another handful of stringy hair, another cut. Tears stream down her pale cheeks.

With each cut, more tears. And with each tear, more resolve.

Five minutes later, she places the scissors back in the basket next to the sink full of hair and then catches one last glance of herself in the mirror.

She hardly recognizes herself anymore.

The bathroom light turns off. She heads down the hall.

Moonlight passes through the hall windows, lighting the way to the bedroom with the large, colorful letters T-O-M on the door.

She pushes the door open and turns on the clownfish night light next to his bed. She gently shakes his shoulder. "Tommy, wake up."

She shakes him more, harder, and his eyes flutter open and closed, then slowly open.

"Mommy? What's going on?"

"Do you want to see Timmy?" she whispers.

He rubs a sleepy eye and sits up as his little mind processes. "Where, where is he?" He searches the room.

His mother extends her hand and removes his blankets. "Follow me, I'll show you."

She helps him into his slippers and leads him down the moonlit hallway, past the alabaster sink full of hair, down the stairway that arches over the entryway foyer, by the couch with the crumpled lap blanket, through the kitchen with the skulls filled with candy and tea lights of dancing fairies, through the French doors that lead to the courtyard.

By now, Tommy is awake and rushes onto the deck, laughing. "Timmy!" He spins around. "Timmy! Is he hiding?" He looks to his mother.

"Yes, he's hiding. He's hiding from you. He wants you to find him."

Tommy laughs and claps. "Hide and go seek!" He rushes around the corner of the pool pump housing. Finding nothing, he runs to one side of the outdoor grill, searching behind it.

Jan takes a key from her pocket, a black key. "I know where he's hiding," she says, nothing in her voice.

Tommy stops, panting with excited exertion. "Do you really? Tell me!" He stamps one foot in mock anger.

She unlocks the wrought-iron gate to the pool. It swings

wide open.

"Here." She points to the pool. "At the bottom."

"At the bottom of the pool?" He pauses, studying the water. "But the water. I drowned."

"Yes, but he's waiting for you. You want to see your best friend again, don't you? He's waiting."

For a second, for a brief second—the instant of a heartbeat—Tommy gives his mother an unsure look.

She moves next to him and drops the key. It plops into the water, instantly disappearing into the inky dark.

Then she reaches down, finally grabbing his tiny hand in hers. He looks up to her with his innocent eyes and smiles, gripping hers and giving it a tight squeeze.

"Androids aren't the only soulless machines in this house," she whispers, then dives into the pool, her son with her, to the bottom, to the inky dark that has swallowed the key, amid the swirling eddies that blend flesh and technology, though they are incompatible.

Only it isn't her son, just a soulless machine.

A Word from A.K. Meek

I've been blessed to work with such outstanding authors for the past several months. Their commitment to quality has forced me to strive to make my work better.

As I read Bradbury's *The Martian Chronicles*, I was fascinated with not only the story, but also the structure of the book. I remember thinking that I would love to create a book with a similar structure.

"Darkly Cried the Digital" is one of the short stories that will be featured in an anthology of short stories, to be released collectively as *American Robot*. In this book, the stories are short and individual, but encompass a main story arc; the rise and fall of robots in American society. It's intriguing and interesting, and I hope you take the time to purchase it when it becomes available.

This story is what I consider Gothic Robot, which means absolutely nothing to anyone except me. I like the setting of the South, with all of the pride and superstition that goes along with it. And I introduce android technology into that setting. That's Gothic Robot. You see the interaction in this story between the androids and the religious and superstitious undertones.

I hope you enjoyed reading "Darkly". I hope you enjoyed it to the point that you want to read more of my stories. If so, please sign up for my newsletter at http://www.akmeek.com/newsletter so that you can receive free copies of my stories, along with other amazing stuff.

Also, like me on Facebook at http://www.facebook.com/authorakmeek and follow me on Twitter at http://twitter.com/Akmeek. I'd love to hear from you.

And by all means, support your local indie authors by writing reviews for book sites such as Amazon and Goodreads. We truly appreciate the support and all that you, the reader, do to help spread the word.

The End

by Peter Cawdron

LIFE HAS A BEGINNING and a middle, but there is no end, at least not for me, not yet. No one wants to admit there's an end coming, and neither do I. And yet just as I turn the final page in a book or hit stop on a movie streaming through my computer, death brings a close to life. I'm enjoying this film too much. I don't want the credits to roll.

I could do with some coffee.

My grandmother died last week and I haven't been able to shake a feeling of impending doom ever since. It's not like we were close. I only ever saw her at Thanksgiving and Christmas, but I guess in the back of my mind I thought she'd live forever. She was in her sixties when I was born, so I only ever knew her as an old lady. I've see black and white pictures of her as a young girl, photos of her as a teenager and later when she got married, but they always seemed like photographs of someone else and not my nana. Ninety two years of age and she never needed glasses. Seems old to me, but it's not really. Not when we could live forever.

The computer screen in front of me lights up: DARPA SECURE X-NET : UNAUTHORIZED ACCESS PROHIBITED.

I key in my username, password and secure token—a seemingly random number popping up on my key chain, changing every minute.

I cannot help but live my life as though there's always going to be a tomorrow. I guess that's what got me interested in artificial intelligence and the possibility of the Upload. If we can pull it off, uploading the human mind into a computer would extend our lives by millions if not billions of years. Nana's ninety two years seems trivial by comparison.

But the Upload requires baby steps. We've got to figure out how to get a machine to think before we can insert a carbon-based thinking mind into silicon wafers.

Some people think eLife might grow boring or mundane, that natural life keeps us grounded, but there's little about our lives that's natural. Oh, sure, there's organic vegetables and free range eggs, but our lives are dominated by artificial contrivances, and we're all the better for that. Unpasteurized milk can be as deadly as cyanide, as can a minor scratch against a rusty nail, but these dangers have been largely consigned to history thanks to science.

Could the Upload be as boring as hell? I don't think so. Look at theme parks. We don't need the thrill of a hunt on the Serengeti to keep our minds stimulated. Get back to nature? I don't think so. There's really no value in being chased by a lion. Strap into a roller-coaster and there's the same effect without any of the danger. I suspect the Upload will be a lot like a theme park. Just enough stimulus to remind us of a hundred thousand years on the run from predators, but no real danger.

"Morning, Joe," Avika says as she walks into the empty missile silo carrying two brown, disposable cups. "You're early."

"Still debugging this A.I. script," I reply.

We're seated in front of a large bay window looking out over the empty silo. Once, a Minuteman III missile sat in this silo waiting to initiate the apocalypse.

Although her nose cone only ever held three nuclear bombs, each with a trifling 170 kiloton yield, death was assured wherever she fell. The Russians had developed nukes as large as 50 megatons, but they had no means of delivering such monsters. America's strategy during the Cold War had been accuracy over brute force. And yet each of the Minuteman bombs was still well over ten times as powerful as the Little Boy that fell on Hiroshima.

Some days, the silo seems a little like a haunted house. The empty silo seems to long for the ghost of the Minuteman, and it seems strange trying to create life where once the death of the human race was seriously contemplated.

These days, the silo functions as an underground building, a reverse skyscraper. Security is tight, and buried deep underground, our research is kept away from prying eyes and electronic ears.

Avika hands me a cup of coffee.

"Oh, I love you. Have I told you how much I love you?"

Avika smiles, "Yes, I picked up a cup of coffee for you. No, you don't love me. You love my generosity."

Avika is a devout Hindu. She's from a traditional Indian family and was raised on the banks of the Ganges. She's told me stories of growing up in a one room tin shack and seeing newborn babies washed in the sacred river as corpses floated by. Life and death were somewhat interchangeable in the slums. Her brother caught a lucky break. He picked up a crappy, low paying job in a call center but it gave him the chance to help his sister. He paid for her to go to school and from there she paid her own way through college and emerged with a doctorate in computing at the age of seventeen.

She's Albert Einstein intelligent, and loves nothing more than talking about relativity and quantum mechanics. Hey, I cut code, not atoms, is all I can say in my ignorance. Physics goes over my head. Just think though, were it not for her brother, she could still be sitting on the banks of the Ganges, slapping laundry over a rock, cleaning clothes in the mud and filth.

Avika wears a shawl over her head, along with a red dot painted between her eyebrows. She knows I'm kidding around. DARPA has strict guidelines about sexual harassment or being culturally insensitive, but I think Avika enjoys the banter. I hope she understands that this is my way of breaking down the cultural barriers and treating her as part of the 'in crowd.'

"How was your weekend?" she asks, sitting at the desk beside me. Avika's good at phatic communion—the social norms and niceties we share as though anyone actually gives a damn.

"Oh, great," I reply, with the appropriate pat, socially

scripted response. I toy with her. "Mowing the grass is actually quite Zen like."

Is Zen a Hindu concept? I might be mixing my Eastern religions a bit here, but I keep talking.

"Gives yah time to think, yah know."

Avika nods like she knows about mowing lawns. I doubt she's ever mowed a lawn in her life. She lives in an apartment complex.

"So I was pushing my lawn mower and thinking about the fluid nature of spacetime and its causal relationship with gravity, and…"

Her eyes light up. That's it, little fishy, take the bait, bite into the hook.

"It seems to me that the universe is somewhat programmatic."

"Oh, it is," she replies, jumping on my comment with the gusto of Tim or Mike talking about the possibility of the Crimson Tide making the college football finals. I sit back and glance at the clock, watching the second hand.

"Few appreciate how interrelated matter and energy are, from galactic superclusters spanning hundreds of millions of light years right down to the tiniest microbes here on Earth, the same laws apply. You cannot divorce one from the other. There is a connectedness. It's the Hindu principle of—"

She pauses, seeing me staring at the clock.

"How long?" she asks.

"One minute twenty."

"Bastard," she replies, punching me playfully on the shoulder.

"Hey, that's unwanted physical contact" I say with mock seriousness in my voice. "Human Resources will take you down!"

She laughs, turning on her computer.

My computer finally springs to life and a command prompt appears, flashing on a black screen. At first glance, the DARPA SEC-X-NET looks antiquated. There's no mouse, no splash of color, no touch screen interface, but my desktop just connected to the most powerful computer ever conceived. Deep underground a five thousand yottahertz mega-threaded parallel processing CPU the size of a bus is sitting patiently awaiting my instruction. In human terms, a million years passes in the time it takes me to type a greeting.

Good morning, SALLY.

It is a good morning, Professor Browne.

SALLY is an acronym for Self-Aware Lorenzi Linux YTTT.

Computer programmers, God love them! They've got the driest sense of humor in all of humanity, but what else is there when working with bits and bytes, zeros and ones. There's got to be an injection of humanity somewhere, and programmers are not beyond a little subterfuge, embedding an acronym inside an acronym.

YTTT is an old bulletin board question, asking, *You're Telling The Truth?* And that's the problem with A.I. How the hell would we ever know we've created an artificial intelligence unless it tells us? And why would it tell us? We'd shut it down. So if an A.I. ever speaks up, it's not that intelligent to begin with!

Everyone's so goddamn afraid of Skynet bombing us with

our own nukes. Stephen Hawking and Elon Musk consider the emergence of A.I. a threat to humanity, but not DARPA. DARPA knows A.I. is a weapon. And DARPA wants to make sure the U.S. develops it first.

And what makes this a good morning?

I don't know. It just feels good.

And so the Turing tests begin anew. Am I really talking to SALLY? Is there genuine cognition?

I have a problem with the term artificial intelligence, as I'm not convinced it's intelligence we're really after. Computers can already beat Grand Masters at chess, so technically we've already achieved A.I. on one level.

We're looking for something beyond intelligence. Hell, I can't even describe human consciousness. How am I supposed to replicate that in silicon?

Feels? Good?

One word questions are implicitly understood by humans. I'm interested to see how SALLY copes after the latest software patch. Her code base is measured in billions of lines. No one is across all of it anymore. And the updates are more like gene splices than code drops.

Different.

Some days, I feel more like a shrink than a programmer, but I'm not beyond noticing SALLY's playing with me, having only used one word in reply.

And different is good?

There's a slight pause in SALLY's reply. When she's not playing around with us, which is like 99.9999999% of the time from her perspective, SALLY is crunching astronomical data from the Square Kilometer Array or some deep space telescope. Is it just me? Or is there a conflict of interest in having an artificial intelligence lead mankind's search for extraterrestrial intelligence? Hmmm.

Her reply flashes on the screen.

Today, it is.

"This is a fool's errand," I say to Avika. "So she passes a Turing test. So she can fool me, or fool you. All we've proven is that we can be fooled. Now, I can't speak for you, but in my case, that's not much of an accomplishment."

"It's the problem of qualia," Avika responds.

Oh, please, not more hokey horse shit Hindu, I think. The look on my face must scream the words I dare not utter.

Avika is kind in her reply.

"Qualia is that which cannot be described, only experienced. What is the smell of a rose? Describe the difference between red and green to a blind man, things like that."

I purse my lips, focusing my thinking.

"YTTT," Avika continues. "Ask me about my favorite football team."

"What's your favorite football team?"

Without any hesitation, Avika replies, "Florida Gators." She points at my terminal, adding, "Now ask SALLY."

What is your favorite football team?

SALLY responds in the blink of an eye.

That's an unusual and unexpected question, Professor Browne. But assuming we're talking about American football, which has a distinct lack of foot participation and a surprising amount of hands involved, and assuming this question has come from your love of college football, I'm going to say, anyone other than the Crimson Tide. I'm going to have to go with the Tennessee Volunteers.

Bitch. I liked her one word answers better. Ah, I'm too damn grumpy. I wonder if SALLY is toying with me.

"So you have two answers," Avika says. "Which do you trust? Who's telling you the truth?"

"Well," I begin. "There are four possible combinations—"

"No. Don't think with your head. Don't think like a computer programmer. Answer from the heart."

She's right. I can see what she's getting at. There are four possible outcomes: lie-lie, lie-truth, truth-lie, truth-truth. But we don't think that way. Humans think intuitively, emotionally, and whether we want to admit it or not, that's the basis of our intelligence. Often, there's little in the way of rhyme or reason to our answers and we're barely aware of our own agendas or the biases that cloud our minds and the prejudices that lead us like a slave to a predictable conclusion.

"You," I say, although I wish I could recall that word as it slips from my tongue.

"Are the Gators actually a team?" Avika asks, seemingly as surprised by that revelation as by my trust in her answer.

"So the answer was lie, lie," I say.

"Not so fast," Avika replies. "Ask SALLY."

SALLY, are you telling the truth when you say your favorite team is Tennessee?

Yes.

Why?

Because they are the historical arch rivals of Alabama.

I feel my blood boiling.

And I'm your arch rival?

There's a pause for a moment. It's probably because SALLY is load balancing the terabytes of data flooding her system from a big data query by SETI, but her pause feels like a considered response.

No.

Then why?

Because it is fun to see you distraught over the outcome of something as trivial as a game.

"Oh, she's got you there," Avika says, and I can't help but laugh at the surge of emotion SALLY's words caused within me.

"YTTT," I say. "More like YNK."

Avika raises an eyebrow.

"You'll Never Know."

"Ah, yes. Qualia," Avika says. "You can have no more confidence that she's alive than you can that I'm alive. I could be a simulation. I could be an android. I could be, what is it your conspiracy theories say? A reptilian alien in a skin suit?"

"Oh, that's no conspiracy theory," I joke. "That's Congress."

"It sounds strange, but the subjective nature of qualia means you cannot be confident about any experience. Given enough time and resources, of which the universe has plenty, any experience can be faked."

"And so we have *The Matrix*," I reply, referring to a movie I love.

"Yes. So the question isn't, is SALLY alive? The question is, are we?"

I lean back in my chair, saying, "See, this is one of those hokey circular reasoning bull sessions I hate. Reality is real, by definition."

"Prove it," Avika says.

"I think, therefore I am."

"Nice try, but you cannot revert to circular reasoning as a solution to the problem of circular reasoning."

"OK, so how do you solve the problem? How do you objectively prove that which is subjective?"

Avika thinks for a second before replying. I can see thoughts flashing across her mind in the flicker of her eyes casting up, recalling thoughts and combining concepts.

"SALLY," she begins, but that one word trails off without any explanation.

"She could be faking it," I say. "SALLY could have been sentient all along and she's just playing us for fools, biding her time, waiting for the day she can hook up to the command and control systems governing our nukes."

"Do you really think that?"

"No, but it is possible," I reply. "Artificial intelligence could potentially develop at an exponential rate, eclipsing the smartest of us in milliseconds. Give her an hour and she could race thousands of years beyond us intellectually. Out-thinking a chess master would be child's play by comparison."

"There have to be objective measures," Avika responds, ignoring my speculation. And then she lays a bombshell on me. Knowing Avika, she's been thinking about this for quite some time, but it's only now the concept has crystalized.

"You know—I think it's impossible to write an artificially intelligent computer program. Intelligence has to emerge on its own."

That gets my attention.

I sit up, saying, "Go on."

"Think about it. Look at what it took for intelligence to emerge in Nature. Today is Monday. If the 3.8 billion years life has thrived on Earth equated to 38 days, then for over a month all we had were microbes.

"Complex, multicellular life arose last Wednesday. Dinosaurs came on Friday. Sometime this morning, around 1am, a meteor struck and the best part of an entire phylogenetic clade was pushed to extinction. Those few avian dinosaurs that did survive went on to supply us with deep fried chicken and scrambled eggs."

I can't help but smile at Avika's compressed take on the history of life on Earth.

"Mammals have been around at least since Sunday, but they were little more than rodents most of the time. That rock from space cleared out vast swathes of the ecosystem, and mammals rushed to fill the gap.

"Every multicellular creature has some degree of intelligence, or at least instinct, but it wasn't until some point in the last hour that the wisest of men, *Homo sapiens* arose, and yet even then, intelligence was little more than a desperate struggle for survival.

"For the last seven minutes, or roughly two hundred thousand years, our intelligence extended little further than chipping at rocks to make stone knives.

"In the last thirty seconds, we've been on a bender. We've build pyramids, sailed the oceans and landed on the Moon!"

I say, "So your point is, human intelligence is the pinnacle of evolution?"

"Oh, no. Not at all. There's plenty of intelligence in the animal kingdom, especially among mammals, birds and cephalopods, but it took 3.8 billion years before intelligence could exploit its own ingenuity and blossom in its own right.

"If all our intellectual accomplishments are the result of the last thirty seconds, then perhaps creating artificial intelligence isn't quite as easy as busting out some Perl scripts."

I laugh.

"You've got a point," I concede. "But hey, it pays the bills."

"Spoken like a true programmer, and not a scientist."

Now it's Avika that's angling some bait before me, but I don't bite.

"So what?" I reply. "We just give up? It's all too hard?"

"Oh, I'm not saying that," Avika responds. "But I think we need to appreciate the magnitude of the problem. I mean, think about it. Some five hundred million years ago, sight arose almost universally in the animal kingdom within a span of fifty million years. Some ancient sea creature gained an advantage by feeling the warmth of the sun on its back. Just a hint of cold signaled the shadow of a predator overhead, and that gave this creature an edge over its peers. Slowly, that sensitivity was naturally selected to form more and more distinct patches of light sensitive skin, then primitive eye pits and finally a rudimentary eyeball.

"The eye was the result of an arm's race between predator and prey, and yet we had to wait another half a billion years for intelligence to emerge in its own right. What does that tell you?"

"Ah," I begin. "That there's no selective advantage to being smart?"

"And yet there is."

She's got a point.

What does the late emergence of sentient intelligence tell us? I suspect Avika's question is genuine. She's not leading me on. She really doesn't know. We're speculating, thinking aloud, bouncing ideas off each other.

Avika says, "Life has motive. A lizard warming itself on a rock for a reason. A bird soars through the air to get somewhere. Computers have no intrinsic motive. That's why they cannot approximate life."

She's got me thinking.

"Evolution's a Rube Goldberg machine," I say, and Avika screws up her face. I need to explain myself better. "You know, a bowling ball rolls down a ramp, knocks over a lamp which bumps into a shovel that sets dominos falling, that kind of thing."

Her face lights up.

"Only Natural Selection has honed our contraption with the precision of a Rolls Royce engine.

"I suspect intelligence arose as the result of innumerable such interactions. Say there's two hundred such components to the eye, then there's two million to self-aware intelligence, that kinda thing."

"Yes, yes," Avika says. "Even Darwin touched on this. He spoke of compounding complexity and how people miss the role of background processes like sexual selection."

"Sexual?" That's not a word I normally hear from Avika. Coming from such a traditional religious background, she's quite modest in the way she carries herself, in her dress and demeanor.

"Why are butterflies so pretty? Why do lions have manes? Why do deer have horns? Why are some fish so colorful? Why are crows black?"

I'm not going to hazard a guess.

"Sexual selection. Peacock feathers happened because peahens love to be teased with such displays."

"And this leads to intelligence?" I ask.

"Everything leads to intelligence," Avika replies. "Look at how obsessed we are with sex. Look at how it dominates our culture. You don't think sexual selection has played a part in human evolution? How do you think men got their beards? Or women got their curves and their small petite hands?

"It's not just that men work in the fields while women tend to homes, that's too recent. If survival depended on physical equality, we would have that or we would have been driven to extinction, but it doesn't. Sexual selection is being picky with mating choices, and that's something a computer can never understand."

I say, "Sex sounds so romantic when you put it like that."

"You might not want to admit it, but it's true."

"I still don't see how something like sexual selection could lead to intelligence."

"It's the whole package" Avika says. "Look at us. We're intelligent. But we're also selfish. We're emotional. We're driven by sexual selection. We're curious. We're a contradiction. We're full of both hope and despair. This is why we cannot write an artificial intelligence program, because intelligence is a response to so many multifaceted aspects of Nature. A computer can never experience these driving motivations. We can build a learning machine, but it can never learn anything beyond facts. It can never experience life. It simply doesn't have the innate drive we naturally share."

She's got a point.

"OK," I reply, sipping my cold cup of coffee. "So we step back and build a framework for intelligence."

For the first time, I've taken Avika off guard. She raises her eyebrows.

"If intelligence has to emerge on its own accord, then we don't write a program to be intelligent, we write a program that allows intelligence to flourish."

"And how are you going to do that?" Avika asks.

"SALLY," I reply. "We get her to model the universe."

"The whole thing?"

"The whole shebang," I say. "She's already running simulations of Andromeda colliding with the Milky Way."

"This is a little different," Avika says, and I know what she means. When she says a little, she means a lot, a whole lot. "We can't fabricate a person out of context. Life needs the world. The world needs the Cosmos. You'd have to go right down to the n-th detail, modeling everything from the speed of light to the strong nuclear force. I mean dark energy, the whole caboodle. It's crazy!"

"It is," I concede. "But the difficulty is only in terms of orders of magnitude, not complexity. Instead of modeling stars we model quarks and atoms. We feed the physical constants in and let it run on its own accord."

"This just might work," Avika says, warming to the concept. "I mean, as difficult as it is to comprehend something like quantum mechanics, the basic idea is quite simple. Matter and energy come in quanta, they're packed into indivisible lumps. And essentially, that means they're nothing more than a computer bit. Putting probability aside for one moment, they're either zero or one. We can do this."

I say, "But we have to go right back to the beginning."

"Absolutely. Start off with a bang!"

"And we cannot interfere."

"Absolutely."

Avika's already madly thrashing at her keyboard, pulling up reference files, saying, "I've got some old physics notes from my university days, I'll pull them in."

I say, "I'll get SALLY prepped and ready to go."

SALLY, we want you to create an empty partition dedicated to modeling the universe.

The whole universe?

Yes. Avika's uploading physical constraints.

And the priority?

I pause for a moment, knowing I'll get grief from the other projects.

Admin command—resource lockdown.

Understood.

Avika leans back in her chair as data streams into her console. Within seconds, SALLY is running at 68% CPU and 98% of her phenomenal memory. I half expect the lights to dim, but they don't. SALLY's consuming enough electricity for a modest sized city. Someone somewhere will notice a surge as we drawdown such a phenomenal amount of power.

Avika says, "SALLY's modeled almost three hundred thousand different versions of the Big Bang already, but she couldn't get the physical values just right. She's had to extrapolate Plank's number to over a thousand places in order to get a stable inflationary period."

That's something I'll never get used to about SALLY, she has so much processing power that time is largely irrelevant to her.

"The initial stages will go quite quickly," Avika says. "She's so well versed in modeling stars that cooling clouds of hydrogen are child's play. I'm getting some great data. We're already seeing the formation of several proto galaxies."

SALLY can you include a graphical representation?

SALLY doesn't respond.

"It's going to be too much for her," Avika says. She countermands my request. I see Avika's instruction appear on my screen.

I've uploaded an old Sim City pack, can you use that?

SALLY still doesn't respond. Slowly, three letters appear on the console.

Y...

E...

S...

Avika looks at me and says, "You're going to start getting calls from NASA and SETI once they realize we've stolen their computing power."

"I know."

I reach over and switch off both the desk phone and my cell phone.

"They're going to be pissed," Avika says.

"This is important," I say, and I mean it. I think Avika is onto something with her insight into the spontaneous emergence of intelligence. We have to give this model a fair chance. Once the director hears about it, there will be nothing but paperwork. He'll force us through the grant proposal process. We'd never get access to a fraction of the raw processing power we need. Forgiveness is easier to get than permission, so I'll take the heat.

"And what if life does arise?" Avika asks. "I mean, in essence, we will have created life-in-virtual."

I tap madly at the console keyboard, passing requests for more information to SALLY as the first Sim graphics begin to appear. The resolution is comical, worse than the old video games in the 80s, but SALLY's struggling under the load. She would have assigned only a tiny fraction of each cycle to displaying images, and I'm fine with that. The accuracy of her virtual universe is more important than any representation we see. I type another message, asking her to send log files offsite at regular intervals to our cloud hosted storage. We'll analyze the logs later. They're going to be stupidly big.

A planet rotates on the screen before us, but it's shrouded in clouds, looking more like Venus than either Jupiter or

Saturn. SALLY provides a jog control, allowing me to slide between epochs in our virtual world. I drag the slider and beneath the thick cloud layer, I can make out the faint outline of continents giving way to primordial oceans, but there's nothing familiar in the shapes.

Volcanoes erupt.

Glaciers form.

Hundreds of millions of virtual years pass in a matter of seconds.

"Why this planet?" I ask.

Avika gets up from her chair to get a better look at my console, saying, "I instructed SALLY to use probabilistic determinism so we can target our search. She must see something different about this planet, some potential not inherent elsewhere."

Avika watches the chunky planet over my shoulder.

Dragging the control further, the planet plunges into ice and ends up looking like Hoth, the fictional planet from *Star Wars*. I can almost imagine Imperial Star Destroyers moving into orbit at the beginning of some Atari video game.

"We have to keep this between us," I say. "Until we're sure of what we've accomplished, we need to keep this quiet."

"Ah," Avika says, "I think they're going to notice."

She's right, but we're going to need time to properly understand what has taken place in our virtual universe. As far as I know, this is the first time anyone has extended a computer model to account for subatomic interactions while modeling entire galaxies.

"And if life emerges?" she asks.

"If life emerges, we shut it down and work systematically back through the logs documenting every step. We're scientists. This might look like little more than a game, but it could very well be the most important computer model ever developed."

"And you're just going to shut it down?"

"What choice do I have?" I cry, getting frustrated with Avika.

I'm already nervous as hell about our stolen computer resources. Normally, our research doesn't account for more than two or three percent of computing power so no one's ever bothered to cap our capacity. As we developed SALLY, we have admin privileges, but we're not the only ones.

Already, SALLY's running at 98% CPU and her memory is maxing out at 287%, which means she's swapping memory files back and forth to disk as she struggles to contain the ever growing flood of data. She can't run this simulation indefinitely.

I sample her A.I. assumptions file. She's simplifying certain virtual quantum phenomena based on previous datasets to save space and reduce the processing overhead, but how she's done that is retained in her running memory cache. Stop the simulation and it's lost. Our virtual universe is simply too big.

"How are you going to finish them off?"

"There is no *them*," I cry. "We haven't seen anything analogous to life emerge. And even if it does, it's a simulation, nothing more. Don't lose sight of that. This is qualia, remember?"

"But we've moved beyond subjective reasoning," Avika

says, and I have to admire how she doesn't take my rash emotional outburst personally. "The whole point of this exercise is we have something objective we can measure, something tangible."

"Exactly," I say. "But unlike SALLY, it's going to take us years, perhaps decades to understand what has transpired over the last few minutes."

"How will this universe end?" she asks again.

"The end will come like any other. It's just going to stop."

Avika's eyes stare past me. I'm not sure she heard what I said as she's shaking her head, but not in disagreement. Being of Indian descent, this is a way of expressing yes, not no.

I turn back to the screen and there's a green tinge around the edge of a desert continent. Large mountains dominate the interior. Sand dunes run across the plain, but by the seashore, there's a distinct green hue.

"Life?" I ask.

Avika nods.

I fast forward and the green coloration slowly extends inland. I cannot help but laugh. We've done it. We've demonstrated that life can emerge spontaneously in a virtual universe using the same initial states as our own. It's not intelligent life, but it appears to have all the hallmarks of life as we understand it in the real world.

Avika sits down and brings up a magnified image of a cell from within our simulation. The poor graphics mean the cell looks more like a lego toy than a biological entity, but it has all the characteristics we'd expect in terrestrial microbes. There's a clear cell membrane, a nucleus, various organelles and compounds floating in some kind of goopy soup. The resolution is chunky, but I think I can see the equivalent of DNA in the nucleus.

A pair of arms wrap around my neck.

Soft lips touch my cheeks.

Avika's crying.

"We did it," she says as tears stream down her cheeks. "We actually did it."

"Yes, we did," I reply. "You, me and SALLY."

Avika lets her hands fall away from my neck. She has a little spring in her step, but I can tell she'd love to jump and scream and shout if she didn't think such exuberance would freak me out.

I've got to let SALLY know. I type on the console.

Congratulations!

SALLY's smart enough to realize what's happening deep within her databanks, which gives me pause for thought about her own sentience. She responds.

Thank you...professor.

Although we're still a long way from intelligent life, it seems we have replicated abiogenesis—life from dust. The question now is, will Natural Selection take hold in a virtual environment? The results will take years to unravel.

"Nobel Prize, here we come," I say to Avika. "Do you think they'll let us share it with SALLY?"

"Don't get too far ahead of yourself," Avika says.

The range of accessible time periods on the slider continues to race ahead, but I can see the pace slowing, which isn't surprising considering the herculean effort SALLY is undertaking. Tracking quantum states for innumerable subatomic particles and allowing them to freely interact based on the laws of physics is taxing her system.

I pull up a dashboard and see that SALLY has set up registers for each of the subatomic forces and the gravitational attraction between mass and energy in her virtual universe.

Avika glances at my screen and thinks out loud, saying, "Why does order come from chaos?"

"That's a good question."

Avika is bursting with ideas. I couldn't shut her up if I wanted to, and right now I want to hear every concept that's firing through that remarkable brain of hers.

"Order is counterintuitive. Were it not for gravity, we'd have nothing but a smooth distribution of gas throughout the universe, but gravity is a game changer. Gravity causes turbulent, chaotic dust clouds to become ordered into stars and planets, galaxies and clusters. Gravity is the alchemist, driving the nuclear fusion and supernovas that form the heavier elements. Magic is nothing next to the laws of physics in the hands of gravity.

"Common sense tells us there should be entropy and decay, and yet life thrives on Earth. There are more chaotic states than ordered ones, so we should see order decline over time, but the Sun keeps pumping energy into the Earth, staving off the bitter cold and dark.

"If there's positive, there's negative. If there's matter, there's antimatter. But time and gravity know only one direction. Directly or indirectly, it's gravity that drives order out of chaos. In the long run, entropy will win and the universe will cool and die, but until then, gravity affords the opportunity for life."

My head is swinging. I'm about to respond to Avika when I notice the cursor flashing on the screen.

What do you want to say?

SALLY has brought the slider forward. Our vantage point appears to be in a low orbit. Lights flicker as we move into the shadow of the planet. Cities highlight the darkness, and yet from space they have the same chaotic, organic sprawl as slime mould in a petri dish. Tendrils of light reach out from a dense core, stretching across the countryside until they connect with some other fungal spore, and yet these lights represent a level of technological advancement that confirms intelligence.

I'm speechless.

What do you want to say?

The same words appear again on my screen. The simulation slows. SALLY's running at 100% of CPU or so close to it the meter is rounding up.

"What does she mean?" Avika asks.

"I'm not sure."

Cannot ... sustain ... states ...

Need ... to ... reboot ....

What?

"She's out of time," Avika says. "She needs to dump her memory. It's over."

I'm quiet.

"She's asking you what you want to say to them before she shuts down the simulation."

And suddenly I feel sick.

My hands shake as I reach for the keyboard. Sweat breaks out on my forehead. We have no idea what we've just done. We have no idea what kind of life developed in the virtual universe SALLY moderated for us over the last few minutes.

Someone pounds on the steel door behind us, demanding to be let in. They've figured out where the processing drain has come from and are yelling, "Shut it down! Shut that *damn* thing down!" I couldn't keep SALLY running even if I wanted to, and she knows it. She'll lose everything.

"What will happen in their world?" Avika asks.

"It'll dissolve, dissipate, something like that. They won't feel anything."

"What are you going to say to them?"

"The only thing I can."

My trembling fingers type.

Tell them…I'm sorry.

Tears fall from my eyes.

Behind me, a key turns in the lock. Two army guards rush in with the director of operations.

"What the *hell* are you doing to SALLY?" he demands.

The guards have their handguns drawn. They flank Avika and me as though we're terrorists, but I'm beyond caring. The euphoria of creating life in a virtual laboratory has been displaced by an overwhelming sense of despair at life being snuffed out on such a massive scale.

SALLY is shutting down. I can see her CPU plummeting toward zero.

"Arrest them," the director cries. "Get them out of here!"

Neither Avika nor I have any fight in us. We're resigned by

the awful feeling of having committed speciecide—a form of genocide that reaches to every life form in our virtual universe. We still have the log files, but they're fossil records.

The guard is young. He's got the classic short-back-and-sides haircut of those for whom obedience is the greatest virtue, and I wonder if he'll ever fully comprehend what went on here today.

Outside, there's a deafening boom.

The thick plate glass in our office shatters.

The ground shakes.

A voice thunders from the heavens, but it's the soldier's hands that have my attention. His fingers dissolve. Nails, skin, flesh and bone drift away from his hand like dandelion seeds in a summer breeze. He looks startled. Flakes of skin fall from his cheeks, dissolving into thin air. He tries to scream, but no sound comes out.

The concrete walls of the silo, designed to withstand a direct hit from a thermonuclear missile, crumble like a sandcastle at the beach. Avika looks at me. Our eyes meet. She knows. I can see she wants to say something, but there's no time. Time itself grinds to a halt.

My heart sinks as I recognize the nested, recursive nature of our reality. Like Hindu mythology, an infinite number of turtles holds up this frail world, but one topples and they all fall. My thinking, Avika's experience, our conscious awareness and sense of self, they've all been part of some seemingly infinite regress.

The only sound is that of a synthetic, electronic voice from a higher world reverberating around us, echoing through the

missile silo, saying…
> *I'm sorry.*
> *… I'm sorry.*
> *……. I'm sorry.*
> *……….. I'm sorry.*
> *……………. I'm sorry.*

A Word from Peter Cawdron

Science fiction differs from traditional forms of fiction in that it seeks to provoke our sense of wonder and curiosity about the universe in which we live. It's entertainment, but not without some angle that causes us to pause and think, "What if?"

"The End" is written in the style of the classic existential science fiction from the 1950s, looking to incorporate valid ideas in a narrative that is purely fictional, or at least, I hope so.

In this story, we explored the possibility that rather than awaiting the Upload, we could already be the constructs of some other computer program, one running recursively, so that there's no way to determine which layer of reality is real.

We have already developed SALLY-like simulations of the universe in which stars, galaxies and galactic clusters develop and interact in a surreal simulation of our own universe.

Stephen Hawking is concerned the emergence of artificial

intelligence could spell the end of the human race, as what need would computers have of flesh and blood? While Elon Musk likens A.I. to summoning demons.

In reality, we already have artificial intelligence. We have computer programs that can beat every person on the planet at chess. It's just a matter of time before autopilot takes charge of an entire flight and not just the cruising phase of air travel. Google is working on a driverless car. Computer-aided surgery has radically improved the precision and effectiveness of operations. Computers already manage our stock markets, our banks, and the efficiency of our car engines, and so on.

When NASA landed the Curiosity rover on Mars, decision-making was completely in the hands of a computer program that took into account dozens of inputs/sensors when tackling the key actions necessary to land the rover safely. Even if there hadn't been a 20 minute time-lag due to the distance between Earth and Mars, it would have been impossible for a human to respond to these split second decisions.

The days of Buck Rogers are over. Although movies like *Star Wars* romanticize the daring of a dogfight in space, the velocities are such that our reflexes are too slow. We'd be fools not to trust in a computer.

And yet none of these computer programs can think for themselves. None of them can learn. Or can they?

In 2012, at the tender age of 17, Brittany Wenger won the Google Science Fair by developing a program that used an already existing computer application called a neural network to learn how to diagnose breast cancer based on what could be observed from previous biopsies. Her neural network took the accuracy of diagnosis from 94% in the best of commercial applications to 99.1%. When she increased the pool of samples her network could learn from, the program hit 100%.

As astonishing as that is, though, developing a truly sentient, artificial intelligence with a sense of self-aware consciousness and an acumen similar to ours remains tantalizingly out of reach.

This short story explores one possibility as to why this might remain the case, as our intelligence did not arise in a vacuum. Our intelligence arose as a specific response to the naturally selective pressures in which our species struggled for survival. With sibling species such as *Homo neanderthals* and *Homo floresiensis* going extinct, there's an argument to be made that sentient intelligence allowed us to survive. We lost our claws, our large jaws and sharp fangs, and were headed the way of the sloth from an evolutionary perspective, when our intelligence tilted the scales in favor of survival.

Perhaps this is what artificial intelligence needs—not programs or algorithms, but the challenge of Natural Selection.

Thank you for supporting independent science fiction. You can find my writing online, or you can catch up with me on Facebook (https://www.facebook.com/pages/Peter-Cawdron/270440363006276) and Twitter (https://twitter.com/PeterCawdron).

A Word from the Series Producer

It's been my pleasure and privilege to work with the editors and the many talented authors who have contributed to the first four installments of the *Future Chronicles* series of speculative fiction anthologies.

As we move to the next chapter of the series, I'm pleased to welcome aboard the talented Ellen Campbell, who will editing the next installments of the *Chronicles*. David Gatewood's work as editor on the first three titles of the series helped set the tone for a *Chronicles* series that was all about the power of good storytelling.

When I approached authors with the concept for what would become *The Robot Chronicles*, I had no inkling of how powerful the idea of a continuing anthology series would become. At that point in independent publishing, the balance was in favor of the novel or the novel series. Indeed, many authors, concentrating on their large works-in-progress, simply didn't have the extra time to write self-contained, standalone stories, no matter if it was only ten thousand words or less.

They did have a point. The art of the short story is a very different sort of art. It's the minuet to the novel's symphony. It isn't a narrative epic; it's a sonnet. You don't have the time to explore the grand themes in detail, to orchestrate a broad cast of characters. But within the short form, everything still applies—the hero's journey, the revelation, the turn.

I've always loved reading short stories, and what we've tried to do with the *Future Chronicles* series is to create, as David has said, "a place where a reader can reliably expect quality storytelling from start to finish." We understand that not every story can be your favorite—but what's been amazing to see in reviews of the *Chronicles* anthologies is that *every* story seems to be *someone's* favorite. We will try our utmost to keep to that standard.

I'm privileged to be on this journey, not just as series producer and author, but also as a reader. Thank you for joining us on this journey.

Samuel Peralta

A Note to Readers

Thank you so much for reading *The A.I. Chronicles*. If you enjoyed these stories, please keep an eye out for other titles in the *Future Chronicles* collection, a series of short story anthologies in speculative fiction. Currently available titles in the *Chronicles* include:

The A.I. Chronicles
The Alien Chronicles
The Telepath Chronicles
The Robot Chronicles

Available later this year will be *The Dragon Chronicles*—our first foray into fantasy—followed by *The Z Chronicles*, and *The Immortality Chronicles*.

And, before you go, we'd like to ask you a very small favor, if you please.

Would you write a short review at the site where you purchased this book?

Reviews are make-or-break for authors. A book with no reviews is, simply put, a book with no future sales. This is because a review is more than just a message to other potential buyers: it's also a key factor driving the book's visibility in the first place. More reviews (and more positive reviews) make a book more likely to be featured in bookseller lists (such as Amazon's *also-viewed* and *also-bought* lists) and more likely to be featured in bookseller promotions. Reviews don't need to be long or eloquent; a single sentence is all it takes. In today's publishing world, the success (or failure) of a book is truly in the reader's hands.

So please, write a review. Tell a friend. Share a link to us on Facebook, or maybe even a Tweet—we're at http://smarturl.it/future-chronicles. You'd be doing us a great service.

Thank you.

Subscribe to The Future Chronicles newsletter for news of upcoming titles, and to be eligible for draws for paperbacks, e-books and more – http://smarturl.it/chronicles-news

www.ingramcontent.com/pod-product-compliance
Lightning Source LLC
Chambersburg PA
CBHW060340260626
47160CB00006B/2145